D1329944

# ANIMAL CONTROL

# THE HERO'S APPRENTICE

Travis Howe

Softpress Publishing, LLC

SOFTPRESS PUBLISHING, LLC
4118 Hickory Crossroads Road
Kenly, NC 27542
www.softpresspublishing.com

*Book design:* William C. Parker
*Illustrations:* Travis Howe
*Cover design:* Isaac Davis
*Optimus Princeps font:* Manfred Klein

ISBN: 1-7322744-2-8
ISBN-13: 978-1-7322744-2-6

This is a work of fiction. Names, characters, businesses, places, events, locales, and incidents are either the products of the author's imagination or used in a fictitious manner. Any resemblance to actual persons, living or dead, or actual events is purely coincidental.

For Nikki

## Prologue

# THE LAST APPRENTICE

Night fell in West City. Fog crept along empty streets, and in the back room of a diner on the forgotten side of town, a badger was dying of a single gunshot wound. He hissed as he clutched the spot, and slid a little further down the brick wall. He felt cold. And tired.

The apprentice crashed into the room, readjusting a ball cap. Avak Tyrell was only a kid, an otter boy with a broad muzzle and forests of whiskers that made him look much older than fourteen. He glanced through the porthole window as the door swung to a stop. "We lost 'em, Sander!" he whispered. "We made it!" Clapping his paws together, he began searching the room for a telephone.

"Tell that to the bullet makin' friends with my kidney," the badger groaned. He tried to stand, but his knees gave out and he slid further down the green bricks.

"Your kidney? All fours!" the otter swore. "All fours, Sander! You're bleeding out!"

"Tell me somethin' I don't know, kid," Sander growled through clenched teeth.

His eyes wide, fixed on the wound, the otter tore his hat off and ruffled his hair. "Alright," he said, his voice sounding shaky yet resolved. "Alright, we need to stop the bleeding." He began rummaging around the room, pulling open the drawers of a cluttered desk, upturning a mesh waste basket.

"With what, a cork?" The badger gave a resigned laugh. "Kid. Kid. Hey, Avak." The otter stopped and looked at the wounded hero. "It's too late. I'm done." His voice was soft now. "You have — you have to get to King. Tell him what we've learned. An s-train. The…" He paused, took in a few shuddering breaths. "The weapon will be on an s-train. Sapply station. Remember — remember that."

Avak stared for a moment. "No," he said. "No, we'll tell King together. We'll go back to Animal Control right now. Now get up."

Sander had slid all the way to the floor. In the faint neon light, the fluid pouring out of him looked as black as spilled ink.

"I said get up," the apprentice repeated, this time not bothering to whisper. "Get up. Get up, you lazy old man! *Get up!*"

But Sander Redding's eyes were lifeless, fixed on empty air. He was dead.

An involuntary sob bubbled up from Avak's chest. Then another. Crouching down, he readjusted the badger's coat collar with trembling paws. He tried to speak, perhaps to say goodbye or that he'd get help, but the only sound that escaped his lips was an anguished gurgle. Knees weak, he began to stand.

But then he stopped.

The body had made a move. It was a strange motion, starting in the badger's chest, as though a string was pulling him upward. Without seeming to push himself he rose to his feet, head slunk sideways, limbs dangling loosely. He began limping toward the exit, brushing past the apprentice as if the otter wasn't even there. Leaving a red print as he pushed through the door, he limped into the empty dining room.

Avak heard the tinkling of a bell as the badger exited the diner. By the time he recovered himself and followed after, the badger was stumbling his way up the foggy city street. It didn't take long to catch up; Sander's movements were slow and labored, and strangely off-balance. He continued on without interruption, even as the otter jogged up next to him. "I thought I'd lost you back there," Avak said, gripping the badger's shoulder.

The face that turned toward him was a mask of death, thrown into sharp relief beneath the red traffic signal. It was stretched, as though every feature was being pulled taut with terror. The eyes were wide, bulging blindly. The lips were curled back in a sneer so extreme, pink gums were completely exposed. A dry tongue dangled out the side of his mouth.

Avak took a step back, releasing his grip. The lifeless badger rolled his head into a shoulder, turned, and continued an awkward stumble along the shimmering pavement.

For a moment, Avak could only watch, numb and shivering, as the undead figure was swallowed by fog and darkness.

Then a memory came to him, a voice so pronounced, he almost looked around in surprise. "*It's not going to be easy,*" King had said, crouching to meet Avak's eyes. The lion was so big, so strong, and yet his eyes were gentle and warm. "*I want you to know that. Sometimes, you'll see things you wish you hadn't. You'll have to do things you'll wish you didn't. I wish I could protect you from the darker side of being a hero, but I can't.*" He had squeezed Avak's shoulder encouragingly, and smiled. "*It's like going into a scary basement. You have to brave the darkness if you're going to turn on the light.*" And then King's voice was gone, and Avak was alone, trembling with fright and staring at the point where Sander had disappeared.

Heart pounding, ears ringing, he gave one last glance to his surroundings, and followed.

The streets were ghost still. Soon they reached the Waterfront, an industrial district that had once been the heart and lungs of Triarch. Now fish markets housed only vagrants, and the great salt factory that once fueled the city's economy stood in disrepair.

Sander had disappeared down a dark stairway at the base of a cement building. Avak made his way down, and found himself in a narrow, unlit hall. He squinted into the space, but despite eyes well-adapted for the darkness of an ocean floor, he could no longer see Sander. If he was going to keep pace down here, he would have to take his other form.

Gritting his teeth and balling his paws into fists, he searched for the feeling. It used to be difficult, but these days it came as simply as conjuring a yawn. It started in his chest, the feeling one gets when gulping down a mouthful of ice water. The sensation spread to his shoulders, his fingertips, at the same time rushing down his back like a bead of sweat sliding along the spine. His paws went numb. His eyes rolled upward. He felt his fur loosening, his skin sliding off his bones like a waxwork in a museum fire. It was not painful, but as every nerve, every cell in his body was turning to fluid, it was difficult to know *what* to feel.

As smoothly as the transition had started, it stopped. Avak lay pooled up on the concrete floor of the darkened hallway. The transformation was complete; he had become water.

He skittered along the chamber floor, his senses melded into one. It was sight and sound, taste and touch, all rolled into a singular cognition. He was not hearing, nor seeing. He did not taste the salt of the floor, nor smell the mildew in the air. He was simply *aware* of these things, as though his mind was storing notes for later recollection. His surroundings became more comprehensible; the vibration of the floor in the direction Sander had vanished; the opening, then closing of a door; the unmistakable stomp of feet descending a staircase. He found the door and slid beneath it, pressed into a wall, and cascaded smoothly down alongside the stairs until he reached the concrete floor. He was ahead now — the badger was still on the stairs. Avak passed beneath the stairwell exit and found himself in another narrow chamber, this one lit by a caged yellow bulb at the far end.

Below the bulb, two figures stood silently watching the door. The first he recognized as Toby Harding, the nervous, shifty-eyed cousin of King of Hearts. The lion was tall and maneless, with a gaunt face and bulging eyes that seemed to border on madness. He wore a cloak, but the hood was pulled back. In this form, Avak could read not only physical appearance, but emotions as well. Toby was terrified, and trying very hard to hide it.

The second figure gave Avak pause. It had registered in his peripheral consciousness as some kind of large bull or ox. Now, he realized that it was neither. In fact, what his senses were telling him seemed *impossible*. The figure was much taller than Toby; cloaked, but with fur. In place of a head, it had only a horned baboon skull, with circular eye sockets and rows of teeth ending in fangs. Long white horns, as thick and curved as elephant tusks, stood out beyond broad shoulders. From beneath its cloak, a skeletal arm extended, its bleach-white fingers clutching a burlap sack filled with something the size and weight of a pumpkin. Unlike Toby, this creature wasn't terrified. In fact, it didn't seem to be projecting any emotion at all. Its bare skull grin leered emptily across the chamber.

*SPLASH!*

All perception spiraled in a thousand directions, a disorienting kaleidoscope of touch and taste, sight and sound, as though he was seeing the world through the broken shards of a mirror. Avak *hated* getting stepped in.

By the time he'd pulled himself together, Sander was more than halfway down the hall, limping in that weird, off-balance manner. It registered to Avak like a marionette bounding along on strings. The thought was both bizarre and unsettling. And there was something else. Where Toby's fear was so pronounced, nearly palpable in its intensity, Sander's emotions were registering as...

Nothing.

There was nothing there. No fear. No anger. No gladness, sadness, discomfort, disdain. Nothing. It was as though he wasn't feeling a single, solitary emotion.

Then Avak felt a focus upon himself. It was so brief, he couldn't be sure. But for a moment, he could swear the horned creature had looked right at him.

"You invited Sander Redding?" the lean lion asked. "He's a member of King's Six. You don't think he'll talk?"

The horned figure said nothing. He turned his back on Toby and walked down a chamber to the right. The lion followed. The emotionless badger took up the rear without having slowed at all.

Avak slid up the wall like an inverse waterfall, then dribbled into a large, reddened cavity in the lowest of the overhead pipes. His cognition gave a shudder; rust registered in his awareness like tin foil on metal fillings. But the pipe allowed him to move without being seen, and he caught up in no time. Their pace was slow, and Toby was speaking again. "We're not going to hurt him, are we?"

There was a shrill laugh. Strangely, it seemed not to come from the skull-headed figure, but from the sack he carried. And then it spoke. "I can assure you, I will not harm Sander Redding in any way."

"And King?" Toby continued. "You won't use my information to hurt him either?"

Another laugh barked from the sack. "How did you think this would end?"

Toby made no response to this. His nature seemed diminished, like a child being scolded by an unfamiliar adult.

As the three came to a stop outside of a large, vault-like door, Toby spoke again, this time directing his question toward Sander. "How do *you* fit into all this?"

The badger, who had come to a sudden and wobbly halt alongside the lion, did not respond, as Avak knew he wouldn't. There may have been a physical presence there, but Sander Redding was as empty as these rusted pipes; nothing but a shell. However it was that he had stumbled his way across the city, the badger's life had ended in that diner.

The horned figure stopped and turned, directing his attention at Sander. He seemed to withdraw something. Not a physical object, but an *intention*; a sense of control. Instantly, the body of Sander Redding fell to the floor. "Sander Redding is dead," said the voice from the sack. "Just as King of Hearts will soon be dead. Come, we will discuss the plan." The door gave a shrill yawn as it was pulled open.

Toby seemed to garner his courage. "You kill Sander Redding right after swearing not to hurt him, and then expect me to trust you?"

The skull turned toward the cat, and the voice from the sack spoke. "You are still needed. I assume you would prefer to stay that way?"

Toby watched as the figure passed through the circular doorway. He hung his head and followed.

Avak remained motionless, his consciousness fixed on the rag doll body of his friend. He considered escaping. He should go and get help, alert King to the danger, tell someone about Sander. But the words from the sack came back to him. *Just as King of Hearts will soon be dead.* Hadn't he better follow, listen in on this plan, and report it back to King? He moved along a bend in the pipe, passed above the vault door and caught up to the pair.

His awareness picked up every aspect of the room, from the shuddering fluorescent lights as they clicked to life, to the long, shallow pool stretching the length of the room. There was enough space around the perimeter for workers to navigate comfortably. The pool wasn't more than a foot deep, and the water only half that. Copper colored bands spanned half an inch below the surface, punched with tiny holes, many closed over with oxidization.

The voice from the sack broke the silence once more, in the tone of a tutor. "Forty-five years ago, this refinery was the soul of Triarch. It employed nearly half the city's residents and made a fair trade overseas." Toby didn't seem to know how to respond, but the sack voice didn't wait. "The secret to its success?" The free skeletal arm gestured toward the pool. "Refining salt is a very unique process. If for example we were refining gold, we would simply heat it, and bring the impurities to the surface. But salt *is* the impurity in saltwater. It must first be extracted if it is to be used."

There was an abrupt, pipe-rattling screech as the horned creature flipped a large switch on the wall. "This country is the salt," he continued. "It is the jewel, the prize. Nikacia is a life source ripe for the picking, but for us to purify it, we must first extract it from the strangle hold of Animal Control. And your cousin stands in the way of that." The pool began to bubble, first slowly, like stale seltzer water, then building up until the entire surface boiled.

The lion's fear was throbbing now, a hammering pulse to match his heartbeat. "So you *do* plan to kill him?" he asked. "To kill King of Hearts?"

"Didn't I already tell you so? But there was a missing piece to the puzzle. A weapon. Thankfully, Sander Redding brought it right to me."

At this moment, Avak sensed many things at once. First, the unmistakable fixation of the horned skull. It was looking straight up at the pipe, fully aware of Avak's presence.

Secondly, the paralyzing numbness of fear, a sense he had never before felt in his fluid form.

Third, he had begun to bubble.

He pushed himself to slide back through the pipe. He must escape. He must warn King.

But he couldn't move. Whether due to his fear or the heat rising from the pool beneath him, Avak was trapped.

His other form! He must turn solid again. He would outrun these two, escape to the streets. Avak knew West City like the back of his paw. He could slip into the shadows, contact backup.

Miraculously, some of his fluid had dribbled through a rust hole. This small movement broke the paralysis. He slipped through the opening, clinging cohesively to the exterior of the pipe. With the greatest effort it had ever taken him, he took his solid form.

For a moment, he hung there ridiculously, like a trapped sloth. The horned creature stared at him. Toby looked terrified at his own feet.

"We know your secret," Avak yelled, sounding much braver than he felt. "We know about the weapon. That it's on an s-train headed for Sapply." He struggled to maintain his grip. The rusted pipe, sagging under his weight, began to creak loudly.

The voice from the sack gave a horrible, shrill laugh. "Fool boy! *You* are the weapon."

The pipe gave way. Avak fell, losing his solid form as he splashed into the pool like an exploding water balloon.

The horned baboon skull grinned down upon the water, an emotionless mask that showed neither satisfaction nor triumph. Evaporation was a slow process, but he had time. He paid no attention to the horrified spluttering of the lion.

## Chapter One

## JACK

Of all the animals, snowshoe bunnies are the luckiest, and of all the snowshoe bunnies, the luckiest by far was Jack Robberts. He wasn't lucky in the sense that he had a good family, or a shiny new bicycle, or a great uncle's inheritance locked away in a bank somewhere. The fact was, Jack had no family, no bicycle, and certainly no inheritance locked away in so much as a buried coffee can.

Jack was lucky in the most basic sense of the word. Things happened to Jack. Sometimes they were good things. Sometimes they were bad things. Luck didn't seem to favor positives or negatives, it just *happened*.

Luck was the reason for most everything that happened to Jack. Why he had no family, why he lived here in this grimy old house on the far end of a grimy old alley.

And it was because of luck that he was confined to his bed in the narrow, tent-shaped attic while the twelve other beds sat unmade and unoccupied.

Jack was small, even for a six year old — a fact that was exaggerated by his overlong ears and big feet. He had butterscotch fur, big, curious eyes that made him look as though he was afraid of just about everything — which, he continuously reminded himself, he most certainly was not — and wore clothing that looked as though it had been handed down five times, which of course, it had.

Currently, Jack sat on the side of his bed facing the window, his v-shaped nose pressed against the glass as he peered down upon the alley three stories below. The other kids had disappeared, off on some adventure while he sat imprisoned for a crime he hadn't committed.

As he stewed over the injustice of it all, he spotted a newspaper tumbling down the alley. It was only one page, the front by the look of it, and it was crumpled and oil-stained, but that didn't bother Jack. Six year old boys don't usually care about things like newspapers, but Jack lived in a city protected by heroes, and the Punts rarely let him watch television. He'd taught himself to read, and was getting quite good at it, just so he could follow their adventures.

*It's too far down*, he told himself. *It's too far down and you won't reach it in time.*

Then something happened. A wonderful something: the newspaper became caught on a milk crate. He didn't need to think twice. He flung his legs over the other side of the bed, practically flew out the door, and began giddily down the carpeted stairs.

It wasn't until he reached the second floor that The Punts entered his mind. She was still somewhere inside.

Mrs. Eloise Punts, the heavyset old owl who never insisted on being called "Mom," had always scared Jack. From her wide circular eyes to her cigarette scented apron, there was little to find redeeming about The Punts. Catching Jack out of his room when he was supposed to be grounded would probably delight her, as it would give her a reason to swat him with her wooden spoon and deny him dinner yet again.

But none of this was what glued him to the stair. He was thinking instead about her zombie head. Or at least that's what the other boys had called it when he told them what he had seen.

It had been about eight weeks ago, on Freedom Day. The Punts had made a casserole to celebrate the occasion, and since dinner here usually consisted of feed and wilted salad, Jack couldn't resist the temptation to sneak downstairs for some midnight seconds. Miraculously, or perhaps luckily, this was also the first night in living memory that The Punts had neglected to lock the attic door. He had just made it past her bedroom at the foot of the stairs when he froze. She was facing away from him in the kitchen doorway, silhouetted against a dim night light.

He had stood unmoving for a moment, his eyes wide and watching. Then he heard a snore. She was sleepwalking! His hungry belly growled, insisting that there was enough room between her and the door jam, but it hadn't mattered anyway. In his excitement, Jack forgot to skip the squeaky panel in the floorboard. The old owl's head had swiveled around until it sat cleanly backward between her shoulders, two glowing yellow eyes glaring widely down at him. He had screamed himself hoarse by the time he'd reached the attic.

Jack shuddered at the memory. He peered between the beams of the railing, trying to catch a glimpse of the front room, ears perked and breath held.

The television crackled, melodramatic voices muffled by white noise. Braving three more steps, he peeked around the wall. There she sat in her favorite smoke-scented armchair, her head resting limply on her shoulder. His heart rose at the sight, but he proceeded cautiously all the same, slowed by visions of The Punts chasing him up the stairs, her head spinning around and around like a police siren.

When he cleared the front room (remembering that creaky board, of course), he closed a padded paw around the door lever, his wide eyes never leaving The Punts as he turned it. After a tense moment in which the old owl dropped the remote control and gave a snort and a lurch, she fell back asleep, and Jack slid through the widest gap he dared make in the oil-wanting door.

Gently, he pulled the door until it clicked shut. He had done it! He was outside! His heart pounding heavily, he leapt down the staircase and landed clumsily on the pebble-strewn pavement, spotting the newspaper instantly; it had escaped the milk crate and was sliding toward the main city street.

By the time Jack reached the crowded sidewalk, the newspaper had taken a left and was picking up speed. "Wait!" he yelled after it, and started pushing his way through a forest of trousered and skirted legs of all colors and sizes.

When he spotted the newspaper again, it was being drawn open by a pair of spindly pink fingers seated at a coffee shop table.

"Oh dear," an aged voice said from behind the paper as the same fingers flicked open a pair of reading glasses. "Well, this changes things, doesn't it?" The voice fell silent as the figure behind the paper put one leg over the other, tossing a long pink tail over his lap as he did so.

Alongside him sat a young fox; a few years older than Jack, and far better cared-for by the look of him. He caught Jack's eye, unabashed, and took a sip from his soft drink.

Jack wasn't going to lose his paper so easily. He'd risked another hungry night for that scrap. "Excuse me," he said as forcefully as a young bunny can.

No response. The fox watched him unhelpfully.

"Excuse me," he said, a little louder. "That's mine."

This time, the page lowered, and an elderly and slender nosed rat peered over it, found Jack's ears and followed them down. "Oh, hello there!" he said in a friendly tone. "What did you say, my boy?"

Jack shifted uncomfortably. "The newspaper," he said sheepishly, trying his best to ignore the impolite stare of the fox. "It's mine."

The rat looked questioningly toward his companion. "Don't know what he's talking about," the fox boy said. "I bought it the same place I always buy it."

"No he didn't," Jack interrupted. "It's just blown over here on the wi…" But he fell short. This newspaper wasn't oil stained or torn. More than that, it wasn't only the front page, but a thick stack of pages. He felt his cheeks grow hot.

The rat folded the paper and lay it on the table before him. "What's your name, son?"

"Jack."

"My name is Dr. Einer Walraven," he continued. "This young fellow," he indicated the fox, who had become interested in a scuff mark on the table, "is Alan Kale, my assistant. Every morning, I send him to purchase a newspaper for me. He's just returned with this one. That said, I can always buy another." He paused thoughtfully. "Why don't you have a seat, Jack?" he said.

When he had flagged down the poodle waitress and ordered Jack a cherry cola, he continued. "You read the news?"

Jack shrugged.

"Let me guess," Dr. Walraven said with a knowing wink. "King of Hearts fan?"

Jack met his eyes for a brief moment. The rat smiled. "Who isn't, right?"

The corners of Jack's mouth twitched.

"I'm guessing you've got a whole collection of these…" But before Dr. Walraven could finish his statement, Jack's eyes wandered to the newspaper on the table, and he gave a surprised yell. Realizing that he had interrupted, he apologized and sank back into his chair.

"That's quite alright," the rat said, rotating the paper so that Jack could read it properly.

## NO MORE SIDEKICKS!

…the headline declared in bold black letters. He read it again, disbelieving. It was Jack's fondest ambition, the thought that allowed him to sleep in that hot, overcrowded attic every night. Becoming a sidekick, tagging along as a hero's apprentice, was *every* kid's dream. No more sidekicks? The headline might as well have read "No More Birthdays," or "No More Ice Cream."

"They can't do this!" he said.

Dr. Walraven looked gravely at the paper. "I'm afraid there really isn't much of a choice."

"But why?" Jack asked.

In answer, Dr. Walraven sipped his tea and nodded toward the paper as if to say, "Read on."

Jack looked back down and continued reading.

Beneath the headline, a subheading read:

## CONTROVERSIAL APPRENTICE PROGRAM ENDS FOLLOWING CHILD'S DEATH

The article featured a black and white photo of an otter in a sports cap. Forests of whiskers framed a comically broad nose and a confident, almost cocky smile; he didn't look older than twelve or thirteen, around the same age as the fox boy. The article continued:

*In a move deemed by some to be long overdue, Animal Control, the famed hero league founded and helmed by the great King of Hearts, has announced the closure of its apprenticeship program following the death of teenage hero hopeful Avak Tyrell. Started more than thirty years ago, the program matched aspiring young hopefuls with AC heroes that could teach and train them to pick up the hero mantle in years to come.* The Future Generations Act *made it possible for heroes to take these up-and-comers — children, mind you — on serious, often dangerous missions.*

*"It's heartbreaking, what has happened," says one expert. "But a surprise? These children are dragged along on capers that* frequently *endanger their lives. Perhaps the only surprise is that it's taken this long for such a so-called adventure to end in tragedy."*

*While authorities continue to search for Tyrell's body, a few factors must be considered. As we reported weeks ago, the body of Sander Redding, better known as White Stripe, was discovered at the location where Tyrell is last known to have been. It must be noted that Tyrell wasn't White Stripe's sidekick, but that of the one and only King of Hearts, which begs the question: What was Avak Tyrell doing in the most dangerous part of the city, with a hero who wasn't even his own mentor?*

The article continued, but something didn't make sense to Jack. "Hang on," he said, looking up. "It says he disappeared, and that he hasn't been found. But the headline says that he's dead. How do they know?"

Dr. Walraven gave an impressed nod. "Very good," he said. "Whenever someone joins Animal Control, they are given a tracker. It's sort of a tag that's implanted under the skin — typically right here," he said, tapping the back of his own left shoulder. "It makes them easier to find, should they ever need backup or disappear mysteriously."

"So can't they find him with that?"

"They certainly should be able to do so, but Avak's tracker has vanished. That in itself isn't too strange. Avak's heightena — that is, his *super power* — allowed him to transform into pure water, and whenever he did, his clothes, his hat," he touched the photograph, "anything he was holding would transform with him. This included the tracker, so he couldn't be traced in that form. His heightena had one tremendous weakness. If he stayed in his water form for too long, or was exposed to the wrong elements, such as an overheated sidewalk, he could evaporate." He nodded at the shocked look on Jack's face. "Avak hasn't been traceable for nearly three weeks now — that's far too long for him to stay in that form."

Jack looked back at the picture of the otter boy and felt a great rush of pity. This was just a kid, one with the same dreams Jack himself cherished. Dreams that came true. Dreams that ended in his death. Jack shuddered.

Dr. Walraven gestured toward the poodle, who strode over and set a small tray with a piece of paper in front of him. "Well, Jack," he said in a formal tone as he extracted paper money from his wallet and placed it on the tray. "Please feel free to keep the paper. It's been a pleasure meeting you today. We have a few things to take care of before catching our s-train this evening, so I'm afraid we must…"

"You're going to ride an s-train?" Jack interrupted. The idea of traveling across the sea in a submersible train was nearly as impressive as the rat's knowledge of Animal Control.

The fox's face drew into a smug grin, as though being impressed by such things was childish, but Dr. Walraven's smile was genuine as he rose from his seat. "I have to get to Sapply for a very important meeting. An s-train is the fastest way to get there."

Setting a briefcase on the table, he popped it open, tucked away the lunch receipt in one of the interior pockets, replaced a spiral-bound notepad, and snapped the briefcase shut again. Jack noticed the gold engraving just beneath the handle: "E.W." The doctor placed a chalk-white Homburg hat atop his head, his ears flattening beneath it. "I suppose we have everything?" he said to the fox, who gave an affirming nod, a supercilious frown on his face as he looked about them. "Well then, Jack," the rat continued, "can we walk you back to your home?"

Jack slid from his chair. Then, as if unable to stop himself, he blurted, "One day, I'm going to be a hero."

Alan scoffed, earning a reproving glance from Dr. Walraven. The old rat met Jack's eyes with a genuine smile. "I believe you will, Jack."

The three of them began down the sidewalk, never seeing the many eyes that followed them from a nearby alley.

## Chapter Two

## THE OTHER BOYS

The Punts was still asleep when Jack returned, and he made it to his room without being caught. But his stomach ached with a new kind of sadness, and he stayed in the attic when the old owl woman called that it was time for dinner.

It was the fox boy that bothered him. A few years older than Jack, but in much newer clothes. And cared for by Dr. Walraven. Most nights, he would envy the bedtime stories.

Tonight, he envied the protection.

When the other boys finished dinner and came upstairs, he feigned sleep, but he knew that it was useless. He'd caused them too much trouble to be left alone. Sure enough, the door had only just given the telltale *click* as The Punts locked it behind them, when a stubby finger jabbed painfully at Jack's ribs. He rolled over and sat up, pressing his back to the window as he did so.

There were twelve of them in total, all bunnies, and all bigger than Jack. The three biggest surrounded his bed, and the remaining nine either watched with interest from their own beds or else pretended to be asleep. The boy that poked him was called Gale. He was the biggest and the dumbest.

"You got a big stupid mouth to go with them big stupid ears," Gale jibed. The other boys laughed appreciatively.

Jack, his eyes wide and his arms hugging his knees, made no response. He could hate the living guts out of these boys all he wanted, but that wouldn't stop them from *beating* the living guts out of him any time *they* wanted.

"Don't got much to say now though, do he?" Gale laughed.

The Ostly twins, tall and slender with narrow faces, leaned against either bed post, but Gale dropped himself down directly onto the mattress. He reached out and grabbed Jack's jaw, pressing his cheeks together and causing his lips to pucker. "All fours!" Gale swore. "He's shaking. You gonna pee your pants, Jack?" At this, the Ostly twins laughed even louder, as did several voices from the surrounding darkness. "Now," Gale continued in his most business-like tone. "We got some things to discuss, don't we? Things like, *why it is a very bad idea to try to get me into trouble.*"

At this point, Jack may have been able to escape the situation unscathed. Gale was mad, but he'd say some humiliating things, make the other boys laugh, and that would be that. But Jack could never keep his mouth shut when someone was in the wrong. "You took Mr. Hargrove's flask while he was sleeping."

"So what if I did?"

Still shaking, Jack rallied his courage and pressed on. "So... so it's wrong to steal. And that's alcohol. You shouldn't be drinking it."

Gale leaned back, putting a paw on Jack's forehead and banging his head against the window. "You dope. That old drunk's the one what shouldn't be drinking it. I was doing him a favor, don't you see? And if drinking alcohol is what I gotta do to help that poor old man, well," he adopted a saintly expression, "then I'll drink it."

The Ostlys tittered stupidly.

"But now, I got nothin'," Gale pressed on. "And even after all your stupid ninny-tattling, The Punts still thought *you* took it!" At this, he let out a forced, heavy laugh.

For a moment, there was silence in the room, as if Gale had run out of insults, or perhaps was getting bored with this game. His attention turned to the torn and faded poster of King of Hearts alongside Jack's bed. "I heard you talking to that *rat*," Gale said, emphasizing the last word as if it were a swear. "We was in the alley. I heard you crying about the sidekick program." He adopted a high-pitched whine. "*Waaah! But I want to be a sidekick! Boo hoo!*" The other boys howled at this. "What kinda super hero would you be, Jack?" Gale continued. "Bed Wetter Bunny? Oh, I know! You could be called *The Snitch*, like how you snitched on me earlier." At this, the humor was lost from Gale's voice, and the smile faded from his lips.

Jack's eyes shot toward the door. It had been a long time since he had actually bothered to get out of bed and check that the door was indeed locked. In living memory, the door had only remained unlocked once, and he'd used the opportunity for nothing more than an attempt to snag leftover casserole. But now, a wonderful idea stole over him. If he could get out that door, he could get downstairs and outside. He didn't know where he'd go, nor what would keep him from being returned by the police the moment he was found, but he didn't care. Adventure and freedom were beyond that door.

But the door *had* clicked, and Jack was locked in for the long haul with three vengeful bullies and nine spectators.

Gale seemed to come alive with an idea of his own. "You know what, boys?" he said, not taking his eyes off the cowering bunny. "I think it's time we summoned Petrillo." The other boys laughed as Gale stood and moved to his own bed in the far corner of the room, reaching beneath the mattress. "It's true what they say, you know," Gale continued, turning again and fondling a closed switchblade. The boards creaked ominously below his weight as he stepped slowly, deliberately toward his prey. "Petrillo is *real*. It comes in the night, and kidnaps naughty boys. Cheats. Babies. Snitches. It drags them away to its lair…" A bone-chilling *chttt!* sounded as the knife snapped open. "And it *eats* them," Gale said, a hungry look in his eyes.

The other boys grabbed Jack's limbs. He fought desperately, but he was no match for even one of them. They pinned him to the bed. When he tried to call out, he got no further than "Mrs. Puh…" before his mouth was full of one of the twins' elbows.

"Oh, hold still," Gale demanded, sounding childish. "We can't summon the demon without a blood offering." The blade gleamed in the blue light pouring in from the window. Jack's eyes were gleaming too, as he tried desperately to pull himself from the strong grips on his limbs. A muffled sob coughed its way out of his dry throat.

Gale's paw was steady as he pointed the knife forward, as though he was demanding an old lady's purse. "*Give it to me,*" this pose seemed to say, and it was at this moment that Jack's right leg escaped its captor and did just that. *Whap!* Straight up between Gale's legs. The boy folded over in a howl of pain, his knife dropping to the floor and slipping between two boards.

In their surprised laughter, and the uncomfortable silence that followed, the twins had loosened their grip enough for Jack to pull free. He bounded around Gale and groped hopelessly at the doorknob.

*Unlocked!*

He could swear he had heard the click, but the door swung open freely. Stairs passed beneath his feet, and he made it to the second floor landing before he heard the three boys giving chase.

When Jack arrived on the first floor, Mrs. Punts had not yet come out of her room. He grabbed the front door handle and tore outside, the others now hot on his heels. Gale's fingers brushed his collar as he descended the front steps. When the older boy's feet hit the pebble-strewn cement, he slipped, tumbled forward and landed hard on his stomach.

Jack reached the city street along which he had followed the newspaper, and found it unusually empty. He looked both directions, not sure if he wanted help or a hiding place. Deciding not to linger on the question, he turned right and sprinted off along the sidewalk. He could hear the other boys coming to the main street now.

Not knowing where to go, Jack let his feet carry him down side streets and across small, neon-lit parking lots, clutching at a stitch that was forming in his side.

As he rounded a corner between two shabby buildings, he found his way blocked by a chain-linked fence. Razor wire was coiled along the top, but it had been lazily placed. One side didn't reach the wall, giving just enough space for Jack to fit through. He climbed the fence, knowing as he did so that the rattling it made would give him away.

Nearing the top, his right leg became hooked in a barb. Desperately he tugged at it, hearing a small tearing sound as the ankle of his pants leg began to rip. He tugged again.

A paw caught his bare foot. "Gotcha!" Gale shouted, pulling Jack's foot down toward him. As he did so, the pant leg became free of the wire. *Lucky break!* Jack thought as he jerked his foot free and dropped down on the other side of the fence.

Up ahead, a maze of train cars sat in a cloud of fog that looked green under the lights. Row upon row were lined up before a tall station building. He ran between two boxcars. To his left, he saw the open bay door of a baggage car at the end of a train. Whether he was cornering himself or not, Jack couldn't run another block. Jogging crookedly to the opening, he pulled himself inside and, as quietly as he could, slid the door shut, leaving himself in blackness.

Heart pounding heavily against his ribs, he backed himself against a shelf along the far wall. His paws groped behind him, finding what felt like a suitcase. Continuing his blind search, he found a gap between a stack of cardboard boxes and a duffel bag, hoisted himself onto the shelf and squished between them.

The crackle of gravel just outside of the car made his heart jump. He held his breath as the footsteps came to a stop.

"Anything?" came a voice from a little farther off; Gale's voice.

"No," said the twin outside. "Nothing over here." The footsteps moved away.

"That's right, Jack Robberts!" Gale called, his voice cracking boyishly as he taunted. "You get your tail out of here and don't you *ever* come back!"

*Don't worry*, Jack thought through angry tears. *I won't*. A dry sob escaped his throat, then another. He began to cry in earnest. It was several minutes before the tears subsided and his lids became heavy. He fell asleep in the baggage car, his head resting on the soft duffel bag which, in the light, would show a tag with the letters "E.W."

## Chapter Three
# THE SAPLING, PART ONE

The Northern Gateway had survived worse storms than this. A stone structure will not stand at the edge of the sea for seven hundred years without facing its fair share of gales, but this storm was different; not in its strength, but its solemn mood. Each flash of lightning painted the Gateway not the blue-gray of the stones with which it was made, but the bleach white of a skull that peered morosely down upon the clashing sea a hundred yards below.

The middle arch was the tallest, a colossal doorway that divided the ocean on one side from a great expanse of grasslands on the other. Second and third arches buttressed outward in either direction, a family of doors linked together along the perimeter of the cliff. The shortest of these could fit two upright elephants standing one on another, but the message was clear from a distance, engraved above the highest arch: "All Are Welcome."

Perched just above this friendly pronouncement, the weasel picked at a tooth with his tongue. It was a nervous tick that came back to him at moments like this; moments with such intentions. He didn't like it. It made him feel weak, to have any sign of nerves. Fortunately, the habit had not resurfaced until now; now that he was in charge and, so long as everything went as smoothly as he'd promised, he need not fear for his life. He had positioned his men above the Gateway's lesser arches, too far below to scrutinize his demeanor. These guys didn't know him. They had no idea that he was shivering with chill and nerves, no idea that he knew — to his very core — that he was in far over his head. From the distance they stood, spread out like candles upon the lower tiers, all they would be able to see was the silhouette of their leader pressed against flashes of lightning in the black sky. He smiled faintly at the thought and licked his sharp teeth again.

His eyes scanned the sea far below. He grabbed at his wrist with a soaking paw and thumbed a button along the rim of his watch. It glowed pale blue. 5:16AM. *Could this take any longer?* He dropped his arms and cocked his head sideways, staring down at the train track that rose out of the ocean and plateaued beneath the highest arch.

A flicker caught his peripheral again. *All fours*, these guys were stupid. He blinked his flashlight back, then to his other side just to be sure everyone got the same message: *Not yet.*

The seconds dragged on, and Frank Magovern wondered if that fish train would *ever* arrive. He licked his teeth.


The luggage car rocked gently sideways, and Jack Robberts opened his eyes. He'd dreamed he was in the belly of a giant fish, swimming lazily through the sea. A nauseousness still bubbled up his chest, the faint odor of sea water still hung in the air.

In the soft red glow of a single light caged just above the inter-car door, he watched a row of suspended backpacks and garment bags click against the metal wall as they swung loosely. The train was in motion.

As the drowsiness ebbed away, he took in the rest of the room. The center floor was made of a single sheet of metal, brown by intention but balding bronze at the center and near the loading and inter-car doors. High up along the loading door, a long and slender window showed nothing but blackness. He watched for a moment, drawn to what he assumed was the night sky. Then something zipped past. Motionless, he waited, and after a moment, it reappeared. It looked like a large bronze sheet whisking past the window. No, whisking *toward* the window, covering it completely, then fading outward again. After several more passes, he noticed something else: bubbles! They swirled in the wake of the whisking object, running along its edges. Some even clung to the window. Elation coursed through him as he realized what it was — an artificial fish fin, propelling the train through water.

He threw his bare feet over the edge of the shelf and dropped down, then selected a sturdy looking suitcase and dragged it over the edge. With great effort, he pulled it across the metal floor and propped it upright beneath the window.

But he was disappointed; beyond the enormous mechanical fin, it was simply too dark to make out anything but particles that glistened red in the window light.

The car began to bank right, so that Jack had to lean against the door. To his left, he could now see golden windows glowing along the rest of the train as it curved. His vision was blocked momentarily as the fin pushed backward. When it drew away, he saw something else. Beyond the train, far ahead, two rows of ghostly green lamps swooped downward on either side of what looked like an unfinished roller coaster track. As the train drew nearer, pointing itself toward the lights, the swooping shape left his field of view, and the train righted itself.

After a moment, there was a heavy grind, both heard and felt. It rattled through the luggage car, dimly at first. Then with a sudden *clap*, the car's motion became rigid, as though it had locked into something. *Tracks!* They had reached the other side of the sea.

As if in confirmation, a voice echoed through the baggage car. "*Weeeelcome* to Northern Nikacia. We're now passing below the Northern Gateway. The ramp can be a bit steep, so please remain seated as we surface."

The water's ceiling drew nearer, a thundercloud of waves into which the train was being drawn. The tinkering patter of rain began to tap menacingly at the roof. A moment later, the baggage car reached the top of the slope, plateauing. It passed below the Northern Gateway, of which Jack only caught a gray flash, and trundled into the vast Bastian Plains of Northern Nikacia.

Seeing nothing but his own reflection staring back at him, slightly blurred in the double pane, he used his sleeve to wipe away the heart-shaped fog his breath had formed, and cupped his paws around his peripherals. This was only marginally better. A black plain stretched out into a black mountain range, silhouetted against a faint gray sky. Morning was approaching. Deciding that weeds and desert brush were the best he'd see, he moved back with a sigh.

He blinked. Something had been moving alongside the train. Once more, he pressed his face to the window.

A pickup truck sped past the window, kicking up pebbles that tinkled against the luggage car. The brakes eased, and the truck began keeping pace with the train. In the bed stood four figures, hanging on to the sides as the truck bounced alongside the track. The nearest of these figures was just below Jack's eye level. He had a bald head with pointed ears. His brows were thick and bushy, and wrapped around a pair of goggles supported by a broad, flat snout.

The rider turned his head quickly upward, and Jack ducked, nearly toppling off of the suitcase. After a moment, he stood cautiously, pressed his forehead against the glass, and cupped the sides of his face. This time he *did* topple off of the suitcase. A pig's face had been level with his own, looking straight in at him! He scrambled to hide beneath the door.

His face next to the suitcase, Jack saw something he hadn't noticed before. A small gold plate was fixed near the handle, engraved with the letters "E.W."

A pair of slender paws seized him at both arms. He felt himself being pulled backward, and in his panic he let out a shrill cry.

"A stowaway, have we?" a mountain-twang voice said as Jack was turned around to face a squirrel in a grayish-blue attendant's suit. "I'm afraid I'll have to take you to the Captain."

Disoriented, Jack began to ramble hysterically. "Pig!" he screamed, pointing toward the window. "He's getting on the train!"

He continued to struggle as the attendant gripped his wrist and pulled him through the inter-car doors. As they entered the rearmost passenger car, sleeping patrons began to stir, looking around to see what all the commotion was about. The attendant seemed to notice, or perhaps he simply realized how little hope there was in dragging a grade-school bunny several more cars to the engine. Relenting, he adopted a reasoned tone. "Alright, listen you. Sapply Station is more than twenty minutes off. Supposing there *was* someone trying to board the train, wouldn't you want to tell the Captain?"

Jack paused, breathing heavily. In his panic, he hadn't thought about what to do. But realization dawned on him: this was a submersible train, and it was heading toward Sapply. "E.W!" he blurted excitedly. "We have to tell Dr. Walraven!" He turned toward the front of the train and bolted off.

"Dr. Walraven!" Jack yelled as he entered the next car, nearly tripping over a white wolf at the doorway.

The doctor, who had been staring thoughtfully out the window, sat upright, his eyebrows raised in surprise. "Jack?" he said as the bunny bounded into the seat next to him. Alan, the fox boy, sat across from the doctor, his feet propped up on the seat Jack now occupied. He jerked a foot angrily from beneath the bunny, grumbling as he shut his eyes. "How did you get on this train?" Dr. Walraven asked.

The squirrel, out of breath, jogged up the aisle. "I'm sorry, Sir. I found him stowed away in the baggage car."

"Is that right?" Dr. Walraven asked, eying Jack. "Well I'll be interested to know *why*," he said, giving the bunny a stern yet not unkindly look. He turned back to the attendant. "Thank you, young man. I'll square away with the line when we get to Sapply."

"Dr. Walraven," Jack burst out. "There was somebody outside. He was a pig. He looked right at me. And then *that* guy grabbed me and I thought he was the pig so I hit him. He deserved it anyway, 'cause you should never grab someone from behind," to which the squirrel rolled his eyes. "The pig was getting on the train!"

Dr. Walraven looked inquiringly at the squirrel, who shook his head. "I didn't see anything, Sir."

A pair of elderly goats had awakened and were watching the discussion with groggy trepidation. Dr. Walraven turned to see that most of the passengers around them were watching as well. "May we speak with the Captain?" he asked.

"I knew *you'd* believe me!" Jack said, throwing a disdainful look at the squirrel.

"Certainly, Sir," the attendant said, gesturing with an open paw toward the front of the train. Dr. Walraven hoisted Jack to the aisle and stood to follow. He paused, turning to Alan, whose eyes were still closed. The fox folded his arms across his chest and made a salivating movement with his mouth. Dr. Walraven turned back toward the attendant, nodding forward, and they moved on.

After several more cars, they entered a hot, loud room bathed in red light. At the far end of the room was a riveted steal door. The squirrel, who had introduced himself as "Nathan," had to shout as he led the two passengers along. "The Captain is right through here," he said, lifting a metal handle.

At the front of the engine, two figures stood before the rain-pummeled windshield, contrasted against the beam of the headlamp. "Sir," Nathan started, "this is Dr. Walraven, a passenger. And this is Jack. He thinks…" he paused awkwardly. "He thinks he saw someone boarding the train."

The squirrel fell silent as the shorter of the two figures turned around, revealing a sharp-toothed grin. A tongue picked momentarily at the teeth. Nathan leapt back in surprise. Under the white captain's cap, the shifty eyes of a weasel turned down to Jack.

"You say you saw someone?" the weasel hissed as he leaned closer to Jack, who pressed into the doctor's legs.

Jack whimpered, his voice soft and unsure. "Yes. It was a pig. He was ugly."

The weasel stood, his eyes half-lidded and his crooked lips turned up into a sneer. "An ugly pig?" he repeated. "Was he as ugly as *this* pig?" He motioned to the other figure, who stepped from the dark to reveal yellow tusks and bushy eyebrows.

Jack cried out as he pressed harder into the doctor's legs. Putting an arm over the boy, Dr. Walraven started, "Now just wait one…"

"That's not the Captain," Nathan whispered.

Dr. Walraven looked to the attendant, then back to the thugs. "I'm afraid the Captain had to step out," the weasel said with a self-satisfied laugh.

"More like 'fly out,'" the pig chortled, but caught the unamused eye of the weasel and stopped short.

"You can join him," the weasel said. "Toss them over the side." He turned again toward the windshield, then paused. "Wait," he said. "Give me the canister first."

"Maybe we could use them," the pig started, shrugging off the shoulder strap of a silver cylinder that resembled an overlarge thermos. "You know, as bait."

The weasel took the canister, fixing his co-conspirator with a cold glare. The pig huffed and threw his belly at the group, shoving them toward the door.


The red walls and overwhelming heat of the engine room put Jack in mind of Hell. It was easy enough to picture this bloated pig in a tight red suit and cape, horns, pitchfork and all.

Slender fingers gripped the bunny's shoulders. "It's going to be okay, Jack," Dr. Walraven whispered.

"Keep moving," the pig said. As they neared the rear of the car, he forced a sudden turn, and they found themselves standing at a metal door with a porthole window, nothing but blackness beyond sideways streaks of rain. He yanked Jack upward by his ears. The doctor made a grab for him, but the enormous pig slapped him to the floor. "End of the line, you runt," the pig said. Without another word, he tore open the door and tossed Jack into the howling rain.

## Chapter Four

# THE SAPLING, PART TWO

It wasn't the thunder that woke Aaron Harding. It was the dream. Well, the memory *of* a dream, but as he burst upright in his hotel bed, he realized that he could no more recall this one than the countless before.

He looked around the dark and disheveled room. A suitcase lay open against the far wall, clothing spilling over the sides. If Evie were here, she'd have something to say. "What would the world think if they could see the great King of Hearts being such a slob?" He smiled at the thought, but his mind was simply too occupied to concern himself with tidiness. Avak had been missing for the better part of a month, which could only mean he was dead. But *why?* Sander, at least, had been a hero long enough to have made some dangerous enemies, but the otter was just a kid; he didn't have an enemy in the world. Could someone have learned Aaron's plan for him?

And then there was this Alan Kale kid. Einer was insistent upon him, and the young fox seemed a suitable candidate. Not ideal, but suitable. Avak had been a perfect fit, and now that the otter was dead, possibly *because* of the plan, how could he justify the use of someone two years younger and far less equipped?

He rubbed an enormous paw over his muzzle and stood, scratching above his tail as he moved toward the bathroom.

As he went about his business, he tried once again to recall the dream. He'd been flying. That part wasn't so unusual — he'd been able to fly since he was nineteen years old. But the *way* he'd been flying was strange, gliding ghostlike through the air, straight toward... something. A stone building of some kind. Maybe a chapel? He was being chased by some enormous thing, like an oblong boulder that had been rolled end-over-end. The object was making a wet, vacuous noise so loud, it might have been roaring through a megaphone. But the harder he tried to concentrate on the details, the hazier they seemed.

Yet he knew, or at least he thought he knew, what these dreams meant. And the dreams were becoming more frequent.

That made the plan all the more urgent.

He washed his paws, flipped on the coffee pot and examined himself in the mirror. *You are getting old, lion,* he thought, taking in the white bristles along his muzzle and the desaturated tone of his dread-locked mane, which hung in ropes around his over-large head.

The phone rang, bringing him out of his reverie. He crossed to the bedside table in two strides and caught up the receiver. "Hello."

"Oh, Aaron, thank God!" said a familiar, yet panicky voice.

"Toby," the lion responded. "What is it? What's wrong?"

"There's trouble," Toby said, his voice breaking. "A train hijacking, right in your area."

Aaron sat heavily down on the edge of the unmade bed. "It's alright, Toby. Just… tell me the details." He listened intently as Toby filled him in, his eyes falling upon the clothing draped over the open suitcase, fixating on the heart-shaped emblem sewn into the fabric.

"Hurry, Aaron," Toby implored.

"I'm on my way," Aaron responded, and he set the receiver down. Rubbing his face with his large paws, he slapped his knees and stood.

As he finished suiting up, he took one last look at his reflection, this time with the slightest hint of a smile. The image of a stone chapel came back to him. And a toppling object just at his tail. And that loud, vacuum-like sound. It seemed to crescendo, coming back to him clearer than ever.

He flicked the coffee pot back off — the aroma would have to suffice. It was going to be a rough day.

Toby had never been a good liar.


Jack Robberts was beginning to lose consciousness. The back of his shirt had caught on something, and he was now hanging like a crook at the gallows, his feet dangling mere inches above the blurred rush of gravel.

Then a shadow blocked out the light.

Looking up and to the right, he could just see the pig climb out through the doorway and grab onto a ladder along the body of the train. Was he coming for Jack? Was he going to kick him loose? Instead, the pig turned upward, climbing toward the roof of the train.

A voice called out. "Jack!"

Twisting his neck as far right as he could, Jack saw slender pink fingers stretching toward him from the same door. He reached upward weakly, but the paw was out of his range. "Lower me a bit," Dr. Walraven shouted. The paw reached down again, getting low enough to brush Jack's shoulder. He raised his arm, a tingling numbness spreading to his fingertips.

The paw closed around his own, and as he was pulled upward, another pink paw grabbed roughly onto his shirt. With a great heave, he rose out of the rain and crashed down on top of Dr. Walraven. The rat was gasping for breath, but flung both arms around Jack and mumbled, "Thank God. Oh, thank God."

Jack trembled and whimpered, looking around the room as he brushed tears down into the fur of his cheeks. Nathan was slumped against the opposite wall, both paws joined over his eyes. He, too, was trying to catch his breath.

Dr. Walraven slid out from under Jack and hobbled to the doorway, leaning out and looking upward. "He's gone," he said. He then turned down to the spot where Jack had been hanging. "Jack, come here," he called, looking back over his shoulder at the bunny and extending a paw.

Jack rose slowly and took small, hesitant steps toward the door. Dr. Walraven put an arm reassuringly around his shoulder and drew him slowly toward the opening. "There!" the doctor said, pointing to the spot where Jack's shirt had become hooked. "You see it?"

A slender, brownish gold protrusion extended out from the body of the train, just below the door.

"It's part of the fin the train uses to swim!" Dr. Walraven laughed. "It seems to have malfunctioned — it failed to close all the way." He moved back into the room, pulling Jack with him, and slammed the door. "I thought we'd lost you." He hugged the bunny. "That was lucky, wasn't it?"

Jack looked up at him, hiccuping another small sob, then rested his head against the doctor's stomach and considered his words.

They moved into the next car, where the passengers were mostly awake and looking uneasily toward the roof. "Yes, we heard it too," a goat woman was saying across the aisle to a grandmotherly finch wearing a bonnet. "It sounded like gunfire."

"That's what I thought," the finch replied.

Jack looked toward Dr. Walraven, who gave him a reassuring smile and crouched down to eye level. "Jack, I need to go and get Alan. It seems the danger is moving in his direction." He looked up toward Nathan. "Would you mind keeping an eye on him?"

The squirrel looked as if he might collapse or vomit, but he gave a rather jerky nod. Dr. Walraven rose and began back down the aisle toward the next passenger car.

Nathan dropped into an empty seat and put a paw over his face. "Two weeks," he mumbled. "Just two more weeks! Spring break. No job. No worries. No all-fours train-jacking." He was shaking all over.

Perhaps Jack had shivered and cried everything out, for now he felt like doing neither. Out the window, the sky was still black, but with a faint blue rim to distinguish the mountains from the storm clouds. Dawn was coming; the storm was ending.

From the far end of the car, thunderous footsteps came crashing along the roof toward the engine, then came to a sudden stop just overhead. The passengers watched the ceiling in anxious silence. There was a muffled yell, then the unmistakable cracking of gunfire, coupled with another yell like a war cry.

Then a louder sound. It began in the ceiling itself, the sound of metal scraping metal. The car vibrated with the noise. The roof began to tear, as though invisible hands were pealing it back. Sparks showered down as the tear grew, exposing the morning sky, opening the car like a sardine can. There was another shout, this one much more audible and profane; the pig's voice. But his cry was cut short with a thud. The metal had rolled up like a carpet, a large lump at its center. The muffled yells of the pig could be heard from inside the roll like a profanity-shouting bulge in an anaconda's belly.

Footsteps thundered once more from the rear of the train, then with a burst, pounded off the rolled up roof, and a shadow flew gracefully across the gap. Jack watched as the unmistakable silhouette, with its brush ended tail and dread locked mane, passed over his head.

Applause had burst out among the relieved passengers. Jack gripped Nathan's arm. "King!" he shouted over the roaring chug of the train engine. "It's King *himself!*"

"Jack?" Dr. Walraven had returned, and was hurrying toward the bunny. "Are you alright?"

Alan walked just behind the doctor, his paws in his jeans pockets as he stared up at the gaping hole in the ceiling.

"I'm fine," Jack nodded. Then he erupted with excitement. "King was here!"

Dr. Walraven turned toward the open ceiling with a look of concerned calculation.

"Is something wrong?" Alan asked.

"Well," the doctor started, "we're getting quite near to Sapply. Another ten minutes and we'll be there."

"That's *good*, right?" Nathan the attendant said hopefully.

"Why aren't we slowing down?" the doctor said. "What was it the pig said?" he continued, more to himself. "'*Maybe we could use them as bait.*' And then after he tossed Jack out the door, the weasel came out and said 'he's here' and the pig climbed to the roof." He fell silent for a moment, then turned slowly toward the front of the train. "It's a trap."

As if in response to these words, a loud roar bellowed through the open ceiling. All heads turned upward. "Wouldn't want to be the hijackers right about now," the goat husband said with a nod to the finch, who smiled nervously.

There was another roar. The crowd around Jack continued to express relief at their salvation, but to Jack it sounded like King was in trouble. Alan seemed to have the same thought. "We need to *do* something," the fox said, looking defiantly up at Dr. Walraven.

The doctor shook his head. "There's nothing we can do, Alan. King is more than capable of…"

He stopped suddenly. The car had given a heavy lurch, which was accompanied by another, even more pronounced *roar*. Passengers jumped to their feet in alarm, filling the aisle. Jack took the opportunity. He pushed his way between the goat and finch, straight through the inter-car doors.

"Jack? Jack! Wait!" But Dr. Walraven's words were drowned out as the second set of doors slid closed.

The light in the engine room seemed even redder than before, bouncing off a thick cloud of steam. Sparks were now falling from the ceiling — he passed below them like a curtain as he entered the room. King didn't know this was a trap. He must be warned.

But as Jack neared the door leading into the control room, the train gave a heavy lurch, paired with the same metallic tearing that had sounded when the roof had torn open. Reaching for the door handle, he lost his balance and tumbled against the wall.

He spun to face the rear of the car. But where the inter-car doors had been, a gaping hole grinned out onto open air. His head spun at the sight. "Wait!" he cried as he ran back to the opening. The engine and first passenger car were now separated by a gap of ten feet, and the divide continued to expand as the passenger cars lost speed. Jack could see Dr. Walraven struggling desperately with the inter-car door, which seemed to be jammed, his wide eyes fixed on Jack's. "No! No! No!" the bunny bleated, his voice choking with horrified sobs.

Overhead, he saw a brush ended tail whisk out of view. "King!" Jack cried.

The train gave another lurch. This one was different, sidelong, as though the engine had been side-swiped by a bus. The room tilted right, threatening to topple sideways, and Jack turned to grab the railing. As he spun round, his eyes fixed on something that had not been there a moment before. Rammed straight through the wall like a harpoon, a barbed pole had pierced the engine, as black as coal and thick as a tree trunk. As quickly as he had spotted it, the pole jerked heavily, its barbs caught the wall, and the train lurched to the left. But this lurch was continual, gradual, as though the pole was being reeled in on a winch. The engine began to lean heavily to the left. The moan of the wheels fighting the track was as loud and mournful as a whale's song.

Legs numb with fright and unsteady on the slick, sloping floor, Jack hobbled toward the gap in the rear of the engine again, moving paw-over-paw along the side rail. Reaching the gap, he sucked in a lung full of smoky air and bellowed with all his might, "King! King, please help me!"

Just as he was inhaling another poisonous lungful, a thick padded paw, larger than Jack's head, reached down from above the gap. "Take my paw!" a deep voice beckoned. "Quickly!"

Jack jumped as high as he could and caught the paw with both of his own. Immediately, he felt himself being jerked upward. He let out a cry as he flew up over the lip of the roof. Another enormous paw caught his waist and pulled him down into a horizontal bear hug. The lion lay across the roof on his back, clutching Jack to his chest as if the bunny were a toddler.

The train continued to tip, steeper and steeper. The wheels gave a final, ear-piercing scream.

The engine derailed.

It was like a dream, a surreal dream where every detail was sharper than it would be in real life. He was gliding through the air, aware of the glint of sunlight bouncing off beads of dew in the grass far below his feet. He could smell the grass, even see little white insects hopping around between the blades. King's arms were wrapped around him, the tight weave of the fabric so clear, it was as if he saw it through a magnifying glass. He could hear the train engine toppling behind them, roaring like a vacuum over sand. And just ahead, he saw a stone chapel. They had been thrown right toward it, much too quickly.

He didn't remember passing out. Nor did he remember vomiting, but the smell of it was the first thing he recognized. He opened his eyes. The air was thick with dust. He seemed to be indoors, in a building made of stone.

As if by an electric shock, Jack was suddenly awake and alert. He was *alive*! Which meant King of Hearts had saved him. He knew he would! His eyes darted around, eagerly searching out his savior. There was movement everywhere. Some of them must be reporters, he considered. King would be talking to the reporters, or else checking with the passengers of the train. Jack rubbed the dust from his eyes, blinking in the haze. It was difficult to see in here. He perked his ears up. Only he didn't hear the sound of reporters asking questions or describing the scene.

What he heard instead were the sounds of chaos. Crackling fire. A stone wall crumbling to the ground. And voices. Scared voices. Some were far off, grinding harshly through walkie talkies. Some were much clearer, sobbing and screaming. Blurry movements soon registered as figures pacing around in front of half-shattered windows of stained glass.

Jack became aware of arms supporting his bottom, and a shoulder on which his head was now resting. Looking down, he saw a long pink tail protruding from below a tan sport coat, vomit dribbling down the fabric. With a feeble groan, he leaned back, craned his neck, and saw the side of Dr. Walraven's face. The doctor turned slightly, returning Jack's gaze. He didn't smile. He simply turned his eyes back to the now-sunny morning and stepped toward the damp grass outside.

Jack looked around again. King *must* be here somewhere.

And then he found him.

The train engine was sunk into the earth, a spider's web of shattered stones at its base.

And from beneath the engine, a brush ended tail lay draped across the stone.

He looked away immediately, his eyes searching for something, anything.

They fell upon a sapling framed in a stone archway like a work of art. A beam of sunlight bedazzled the gemstones of dew on its little leaves. It was a weak, lonely little plant, but the sight of it protruding from the rich brown soil filled Jack's heart, took the tremors from his paws, lulled him once again to sleep.

"You look very handsome, my boy." Dr. Walraven had said this three times already, and while he knew the rat was trying to ease the silence, Jack couldn't help frowning at his own reflection.

He looked stupid. Everyone looks stupid in a bow-tie, but he looked worse, like a long-eared ventriloquist's dummy. He turned his head and looked out the hotel window into the sunny morning, a sight in stark contrast with his own screaming insides.

King was dead. His body retrieved, placed in a box to be planted in the ground. And all because of Jack. If he had stayed in the passenger car, if he had minded his own business, if he hadn't needed saving, King would have had time to get to safety. He, Jack, had taken away those precious seconds and cost King his life. He looked again at his own reflection, hating himself and the stupid way he looked. Tears poured into his furry cheeks.

"Hey, now," Dr. Walraven said as he knelt beside the bunny.

"I don't want to wear this," Jack said. "I hate this stupid tie. I wouldn't have to wear it if I had stayed with you. I wouldn't have to be in this stupid tie! You wouldn't either. Nobody would. No ties. No flowers. None of it, if I had just… just stayed with you." He began to sob, and fell against the doctor's shoulder, his arms stiffly at his sides. Alan, who sat at the edge of the nearest bed, watched them silently, hardly seeming to breathe.

"No. No," the doctor said, drawing the bunny into a tight embrace, then pulling him away to meet his eyes. "None of this was your fault. I know you won't understand this now, but sometimes… sometimes you have to lose in order to win." He smiled, but seeing the confused look on Jack's face, he continued. "King died to protect *all* of us. Nothing you did changed the way things would have turned out. Do you understand?"

Jack nodded, although in truth, he didn't understand at all, and he didn't think Dr. Walraven did, either. He was the boy who killed King of Hearts. The tears came again. "Will you make me go back?" he asked between hiccups of breath. "Are you going to take me back to Mrs. Punts?"

Dr. Walraven gave Jack's bow-tie one last tug, then put both paws on the bunny's shoulders. "No, Jack," he said, looking toward Alan with an encouraging smile. "You're with us now."

## Chapter Five

# THE HONEY SAP GRILL

Five years passed, and despite common fears, King's death did not bring about world-altering change. Animal Control remained strong. The citizens of Nikacia remained safe. And in the quiet country town of Hadensburrow, four hundred miles north of Sapply, the mail still came only once a week; on Tuesday at precisely two in the afternoon.

The residents of Living Oak Drive treated mail day as some might treat a book club or knitting circle. They would huddle in conversation around the wall of stacked and mismatched mailboxes, sometimes staying hours after the mail had arrived. Lately, the discussion centered around the earthquakes. There had been quite a few in the recent months; some strong enough to knock picture frames from the walls; some so subtle, only the underground dwellers of the neighborhood would have felt them at all. The strange thing was, nobody could seem to remember a single quake in Hadensburrow's history — not until this year.

"Been here since I was just a cub," Mr. Tramontozzi said gruffly, leaning into his walker with his large paws. "And I can't recall so much as a leaf falling to the ground without a proper wind to explain it."

The neighbors all nodded in agreement — all except one. He said nothing, watching the approaching mail carrier.

"My Frederick, God rest him," started Mrs. Beeberson, a plump cavy in a floral dress and bonnet, "never did much care for the quakes we used to get in the South. Had I known they'd start up here, I'd never have put him on the mantle."

Again, everyone grunted in agreement. All except for one. He watched as the mail carrier deposited a package into his red painted mailbox.

"There was another one last night," Mr. Feedler harrumphed. He was a bear like Mr. Tramontozzi, although significantly slighter in build, with blue-gray fur wrapped up in a flannel coat that smelled strongly of tobacco. "I've about had it with bein' woke up every other night."

Several of the others nodded. As the mail carrier finished his work, the silent resident stepped forward.

Mr. Feedler saw him approaching. "And what do you make of these quakes, Dr. Walraven?"

The rat kept his eyes on his mailbox. "I think the quakes will continue," he said in a friendly but uninvolved tone as he pulled the little red door open. "Or they won't. But I can't see that your grumbling is going to persuade them to do one thing over the other."

Several of the others laughed, including Mr. Feedler. Dr. Walraven stuffed the package beneath his arm without a second glance, wished them all a "Good day," and started back along the dirt road.

When his neighbors were out of sight, Dr. Walraven withdrew the package and turned it over. From the outside, one would never know it was anything but ordinary; in fact, it was quite plain. It was about the size of a clock radio, wrapped neatly in brown paper (and an overly-cautious amount of packing tape). Aside from his address and the postage, the only marking was a single word scribbled into the corner where a return address might typically go: "Stronger". The word brought a smile to his face.

But the smile was short lived. In his heart, he knew that the arrival of this package meant dark days were ahead. Dark for him; certainly dark for Jack.

He sighed as he approached the rickety old watermill. It was gnarled and crooked, shaded beneath a giant oak tree along the bank of a slow-moving river. A large wooden wheel turned with a moan as it was pushed by the calm water of the Bristlin.

"Jack?" he called as he entered, unbuttoning his coat and hanging it on an antique rack. He set the package down on the dining table. "Jack?" he called again. *Now where could that boy have gone?*

In truth, he already knew the answer. All he could do was hope Jack wasn't getting himself into any more trouble.

But of course he was. As a matter of fact, for a boy of only eleven, Jack Robberts was probably the keenest trouble-maker the quiet country town had ever seen. Many of the locals remembered his arrival, because it had been around the time of that famous train wreck, the one that had killed King of Hearts. Expecting this new bunny to be as friendly and well-mannered as the fox boy that already lived with Dr. Walraven, they had graciously welcomed Jack into the community. Quieter than the fox boy, if not as well-mannered, he would follow Dr. Walraven around town, watching his own feet, and nobody could help but feel sorry for him.

But after a few years, the local police were delivering him to his watermill home on a regular basis. He'd been hiding in trees and flinging marshmallows at porcupines, or else pouring soap flakes into the Hayward family dam. When he turned eleven, he replaced Mr. Feedler's cigars with fire crackers, and spent the afternoon at the police station. One more misstep, he was told, and he'd stay there overnight. It was for this reason that Jack now vented most of his pent-up mischief here at the Honey Sap Grill, where he now sat across the table from a barrel-chested rat in a flannel shirt.

"You're *lucky*," the rat repeated, disbelieving.

Jack was shuffling a deck of cards against the table. "Yes sir," he said as he divided the deck and shuffled again. "Luck of the rabbits; it's all in the feet. And I can correctly guess your card *every time*."

"Aren't you a little young to gamble?" the rat asked.

Jack smiled crookedly. "Yes sir," he said. "But this isn't gambling. Think of it as... *street magic*. You pay five bucks and I'll guess your card correctly. And if I can't..." he added, holding up a paper bill and placing it on the table.

The rat picked up his drink, swirling it around gently. "Alright, kid. You're on."

A manic looking opossum, much smaller than the rat, grabbed his arm. "No, no Chuck! You'll lose for sure! You heard him! He's lucky!"

The rat yanked his arm free, then reached into his pocket, withdrawing a crumpled wad of cash. "He's just a kid, Stew. And it's five bucks." He extracted a green bill and placed it on the table alongside Jack's.

"That's the spirit," Jack said. "And I'll tell you what, *Stew*," he added, meeting the opossum's bulbous eyes and offering the deck of cards. "Why don't *you* do the honors? Hold these out, let your friend pick a card. Mark it with this pen," he extended a black marker, "and reinsert it into the deck anywhere you like." The opossum was eying him distrustfully. "I'll even turn my back," Jack said, making a bit of a production out of covering his eyes and turning around.

There was a silent moment, the sound of cards being shuffled, and then the rat said, "Alright, let's see this luck of yours."

Jack turned around to see the opossum fanning the deck of cards toward him. He extended a paw, touched one of the cards, then shut his eyes as if in concentration and shook his head, touched a different card, nodded with a smile, and withdrew it. "Is *this* your card?" he asked with a knowing smugness as he held it up.

The rat let out a barking laugh. The opossum joined in. Looking at the card, Jack's smile dropped; there was no mark on it.

"Thanks for buying my drink, kid!" Chuck laughed.

"I don't understand," Jack muttered, rifling through the deck until he found a Three of Diamonds with a black *X* in the corner. Defeated, he leaned back into his chair.

The burly rat stood and grabbed up his winnings from the table. Suddenly, Jack's paw caught him around the wrist — barely wrapping around half of it — and their eyes met. "Ten to nothing," Jack pleaded.

"Ten?" the rat chortled. "That's a hundred bucks on the table. Are you crazy?"

"If I am, then you've got nothing to lose."

"And I suppose you've got fifty bucks just lying around, do you?" Chuck asked, his tone half mocking, half hungry.

Jack reached into his coat pocket with a jingle and pulled out a fistful of coins. Counting out five of them, he laid them on the table without hesitation. His eyes shot imploringly back to Chuck's.

The rat considered him, then smiled greedily and dropped back into the wooden chair. "Ten to nothing," he consented.

With an expression of nervous modesty, Jack slid the deck of cards toward the rat, who shuffled only once before extracting a card, marking it discreetly, and replacing it in the deck. "Let's make it twenty," he said, adding several crumpled bills to the pile.

Hesitantly, Jack pulled another paw full of coins from his pocket and, with a look that suggested this was causing him great inner turmoil, dropped them into the pile.

Chuck fanned the deck toward Jack, who shut his eyes, reached forward, and extracted a card. He opened his eyes and held his breath as he turned it over.

The Knave of Hearts, with a small black "X" in the corner.

The rat looked as though he had been clubbed over the head. As Jack swept the huge pile of coins and bills into a cloth napkin on his lap, the rat spat a tirade of profanities, kicking his chair over backward. The nervous little opossum was giving him a sermon of "I told you so"s, which only angered him more.

Drawing the corners of the napkin together and tying them, Jack stood. The rat grabbed at him, his paw cuffing Jack's entire forearm. "Now wait just one..." he began, but paused, looking at Jack's arm. Grabbing the bunny's sleeve, he yanked it back, revealing a wire apparatus wrapped around Jack's wrist like a watch. The tinkering of glass and conversations around the crowded room silenced at once. "Cheating," Chuck hissed, his grip on Jack's forearm tightening. "Seems you've been making your *own* luck, bunny," he growled, drawing a balled fist backward, "and it's just run out."

Jack's free paw shot to the wire apparatus, flicking a catch along the side. An armature extended like an accordion, jabbing Chuck's paw. With a roar of pain, the rat's grip immediately loosened. Jack dropped his weight and lunged forward, ramming a shoulder squarely into the rat's stomach, toppling him over the much smaller opossum. Pushing his way through the now standing crowd, Jack burst through the front door into the breezy day.

The sky was blinding after the dimly lit dining room, and by the time Jack's eyes adjusted, the entire populous of North Street was watching him. He ran to the edge of the patio and leapt to the sidewalk, bumping his way between two squirrels at the foot of the stairs. Excited laughter escaped him as he disappeared around the vine-covered side of the building.

A breath later, the heavyset rat threw the saloon doors wide and stomped down the stairs. "Which way did he go?" he demanded of the dissipating crowd, to no response.

The sudden roar of an engine barked from behind the restaurant. He turned just in time to dodge a small motorcycle as it peeled past him, kicking up dirt and oak leaves until it found the red brick road. A boyish laugh echoed down the steep hill of North Street as Jack looked over his shoulder at the rat, held up his paw, and made a less-than-friendly gesture.

## Chapter Six

## AT THE WATERMILL

He'd hardly reached the bottom of the hill before the smile faded from Jack's face. Rhoda, the Honey Sap's owner, must already be giving Dr. Walraven an earful about his behavior. His mind wove through eloquent phrasing that might convince the doctor it was no big deal, but he nevertheless found himself silencing the engine and walking his motorcycle the last half mile home.

When he had propped the bike against the oak tree at the southern corner of the mill, he ducked below the window, tiptoed up the front stairs and inched the door open as gingerly as a runaway, edging his way inside.

The living area was small, with a worn blue couch and Dr. Walraven's favorite floral arm chair forming an *L* around a rustic coffee table. The floor was made of gray, knotted boards covered in part by a faded and frayed maroon rug. On the far end of the room was a small kitchen and dining area, with a similarly knotted table and three chairs, and a sink that pumped directly from the river outside. Around the corner, wooden stairs led to a second floor, where Jack's and Dr. Walraven's bedrooms were, along with the empty room that Alan used to occupy.

"Hello, Jack."

Jack jumped and turned. "Er… hi."

Limping down the stairs in his arthritic manner, Dr. Walraven moved to the dining area and lowered himself into one of the chairs. "I spoke with Rhoda," he said. His tone was not accusatory, but he looked at Jack as if waiting for a response.

Jack shrugged, looking down at his own feet as he dropped into the adjacent chair.

Dr. Walraven spoke to the side of his head. "Son, you will be twelve years old this week. Nearly a teen. It's time you put aside this childishness and…"

"And what?" Jack said, turning to the doctor with a gaze that was both frustrated and miserable. "And 'grow up'? Why should I? It's not like you're ever going to take me to Triarch. You work for Animal Control, and yet you've never taken me. Not once!"

"Jack…" Dr. Walraven reached out to squeeze Jack's shoulder, but the bunny pulled away. He sighed and continued. "I don't *work* for Animal Control. I consult for them. I sit in conference rooms with a bunch of old men. You'd be bored to tears."

"You took Alan all the time," Jack said. "Now he's working for Animal Control, and you haven't spoken in two years. I thought we were a *family*."

"Alan and I had a very different relationship," Dr. Walraven said.

"Shuh," the bunny grunted.

There was a moment of silence between them, and then Dr. Walraven fixed Jack with a serious look, seeming to decide on something. "I'll make you a deal. I will take you to Triarch..." Jack looked up, but Dr. Walraven held up a paw and continued. "But you will have to earn it. You have to stop behaving like you did today. Hustling tourists. Cheating, no less."

"But I wasn't cheating!" Jack interrupted.

"Please let me finish," the doctor said. "If you are going to come with me to Animal Control, I need to know that you can behave like an adult. It won't be a sight-seeing tour. You'll need to behave responsibly." By this point, Jack's eyes were fixed on the doctor's, his heart pounding. "Which means that for now, you'll need to take on some responsibility."

His heart still inches higher in his chest, Jack tried his best to keep the smile off of his face as he asked, "Responsibility? Like what? Find a job or something?"

Dr. Walraven allowed a small smile onto his own face. "As it happens, I've already found you one."

"Really? Where?" Jack asked.

"I had a nice talk with Rhoda, and she has agreed to let you work for her. You spend most of your time at the Honey Sap anyway; we might as well get some use out of your time there. And, if you work hard, and can give me six months without any reports of you causing trouble, I will take you to Triarch with me."

Jack slapped his paws together exuberantly. "Yes! Thank you. I will. I mean I won't. I mean, I *will* work hard and I *won't* cause any trouble." And with that, he did something he had not done in years – he hugged the doctor.

October evenings came too quickly in Hadensburrow. Darkness fell long before the day had run out of possibilities —

to Jack's mind, anyway. He now found himself perched in the tree flanking his rickety old home, watching the first stars sparkle above the forest on the opposite bank of the river. The few clouds that patched the dusk sky were purple and slow moving, like sailing ships in an ocean of glistening diamonds. He rested his head against an upright branch, his bare feet dangling as he took another acorn from the cluster in his paw and threw it to the river. A gentle *plunk* sent a series of ripples outward.

Jack inhaled deeply the scent of damp, mossy wood, sighing contentedly as he exhaled. Six months of "good behavior" — shouldn't be too difficult. That rat had been too aggressive; Jack should have spotted it right off the bat. He wouldn't make that mistake again. Only safe-looking travelers. Rich ones who could stand to lose their money. Anyway, it wasn't cheating. Not really. Not when he'd changed the card out on the first round. Losing on purpose wasn't against the...

His ears perked upward, and his head turned quickly toward the road. Lost in thought, he hadn't heard the approaching car until its headlights were visible behind the trees. Living Oak was a private road, and the Mill was at the end of it. Who would be coming here this late at night?

Jack leapt from the oak branch and, landing in a stride, hurried to the front door. The car's engine sputtered as it finally came to a stop in front of the mill. The headlights went out, seeming to fade away until the car was completely hidden in blackness. There was the sound of a door opening, then slamming shut. Footsteps crunched in the leaves, and slowly, a figure became visible in the light of the front doorstep. Tall, broad shouldered, and wearing the same type of homburg hat favored by Dr. Walraven, he came to a stop when he spotted Jack.

"Hello! You must be Jack," said a confident, booming voice. "Glad to see I'm in the right place. It's a long drive from Animal Control."

## Chapter Seven

# MR. BEHR

The newcomer introduced himself as Robert Behr. He was a canine, with chocolate fur turning silver across his brows and muzzle. Clutching his hat in his paws, he stooped as he followed Jack through the doorway. Although his eyes and jowls had a mopey droop about them, he looked around the place with an appreciative nod. "Somehow, I always pictured this is how it would look, Einer," he said as he extended a paw toward the rat.

"Well, Bobby, it's about time you made it up here to see it," Dr. Walraven responded as they shook, although Jack thought there was something stiff and reserved about his tone. The doctor took Behr's hat and hung it on the coat rack near the door. "I see you've met my other boy. Jack, Mr. Behr here is the director of the Department of Enhanced Nature at Animal Control."

The dog smiled. "I can't believe how much you've grown. My goodness! King's funeral, you were about five then, weren't you?"

Jack fidgeted. "Six."

Behr nodded. "Ah, well. Sad times, sad times. But," he clapped the bunny on the back, "all is not lost. Thank God for the sapling, eh?"

Jack wasn't sure what this meant, but was saved from the need to respond by Dr. Walraven. "Can I get you something to drink, Bobby? Tea?"

"Tea, yes. Thank you."

As Dr. Walraven busied himself in the small kitchen, Behr fixed Jack with a considering gaze. The bunny pursed his lips and looked uncomfortably around the room.

"You know," Behr started, "I haven't been to Hadensburrow since well before you were born. I seem to remember a rather good pub on North Street. Tom Something-or-other's. It's where I stayed the few times I visited, in a room upstairs. 'Course, I don't suppose pubs mean much to you just yet."

"As a matter of fact," Dr. Walraven said, returning with a steaming mug and handing it to Mr. Behr, "Jack just got a job at the Honey Sap, just up the street from Tom's. You remember the place. Malcon deplored it."

"*Too much dagged noise. Are we having a meeting or a carnival?*" Behr laughed. "Well, good for you Jack. A little hard work can go a long way."

"Speaking of going a long way," Dr. Walraven said, "why don't you tell us what brings you to Hadensburrow this late at night?"

"Ah, yes," Behr said. He licked his chops, clutching the warm mug between his paws. "Well, Einer, there's no easy way to go about this, frankly."

"There's always an easy way between friends," Dr. Walraven said. "Let's have a seat."

The dog dropped down into the low couch at the center of the living area. Dr. Walraven stooped into his favorite armchair. Unsure of where he should go, Jack lingered in the space between the dining and living areas, fiddling with a single acorn he'd maintained from outside.

"Well I'll get right to it," Behr said as he leaned into his knees, placing the mug on the table before him. "Animal Control has been robbed."

Jack looked sharply to Dr. Walraven. The rat's brows furrowed slightly and he nodded, but he gave no indication that this news was either surprising or of vast significance to him. "I see," he said. "And what was taken?"

The dog's eyes darted fleetingly toward Jack, then back to Dr. Walraven. "It's top secret, not supposed to say in front of… well, it's a certain brass item of importance to keeping the sapling locked up." As he said this, he made a gesture with his paw as if attempting to start a car engine.

Dr. Walraven laughed. "I think my boy knows what a key is," he said, but his tone was not mocking. "So the Revelation Key has gone missing. *Minds of mice.* That *is* significant news."

Behr looked extremely uncomfortable, shooting glances in Jack's direction. "Now, I wasn't supposed to… that's top-secret information, you understand."

"Oh, don't worry. Jack can keep a secret; isn't that right, Jack?" The bunny shrugged, examining his acorn a little too intently. Dr. Walraven leaned back into his chair, looking out the darkened window to his right. He sat in silence for a moment, contemplative. His eyes didn't leave the window as he spoke. "Triarch is such a long way from Hadensburrow. Must we leave right away?"

It took a moment for the question to set in. Jack looked at Dr. Walraven. "Leave? Leave; what do you mean? You can't mean…"

"It's alright, Jack," the doctor said, turning toward him with a relaxed smile. "Mr. Behr drove a long way. Let's not make this harder for him. Now I imagine there are one or two more men waiting in the car?"

Behr's posture had become rather rigid, his smile fixed. "Just Vincent. Now listen, Einer, you know Brisk. He wanted to send a whole platoon up here to bring you in. Anaxopters, guns, the whole thing. I came because," he faltered, cleared his throat, and continued, "because Animal Control owes you more respect than that. Now, I don't know… I won't insult you by asking if you did it. If you did, well you have your reasons, and if you didn't, then this'll all be cleared up right away." He reached into his coat and withdrew a folded piece of paper, passing it to Dr. Walraven. "But one way or the other I still gotta bring you in."

"Bring him in?" Jack half laughed, half shouted. "Did what? Stole the Resolution Key or whatever the stupid thing's called? Are you crazy?"

"It's okay, Jack," Dr. Walraven said, unfolding the paper and sliding his glasses further up his nose.

"No, it's not okay," Jack said, gesturing toward Behr. "This guy comes into our house and accuses you of stealing from Animal Control. You haven't even been out of Hadensburrow in a month."

The doctor was silent for a moment, scanning the page. A faint sadness seemed to touch his eyes, and he let out a low sigh as he folded the letter once more and turned to Jack. "Exactly," he said. "Mr. Behr isn't accusing me of anything. It's procedure to question anyone with a motive when something like this happens."

"And you have a motive?" Behr asked.

"Of course I do. I don't like the idea of that key being within a hundred miles of Alexander Brisk, and now that he's been sworn in as Animal Control's new President, the key is at his disposal. Or at least it *was*." Smiling, he set the paper down on the side table next to him. "But then, as Jack says, I haven't left Hadensburrow in over a month. Now, if I were to guess, I'd say I'm not alone in my feelings regarding President Brisk. But no matter." He stood, looking down on Behr. "This whole uncomfortable business will be cleared up in a few days. I appreciate your generosity in coming this far on my behalf. I will repay the favor by not putting up a struggle."

Behr stood, too. He nodded. "As far as I'm concerned, Einer, this isn't an arrest."

"No," the doctor agreed. "Nor is it the first time you and I have traveled together from Hadensburrow to Triarch. It'll be just like old times." He strode to the closet and took his emergency travel bag from the top shelf.

"I'm sorry, Jack," Behr said as he put his hat back on, and he truly looked it. Of course, with those droopy eyes, he must *always* look it, Jack thought. The bunny made no response.

"I should be back day after tomorrow, I guess. Oh," Dr. Walraven halted halfway through putting on his coat. "That'll be your birthday, won't it." He finished with the coat, then plopped a white homburg onto his head. The door opened, and the two stepped into the night. Before he disappeared, Dr. Walraven added with a smile, "It'll be alright, Jack. Remember, good behavior."

It was never easy falling asleep when Jack was home alone. Every creaking board or branch scratching at the roof was far more unnerving without another body in the house on which to blame it. For this reason, Jack usually slept on the couch whenever the doctor was away. It was actually noisier down here, but at least the noise could be excused by the crickets and the slow turning mill wheel. The rhythmic moan was rather soothing, Jack thought, and it was usually enough to hum him to sleep.

But tonight, he kicked his blankets off with an aggravated groan and sat upright.

It was that prickling sensation at the scruff of the neck, as if he was being watched. He looked to the empty chair by the window, where Dr. Walraven had been sitting only hours ago. He'd gone so peacefully. It was as if he'd expected it from the moment Behr had arrived. Maybe even *before*. It wasn't until he'd been handed that letter that Jack had seen the faintest glint of sadness cross the doctor's face. It had been fleeting, but it was definitely there.

Jack's eyes fell upon the letter resting on the side table. He stood and walked toward it, reaching into the shade of the table lamp and clicking it on. The paper was folded, but trying to remember its original shape, and under the yellow glow of the light, a scribble on the exposed inner side caught Jack's eye; a scribble that looked horribly familiar. He snatched the sheet up, disbelieving, and swore loudly. Seething, he read the letter in its entirety.

Dr. Einer Walraven,

It is with great regret that I must inform you that certain artifacts have been stolen from the archives of Animal Control. Due to the sensitive nature of this theft, the items in question shall not be identified here. However, we have reason to believe there may be a connection between their disappearance and your most recent visit this past month.

It is not left to me to accuse you of anything, and I certainly hope you had nothing to do with this betrayal. However, it is my unpleasant duty to request that you accompany Mr. Behr to our headquarters, where a full investigation may be carried out. Should you refuse, I must warn you that more aggressive action shall be taken. Given our history together, I would greatly appreciate your compliance.

Until our next meeting,

Alan Kale
Assistant to President Brisk

Jack read the letter through several times, his heart pounding. He remembered the argument that had driven Alan from their home. Alan had announced at dinner that Alexander Brisk, then Vice President of Animal Control, had expressed an interest in bringing him on as his personal assistant. Dr. Walraven had been less than enthusiastic, implying that Brisk would be interested only in using Alan to keep tabs on Dr. Walraven, with whom he had a decades long rivalry. The argument escalated, until Alan threw a glass across the room, shattering it, and stormed out.

Just like that, Jack lost the only brother he'd ever had, without so much as a goodbye. Dr. Walraven had gone after him, of course, but it didn't do any good.

# CHAPTER SEVEN

These thoughts continued to swim through Jack's mind as he lay in the dark an hour later. The groaning wheel did not soothe him; not tonight. Tonight it made him feel as if he wasn't alone.

# Chapter Eight
# VANGUARD

It was the night of October 13th, Jack's birthday, when he got his first glimpse of an anaxopter. Riding toward the Honey Sap for his second night of work, he heard a rhythmic, chopping sound very different from the growl of his motorcycle's engine. Thinking the strange noise might be something caught in his wheel, he slowed to a stop along the forest road. Just then, the anax passed overhead. The vehicle looked like an enormous dragonfly gliding above the oak trees. In the darkness, Jack could only make out its shape between the blinking red and green lights of its body. As far as he knew, anaxopters were only used by Animal Control. What was one doing here in Hadensburrow?

The Honey Sap was aglow with light from a log fire and buzzing with conversation. At a table in the center of the room, a group of badgers and birds played a game of low stakes poker. Another group, mostly bunnies and squirrels, yelled encouragement as they watched a wiry rat try to hold his liquor against an opposing black bear. The rat reached for another shot glass with a trembling paw, but had only touched it to his lips before toppling headlong into the table to the pleasure and dismay of onlookers.

Jack, a brown apron tied around his waist, did his best to navigate the room with an unsteady tray of drinks. A ginger-colored liquor was lifted from the plate by the victorious bear, who swigged it down in one. Jack worked his way around the card table, delivering drinks to the players. They grunted thanks, drawing their cards close to the chest as he passed.

A bell tinkled, and every eye was drawn to the door as three new arrivals entered. They were out-of-towners, but certainly not out of their element. The first to enter was a greyhound, tall and slender, with sleek silver fur that glimmered in the firelight. He gazed imperiously down upon the crowd through oval-shaped glasses, stepping smoothly into their midst.

Following behind the dog, stooping low as he passed through the door, was a monster of a bull. His horns reached beyond his broad shoulders, and he had to step sideways as he entered. A gust of air snorted out of his fist-sized nostrils as he looked around the room.

The third, and certainly the most at ease, was a handsome falcon. He was not as tall as the others, nor as powerfully built, but they turned to look at him, and not until he gave a satisfied nod did they follow him to a table near the center of the room. It was not unoccupied, but the two rats quickly vacated their seats and stood watching with the rest of the atypically silent crowd. Even Jack, forgetting his duties, watched the newcomers with a slightly opened mouth. There was something familiar about this group, particularly the falcon, although he couldn't immediately place it.

The falcon sat first, looking around the room with a relaxed and friendly smile. He gave a genuine nod of greeting to several patrons, unfaltering as each turned away.

The bull, sitting in a chair far too small for him, looked like an over-sized child on a time-out. He furrowed his heavy brow as if scanning the room for something to punch. As he let out another blast with his nostrils, the crowd took their cue and went back to their conversations.

"Welcome to Hadensburrow," Jack started, reciting the greeting Rhoda had prescribed for out-of-towners. "Where you folks coming from?"

The greyhound looked Jack up and down, then looked away smugly, leaning into his elbows. Nonplussed, Jack turned to the others. The bull, who sat nearest, was stone-faced, watching the bunny as if expecting him to turn around and moon them at any moment. The falcon was the only one to respond. "Triarch," he said. He unzipped his jacket and shrugged it off, revealing a falcon insignia on his shirt.

Jack nearly dropped his pad and pen. "Isn't that the Animal Control logo?" he asked, his voice a little higher than usual. "I thought only Animal Control heroes were allowed to wear it."

"That's right," the falcon smiled.

Jack's lungs felt heavy, as though the air had suddenly become thick in the dining room. "That anax. That... was that you?" And then, like puzzle pieces locking together, it came to him; he'd seen this falcon on TV, being interviewed by reporters. "You're Firebird!"

The falcon nodded.

Disbelieving, Jack looked at the others. "And that makes you Bullet Hound," he pointed to the greyhound, "and Ford," he said to the bull. "You're Vanguard! You're Animal Control's best team!"

"Only when we're working," the falcon said with a satisfied smile. "What's your name, kid?"

"Jack," he stammered. "Jack Robberts."

"Jack Robberts, I'm Grayson Conway. This is Edward Dixon," he gestured toward the greyhound, "and Hugo Ford," he motioned toward the bull. "We're just passing through, staying down the road at Tom Pillinger's. Nice place, but a little quiet for our liking."

In an effort to keep his cool, Jack flicked open his pad and clicked his pen. "Well, welcome! What can I get for you?"

"Whatever dark beer you've got is fine for myself and Hugo here," the falcon said, flicking a flight feather toward the bull.

Jack turned to the greyhound. "And for you, sir?"

"Red wine. Mouse if you've got it," the dog said, casting a half-lidded look around the Honey Sap, as if its ability to supply mouse-made wine was doubtful.

Jack gave a small nod and turned to walk away, but at that moment the door burst open with a crash and a tinkle. "I don't care, you bug-eyed little pansy! That's his bike, so he's in here somewhere." Recognizing that voice, Jack turned toward the door to see Chuck, the over-sized and bad-tempered rat, stumping into the room. By his tone, Jack guessed that he hadn't quite gotten over their card game, and sure enough, when his eyes locked onto Jack's, he let out an angry yell and began shoving his way through the crowd.

"Friend of yours?" Conway asked, leaning back into his chair and watching the rat with mild interest.

Chuck forced his way through the crowd until he reached the bunny. "You and me, we got unfinished business," he growled through gritted teeth as he wrapped his fingers into Jack's shirt collar.

"Excuse me," Rhoda called. The badger woman marched out from behind the counter, brandishing a wooden spoon at Chuck. "You can just turn around and walk right back out that door. This isn't a place for trouble."

"Shut up, you old bat," Chuck slurred, his rancid breath spraying into Rhoda's face. He turned again to the bunny and drew back a balled fist.

Jack clenched up, waiting for the blow. Instead, he felt a sudden warmth across his whole body. Opening his eyes, he saw Chuck haloed in yellow-white light emanating from behind him. Everyone around was shielding their eyes, and the rat turned slowly, his fingers leaving Jack's collar.

"That wasn't a very courteous thing to say, now was it?" said a god-like voice; it seemed to come from everywhere, echoing, filling the room. A glowing figure was standing atop the table, flickering like a holiday sparkler and looking down upon the rat through white-hot eyes. "Apologize."

The rat looked as if he was seeing his own brain pop out of his head and tap-dance across the table. He stumbled backward, tripping over a chair.

"I said," the angelic voice repeated, "apologize to the lady."

Chuck struggled to a standing position and turned to Rhoda. "I..." he tried, speaking to the side of the badger's head as she squinted up at the glowing figure. "Sorry."

The light dimmed, and Grayson Conway stepped down from the table, small flames licking out from beneath feathers. He pressed his beak against the rat's nose. "Now get out," he said, his voice normal once more.

Chuck tripped over his own feet, as well as his opossum companion, as he ran for the door, throwing one last terrified glance over his shoulder.

"Thank you," Rhoda said, clutching her chest. "That was very chivalrous of you, stepping in like that."

"It was nothing, ma'am," the falcon said, his eyes still fixed on the door through which the rat had disappeared.

"It most certainly was not 'nothing,' whatever it was," the badger insisted. "I don't think I've ever seen anything like that; not since... well, in any case..." She looked around the room, flustered. "Oh, go on then," she announced to the room at large, brushing at them with her paws. "It's all over, so carry on."

Since the trouble had been in relation to him, Jack took this moment to slip away and escape a reprimand.

It was well past midnight when Jack leaned his motorcycle against the oak tree and stumbled in the darkness to the front of the mill. With what he had made in tips tonight, keeping his promise to Dr. Walraven would be a breeze. Smiling with sleepy contentment, he rubbed the space between his ears with one paw and reached for the door handle with the other.

He stopped mid-reach, all drowsiness shaken from him as his heart jolted. The front door was open.

Frozen and staring, he tried to reach back to the moment he'd left. Hadn't he shut it? Maybe the wind blew it open? But this didn't seem likely, either. Turning, his wide eyes scanned from the forest on the opposite side of the road, all the way down to the bank of the river. It was a dark night, unusually quiet. He thought of his motorcycle, propped against the tree. But where would he go? Even Tom Pillanger's would be shut down by this time. Tom Pillanger's, where Grayson Conway and his fellow heroes were staying. How childish they would think him if he showed up in the middle of the night, scared to go into his own house because the door was open — when in all likelihood he'd left it open himself.

It was with this thought that he spun to face the door again, pressed his paw against it and entered.

The mill was ghost still. A slim shaft of moonlight shone in through the kitchen window, blanketing the fallen bookshelf at the far end of the living room. Volumes of books had been spilled out across the rug. Jack peered wide-eyed into the room, not crossing the threshold. "Hello?" he called tentatively, his ears and whiskers on end. With a trembling paw, he patted around until he found the light switch, flicking it on without blinking. The lamp, which lay on its side on the floor, cast long shadows around the room. Couch cushions were upturned. The coat rack near the door lay on its side, clothing items scattered around it. Jack's eyes fell on Dr. Walraven's favorite windbreaker. Its pockets were turned outward.

He scooped up an umbrella from the mess, brandishing it like a sword as he continued cautiously into the house. But after a thorough and very slow search, he was satisfied that the house was empty. Still shaken, he returned to the front door and locked it, then turned on every light, both upstairs and down. He made an effort to clean up some of the mess, but became distracted by a surprising and rather intriguing discovery.

He had just finished propping the bookshelf upright, and was dragging it to its place in the corner. With his back pressed against the wall, he gave the bookcase one last heave, lifting it slightly upward to get over the corner of the maroon rug, when he felt a click in the wall behind him. As he stepped away from the wall, part of it seemed to come with him. He turned to see that a panel had indeed fallen outward. It hung open like a laundry chute; a secret compartment hidden in the wooden boards behind the bookcase's normal resting place. Peering inside, he found a small collection of items piled at the bottom.

The first of these items was a fedora, wide-brimmed and black. There didn't seem to be anything special about it. He set it aside and reached in once more, this time withdrawing a brown paper package. There was nothing unusual about this item either, except in the amount of tape used — it was practically waterproof. It had very few markings, save for the address to the mill, the postage, and a single word scrawled into the upper left corner: "Stronger".

When he had considered the package for another moment, shaking it next to his ear like a present and unable to guess at its contents, he set it aside as well.

The third item he extracted was a gold colored envelope. It was shaped like a birthday card, rather than a letter, and to Jack's surprise, it was addressed not to Dr. Walraven, but to Jack himself. It *was* his birthday, after all, and perhaps Dr. Walraven had planned to give it to him today. Yet it had been mailed, so it couldn't be from Dr. Walraven. But who would send him a card? His only friend outside of Hadensburrow was Alan, and he hadn't spoken to the fox in two years, not since he had stormed out and moved to Triarch.

He worked his thumb under the flap, and tore it open. It was, indeed, a card. But instead of "Happy Birthday" or some funny cartoon on the front, there was something else. Something that made Jack's heart skip.

It was the blue silhouette of a falcon, with its wings extended in either direction and its head turned to one side. It was the insignia of *Animal Control.*

And in gold letters above the falcon, it said:

THE SIDEKICK PROGRAM IS BACK, AND WE
WANT YOU!

## Chapter Nine

## THE WOLFGANG

"Rise and shine, Jack; it's almost noon."

Face down on a throw pillow, Jack lifted his head groggily and squinted up at Dr. Walraven. The rat was looking around the living room, where coats, books, and papers were still scattered around. "House party?" he asked.

"Mmmmm... what?" Jack mumbled, following the doctor's gaze. He saw the mess, and everything came back to him. "Oh!" he said as he sat upright. "No! It was like this when I got home last night. Someone searched the mill!"

The doctor nodded as if he'd somehow expected this. "Well, never mind that now," he said, unshouldering what Jack had taken to be his traveling bag and extending it toward the bunny. "Happy birthday."

The lack of ceremony catching him off guard, Jack sat up, wiped the saliva from the corner of his mouth, and accepted what he now saw to be a military green messenger bag.

Last night, after discovering the letter and the brown package, Jack had wondered — better said, he had *hoped* — that Dr. Walraven was reserving them for his birthday. He fell asleep with the wonderful idea that the whole "six months of good behavior" thing was a rouse to throw Jack off the scent, that his real plan had been to take him along to Animal Control this very week.

And here he was, handing Jack a messenger bag, perfect for travel. He accepted the bag, weighing it curiously before unfastening the buckle and peering inside.

It was empty.

Confused, he looked back up at Dr. Walraven, who appeared slightly embarrassed. "It used to be mine," the doctor said with a hopeful smile. "Military issue."

Jack looked back down at the bag. It had only the one pocket, which closed with a buckle. A dark gray patch was stitched into the frayed overhanging flap, and a long strap connected at either side, giving the bag the look of a large, masculine purse.

"Um," he started, trying to hide his disappointment. "It's great. Thanks."

Looking back down at it, he considered the patch. It was an angular representation of a hawk, or some other bird of prey, its outstretched wings and pointed tail forming a downward facing triangle. In truth, he thought it looked like a poor knockoff of the Animal Control insignia. "What's this?" he asked, thumbing it to feel the stained fabric.

"That," Dr. Walraven smiled, "was the sigil of our company. It was designed by Aaron Harding himself."

Jack examined it more closely, disbelieving. "King of Hearts designed this?" he asked.

The doctor nodded encouragingly.

Jack knew his adoptive father had served in the military alongside King of Hearts, long before there was an Animal Control, but somehow that seemed like information belonging in a history book, not here in his paws. "Then, does that make this…" he looked up with excited wonder, then back down at the patch. "Does that mean this was the first version of the Animal Control logo?"

"It sure does," Dr. Walraven nodded. "Aaron stitched that patch when we were holed up in Pretty Fishes."

"There's a place called 'Pretty Fishes?'" Jack asked.

"It's right next to a town called 'Your Friend,'" Dr. Walraven laughed. "Anyway, one of our company had been killed just two days before. He had left his coat with Aaron just before it happened. I guess Aaron thought it would be the best way to honor him, so he cut up the coat and put a patch on each of our bags."

Jack looked again at the bag. Tattered though it may be, it certainly had a history to it.

"I thought it might come in handy for our trip," Dr. Walraven said.

Jack's heart leapt in his chest, and his face flicked upward.

"I had intended to wait until after your shift tonight to tell you."

*I don't want to wait! Tell me!* Jack thought eagerly.

"We'll be leaving tonight, just as soon as you get home," the rat continued.

*I'm finally going!*

"Now I want to warn you: it will be a long trip."

*I don't mind! Animal Control is worth the wait!*

"I have to visit a friend in Pine Creek, and I'd like you to come along."

A balloon was punctured in Jack's chest. Pine Creek, he knew, was up north in the Moledun Mountains, along the Helmet Range that formed the northern border of Nikacia. In other words, it was as far from Triarch as one could get without crossing into carnivore territory.

His disappointment must have been showing, because the smile slowly faded from Dr. Walraven's face. "You do want to go, don't you?" he asked.

For a moment, Jack considered a flat *no*. "I dunno," he said. "I was hoping you'd say Triarch."

Seeming to have expected this response, Dr. Walraven sighed. "Now Jack, we *did* talk about visiting Triarch," he said. "I told you I will take you in six months, once you've worked for a bit and proved you will behave responsibly."

"Right," Jack said, extracting the golden envelope from his pocket and holding it up. "Is that why you kept *this* hidden?"

If the doctor was surprised to see the invitation, he did a good job of hiding it. "Yes," he said with a sigh of resignation. "I kept that from you because I didn't want you to be disappointed that I can't allow it. Not yet."

"Not *yet?*" Jack echoed. "You took Alan practically every other weekend when he was my age. Of course, Alan never killed any superheroes, did he?"

Dr. Walraven bowed his head, let out a breath, and continued in a calm tone. "The truth of the matter is that this is quite urgent. And last night's break-in makes it clear to me that I can wait no longer. I *must* get to Pine Creek, and I need you with me."

As Jack strode to the door, Dr. Walraven continued. "I've already arranged everything with Rhoda. You will take three weeks off. That should give us enough time to get up there, take care of my business, and spend a little time enjoying the mountain air before you have to work again. I know you'll love it."

Jack jerked the door open.

"Come now, son," Dr. Walraven said.

Jack groaned irritably. "Please stop calling me *son*," he barked. With that, he stepped outside and slammed the door behind him.

He didn't know why he'd said it. The words just sort of came out. It didn't take long for guilt to catch up, and he brought his motorcycle to a stop at the end of Living Oak. He placed a paw on the seat behind him and turned to look back down the gravel road, then let out a long sigh. Why had he been so upset? Dr. Walraven *had* agreed to take him to Triarch in six short months. Besides, from the little he knew about the Moledun Mountains, they sounded pretty exciting. He'd heard stories of feral bandits, travelers buried alive in the snow, even carnivorous creatures that lived beneath the ice. He wasn't sure he believed that last one, but it sounded a whole lot more exciting than sitting around Hadensburrow on good behavior.

And then there was the way that he'd treated Dr. Walraven. *Please stop calling me son*, he had said. Was that really how he felt? No, he told himself, of course it wasn't.

He looked back up the road, in the direction of the Honey Sap. His shift didn't start for a few more hours. There was plenty of time for him to return home and patch things up.

But as he waddled his bike around to face the opposite direction, he came to a halt.

CHAPTER NINE

Standing in the middle of the road was a gray wolf. He wore a sleeveless black shirt and jeans, and his lips were turned up into a smile. "Hello, Jack," he said. "Pleasure to finally meet you." His voice wasn't particularly deep, but there was an oiliness to its tone. His piercing silver eyes seemed to stare right through Jack.

Two more wolves walked out from either side of the road, their similarly silver eyes hungrily fixed on Jack. The first wolf's smile grew broader at the obvious terror on Jack's face. "I suppose there's no point in pretenses," he said. "Your Dr. Walraven has something. Something we want very much. And we're here to get it. Truth be told, we had no interest in you. We were going to let you pass right by. It's just dumb luck that you delivered yourself right to us, and obviously we can't just let you go." He crooked his head sideways, sizing Jack up as if he were a meal. "Boys," he said. "Sick 'em."

The wolves laughed menacingly, licking their lips as they approached. Jack's legs had gone numb, and when he attempted to put his bike into gear, the engine sputtered and died. The nearest of the wolves reached a paw toward him, his claws as sharp and black as talons.

But he stopped suddenly, as did the others. The earth had begun to shake. It was subtle at first, but the rumble grew until they were all unsteady on their feet. Jack's bike nearly fell over, and the groping wolf, missing his aim, toppled to one knee. Seeing his opportunity, Jack kicked the motorcycle to life and tore back down Living Oak toward the mill.

He dropped his bike at the foot of the stairs and raced inside. Dr. Walraven was sitting at the cluttered kitchen table, his paws folded in front of him. When he saw Jack enter, he stood. "I felt the quake," he said, looking Jack up and down. "Are you okay?"

"I'm fine," Jack said. "We have to go! Now!"

Dr. Walraven was still searching Jack as if for wounds. "Did you get hurt at all?"

"I said I'm fine!" Jack argued. "There were these wolves. They tried to attack me..."

"Wolves?" Dr. Walraven exclaimed. "Where?"

"Just at the end of the road, by the mailboxes."

Dr. Walraven moved swiftly to the bookshelf in the corner and toppled it over. He pressed both paws against the wood panels of the wall, then pushed in and lifted upward. The panel fell open like a laundry cute, revealing the narrow compartment Jack had discovered the previous night. He rifled around, elbow deep in the opening, and extracted the taped-up package, replacing the black fedora. "This is more urgent than I'd feared," he said as he clicked the compartment shut and turned to face Jack. "There isn't much time, so I need you to listen carefully. There are things you need to know."

"Now's not the time," Jack said, moving to grab the doctor's arm.

"Now may be all we have, my boy," the doctor responded. "I need you to think back, Jack. Back to the day King died."

"To... to what?" Jack said, his stomach plummeting.

"When King died. Jack, think. Do you remember that day?"

A hollow feeling spread through Jack as he saw, in his mind's eye, the lion's tail protruding from beneath the fallen train engine. "How could I forget?" he said in a quiet voice.

"Do you remember the sapling?"

"The what?"

"The sapling. The sign King left when he died."

*The lion's tail had made Jack dry-heave. He had looked away, his eyes searching for something, for anything to latch onto. And they had fallen upon a small sapling framed in a stone archway. It was the last thing he had seen before he had passed out again.*

He nodded. "I remember."

"That sapling is the key to everything, Jack," Dr. Walraven said. "King's heightena was unique. It was transferable. And when King died, he transferred his power into that sapling. It's what we call 'permeation'. The moment I saw it, I knew. I uprooted it, took it to Triarch, and planted it in the Animal Control campus. We built an impenetrable safe around it, and put the key under the highest level of security we could give it. And the highest level at Animal Control is saying something."

"The key that Behr says got stolen?" Jack asked.

"Precisely," Dr. Walraven replied. "King's power cannot fall into the wrong paws. That's why it is critical that we get this package to Pine Creek as soon as possible."

"Pine Creek?" Jack said, looking at the package quizzically. "What's in it? What could possibly be stronger than King's heightena?"

"Never mind that now," Dr. Walraven shook his head and grabbed up the messenger bag from the floor, nimbly unfastening the buckle. He stuffed the package inside and fastened it shut once more, then threw the strap around Jack's shoulder. "There we are," he said. "Safe and sound. Now, let's get you out of here." Grabbing a black traveling bag from the table, he ushered Jack toward the front door.

Jack would never remember which of them had opened the door. He would never remember the exact swear he had blurted. All he would remember of that moment was those silver eyes, and that crooked, sharp-toothed smile.

Dr. Walraven slammed the door in the wolf's face, then slid the deadbolt into place and pressed his back to the jam. He lurched forward as the wolf on the steps kicked at the nob. His voice was audible, but Jack couldn't understand the snarling language he spoke. Apparently Dr. Walraven had understood. "Jack! The window!"

The window next to the door imploded as a stone came crashing through. A second later, a bottle soared in through the jagged hole, a flaming rag protruding from its neck. It shattered on the floor, liquid splashing across the wood, igniting instantly. Much of the fuel spilled beneath the floorboards, and a candle-like flicker began to glow between the cracks.

More bottles were shattering outside, each crash paired with taunts and barks, and soon flames were licking their way in through the window and beneath the door. Jack looked up at the ceiling to see the same fire glow overhead. Flaming raindrops dripped down between the cracks.

The mill gave a sudden heave. Another earthquake, but the tremor was continual. The coat rack toppled over, and a loud cracking sound barked from overhead. With no more warning, a heavy support beam fell from the ceiling and crashed down directly between him and the doctor. As it hit the floor, one end broke through, so that Jack was now blocked by a flaming beam on one side, and a gaping pit in the direction of the door. He was trapped.

The door burst open with a sound like a shotgun blast. The lead wolf had crashed into it with his shoulder. He landed heavily on his side atop the fallen door, letting out a howl as he gripped his dislocated arm. "Ready or not!" the second wolf snarled, stepping over his fallen leader and into the flaming room. The third wolf followed. Their silver eyes fell on Jack. The nearest wolf gave a half chuckle, half growl. He said something in that strange language as he sniffed the air, savoring the scent.

But suddenly, his eyes shifted, then his whole attention, toward the kitchen area. The other standing wolf turned his attention as well. Jack's eyes followed. A kitchen knife was gripped tightly in Dr. Walraven's paw. At first, Jack thought he was going to fight the wolves, and nearly called out.

Then he saw Dr. Walraven's wrist.

Blood dripped from just below his paw as smoothly as wine from a bottle. He held his arm out toward the intruders, his empty fist clenched as if squeezing every drop of liquid from a sponge.

The wolves began to salivate heavily, unable to resist the scent of Dr. Walraven's blood on the air, losing interest in Jack altogether. The bunny opened his mouth, but never knew if he was screaming, or indeed if he was making a sound at all.

One after the other, the two standing wolves leapt at the doctor, tackling him straight into the kitchen wall, smashing the overhead light as they did so. The sound of their ravenous snarling was pronounced over the roar of the fire and the creaking of weakening wood. The last thing Jack could see in the fire glow was the flicking of two tails, weaving playfully before disappearing behind a downfall of burning ceiling debris.

At that same moment, the ground gave another heave, and the floor beneath Jack's feet gave way. A sense of vertigo brought him back to reality for the space of one breath; he was falling.

And then he was swallowed by the river.

# Chapter Ten

## STRAY

Jack moved with the river's mild current, aware of nothing but the brilliant blue sky at which he was staring. He didn't know how long he'd been floating. He hadn't even realized that he was awake. The messenger bag around his neck became caught in an overgrowth of blackberries, and he came to a stop, fixating blankly on a vine just above his face. Jagged thorns formed a row along its edge, curved and pointed, just like teeth. Like snarling, hungry...

*Teeth!*

He flailed his arms backward, spluttering to consciousness as he ingested a mouthful of water. His feet found the stone embankment, and he attempted to kick away, but the bag was hooked in the thorns, and the more he struggled, the more entangled he became. He tried taking it off, intending to leave it behind, but couldn't do so without going deeper into the bramble.

*Calm*, he told himself. He drew in a breath, held it, and perked a long ear up. Hearing only the trickling movement of the water, he got to work untangling the bag.

As he delicately unhooked the barbs, he took in his surroundings. Upstream, the river passed around a bend, both banks completely obscured by blackberries. In the distance stood a range of forest-covered mountains. They weren't familiar. He turned the other direction. About fifty feet downstream, a stone bridge arched over the water, ornamented with iron lanterns along its edge. If there was a bridge, there must be a road.

Finally freeing the bag, he pushed off the sloping embankment. He wasn't much of a swimmer, but had no trouble keeping his face above the water as he bounced weightlessly below the refracted light dancing across the bridge's underbelly.

There were brambles on the other side, but with a reasonably broad gap between them and the bridge. The bank was steeper than expected, but a few sturdy roots aided his climb, and he pulled himself onto the level earth alongside a gravel road, then collapsed into the dust.

The urgency of escaping the river had washed all else from his mind. Now it came flooding back like a horribly vivid nightmare.

Dr. Walraven was dead.

There was no question about it. Even if the wolves hadn't finished him, the fire would have.

He shook the thought — and a spurt of water — from his head and pushed himself to a sitting position. Unfastening the buckle of the messenger bag, he pulled out the package. It was nothing special; if anything, it was as plain a package as Jack had ever seen. Brown paper that looked like it had been cut from a paper bag, completely wrapped in tape, and addressed to...

He wondered if the contents had been destroyed by the river, or whether the tape might have protected it. Then he decided he didn't care.

He turned it over, mindlessly eying every side. Protecting this package had been Dr. Walraven's final act, but now, as Jack pondered its contents, he had to fight a desire to toss the wretchedly simple thing into the river. Instead, he began working at the tape. After a moment of uselessly scratching at it, however, he gave up and started scanning the ground for a suitably sharp rock or stick.

"Hey! Boy!"

Jack dropped the package and spun around, ending up in a crawling position. Lost in his thoughts, he had not heard the approach of a large blue tractor. As he took in its enormity (it narrowly cleared both edges of the lantern-lined bridge), he marveled that he had not heard the loud, uneven banging of its engine.

A broad-shouldered farmer was leaning out the window of a cab between the large rear wheels. His face was mostly hidden by the shadow of a wide-brimmed hat, but his long whiskers and thick muzzle identified him as some large breed of cat.

"You alright, Son?"

His voice was deep, booming, and although he sounded kindly, his lips peeled over razor-sharp teeth as he spoke, and Jack was seized by an uncontrollable trembling. Nausea spread from his temples down to his stomach, and everything grew dim.

A sudden jolt woke him. He was slumped sideways, his cheek pressed against glass. Too dazed to react, whether in alarm or otherwise, he sat slowly upright and turned his head lazily, observing his surroundings. He seemed to be in the cab of the big blue tractor; through its windscreen he could see its boxy blue nose bouncing along a path that cut between oaks and evergreens. His clothes were still soggy, but had dried to some extent. By the fading light of the sky, it was setting on evening — was that even possible? Blinking drearily, he turned his head to the left. The farmer was staring straight ahead, firmly gripping a large black steering wheel. He looked out the corner of his eye and gave a smile. "Ah! You're awake! How do you feel, boy?"

Jack glanced away.

"From the looks of things, you seem to have been swimmin' in the Bristlin." He laughed. "Bad idea, that. The Bristlin *looks* slow, but it's got a mighty undercurrent. You want to be careful."

Jack's head bobbed with the movement of the tractor. He turned to look out the window. Here and there, they passed homes so ornately trimmed, they looked like gingerbread houses. "Where are we?" he asked in a flat tone.

"Ah, he breaks the silence!" the heavy cat guffawed. There was warmth in his voice. "This," he said, "is the beautiful town of Bristlin, namesake of your river."

Jack felt a swell of relief. Bristlin, he knew, was a great journey away from Hadensburrow. Whatever danger still lurked there, it was behind him; *hours* behind him. But how had he come this far? And why had the cat taken him so far from where he had found him.

This last question he voiced, hoping only later that it had not sounded rude.

The cat laughed again, and then tipped his hat back slightly, though his face was still shaded. "Well, you *did* tell me you had to get to Triarch."

"I… I did?"

"Several times, boy. Said you knew somebody there. If that's not the case, I can certainly take you back the other way, though we'd best find a place to stop for the night."

Jack watched the trees passing by. He did know somebody in Triarch, and now, Alan Kale was the only family he had left. "No," he found himself saying. "I *do* need to go to Triarch."

"Well, then," the farmer turned his head fully toward Jack for the first time, "we're headed the right way."

In the distance ahead, Jack could see a long row of high-standing lanterns lining the path. Just beyond, he saw a large building, brown with white trim, in that same gingerbread style. He was out of danger.

## Chapter Eleven

# SPRINT AND HOOVER

Once again, Jack woke to find himself in a strange place. He sat bolt upright, blinking in the dim light of an unfamiliar room. Disoriented, he tumbled out of the bed, scrambled to a sink against the far wall, and splashed water into his face.

Wiping his muzzle with the back of a shaky paw, he examined his reflection, then turned to face the room.

A thin shaft of sunlight peeked in from between curtains, slashing a white line down the center of what was unmistakably a hotel room. A television sat on top of a chest of drawers opposite the bed. The sink area at which he stood was furnished with a rack of bleach white towels and a coffee pot, and opened at one end into a closet-sized bathroom.

At the foot of the bed, his folded clothes lay in a neat pile. They looked not only dry, but clean. Seeing this, he turned to the mirror to take himself in. He was wearing a new pair of blue pajamas, seemingly tailored to his exact size.

As he tried in vain to recall how he had arrived in this room, with these new clothes, his eyes fell upon a plain white card standing like a tiny paper tent next to the television.

"Good Morning" was written across the front. Next to the card was a small cloth sack. He strode across the room and snapped up the card.

In messy writing scribbled in ballpoint blue, a message inside read:

*Good morning, my mysterious friend,*

*Room is paid for. I wish you the best of luck in your journey, and hope that this small contribution will help you on your way.*

*-TOM*

*PS. Sometimes you have to lose in order to win.*

He read this last sentence several times. Not only did it seem to make no sense in the context of this card, but there was something strangely familiar about the words.

The cloth sack was about the size and weight of an apple, and jangled when he shook it. Money. A good amount, by the feel of it. Wishing he could thank *Farmer Tom*, he dressed in his newly washed clothes, then packed the pajamas alongside the brown package in his messenger bag. To his surprise, the gold envelope, which had been in his pocket when he'd gone into the river, was already in there.

Giving one last glance around the room, he stepped outside and pulled the door shut behind him. It locked automatically. He found himself on a slender balcony overlooking a parking lot bordered with pine trees, and in which a large tour bus sat idling. A group of school-age animals were filing out of the bus and into a diner at the corner of the first floor. They were excitedly jostling each other, snapping pictures of the hotel and surrounding forest, and chatting animatedly.

This group was unusual, though, and it was instantly noticeable. Normally, crowds coming from a certain area would be made up of a certain type of animals. Coming from Hadensburrow, a crowd would most likely consist of foxes, rodents, badgers, and birds, with an exception or two. Coming more from the far north, a crowd might consist of falcons, apes, and bears. But this crowd was different. A giraffe in a blue and white letterman jacket had to stoop low as he entered the diner. A lime green gecko, about a third the giraffe's height, was looking over a map as he walked alongside a brilliant red macaw. An anteater, with a long tapered snout and bear-like claws, debated with a squirrel who was fishing into a bag of peanuts. It was, in short, the most diverse crowd Jack had ever seen.

He passed room after room, squeezing by a housecleaning cart and descending the stairs. Following the last members of the crowd into the diner, he was instantly overwhelmed by the noise. The room was buzzing with excited conversation, every corner filled with kids taking each other's pictures, slapping each other high fives, or putting someone in a headlock. Jack, who had been home-schooled by Dr. Walraven, was not used to being around so many kids his own age, and certainly not so diverse a crowd. But they all looked perfectly at ease with each other. A teen lion, with a patch of orange hair atop an otherwise maneless head, was arm wrestling a short, plump toad. The gecko and macaw were joined by the giraffe, who had to stoop so low beneath the ceiling that he looked like a hunched old man. Having never seen a giraffe in person before, Jack couldn't take his eyes off of him.

"You keep staring like that, you'll get a nosebleed," said a voice to his left. The peanut-eating squirrel was eying him with an upturned brow. He had a fluffy brown tail that arched higher than his pointed ears, and a mischievous face with teeth far too large for his mouth. "Anyway, what's your deal? He's a giraffe, not a unicorn."

Jack felt his cheeks burn, and looked away.

"I didn't see you on the bus," the squirrel said.

Jack turned back toward him. "I... what?"

"The bus," the squirrel repeated. "I didn't see you on it before."

"Oh," Jack said, awkwardly shifting to move past the squirrel. "I... uh... No, I... I'm not a tourist."

The squirrel laughed. "Tourist? You think all these fine folks are tourists?" His tone wasn't aggressive; he seemed more amused than offended, as though he was enjoying some piece of information Jack didn't have. "My friend, this crowd you see before you," he said, throwing an arm around Jack's shoulder and sweeping his other paw dramatically across the room, "are *the future*. Mind, I include myself in that. But," he added, tilting his head toward Jack, "I didn't see you on the bus, and I'm just curious... if you're not with us, then what is a grade school bunny doing on his own at a hotel?"

"Who says I'm on my own?"

"Please," the squirrel said, releasing Jack's shoulder and stepping back as though to get a better view of him. "Traveling bag, lost child look on your face. Plus, the only adults I see are either in aprons, or with us."

"So?"

"So, you're by yourself."

"And if I am?"

"Just making conversation," the squirrel said. "However, if someone your age can afford to stay here by himself, it stands to reason you might have a few bucks on you. My friend and I were

93

discussing the importance of a good breakfast, but we're also rather low on funds, and…"

"You want me to buy you breakfast?"

"Oh, no!" the squirrel said. "No, not at all. But I wondered how you might feel about a friendly game of cards."

"Cards?"

"Yeah, you know," the squirrel said. "Cards. Flat, rectangular objects with numbers and shapes on them. If I win, you pay for our breakfast. If you win, we'll pay for yours."

Jack moved once again to step past the squirrel. "I'm fine, thanks."

"That's alright," the squirrel said, stepping out of Jack's way. "If I'm honest, you didn't stand a chance anyway." He smiled crookedly, and started to walk away.

Jack had spent too much time conning travelers at the Honey Sap not to recognize a professional at work. Still, the idea of shying away from a game he knew he would win — especially against such a smug opponent — was like a nagging itch. "Wait," he said. "I'll play."

The squirrel turned toward him and smiled. "Atta guy," he said, and he led the way across the crowded room to a table at which his anteater friend was already seated.

While Jack could recognize a con the moment it appeared, he could just as easily turn on the scheming gears himself. "I should warn you," he started as he sat. "I don't think it'd really be fair. To you, I mean."

The squirrel scooted his chair closer, his eyes gleaming, and laughed. "Oh yeah? Why's that?"

"Because I'm lucky."

"You're lucky," the squirrel repeated.

Jack shrugged. "Just think it's fair to let you know. What are we playing? Poker?"

"Poker?" the squirrel leaned back in his chair. "Shoot, I'm just a simple country squirrel. Only game I know is Pickup."

"Never heard of it."

"I'd be surprised if you had. Made it up myself. It's basically go fish, only *just* the go fish part. Deal us each five cards, then split the deck into two stacks. Pick up from either stack, and then discard. We play until the deck is gone. Player with the most four-of-a-kinds wins."

Jack shifted uncomfortably in his chair. The game seemed to fit his luck well enough, but he felt uneasy betting on a game he'd never played, particularly one invented by his opponent.

"Luck is all in the mind, you know," the squirrel said to his anteater friend, withdrawing a deck of cards from his pocket. "All animals have some sort of defense mechanism. A turtle has a shell, a bird can fly, and a... whatever you are... elephant rat has claws."

"They're for digging," the anteater responded, looking down at his claws as if wondering whether he'd been using them wrong.

"Squirrels, we're rather quick, and rabbits, such as this specimen you see before you," he gestured to Jack as if he were a drawing on a white board, "their defense is to lie." Jack made an affronted shift, at which the squirrel quickly continued. "*Bluff,* if you like. Maybe that's gentler. Point is, this rabbit believes he can influence my card playing abilities by falling back on the old long-ear line, 'I'm lucky.' I've heard it before, 'the luck of the rabbits', but I don't buy it." As he said all of this, he shuffled the deck, dealt, then divided the remaining cards into two equal stacks, which he placed at the center of the table.

Jack eyed his hand. It was almost perfect for this particular game, as he knew it would be. Four 9's, along with a 5 of clubs. "How do we start?"

The squirrel gestured toward the two stacks with an open paw.

Hesitantly, Jack reached toward the stack to his right.

But he stopped, his paw hanging stupidly in mid-air. The squirrel had begun to move so quickly that he became little more than a reddish blur. As Jack watched, dumbstruck, the two stacks of cards seemed to shrink under a flurry of movement. When a stack was gone, a discard pile would flip over, and slowly begin to shrink again. Through it all, a breeze blew toward Jack as if from a fan. In less than fifteen seconds, ten small stacks of cards were lined up in a neat little row before the squirrel.

He held out the three cards still in his paw. "Here you go. I imagine you've got a 5 in there somewhere."

The anteater accepted only a paltry meal of toast and an apple, which he diced into even little chunks and ate daintily with a fork. The squirrel was less modest. Walnut pancakes, hash browns, fried plantains, waffles with strawberries, a bowl of chopped fruit, all washed down with a large chocolate milk. He finished well before the anteater, despite the hefty order and the fact that he was speaking to Jack the entire time. His real name was Miles Greenacre, "but my friends call me *Sprint*. Doesn't take a mouse to figure out why," he said through a mouthful of waffles.

"Not exactly," Jack agreed, failing to hide the amazement in his voice. "That was really... something."

"Yeah, it's great for cards," Sprint said. "Real mess maker doing the dishes."

The anteater, who silently munched on his apple bits, was called Hoover Fennelman. They came from Pear Valley, a suburban town several hours east of Hadensburrow. "We left a few days ago. Had a little... mishap with our bus," Sprint explained, and for some reason, he glanced sideways at Hoover when he said this. "But another group of recruits were coming from the same direction, so we all crammed onto their bus in New Castle, and here we are."

"Recruits?" Jack asked.

"Well, *hopeful* recruits," Sprint amended. But before he could elaborate, a lizard woman near the door shouted for attention.

"Alright," she projected, "I want everyone on the bus in three minutes. Let's go."

"Ready, Hooves?" Sprint asked the anteater, standing. "Like I said, it's crammed on the bus," he explained to Jack, "and I'd rather not get stuck sitting behind the driver again." Hoover finished his toast in a hurry, the two of them said goodbye to Jack, and were off. The room cleared out quickly, leaving a goat in an apron to stare exasperatedly around the trash laden dining area, a bus tray hooked under one arm.

As the last young travelers filed out of the room, the lizard held the door open, looking to Jack. "Let's go, rabbit."

"But I'm not..." Jack started, surprised.

The lizard cut across him impatiently. "Not what? Done? Ready? I don't care," she snapped. "It's a full night's journey to Animal Control. We will not be late to the harbor because of you."

Jack's heart skipped. He thought of the golden envelope in his messenger bag. Drawing the strap tight over his shoulder, he stood and smiled. "Yes ma'am."

## Chapter Twelve

# THE HARBOR

The bus was crowded, noisy, and stiflingly hot. Jack was crammed between Sprint and Hoover on a bench near the middle. He unclasped the messenger bag between his feet and replaced the invitation, which he had been showing to them. They had identical ones, although Sprint's was worn and creased, as though he'd read it a thousand times, while Hoover's looked brand new.

"So what's your power?" Jack asked as the anteater replaced his invitation in its envelope with gingerly care.

Hoover shrugged in response, but before he could speak, a voice piped up from across the aisle. "He's the reason this bus is so crowded." Jack turned to see a heavyset groundhog leering across the aisle beyond Sprint. "Bazooka Breath here had to sneeze. And instead of sticking his snout out the window like any sensible non-idiot, he tried to hold it in, failed, and blew the whole bus up. We had to wait three hours for one of the already-full busses to come get us." He shook his head and looked at

Jack. "Honestly, I can't believe how many fan boy wanna-bes they've invited. Nothing but a bunch of talentless Control Freaks. Surprised none of them did a Gary Green." He waited for a response, and when Jack made none, he prodded. "Gary Green? Tell me you've heard of Gary Green."

"Just tell us, Cal," Sprint, who sat along the aisle nearest to the groundhog, said in annoyance. "Get it out of your system so you can shut up." He gave the seat in front of him a shove with his foot as he repositioned himself against his pillow-like tail. A pair of eyes raised over the seat, glowered at him, and then dropped back down.

Cal pretended not to hear him. "Couple of years ago, there was a kid about our age, maybe a bit younger, named Gary Green. One day, Gary's walking through his house, trips, and stumbles right through a wall, ending up outside. Only the wall hadn't broken. He'd just passed right through it. This terrifies Gary. Think about it. If he can pass through walls, what's to stop him from passing right through the ground below his feet? He becomes obsessed with the idea, terrified that he'll lose control of his power. One night, lying in his bed, the panic becomes too much. He screams for his mom and dad. By the time they get there, only his paws are visible, sticking straight out of his mattress as though it's made of quicksand. And before they can get to him… *Thwoop!* He's gone. Right down into the earth."

He laughed, then dropped his voice sinisterly. "You never know. One night, you could be asleep in your bed, when arms rise out of the mattress… *and grab you!*" A pair of paws gripped Sprint's shoulders from behind. The squirrel jumped, flailing his legs and kicking the seat in front of him.

"Okay, seriously," a girl's voice barked out from the seat Sprint had bumped. A doe's head poked up from behind the bench, those same eyes glowering at him from beneath the bill of a gray patrol cap. "If you bump my seat one more time, I'm gonna stuff that fluffy tail of yours down your throat."

"Easy there, Prancer," Sprint said. "It was an accident."

"Okay first," the doe started, "my name is not Prancer. It's Maddie. Second, this bus was made to fit a *giraffe*." She gestured toward the rear of the bus, where the letterman giraffe sat in conversation with the red-haired lion. "If you can't fit comfortably without *accidentally* hitting my seat, I suggest you move to the back where there's more space."

"Alright, alright," Sprint said, holding his paws up defensively. "Relax. It won't happen again."

The deer spun around and disappeared behind her seat.

Sprint turned to Jack with wide eyes. "Somebody's antlers are growing in the wrong place," he whispered.

"I heard that," the doe grumbled.

The hours passed by in conversation. Sprint and Hoover had been friends since childhood, had gone to the same school and lived in the same neighborhood all their lives. Hoover's father, who was a writer for some well-respected hero magazine, had submitted both of their names for an apprenticeship at Animal Control, and because of his connections, they'd been invited to try out immediately.

"There are forty slots," Sprint explained. "Forty kids will get to be sidekicks for a hero, to learn from them. I hope I get matched up with Kenja Hawari. Fastest woman alive."

Jack nodded in agreement, although he'd never heard of Kenja Hawari. He wondered whether most of these kids *had* heard of her.

But something else was bothering him. If Hoover's father had submitted their names, that meant someone must have submitted *his*. But who? Dr. Walraven didn't seem too keen on the idea. Maybe Alan? But why?

The bus began to descend a reasonably steep hill. The sea was now visible over the tops of the buildings ahead, glittering in the afternoon sunlight.

As they neared the harbor, a dozen identical buses were lining up before a guard booth, a candy cane striped bar raising and lowering to let them in one at a time. When it was their turn, the bus driver opened his window, said something to the guard, nodded, and drove through.

Beyond the gate was an open parking lot, thousands of empty spaces marked in white lines, with orange traffic cones weaving makeshift roads across them. The bus followed a path to the left, trailing the bus ahead, and they slowed to an idle as they passed under the shadow of what Jack originally took to be a building. Looking again, however, he saw an enormous white and silver ship looming over them, the familiar blue falcon emblem painted across its side, with a wingspan of more than twenty feet. The kids all piled to their side of the bus, gazing in awe at the vessel.

The train of buses continued again, moving up a ramp and through a huge bay door in the side of the ship. The interior area was high roofed, filled with large boxes and tarp covered crates, and crowded with excited kids whose buses had already parked. A goat in an orange workman's vest flagged them into an open space, the air brake hissed, and the lizard at the front of the bus stood. "Alright, Team Yellow. Remember that name, and look for *this* sign." She held up a yellow card on a stick. "When we exit the bus, we're going to make our way to the deck. Do not lose the group. This is a big ship, and we want to make sure you're all accounted for. Now grab your things, and let's go."

Jack threw his messenger bag over his shoulder and followed the group off the bus. They moved through the enormous cargo bay and into a stairwell that echoed with the thunder of their footsteps.

Since he had not made a reservation, checking in was rather difficult. The attendant behind the counter handled his soggy and misshapen invitation with only two fingers, and irritably informed him that without a reservation, they wouldn't have a room for him on the ship. She was about to inform security of the issue when Sprint stepped in, offering to let Jack stay in the room he was sharing with Hoover. Mollified, the agent stamped his invitation and directed the three of them toward the sleeping quarters.

Room 4816 was a small space, nothing more than a narrow gap between a bunk bed and a blank gray wall. There wasn't even a window. "Well, look on the bright side," Sprint said as he threw his bag onto the top bunk. "We're not elephants."

When they had settled in, using an extra blanket to make a bed for Jack on the floor, they left the room and climbed a stairwell to the main deck. The rails and light posts of the deck had been wrapped in string lights, and tables of food were arranged along one end. Jack stood along the rail, watching the last sliver of sun disappear behind the horizon, leaving a vibrant pink and orange sky.

But he barely saw the sunset. His mind was entangled in a strange mixture of excitement and guilt. Here he was, headed for Animal Control, just like he had always dreamed. Was it wrong to feel excited? What about Dr. Walraven? Had he been wrong not to go back, not to seek help?

He didn't know how long he'd been in the river, but he did know that Dr. Walraven was well beyond his or anyone's help. There was nothing that could have been done, right? Then why was he feeling this guilt? Was it because deep down, he was *excited* to be on his way. No, he told himself. This wasn't a pleasure trip. He knew once he got to Triarch, he'd feel differently. He'd used his invitation to secure a ride, but the moment he got there, he'd seek out Alan. Sure, they hadn't spoken in two years, but Alan was the only family Jack had left – if indeed he could be called that – and as the fox was eighteen, Jack supposed that made him his legal guardian.

A shrew suddenly appeared, vomiting violently over the railing next to him. He was in his early teens, with wire rimmed glasses atop a long, pointed snout, a blue and white checkered shirt tucked into his pants. Wiping a shaky paw across his muzzle, he turned to walk away, halted, then returned and vomited again.

"You do realize we haven't started moving yet?" came a familiar voice. Jack turned to see a short, pudgy groundhog approaching, smiling maliciously at the shrew. "Soon we'll get out on the open water, with the ship rocking back and forth, back and forth, up and down," he gestured with his paws as if they were waves. The shrew, looking horrified, ran back to the edge and threw up again.

"Rookies," Cal said, rolling his eyes. "Seriously, how can you be Animal Control material if you can't even handle a rocking boat?" He flexed his shoulders and leaned against the railing, turning toward Jack. "I'm pretty much a shoo in, myself. If being related to Winter Crier wasn't enough," he paused, waiting for a reaction, but Jack had never heard of Winter Crier, whoever that was, and apparently the groundhog could tell. He huffed, then pointed out over the water as he continued. "I can also do *this*."

Jack turned toward the open sea in the direction the groundhog was pointing. At first, he saw nothing. But after a moment, something caught his eye. About fifty yards out, a small cloud had begun to form, and within seconds it had swelled to nearly the size of a bus.

"You can make clouds?" Jack asked, impressed.

"Controlled condensation, yeah. But that's nothing. Watch this." With a point of his other paw, a second cloud slowly materialized. As he swept his arms together, the two clouds followed, blending into one. He seemed to be crushing something between his paws. There was an electric *CRACK!,* and Jack jumped as a blue streak of lightning shot from the cloud, followed by a *BOOM!* of thunder that shook the deck.

"Hey!" called a bird wearing a blue *STAFF* shirt. "No powers on board."

Cal nodded and waved in acknowledgment.

The shrew ran back to the ledge and heaved once more over the side.

## Chapter Thirteen
# DEAD IN THE WATER

The following morning, Jack was the last one out of the room. Sprint was up and ready in less than a minute, complaining that he was hungry. Hoover, who had been dressed before Jack had even woken up, said that he could use the fresh air after being cooped up in this small quarters all night. "It smells like a swine's sock in here," Sprint had agreed, and the two of them had left Jack to dress.

When he was finished, he put the messenger bag over his shoulder and stepped into the empty corridor. The previous night, this hallway had practically been a party, almost impassably thick with excited, mingling bodies. The three of them had found it difficult getting to their room, and it was only when Sprint had announced loudly, "Porcupine, coming through!" that a path had been cleared enough for them to navigate. By contrast, this morning the chamber was entirely deserted; a burgundy rug stretching endlessly in either direction.

Nearing the stairs to the main deck, he heard the rhythmic crashing of ocean waves. The sound was pleasant and inviting, and he took the stairs two at a time, eager to enter the sunshine. But he slowed to a halt, perking his ears up and listening intently. He could hear the waves clearly, splashing against the hull of the ship. Shouldn't such noises be drowned out by the excited voices of the passengers?

Halfway up the stairs, Jack found his way blocked by a goat in crew attire, facing away from him with a tray of drinks perched on one hoof. He stood completely still, and made no acknowledgment that he recognized Jack's presence. "Ahem," Jack coughed. Nothing. "Ahehem!" Jack coughed again, much louder. Still no response. Finally, he ducked beneath the tray and moved around the goat, who didn't budge, nor did he blink as Jack waved a paw in front of his face.

Wondering what held the goat's attention so raptly, Jack turned out toward the deck, expecting at the very least to see someone dancing around with their pants on their head. Instead, what he saw sent his eyes darting around the deck, touching on every single occupant of the open space.

They were all similarly frozen, a crowded maze of wax figures wearing stupefied, blank expressions. Some were balanced mid-stride. Some held their arms up in gesture, as if they'd been turned to statues mid-conversation.

Jack stared wide eyed around, trying to think of a possible explanation. This was obviously some kind of stunt, perhaps a group activity for which he'd been too late to participate. Any moment now, a whistle would blow, or a voice would call out, and the waxwork expressions on everyone's faces would melt away, turning to cheers, or perhaps even laughter at the dumbfounded look on Jack's face.

Only no whistle blew. The sun bore down upon the shadeless deck, and Jack's confusion quickly turned to panic.

Several minutes passed. He was forced to accept that this was not a stunt when he discovered the sea-sick shrew from the previous evening. The shrew had rather sparse fur on his face, and his pink skin had begun to turn tomato red under the harsh sunlight. Blisters had even begun to form on his snout.

Jack placed a paw on either shoulder and gave him a heavy shake. His body was rigid, as if carved from wood, and he made no response.

Heart beating heavily, Jack turned and jogged among the passengers, desperate for any sign of life. "Hello?" he yelled, hearing the fear in his own voice. "Is anyone… awake?"

No response.

Calling again, he fell short when his eyes traveled beyond the deck and landed on something that made his legs go numb: the shore. They were nearing the city, the tallest of the buildings standing like beacons along the cliff-faced horizon. He could now see sail boats and small steamer vessels puttering around in the open harbor.

He swiveled around and looked up to the flat window of the bridge. Shielding his eyes against the sun, which was bouncing harshly off the glass, he could just make out the captain behind the blinding white glare, his white hat proudly perched between five-point antlers. Jack squinted up at him and realized, to his horror, that the captain was just as incapacitated as any of the passengers.

With another glance toward the shore, he bolted for the stairs leading to the captain's bridge. *I'll speed us up,* he thought, taking the steps two at a time. *I can't dock this thing, but I can get us nearer, then stop and radio for help.* Rounding a corner, he found the door leading to the bridge, and gave it a shove. It opened only a half an inch, and then halted as if striking a wall. He pushed again. There was definitely something — or someone — pressed up against the opposite side of the door. He put his full body into a third push, but he knew immediately that it was no use. Whoever was blocking the door seemed to weigh as much as a rhinoceros, and with all of his strength, Jack couldn't move it an inch further. Kicking it in frustration, he ran back down to the deck. In the seemingly short span of time, the harbor had drawn much closer, a sheer cliff face against which he could now see a white line of breaking water. Above the cliff, the details of the cityscape were becoming distinguishable, no longer a jagged mass, but individual high rises and steeples, water towers and one buttressed cathedral, atop which Jack could even make out the silhouettes of five gargoyles looming down upon the sea.

The call of a harbor gull reached the ship. Having seen this behavior as they had disembarked, he understood that the gull was calling to acknowledge their approach, and that someone on board was meant to reciprocate. But the gull on board would be unable to respond.

"Help!" he bellowed, flailing his arms. "Help!" But he was no gull — his calls were soft, lost on the wind, and he knew they wouldn't reach the gull on shore.

The harbor was getting dangerously close. That cliff face was only minutes off; he could now properly count the gargoyles along the rim of the cathedral — four, not five.

Row upon row of piers stretched out over the water like banded wooden fingers, nearly all teeming with crowds of seals basking in the sunshine. They were so close, Jack could hear their barked conversations.

"Help!" he called, throwing his upper body over the railing as if hurling the words at them. A few lifted their lazy heads.

The shoreline gull was joined by several others, the calls becoming much more frequent and shrill.

The nearest of the piers was so close now, he could make out the individual barnacles creeping up from the water. "Whoa! Whoa!" the group of seals cried as they scrambled over one another and into the water. The boards snapped loudly as the ship's hull wedged into the pier, sending splinters to the air and seals cursing into the waves. The vessel rattled at each beam, but made no sign of slowing.

Having struck the pier at an angle, the ship shook free and trundled on in the direction of the rock face, the vulgar swears of the seals still audible from below.

The cliff drew nearer and nearer. By this point, a crowd was gathering at its edge a hundred feet up, pointing toward the ship.

"Help!" Jack called to them, but he knew it was no use. What could anyone do? Even if the captain were to wake up and put the ship into full reverse, at this speed they were *going* to hit the wall.

But as he braced himself and let out a frightened hiss of air, his breath formed a swirling cloud that rose before his eyes. The exposed skin of his inner ears and nose became chill, and he felt his body tremble with the sudden cold.

A musical crunching sound, like the slow cracking of glass, rose from over the deck's edge. The ship's hull rattled and whined loudly, fighting against some obstacle. Jack ran to the railing and looked over.

A field of enormous icy shards coated the surface of the water, an alien terrain of ten-foot-tall crystal barbs that started at the ship's hull and stretched out over the water — and it was working! The shadow of the cliff began to creep over the deck, but had only reached the bridge before the ship came to a halt, the engines roaring in vain.

Beneath the shade, a change came over the passengers. All at once, they seemed to break from their trance. Some looked confused, disoriented. Others looked horrified. The shrew let out a bellowing shriek and dunked his head into the punch bowl.

As the passengers rubbed their heads and looked around in confusion, that same musical crunching sound could be heard overhead, like the tinkling of a crystal chandelier. Looking up, Jack was astonished to see what could only be described as a bridge being formed from the same splinter-like shards of ice. It stretched from the top of the cliff high above, materializing from thin air, sloping until it touched down on the deck of the ship. And stepping coolly across its surface, passing impressively over their heads, an emperor penguin glowered down upon the crowd. Jack recognized him from the countless times he had appeared in newspapers and on television. He wore a silver vest and pants, with a blue tie that bulged beneath his chin. He stopped ten feet above the deck, his gaze sweeping across the now silent crowd.

"Who did this?" President Alexander Brisk demanded.

A moment of silence passed as the passengers looked amongst themselves. Then, raising a quivering hoof, the unfriendly doe, who had been so irritated by Sprint bumping her seat, stepped forward.

## Chapter Fourteen

## ANIMAL CONTROL

"Think she'll get kicked out?" Hoover asked with a tone of concern. They were following the crowd up a noisy concrete stairwell inside the cliff.

"Who cares?" Sprint, who had lost his balance and toppled when the spell had lifted, was hobbling up the stairs with a pronounced limp. "I just wish I knew how she did it," he muttered. Despite the fact that the paralysis had affected everyone aboard the ship — everyone but Jack, at least — Sprint seemed to take the event personally. Maddie had, after all, been very rude to him on the bus. Mostly, however, Jack suspected the squirrel was so angry because although she was likely to be sent back across the sea — if not arrested — her heightena was undeniably impressive.

"I don't know *how* it happened," Hoover said, "but just *before* it happened, there was an announcement that she had received a phone call."

"That's right! She... hey!" Sprint exclaimed, then dropped his tone conspiratorially. "Hey, you don't think that was some kind of a cue, do you? Like a signal?"

"I don't know," Hoover said. "I don't see why she would *want* to cause all of that. After all, if the President hadn't shown up... well, she was on the ship too."

"Then maybe she was attempting to pull off some big stunt to make an impression, and it went wrong."

Jack shook his head. "I don't think so. I saw her when I was walking around the deck. She was staring right up at the bridge, just as frozen as everyone else. I think it was an accident, whatever it was."

They reached the top of the stairs and followed the crowd of teens into the open air again. Instantly, the three fell silent as they found themselves on a bustling city street between towering skyscrapers. Jack had never seen buildings so tall. The fur along his spine stood as he tilted his head up at them.

"Triarch!" Sprint said, his face exultant. "Wow, it's better than I'd imagined!"

"I wish we were here at night," Hoover said. "I've seen pictures — it's all lit up like an enormous arcade."

The guides were shouting for attention. The yellow sign poked up above the crowd, waggling back and forth. They took a left, following the group along the busy sidewalk. Jack looked around in amazement. There was simply too much to take it all in.

A goat in a velvet vest stood at the box office in a concave theater entrance, grumbling to his collie companion. "...Well then there should be a lah-ah-aww," he stuttered. "Porcupines should remain in *standing rooms* only. You wouldn't believe my upholstery bill."

An exasperated looking mother cat was walking along the sidewalk in the opposite direction, pulling the hem of her skirt away from her young children. "Can't you kids give it a rest for two minutes?" she snapped. "For the last time, this is my favorite skirt. It's not a curtain for you to claw at!"

Vertical neon signs marked hotels and restaurants. Vending carts and taxis drawn by gruff looking horses lined the cobblestone streets. The alluring smell of hot fries wafted out of *Hibernation Headstart*. The acrid scent of metal tinged Jack's nostrils as they walked past *Sure-Hammer: Shoes for Quadrupeds*. A deep humming sound poured through a plastic screen covering the entrance of *Buzz On In: Wax and Honey to Go*. As he watched, a suffocating swarm of bees loomed around several protectively dressed patrons, and a badger woman at the door was offering the same protective gear to an interested looking brown bear.

They reached a corner, across from which stood a vibrant green park. The throng of teens came to a stop, waiting for a signal light, and then crossed to the lawn, where a stone path led into the park. Once the entire crowd had crossed, they broke into their color groups on the open lawn. "Listen up!" the lizard shouted. Several kids continued to chatter, so she clapped loudly and yelled again. "Listen up! We're headed toward North Gate. We'll walk *single file*, and line up at the gate. You'll be asked to show your invitation at the kiosk. Please have it ready. Now let's move."

The yellow group began moving again, forming a line just behind orange. They followed the path as it curved its way beneath the shade of trees. Soon, they were walking between perfectly manicured cone hedges. The pathway itself was immaculate, with gray patches of moisture where the morning power wash had not yet dried.

The hedges ended at pillars of red brick, an iron archway stretching between them. At the center of the arch, the famous falcon insignia was cast in black iron, on either side of which were two-foot-tall letters that spelled the words:

## ANIMAL CONTROL

The archway let onto a large, open esplanade paved with those same red bricks, and populated with lamp posts, park benches, and here and there a small fenced off island of flowers and bushes. The area curved mildly in both directions, skirting a hedge fence on the opposite side. The other groups had already formed an orderly line before a pearl white kiosk, like a ticket booth for a fancy amusement park.

"Fennelman, Hoover?" the anteater spoke through the glass window of the kiosk, sounding uncertain of his own name. He slid his invitation beneath the window.

The sheep behind the glass adjusted her horn-rimmed glasses and eyed the invitation, then flicked through a stapled stack of papers. "Ah, yes. Here you are, dear," she smiled as she scribbled his name onto a card. She unwound a lanyard and fit the card into a plastic sleeve at the end, then pushed it beneath the glass. "Please wear this around your neck at all times while on campus." She gave him an encouraging smile. "Good luck, dear."

Jack suddenly realized that he was next. With everything that had happened, he hadn't thought about *why* he was here since he'd fallen asleep last night. It had been so easy to feel like a part of this group, just another one of the invitees. But that time had passed.

"Honey, your invitation?" the sheep said, looking at him over the top of her glasses.

"I… right," he said, unclasping his bag and fishing the envelope out. He slid it beneath the glass, then drew in a breath. Sprint was standing close by. It would be difficult to say what he had to say without being overheard. "Listen," he started, lowering his voice. "I'm not really here for the tryout. I came because I have an… emergency."

The sheep stared uncertainly. "Emergency," she repeated.

"Yes, I… well, there was an earthquake, and these wolves. It's all kind of jumbled together, but my house caught fire, and…"

"Dear, if you have a house fire, you need to call the fire department. I can put you in touch with…"

"No!" Jack burst out. "Sorry, it's just… It's not like that. Wolves attacked. They killed my father. Dr. Einer Walraven." He said the name slowly, hoping for recognition, and it seemed to work. Her eyes lit, and she leaned slightly forward in her chair. "Dr. Walraven is… dead?"

It was the first time Jack had heard the words, the first time he himself had vocally acknowledged it, and his voice caught in his throat. He simply nodded.

There was a moment of silence as the sheep considered this information. "I'll need to get you in touch with dispatch. If you can just stand over…"

"I need to speak to Alan Kale," Jack interrupted. "He's the President's Assistant."

The sheep looked uneasy. "Mr. Kale is a very busy man."

"He's also the only family I have left," Jack said. "Please. He'll want to know about Dr. Walraven, and he'll want to know I'm here. Jack Robberts."

The sheep considered him for a moment. She picked up the receiver of a phone and hitched it in her shoulder, then pulled four numbers in the rotary.

"You were attacked?" Sprint asked.

Jack turned to him and nodded.

"Why didn't you say anything?"

Jack shrugged. "I dunno. I just... couldn't."

The sheep thanked the voice on the other end, then hung up the phone. "Alright," she said as she scribbled something onto a card, then slid it into the plastic sleeve of a lanyard and passed it beneath the glass, along with his invitation. "Mr. Kale will see you." Jack picked up the lanyard and read, "Jack Robberts," and below, "Visiting Alan Kale." The sheep leaned forward in order to gain a clearer view of the walkway beyond the gate, then pointed. "Take the left path. Stick to it until you come to a stone building with a big staircase in front. Mr. Kale will meet you in the lobby."

"Left path, stone building," Jack repeated, lifting the lanyard over his ears as he started through the gate. "Thank you."

He turned toward the squirrel, and their eyes met. An awkward silence hung between them. "Good luck," Jack finally managed.

"Thanks," Sprint shrugged. He turned and slid his invitation beneath the glass. Jack continued through the gate, nodding goodbye to Hoover as he passed.

The diamond patterned walkway followed along the hedge fence, occasionally passing a building or branching off to the right. He stuck to the path, and eventually it curved in to the campus.

Not far along, a worker wearing disposable coveralls was scrubbing at a brick wall. A steel falcon stood out from the wall;

another Animal Control logo. This one, however, appeared to have been defaced. Spray paint marked the steel and the wall behind it, turning the falcon into an elephant head. Its wings were now ears, its tail a trunk. Black paint also formed eyes and tusks. Above this strangely transformed logo was a single word, done in a scribbled, graffiti style. **STRONGER.** Something about this word struck Jack, and he stared at it as he passed.

"Morning," a voice called, and Jack spun around just in time to see a tram car come up on his left side, three empty passenger trailers in tow. It passed him by and continued up the path. He saw few others, save for two goats wearing aprons and pushing a trolley of covered platters, and a gazelle in a skirted suit and heels, scribbling away on a clipboard as she clicked past him.

The path forked in three directions, with the one in the middle leading directly to a wide staircase at the base of what Jack would have guessed to be a courthouse. The building was made of stone, with tall white pillars before three doors of varying sizes. A small door, just big enough for Jack to fit through, a medium sized door, which looked a little too big for him, and one between them so tall, Jack wondered how it could possibly be useful.

His question was answered as he reached the top of the stairs. The large door at the center swung open, and out stepped an enormous bull elephant, his flat palm pressed against the wooden door, holding it open for his smaller companions, a goat and a lizard. Jack must have been staring, because the elephant threw him a friendly wink as he stomped past.

Feeling slightly humiliated to use the small door, Jack stepped into an open lobby. A stone fireplace crackled at the center of the room, beside which a tropical bird in a white blouse was tapping away at a word processor.

"Hello, Jack."

Jack turned to see Alan descending a stairway to the left. He had grown in the past two years, a full head taller than the last time Jack had seen him. And of course the suit and tie didn't hurt the impression of maturity. "Hi, Alan," he responded, moving to hug the fox as he approached. Alan embraced him reluctantly and released after one pat of the back.

"Now, I was told Dr. Walraven is dead." His tone was impassive as he said it, as though he was talking about a flat tire.

Jack nodded. "Yeah, he… a few days ago. We were attacked by wolves."

"And you were unable to save him?" Alan asked, fixing Jack with a cold gaze.

Jack didn't know how to respond. Whatever he had expected Alan to say, it certainly wasn't *that*.

Alan swept his ears back with a paw and let out a resigned laugh. "I'm sorry," he said. "Let's just say Dr. Walraven would expect me to make an inappropriate joke at a time like this." He put a paw on Jack's shoulder and smiled; a smile that didn't quite reach his eyes. "You're safe now, and that's what matters.

"Kat," he added, turning to the tropical bird at the desk, "I'll be out for a while. Please reschedule my appointment with President Graizer."

"Yes, Mr. Kale," the bird responded, giving Jack a warm smile as they left.

They had only just stepped back into the daylight when there was a loud *crack*, followed immediately by a splashing sound. Jack looked to the left. Just below the stairs, a brown dog, maybe a year or two older than Jack, was wading around in a circular fountain. He swore in frustration as he adjusted a backward ball cap, then looked up and spotted the pair of them. "Ah! Mr. Kale!" he yelled. To Jack's surprise, he instantly vanished, then reappeared with another loud *crack* at the top of the stairs just in front of them. "There you are!"

"Hello Jay," Alan said in a rather bored tone. "This is Jack Robberts. He's a guest of mine, visiting Animal Control for the first time. Jack, this is Jay Behr. He's a porter."

Jay shook the water from his clothing with a jovial shudder, sprinkling the other two. "It means I carry messages and stuff around the campus," Jay said, jabbing his own chest with a thumb. "*Porter*, I mean. Course, I can also *tele*port, so I suppose I'm a porter in more ways than one. It's one of the more dangerous heightena, you know," he added. "For myself and for others. Imagine if I teleported right where you're standing." He clapped his paws together in Jack's face. "POP!" he said, laughing boyishly.

"Yes, charming," Alan said with a frown. "You were looking for me, Jay?"

"Right," the dog said. "Er… President Brisk is looking for you. He heard you have a visitor," he eyed Jack with interest, "and he wants to meet him."

Thanking Jay, Alan began down the stairs, and Jack followed. There was another loud *crack*, another splash, and Jay yelled in frustration.

## Chapter Fifteen

# A PENGUIN WITH HORNS

The President's estate was located at the far end of a sprawling grass field, along which several rows of suburban houses were positioned.

Alan hadn't said much since they had left the building, but now, standing at the iron gate of the mansion, he broke the silence. "President Brisk is a very important man. If he wants to see you, he has a reason." He looked at Jack meaningfully as he slammed his palm against a square button on the gatepost. In response, the gate clicked, and there was a motorized grinding sound as it began to swing inward. A steel falcon insignia at the center of the gate was divided in half as it opened.

"Which is what?" Jack asked. After the penguin's impressive display this morning, and the cold glare with which he had fixed the doe, Jack was very nervous about meeting the President.

Alan stepped through the open gate, and Jack followed. "I've gotten to know President Brisk very well over the past two years," Alan said. "He is brilliant and powerful. He wastes no time, and doesn't like being lied to." He paused briefly, but before Jack could respond, he started again. "Dr. Walraven died in a house fire. A tragic accident. You weren't there."

"Yes, I was," Jack protested. His blood had immediately boiled at the words. "You haven't asked me *anything* about Dr. Walraven's death, except to imply that I should have saved him. And now you're going to say it was only an accident? I *was* there, Alan. We were attacked."

"You're not hearing me Jack," Alan said, stopping the bunny with a paw to his chest. "It was an accident. You saw nothing. You saw nobody."

"I…" Jack started.

"After the mill burnt down, you came here to find me." He began walking again. "I *am* your new legal guardian, after all," he added coldly.

The cobblestone driveway curved around a large oak tree before the biggest, nicest house Jack had ever seen. Three stories tall, every window and door wrapped in stone arches. Construction scaffolding hid the entire left side of the house; the exterior seemed to be going through a remodel.

The wooden double doors were as tall as the one the elephant had passed through in Alan's building. Medium and smaller doors were carved into them.

Alan lifted a fist toward the door, looking at Jack. "Remember," he started.

"I saw nothing, I saw nobody," Jack muttered. The words felt like a betrayal as they came out of his mouth.

"Nothing and nobody," Alan agreed, and he rapped on the door.

There was silence for a moment. Then a lock clicked, and the inset door on the right creaked open, slowly at first. The pleasant but quizzical face of a bespectacled penguin peered out. She eyed Jack first, looking him up and down, and then spotted the fox.

"Alan!" she said, and pulled the door wide. "Back so soon. That business this morning. That could have been a disaster!"

"Hello, Mrs. Brisk," he replied. "Yes it could have, but all is well now, as I understand it." He ushered Jack forward. "This is Jack Robberts. You might say he's my kid brother. Jack, this is Mrs. Dulcanae Brisk, The First Lady of Animal Control."

"Hello, Jack," she said as she extended a flipper toward him. Never having met a penguin in person before, he reached forward uncertainly and pinched the end of the flipper between his fingers. "Alan is always so formal," she laughed. "Please, come in."

It must have been twenty degrees cooler inside. Appropriate for penguins, he considered. The cylindrical entryway was nearly all marble, with pillars that stretched up to a high ceiling from which a crystal chandelier was suspended, adding dramatically to the icy feel of the space. A large painting of a squat, stern looking bull rested on the floor next to a fireplace, glowering out upon the room with a furrowed brow. To the left of the mantle, a stairwell of deep mahogany curved up to the second floor.

Mrs. Brisk shut the door behind them, then turned and pressed the tips of her flippers together. "Alexander is in a meeting right now, and, well," she paused, as if biting back her words.

"Ah, is Mr. Gordon here, then?" Alan asked.

Mrs. Brisk looked about her distractedly. "Yes," she said, picking up a half empty water glass from the mantle and dusting below it with the blade of her flipper. "He arrived with his assistant about fifteen minutes ago, just after Alexander returned. I think there's quite enough for Alexander to be dealing with today, and what that man expects him to do about… well, anyway, they should be finishing up soon. Why don't you boys just…" she laughed dismissively as she touched Alan's paw. "You know where you're going, don't you," she tittered.

Alan thanked her, then ushered Jack to the mahogany stairway.

The stairs opened into a long, narrow hall. A door at the end was slightly ajar, spilling blue daylight across the dark wood floor. As they drew nearer, Jack could hear a deep voice from behind the door.

"…don't have the resources to investigate it ourselves. This is the fourth one, Mr. President; it's not an isolated incident. It's…"

"I understand your situation, Mr. Gordon," said a second voice, which Jack recognized as that of President Brisk. "But I'm afraid this matter does not fall under the protection agreement of Animal Control. It's a matter for your local police to handle."

"The police? But surely this is…"

"I'm sorry, Pontificus," Brisk cut across him, "but there is nothing more that I can do for you. There really is nothing else to be said." There was the sound of a chair scraping across wood, and Brisk continued. "I truly am sorry, old friend."

"As am I," the deep voice responded, and another chair was moved across the floor. The door opened abruptly, and a tall hawk entered the hall, stopping short at the sight of the fox and bunny. Just behind him followed a gangly white wolf with a stooped posture. Jack took a step back instinctively, but the wolf's mannerism was so meek, he relaxed immediately. This wolf was the wrong color anyway, he considered.

"Ah, hello Alan," the hawk said, his tone instantly warm.

"Hello, Mr. Gordon," Alan responded. "How was your flight?"

"Long," the hawk said. "…And boy are my wings tired!"

"Two years later, it's still not funny," Alan said, although he betrayed a smile.

The hawk sighed. "Ah well. One day, you'll develop a sense of humor. I intend to be a witness." He chuckled, then turned to Jack. "And who is this?"

"Mr. Gordon, this is Jack Robberts," Alan said. "Adopted son of Dr. Walraven. Jack, this is Pontificus Gordon. Mr. Gordon holds a similar position to my own; he is assistant to Lady Claythorne in Safehaven."

"I'm merely her gopher," Mr. Gordon said with a wink. "But adopted son of Dr. Walraven, you say? My dear boy, I've only just heard of your loss. My deepest sympathies."

Wondering how he could already know about Dr. Walraven, Jack nodded uncertainly. "Thank you."

"Dr. Walraven was a fine rat; a hero above nearly all others. This will only add to the bad news I must bring back to Her Ladyship. Good day to you both," Mr. Gordon said. "Peter, come along," he added, and the wolf followed him to the stairs.

Alan wrapped on the door frame with the back of his paw. "Hello again, Alan," the penguin said, standing as they entered. "Yes, Carla told me you had a visitor this morning. This must be Jack." He fixed his eyes on the bunny and stepped around his desk.

"Yes sir," Alan nodded. "This is Jack Robberts. Jack, I'm sure you already know who this is."

"It's a pleasure to meet you, son," Brisk said. To Jack's great relief, he did not extend a flipper.

"Pleasure to meet you too, sir," Jack half mumbled.

"I returned through the North Gate this morning," the President explained, leaning a hip against the edge of his desk. "Carla tells me you brought some rather terrible news along with you." He paused, perhaps waiting for Jack to respond. Jack managed a small nod. "A house fire," he said, disbelieving. "Were you there? Did you see anything?"

Jack didn't respond immediately. He looked sideways at Alan, who did not meet his eyes. "No sir," he said finally. "I wasn't there."

The penguin clicked his tongue, shaking his head regretfully. "I'm very sorry, Jack. He was a great friend of mine, and a true inspiration to us all.

"Alan," Brisk looked to the fox. "I'll need a word with you. Excuse us, Jack. Please take a seat." He placed a flipper around Alan's shoulder and the two left the room, shutting the door behind them.

Jack dropped into a chair before the desk, his eyes wandering around the office. Several stacks of cardboard boxes filled one corner. The walls were empty, with several different paint swatches brushed here and there, as though President Brisk were in the process of selecting a wall color.

Another cardboard box was sitting on the President's desk alongside a gold-trimmed carriage clock, and on top of that was a golden letter opener.

*A letter opener.*

Jack looked over his shoulder. The faint voices of Alan and Brisk could be heard just outside, deep in conversation. He lifted the strap of the messenger bag over his head and withdrew the brown paper package.

He considered the word written in the upper left corner. "Stronger." Whatever was in this box, it was meant to protect Nikacia from the possibility of the stolen key falling into the wrong paws. What could possibly be stronger than King's heightena? And why was that same word painted onto the wall above the defaced Animal Control logo?

There was so much tape, piercing it took some effort, but after short work, he managed to slice an "I" shape along the top edges of the box. Heart pounding, he looked over his shoulder again. The conversation didn't seem to be slowing.

He slid a paw into the opening and fished around in the bed of foam peanuts. His finger brushed a solid object, small and slender. It was cool as steel and about the size of a pen. He withdrew it.

*What could possibly be stronger than King's heightena?* Jack had asked. What could protect the world from that key falling into the wrong paws?

And here was the answer, resting on his open palm as he stared at it in disbelief.

*Nothing.* It wasn't a safeguard from the key falling into the wrong paws.

It was the key itself.

Alan and Brisk seemed to be ending their conversation outside. As quickly as he could, he stuffed the key into his pants pocket. The door began to open.

The box! He'd nearly dropped it in his scuffle to hide the key. He threw open the flap of his bag, and stuffed the box inside.

"My apologies," Brisk said as he reentered the room. "My schedule is quite full today, as I'm sure you can imagine."

"Mmmm," Jack grunted, forcing a grin and folding his paws over the messenger bag in his lap.

"We nearly lost an entire ship full of potential recruits. Children, I should say," he added. He paused for a moment, then turned his eyes to Jack as he dropped into his own chair behind the desk. "You know, if that deer hadn't come forward, I might have thought *you* had caused it all."

Jack's heart leapt. Was this why he had been brought here? Was he somehow in trouble? "I don't, uh…"

"I saw that ship plowing through the pier, a deck full of mannequins, and one bunny, running around like a martyred chicken." He considered Jack. "Then that deer came forward. What a way to make an entrance," he said with a soft laugh.

Jack smiled stiffly.

"What I find remarkable," Brisk continued, "is that you were the only one unaffected by her heightena. The *only* one," he emphasized the word, almost accusingly. "Could it be," he said, tilting his head with curiosity, "that you possess the fabled luck of your species?"

Jack shrugged. "Dr. Walraven always thought so. I dunno, though…"

"Einer thought so, did he?" Brisk asked, raising a brow. Jack remembered how Dr. Walraven had felt about Brisk, and wondered whether the feeling was mutual. "Well," the President said finally, swiveling toward the bay window behind him, "Einer was a very wise man. I'm quite sure he was right in this matter. What else could explain it?"

Jack watched the back of the President's chair, wondering if he had somehow offended him. Then the chair swiveled around, and Jack was surprised to see tears welling in his eyes. "Dr. Walraven was someone I respected greatly," he said. "His death has… well, it's been a punch in the gut, to be frank. We had our differences, it's true; but then what true friends haven't?" He coughed, smiled at Jack, and continued. "Still, it's the things we regret that we remember the clearest, isn't it. Last time I saw him, I called him a," he paused, then finished in a tone of self-loathing, "a *raving rodent.* Suppose I'll live with that forever."

This confession from the stern, intimidating President took Jack by surprise. After Alan's cold indifference, the President's words felt... well, a lot like a hug. "Yeah," he said, his voice a little shaky. "I know exactly what you mean. He'd wanted to go somewhere... Pine Creek, I think, and he'd wanted me to go with him. I was mad about something stupid, and I threw it all in his face." His eyes burned with unfallen tears, the first tears since the attack, and he buried his face in his paws.

"Oh, Jack." Brisk rose from his seat and stepped again around his desk. He rested a fin on the bunny's shoulder. "He knew how you felt. He knew you loved him."

"I told him to stop calling me *son,*" Jack said, his voice cracking. It felt strange to be so emotionally exposed in front of someone so important, someone he'd only just met. But now that the words were coming, they seemed to flow effortlessly. "It wasn't until he was gone that I understood how much that word meant to me."

"That's how it always is, my boy," Brisk said. "We never realize what we have until we've lost it."

Tears came in earnest now, and it was only by an effort that Jack choked back a sob. Brisk smiled encouragingly, then turned toward the stack of cardboard boxes in the corner. "I have a picture here, somewhere..."

As Brisk dug through the boxes, Jack slid a paw into his pocket, gripping the bronze key. Dr. Walraven had been so distrustful of President Brisk; enough, apparently, to somehow steal this key. And yet here Brisk was, more encouraging and kind than anyone had been to Jack since the doctor's death. Surely he could be trusted.

"Ah," Brisk exclaimed, stooping to reach into one of the lower boxes. "Here it is!" He stepped back over to Jack, holding out a small, unframed photograph. It depicted a slightly younger Dr. Walraven standing near, but not next to, President Brisk. A third figure, a tall lizard with pinkish white scales in stark contrast to his black tuxedo, stood between them. The three of them held up champagne glasses in an apparent toast toward the camera. "I want you to have this," Brisk said.

With his free paw, Jack reached for the photograph. But just as his fingers brushed the President's fin, there was a sudden shift; a hideous change had come over the President. The black feathers of his face had become sparse, patched, exposing pale white skin beneath. His eyes sunk back into his skull, leaving only empty sockets. And from his temples, a pair of enormous black horns had sprouted, so large they seemed unsupportable. "I need more power!" the demoniacally transfigured president shrilled, leaning toward Jack. "Red teeth! Red teeth! Red teeth!"

Jack tumbled over the back of his chair. He scrambled to his feet, his arms wrapped around his head defensively.

But the only sound he heard was the gentle ticking of the carriage clock. He opened his eyes, but instead of the rancorous perversion of President Brisk, he saw only the bewildered penguin, perfectly whole, staring back at him.

Brisk's look was half appraising, half concerned. After a moment, he spoke. "It's only a picture," he said, his tone reassuring. "I apologize if it upset you."

Still half crouching, Jack looked around the room.

The clock continued to tick.

He rose slowly. "Er… no," he said. "I'm fine. I just… lost my balance." It was a lame story, but Brisk nodded.

"Well, in any case," Brisk said, looking at the carriage clock on his desk, "I hope you will forgive my abruptness, but I do have matters to which I must attend." He smiled, took a step toward the door, and then paused. "I have an idea," he said. "Why don't you accompany me to the trials today?"

Still shaken, Jack hesitated. But Brisk now stood between him and the door, and he found it impossible to say no. "Sure," he said finally. Thinking to save face, he added, perhaps a little too enthusiastically, "That sounds great!"

"Wonderful," Brisk nodded, all signs of misgiving faded. "Well then, let's be on our way."

## Chapter Sixteen

# THE CONVENTION CENTER

When they returned to the marble entryway, a small crowd of official-looking adults were gathered and conversing. "S'about time, Brisk," a black bear jibed. "Let's get this show on the road."

"In good time, Ty," the President said with an indulgent smile. "We have a special guest with us today, and I'm afraid I have some bad news." He introduced Jack, and divulged Dr. Walraven's death to the group. They responded with gasps and groans, looking amongst themselves. Mr. Behr, the brown dog that had arrested Dr. Walraven, looked to Jack in stunned disbelief.

"Unfortunately," Brisk continued, "we don't have time for grief just yet. I believe our young visitors are already at the Convention Center. Let's not keep them waiting any longer." He gestured toward the doors, and the crowd began to file outside.

Alan, who had been standing at the back of the room, strode next to Jack as they entered the daylight once more. "How did it go?" he asked.

The monstrously transfigured face of President Brisk still seemed to loom before Jack. Had it been a hallucination? Maybe the events of the last few days finally catching up with him? Alan's cold reception didn't exactly give Jack much confidence that he wouldn't think he was crazy. Or maybe he still hadn't forgiven him for Dr. Walraven's arrest. Either way, he shrugged. "It was fine."

They walked around the edge of a glass lake, and finally arrived at what looked like a military warehouse. A three-story tall sliding door was pushed open, with letters stenciled across it that read *BLDG E4*. Just before the doors, the crowd of invited applicants were gathered. Their numbers seemed to have doubled; there must have been a thousand of them. Jack considered that many of these kids would have come from the south.

"Attention!" an adult voice called from among the crowd as the President's entourage approached, and a gradual hush fell, all heads turning in their direction.

Brisk made a forward motion with his flippers, and crystal shards began to form along the ground. The shards ramped upward, and the small group moved onto the slowly materializing platform of ice. Jack hesitated, but Alan put a paw on his shoulder and guided him forward. The crowd before them began to talk excitedly amongst themselves. "Silence," the same voice called out, and the hush returned.

"Welcome," Brisk projected, beaming down upon the crowd. "We thank you for joining us on this exciting occasion. For the past five years, the sidekick program has been shut down. Today, we open it back up. You have all been invited here because you are the *best*." Applause erupted, and Brisk smiled indulgently before continuing. "We are honored by your presence, and wish every one of you the very best of luck. And remember," he paused for dramatic effect, "we seek not your power, but your will. All of you have shown that will by being here today, and for that, we thank you." The crowd erupted once more.

President Brisk stepped back, nodding to Alan, who replaced him at the front of the ice stage and spoke in a dry, matter-of-fact tone. "You will be competing for an apprenticeship with one of our brave heroes. This morning, you will participate in the first of two trials. Those that succeed will move on to the second trial, after which our department heads," he turned and indicated the crowd on the platform, "will make placement decisions. You will use your skills and heightena to complete these tasks. As long as you do not harm your fellow competitors, you are encouraged to do whatever it takes to succeed."

"So who's ready?" bellowed the black bear. The crowd burst into excited applause once more.

Alan waved them down. "Allow me to explain how the first trial is going to work." He gestured beyond the crowd to the large open doors. "You stand before the newly refurbished Convention Center. Inside, you will find a large warehouse floor filled with obstacles and training instruments. Our staff have placed envelopes, similar to the invitations you received, throughout the space. Think of it as an egg hunt. These envelopes will be difficult to reach — you will need to complete a task in order to access them — so don't go looking under a mat or behind a box. Explore the room until you find a task that suits your skills. Collect an envelope, and you will be directed to the second task."

"So let's get this party started!" the bear yelled. The crowd cheered, and began jostling each other as they filed in through the giant door.

"Jack, I can't tell you how sorry I am," Mr. Behr said as they followed the President under the shadow of the building and into a large, sprawling gymnasium. "I just want you to know, it's a loss for all of us. Animal Control won't be the same without Dr. Walraven."

"Mmmm," Jack mumbled with a stiff nod. He wasn't angry with Mr. Behr. But he'd defended Dr. Walraven, and now he knew he had been guilty. Facing his accuser was a bit awkward. He was saved from having to make a further response by a fight that had broken out just ahead.

"Because you're an all-fours cheater," a blue jay swore, pressing up against a much smaller frog. "That envelope is mine, and you know it, you slimy little punk."

"If it's yours," the frog taunted, "why am I holding it?" He wagged the envelope in the bird's face. Several of the bird's friends protested angrily.

"What's going on here?" demanded Mr. Behr.

"This little punk is a cheater," the blue jay said, bumping chests with the frog, who pushed him back. "I was flying up to grab that envelope. It was on a wire between those two poles." He pointed up to a cable sixty feet overhead, spanning between two support beams. "This little pond dweller jumped onto my back as I was flying, then jumped *off* of my back and grabbed the envelope before I could reach it."

"Worked, didn't it?" the frog sneered, holding his arms wide as if inviting an attack. The jay shoved him again, his friends once again yelling angrily at the lone frog.

"Hold on, break it up," Mr. Behr said. The frog and jay broke apart, turning toward the dog. "Now it sounds to me like…," he started, then leaned in to read the badge hanging from the frog's neck, "*Willie* here used his skills to reach the envelope first. I regret that he used physical contact, but it's not technically against the rules. Wouldn't you agree, Mr. President?"

Brisk stepped to the front of the crowd, looking between the two. "Most impressive," he nodded to the frog. "You've shown initiative and resourcefulness. Just what we're looking for."

"But, sir," the jay protested.

Brisk cut across him. "You can stand here and complain, or you can move on and look for another envelope. I recommend you get going. All of you," he added, looking around at the crowd. As they dispersed, grumbling, he turned to the frog again. "Good luck in the second task, *Willie*," he said with a nod, and he led his group past the beaming frog.

They walked slowly through the warehouse, observing groups of kids attempting every imaginable task. Some were racing through transparent pipes filled with water. Others transformed their bodies to fit through impossibly small gaps in walls, or else passed through jets of flame emitting from torches set into the floor. Jack watched as a group of teleporters took turns attempting to pop into a ten-foot bell jar with an envelope on a podium inside. With each failure, they roared in frustration and slammed their fists against the glass, until a teenage bear hooked his claws beneath the jar, toppled it with what must have taken immense strength, and snapped up the exposed envelope to the disbelief of the onlooking teleporters.

At the far end of the gymnasium was a row of glass walls like enormous microscope slides. They formed transparent hallways that each led to a steel door in the gymnasium wall. Two familiar figures were outside the leftmost hall. Sprint was crouched like a marathoner waiting for a gunshot, pointed into the hall. Hoover stood behind him, watching apprehensively.

"You're going to hurt yourself again," Hoover warned, clicking his claws together.

"No pain, no gain, Hooves," Sprint responded.

"I don't think that term is referring to broken ankles," the anteater said uncertainly.

Jack broke away as the President's group filed past, stopping next to Hoover. "Hey," he said.

"Hi, Jack," Hoover said, not taking his nervous eyes away from the squirrel.

"Mr. Robberts," Sprint acknowledged in a tone that suggested he did not wish to be disturbed.

"What's all this about?"

Hoover sighed. "Oh, well. He discovered switches on the ground. When he steps on one," he pointed toward the steel door at the end of the hall, "the corresponding door slides upward. There's a podium inside with an envelope on it." He looked back toward Sprint, clicking his long claws together nervously. "But the moment he releases the switch, the door slams shut."

"Couldn't you just... go in and grab it while he's standing on it?"

"You, too?" Sprint said. "A little faith, please? We can't all sneeze our way into the next trial."

"Sneeze?" Jack asked.

"Yeah," Hoover said, withdrawing a silver envelope from his pocket and holding it up. "I got this earlier, sort of by accident."

"By *accident*," Sprint said, shaking his head.

"It was inside a big cement block," Hoover explained. "I got some dust in my nose as we were passing it, and… well, anyway." He looked back at Sprint with concern. "His leg is pretty bad from that fall earlier. He's already crashed twice. I think it's getting worse."

"I'll show you *getting worse*," Sprint grumbled. He stomped on a square switch in the floor, and the steel door at the opposite end slid upward. He crouched so low, his chin was nearly touching the ground, his tail arched high.

And then, with a sudden *woosh,* a reddish blur zoomed through the glass hall. The steel door dropped instantly, slamming to the floor like a guillotine, but not before a loud *clang* could be heard, like a wooden spoon banging on a pot. A moment passed, and a door within the door swung open. Sprint came limping out, the envelope held high over his head. His eyes were shut and he wore a pained grimace on his face. "Am I holding it, Hooves?" he winced through gritted teeth.

"Ye… uh… Yes."

"Good," he said as he opened his eyes and dropped his arm. "Because I'm gonna need a medic."

When the pair had limped away, Jack turned and jogged to catch back up with the President's group. They were standing near an open space in which a strange kind of obstacle course was constructed. A raised balance beam stretched across the space, the kind upon which a gymnast would perform. Wagon wheels rotated around the beam, with gaps between their spokes through which a fast mover might pass. From below, foam pads swung up on curved arms, punching empty air in the spaces between the wheels. At one end, a staircase led onto the beam, and at the other end, yet another envelope podium was positioned.

A burly ape jogged up the wooden steps, to the encouragement of a small group of onlookers. "Come on, Fred," one of them called. "You got this."

The ape took a tentative step out onto the beam, waited for a gap in the first wheel, then charged forward. He stopped, arms flailing to catch his balance, waiting for the next wheel. Dodging through, he stopped again, then darted forward. This step was mistimed, and he took a padded punch to the hip. For a moment, it looked like he might recover. He stuck his hairy brown arms outward again, standing completely sideways on the beam. But the spoke of a wheel caught his extended arm, knocking him off balance, and he fell to the blue mat below.

"Too big," Brisk said. "The Gauntlet isn't meant for the jock type. It needs someone smaller, quicker."

"Someone like Jack," Alan said.

The President met Alan's eyes, then turned and observed the rabbit. "Yes," he said in agreement. "Yes, someone like Jack."

Jack's heart skipped. "I... no, I couldn't..."

"Skill and timing are only a part of it," Brisk said, stepping toward Jack. "There's another element: guts." He jerked his head toward the course. "Give it a try."

The eyes of every Animal Control official were on him now. Some, such as Behr, gave encouraging nods. A slender, sharp faced cheetah woman frowned doubtfully at him. He took a deep breath and stepped onto the mat.

From the top of the stairs, the Gauntlet looked even more impassible than it had from below. Spokes turned and battering arms swung with such consistency, it was impossible to see the podium on the other side.

"Hurry up, man," the ape called from the foot of the stair. "I want to give it another go."

Jack looked at the nearest wheel. There was just enough room between the spokes for him to fit. Brisk was right; it was remarkable that the ape had made it through the first wheel. Well, if he was going to fail, he thought, he might as well fail fast. He bounced on his toes, took a breath, and darted forward.

He made it. A spoke brushed the back of his shirt, but his big bare feet made balance simple. Wide eyes fixed on the next wheel, he took another breath, and darted through this one as well.

Filled with a new confidence, Jack made it through the next obstacles without error. But it became increasingly challenging the further along he got. In the final section, the wheels and punching arms were positioned so close together, there was no space to stand between them. Once he started, he wouldn't be able to stop without getting knocked off. The podium was just visible, the silver envelope perched on top.

*Fail fast*, he thought to himself. He crouched, held his breath, and rushed forward.

He passed the first wheel. Then a punching arm. Narrowly made the gap in the next wheel. The podium was only feet away. A punching arm clipped his shoulder. He flailed, but caught his balance without stopping. The envelope was just beyond his grasp. A few more inches.

*Wham!* A spoke of the rotating wheel caught his side, and he toppled sideways. As he fell, a punching arm swung upward, striking him directly in the face. It was padded, but he saw a flash of light as it connected with his muzzle. He was flipped around, banged his head on the beam, and dropped to the blue mat. The wind was knocked out of him.

Then, as he lay on his back, gasping for air, something slapped against his face. Something made of silver paper.

"Well done, Jack," Behr said. "It wasn't exactly Eddie Dixon, but you managed." He extended a paw and hoisted Jack to his feet.

"Well if that wasn't the luck of the rabbits," Brisk said as his entourage approached, "then I'm a pigeon."

Jack looked down. In his paw, he clutched the silver envelope. "But... how? I didn't make it to the podium."

"When you were knocked back by that pad, you collided with the beam," Behr explained. "I guess you must have knocked the envelope loose."

Jack looked up at him. "But it's not mine then. I got it only by chance."

"Whatever it takes," the black bear said, smiling over Brisk's shoulder. "Looks like you're moving on to the second trial."

## Chapter Seventeen

# THE NEW TEAM

*At E9 where you must head,*
*You'll have to use your wit.*
*Solve the riddle found below,*
*And prove that you're a fit:*

*Together we're a spid'ry bunch,*
*But you must get a grip,*
*We stand together, side by side,*
*We fold, and flick, and flip.*

*A monkey has the right amount.*
*A panda has too many.*
*We lend some help to show the way.*
*Though serpents won't give any.*

Jack read the card over and over again, but he could make no sense of it. Whatever the answer was, at least he knew where he needed to go.

"Alan," he said as he approached the fox. "I… it sounds like I have to get to Building E9. Do you think Brisk… I mean President Brisk would mind if I left?"

"He wanted you to go for the envelope, didn't he?" Alan responded without looking at him.

Jack nodded, started to walk away, then paused. "Where's the medic?"

"In that corner, by the entrance," Alan said, pointing distractedly toward the open hangar door.

"Thanks," Jack said, bristling at the fox's indifference, and he walked away.

The medical quarters looked as though it did not typically serve that purpose. Rolling partitions were placed around the room, giving privacy to groaning children lying on portable beds. A sheep in a nurse's gown allowed a yellow bird to cry into her shoulder. "I've passed through walls a thousand times," the bird sobbed. "The one time it matters, *BAM!* I smack right into it."

"It's perfectly normal, dear," the sheep consoled her. "You just got nervous. It happens."

Three beds down, Sprint was sitting on the edge of his mattress as a goose in blue floral scrubs scribbled onto a clipboard. "And I must insist that you not push yourself too hard," she was saying. "You should rest for the next few weeks, keep off that leg."

"Right," Sprint said as she waddled away. "Keep off my leg. Not like it's an important day or anything." He lit up as he looked past Hoover and saw Jack approaching. "Jack! Come to cry over my remains?" He slid off of the bed and snapped up his silver envelope. "Well, I'm afraid you'll have to feed me grapes some other time. Just got the clean bill of health from Mother Goose over there, so we're off to the second task."

Jack held up his own envelope. "Care if I join you?"

Sprint's eyes widened, and a smile stretched across his face. "Shoot! How'd you pull that off?"

"Long story…" Jack said. "Have you guys figured anything about the riddle yet?"

"You mean other than getting to E9?" Sprint asked. "Nah. We figured we'd head that way and see what happens. I *guess* you can come with us," he added sarcastically.

"Oh, *thank you, Your Grace*," Jack returned the sarcasm.

"Commence with the grapes, Peasant," Sprint said as the three of them began toward the door.


Building E9 would not have been difficult to find even without the trail of kids walking ahead of them. Instead of a warehouse, as Building E4 had been, E9 was a great oval shaped stadium. A zig-zagging cement ramp lead to an entryway framed by vast iron elephant tusks. They jutted out from the walls, swooping upward like the frameworks of a suspension bridge. Two guards stood between the tusks; a raccoon and a fox. They shouted over the crowd, repeating the same answers again and again. "If you have a pass for the second task, enter here and you'll be given further instruction. If you have a pass for the second task…"

The three friends flashed their silver envelopes to the guards and followed the line of kids into a broad hallway. The steel walls were decorated with newspapers and posters, depicting the brave acts of heroes both past and present. A *Daily Call* headline read "Deadly Sea Serpent Rampage Ends With Brisk Encounter."

Grayson Conway, the fiery falcon that had visited the Honey Sap, looked immaculate on the blown up cover of *Phylum Magazine*. "Firebird: The Inside Scoop on AC's Hottest Hero," the magazine declared in bold orange text.

A frame halfway along the hall caught Jack's attention, making him do a double take. It was a newspaper, a front page yellowed with age. The headline read:

WAR HEROES TEAM UP!

...with the subheading:

FRIENDS BECOME FOUNDERS OF NEW LEAGUE, CALLED 'ANIMAL CONTROL'

It was the picture that had stopped Jack in his tracks. It was an old photograph, over-exposed in black and white, but the two figures were unmistakable. On the left was a very young Aaron Harding. He wasn't dressed in his famous costume, just a button down shirt and slacks. His mane was neatly combed, not the tangle of knots for which he would eventually be known. And his thick arm was draped over the shoulder of a young, bespectacled rat wearing a dopey grin. Jack stared at the image in disbelief. *Dr. Walraven was one of the founders?*

"Jack, come on!" He blinked and looked down the hall. Sprint and Hoover were several paces ahead. Taking one last look at the photo, he jogged to catch up.

The hall ended at a brick wall adorned in yet another falcon logo, this one made of brushed steel with a six-foot wingspan. It stood several inches out, with blue light splashing onto the bricks behind.

"Welcome to the second trial," a gazelle woman projected, standing before the logo. "Please take the stairs to the right or left. It doesn't matter which path you choose, there is no difference between them."

The three exchanged glances. Sprint shrugged and moved toward the stairs to the left. As they followed the group ahead of them, they heard the gazelle begin her recital again. "Welcome to the second trial. Please take the stairs to the right or left..."

After climbing several floors, they found themselves in a curved hallway. The inside wall was one long window looking out onto an oval-shaped arena. Thousands of empty seats wrapped around what would typically serve as a field for sporting events. Instead of a field, however, a labyrinth of thick iron walls had been constructed. Jack's spine tingled at the sight, and the three of them stood at the glass, staring in awe with the rest of the excited crowd.

"It's a maze," said Hoover.

"Keep it moving," called an adult voice, and the spell was broken. They continued along the curving path. Opposite the glass, the outer wall was lined with open doors. They were as large as the biggest doors of the President's mansion or Alan's building, and seemed to have slid open like the doors of an elevator.

Sprint, who was walking nearest the wall of doors, poked his head into one.

"No!" barked a familiarly boyish voice. "Not you newbs." Cal, the heavyset groundhog, stepped from the room, gesturing for Sprint to keep walking.

"Easy, guy," Sprint said, raising his paws and backing again out of the room. "Just looking."

"Yeah, well, look somewhere else," Cal said. "We don't need pathetic little forest critters on our team."

"Pathetic?" Sprint said indignantly. "Cal, you're a groundhog. Notoriously afraid of your own shadow."

"Say that again," Cal said, puffing out his chest and taking a step toward Sprint.

"You want me to repeat myself?" the squirrel asked, smiling as he backed away. "I feel like there's a groundhog joke there too." He turned, and the three of them continued along the path, leaving Cal looking confused and irritated.

"What do you think he meant by *our team*?" Jack asked.

"Who cares," Sprint said. "Can't stand that guy. Let's try this one."

They stepped into the next room, this one empty. It wasn't a large space, with only black walls beneath four can lights. A strange pattern was set into the floor. It looked like a paw print, with a large metal circle at the center of the room, and five smaller circles on its far side. The smaller circles were elevated two inches off the floor, while the larger circle was recessed *into* the floor, like a ten foot wide access hole cover.

"It looks like a door," Jack observed. "Think we have to open it?"

Sprint nodded. "Stand back, Jack. Hooves, want to give it a shot?"

Hoover stepped to the edge of the plate as Sprint and Jack pressed against the wall. The anteater's chest expanded as he drew in a deep breath. He held it for a moment, then, pointing his snout directly at the opening, he expelled a blast of air as loud as a cannon. Jack's ears immediately started to ring, and he coughed as the air became suffocatingly thick with dust.

But the plate hadn't budged.

"It won't open like that, you idiot," said a gruff voice. The frog from the fight earlier was standing in the doorway. *Willie*,

Jack remembered. By himself, he looked rather small, only coming up to about Jack's chin. He was green, with a slight build, tiny little muscles bulging at his biceps and calves. He wore an impatient expression, as if he'd dealt with enough *idiots* for one day. Striding across the room, he stepped onto one of the smaller disks as though weighing himself. Nothing happened.

"Zing!" Sprint said. "Really made us look stupid."

"It's what they did in the room next door," Willie said, stepping off the pad, then back on. "Not sure why it's not working here."

Sprint walked over to one of the disks and jumped up and down on it. Nothing happened.

Jack took the card from his pocket, rereading it. "The answer must be in the riddle," he said. "Here, listen to this: *A monkey has the right amount. A panda has too many.* But what does a monkey have that a panda has more of?"

"Weight," Willie said.

Sprint rolled his eyes. "You wouldn't tell a panda, 'I'm sorry sir, your weight is too *many.*'"

"Then you give an answer, undertail," the frog shot back.

"Fingers," said a girl's voice from the entrance. To Jack's surprise, it was Maddie, the doe that had caused all the trouble on the ship.

"What are *you* doing here?" Sprint asked.

"The answer is fingers," the doe said as she walked into the room. "I can't believe none of *you* got that," she added, holding up her hoofs.

"We *would* have. Eventually," Sprint said.

Maddie scoffed. "They're spidery as a group, but not individually. They stand together, side by side. A monkey has five

147

of them. A panda has six. They can't help a serpent point the way, because he doesn't have any."

"Okay, so fingers," Sprint said. "So how does that help us?"

"A monkey has the right amount," Maddie repeated. "Five. Five is the right number. Five of us have to step on the plates at the same time. They're getting us to team up."

"Team up?" Hoover asked.

"Huh uh," Sprint dissented. "Not with you." He strode toward her, exaggerating his limp as he moved. "See this? You did this to me. We'll wait for someone else to show up."

In response, Maddie moved to the far end of the wall and stood on one of the plates. "Go ahead and wait," she said, smirking and crossing her arms. "But unless you plan to drag me off of this plate, you'll have to wait somewhere else."

Sprint looked furious. "Hoover. Blast her."

"Come on, guys," Jack said, moving between them. "There are five of us. We *all* want to get into that opening. So just… everyone get on a plate."

Willie shrugged and strode to the plate next to Maddie. Hoover followed. Sprint looked at Jack as if he'd been betrayed, but strode to the next plate.

As Jack mounted the fifth plate, two things happened in sequence. First, the outer doors slid slowly closed. Then the large plate in the floor spun open like a camera lens, revealing a black pit beneath.

They stepped to the edge of the pit. It might have been a hundred feet, or only fifteen; it was too dark to see anything beyond its cement mouth, into which the shuttering doors had disappeared.

"You think we're supposed to go in there?" Sprint asked, his voice echoing in the closed space.

"No, I think we're supposed to toss our recyclables," Willie spat.

"There is *no way* I'm jumping down there," Maddie said, holding up both hoofs.

"Me neither," Hoover agreed.

"Fine, stay here," Willie said, and without further comment, he pencil dived into the pit. They listened, but heard no sound.

"You okay down there?" Sprint yelled. The frog made no response.

Jack looked between the remaining three. "I'll go," he said, trying to keep the nervousness from his voice. The task was created for kids. They wouldn't have built it to cause them any harm.

*Right?*

The others looked at him in silent anticipation. He drew in a breath, and jumped.

# Chapter Eighteen
## INTO THE MAZE

Jack fell for the space of one breath, then plopped softly into a pit of foam bricks. He struggled to sit upright and looked around. It was dark, but the rim of the pit was just visible, and he half rolled, half crawled to its edge.

"Jack? You alright?" Sprint called, his voice surprisingly far away. Jack turned his head upward. Three shadows peered down at him from the circular opening.

"Yeah, it's safe," he yelled as he reached the side. One by one, they dropped down into the foam bricks, and soon they were all standing on the cement floor surrounding the pit, letting their eyes adjust.

This room was only slightly larger than the one above, with dim white lights notched into the walls. There was a door, sealed, and a flat rectangle mounted high up along the wall next to it: a television. The screen was black, but it cast a glowing halo of light.

"Now what?" Sprint asked, pressing his paws against the unmoving door.

As if in answer, an electronic melody sounded, and a bright light from the television drew all of their attention that way. "Hello," said a pleasantly voiced woman, some sort of exotic deer. She wore a collared blue uniform beneath a face of light brown fur, with heavy eye shadow that pronounced her over-large eyes. "And congratulations on making it to the final trial. In a few moments, the door before you will open, and you will enter the playing field." She spoke as though reading her lines from a teleprompter. "As you enter the maze, you will find a flag of either red or blue. Your job is to defend this flag without moving it, while locating and capturing the flag from the opposing team. You are encouraged to use your heightena and skills in this task, but you are *not* allowed to harm your opponents. Keep in mind: you are being considered now as a team. You succeed or fail together. Good luck," she finished with a smile. The same electronic tone played, and the screen went black, leaving only blue text with the words "Stand By..."

Sprint looked away from the TV. "Considered as a *team?*" he groaned. "Great. Wish they'd told us that before we joined forces with Our Lady of Rigor Mortis."

Maddie shot him a venomous look. "My heightena won't work in this case anyway," she said. "We'll be in an iron maze. My power is blocked by iron, so unless I can look directly into sunlight while being in the same part of the maze as the other team..."

"Oh fabulous!" Sprint cut across her. "So instead of turning us all into mannequins, you'll be completely useless."

"No I won't," she snapped. "Being a hero is not about heightena, it's about heart."

"That's beautiful. When the other team gets here, why don't you recite some more poetry to *them*."

"It's not poetry. That's Aaron Harding; King of Hearts. Maybe you've heard of him?"

"Would you two shut up?" the frog barked. "We need a strategy." He looked between them. Neither argued. "Some of us will need to protect the flag. Some of us will need to go find theirs. So what can you all do?"

"I'm going out there," Maddie said. "I wouldn't be any use protecting the flag; not without sunlight. At least I can look around."

"I'm going too," Sprint said. "I can run the flag back in a second. Because, you know, I don't require sunlight to do my job."

"Great," Willie said. "Well, I'm staying at the entrance and protecting our flag. So which of you is staying, and which of you is going?" he asked, looking between Jack and Hoover.

"I'll stay," Hoover said.

"Looks like you're with me," Sprint said. Jack nodded uncertainly, not feeling like he'd be of much use to *either* team.

A silence fell between them, and they stood in the semi-darkness, watching the door like race horses at a starting gate. But the silence dragged on and on, seconds turning to minutes. Minutes stretched into an hour, until finally...

"It's changed!" Maddie said with a start. "Would you two get your tails out of that foam pit. The TV says we're next!"

Jack, who was just about to lob another foam brick at Sprint, turned toward the monitor. Sure enough, the text had changed from "Stand By" to "Your Team Is Next." They climbed awkwardly back out of the pit just as the television came to life once more.

"In just a moment," the same deer woman said, "the doors before you will open, and you will enter the arena floor. You will have fifteen minutes to navigate the maze and return with the opposing team's flag. Good luck."

The screen went blank again, and they stood in nervous silence, Jack next to Sprint, Sprint next to Maddie, ready to bolt into the maze. Just when Jack began to wonder how long they would have to wait, a tone sounded, and a blue number appeared at the center of the screen. "3".

He felt as if he'd forgotten how to swallow.

Another tone. "2".

He looked back at the door.

"1."

The door slid upward, and a horn blared somewhere beyond. There was a flash of motion, blowing Jack's ears sideways. He turned to see only Maddie looking back at him. She raised a brow in surprise, and Jack smiled despite his nerves.

They ran as fast as they could through the open space. A field of grass surrounded what looked like an enormous silver block, about thirty feet tall, with rivets running along its seams. At the center, a gap in the construction extended from top to bottom, opening into the maze. Sprint had already disappeared inside. As they drew closer, Jack could see a red flag mounted into the left wall of the entry chamber.

The air was cooler in the shade and silence of the maze. The sound of their heavy breathing reverberated off the iron walls, which opened high above them to blue sky. They reached the end of the chamber, a T-junction splitting in opposite directions. "Guess we'll have to split—" Jack started, but Maddie had already picked up pace along the path to the right. He sighed, turned to the left, and started off again at a jogging pace.

# CHAPTER EIGHTEEN

Having no idea what or who to expect, Jack allowed his feet to carry him through the wide corridors. First a right. Another right. A left. He worked deeper into the maze, taking this turn or that without any conscious reason. He quickly became turned around, uncertain even of the direction he was heading. Was he running toward his own flag now? It all looked the same in here — dirt floors and pewter walls that opened to the sky. He took another left. A right. Right again. Straight past an opening, then through the next one.

As he rounded a corner, he found himself in a familiar space. The corridor opened onto a grass field, a wall of doors at the opposite end. He was back to the beginning.

Frustrated, he started to turn around, but his eyes fell on the flag and he halted.

It was blue!

He'd done it! He'd found the other team's flag! Admittedly, he had no idea *how* he'd done it, but there it was, undefended and untouched.

But as he took a step toward it, something moved in the opening. It started from beyond the walls, a yellow line stretching deliberately across the pathway. Then a second one stretched across the first. The two of them formed a yellow X like tape around a crime scene. "Not so fast," a voice said, and a head moved like an anaconda around the edge of the opening. It passed below the X on an over long neck, smiling up at Jack, who recognized the face of the letterman giraffe from the bus. His neck zigzagged back and forth, looking much too long and limber, even for a giraffe. Jack looked at the X and realized it was the giraffe's outstretched arms, pulled like bungee cables across the entryway.

The giraffe grinned menacingly. "You want our flag, you'll have to get past me."

From Jack's left, there was a blur of motion, zipping beneath the *X* and out again in one swift move. "No problem, Princess," Sprint goaded, holding the blue flag over his head.

"Princess?" the giraffe yelled. "Hey, I'm a guy!"

"If you say so," Sprint laughed. He looked at Jack, nodded back into the maze, and took off once more. Smiling at the thunderstruck look on the giraffe's face, Jack turned and bolted back up the chamber.

Now to find his way back. The first turn had been a left, which meant he needed to turn right. But he felt less certain as he passed an opening to his left. Had he come from there? Or from the next one? He started down the nearest one, second guessed himself, and turned back. He took the next path, trying his best to recognize any of his surroundings. But every hall was that same dark iron, indistinguishable from any of the others.

"Watch it!" someone yelled, and he was knocked to the ground. Sprint came to a skidding halt, stomach first in the dirt. The flag landed a few feet away. "Ah," the squirrel groaned as he pushed himself to stand, then hobbled over to help Jack to his feet. "Sorry guy," he said. "I solved the maze by running down every chamber, but I couldn't remember how to get back, so I just started doing the same thing again. Guess I should have been watching where I was going."

As Jack brushed himself off, a glint caught his eye. *The key!* It had slipped from his pocket as he fell. He stooped down and picked it up, shooting a nervous glance toward Sprint. Fortunately, the squirrel had been distracted by a familiar voice.

"Why are you guys just standing there? Is — is that the flag?" Maddie came jogging up the hall.

"Yes," Sprint said, striding over to the fallen flag and snapping it up. "*We* found it."

"Good for you," Maddie sneered. "Were you gonna take it back to our base, or claim this land in the name of the squirrels?"

"Funny," Sprint started, but he was interrupted as someone else rounded the corner.

"You!" said an angry voice. It was the sunburned shrew from that morning. He was shorter than Jack, with beady eyes behind round spectacles, and the same kind of collared shirts Hoover wore. His expression was murderous as he strode toward Maddie. "You're the one that pulled a Gary Green on the ship. What are *you* doing here? I thought they kicked you out, you loser."

Maddie had looked surprised when he'd singled her out, but her eyes narrowed at these words and she took a step forward, towering over the shrew. "What did you call me?" she growled.

Jack rushed between them. "No!" he yelled. "The team is being evaluated *together*," he said. "If you get disqualified, we *all* get disqualified. Just let him..."

The rest of the words caught in his throat. In his effort to separate them, he had gripped Maddie's arm, and in an instant, a horrible change came over her. Her eyes seemed to grow three times larger — solid black orbs that made her look like an insect. Her skin became loose and wrinkled, as though the flesh beneath it had withered away. Ribs were visible beneath her shirt, and her hips became so gaunt, she looked nearly skeletal. She even seemed to have trouble standing, wobbling around weakly as she turned her overlarge eyes on Jack. "How could you possibly understand, you stupid *boy!*" she said in a frail whisper. "I'm bossy or I'm just a *girl*. I'm *looking for attention* or I'm dressed like a slob. I have to be *perfect all the time*, but they all think I'm fat. They all think I'm weak. They all think I'm a loser!" She wailed this last sentence as though in a bad impression of a ghost. Terrified, Jack became tangled in her bone-thin limbs, and they toppled over together. There was a sudden burst of light, like the flashbulb of an old camera, and he landed with a thud on the dirt floor of the maze. He felt as rigid as a statue, completely paralyzed.

He was trapped.

## Chapter Nineteen

## THE LOSERS

Jack felt so stupid. He was lying face down in the dirt, his rear end pointed straight at the sky. His limbs seemed to have turned to stone, a horrible tingling numbness spreading through him, as though he'd fallen asleep on his arm. Only it wasn't just his arms; it was his *everything*.

He focused hard, trying to curl a fist. To bend an elbow. If he could make even the smallest movement, he knew he could break free. But it was useless; he could no sooner bend a single fingertip than float into the air and levitate around.

Another minute or so passed, and a horn blared in the distance, signaling the end of the match. But the paralysis didn't change. He remained as motionless as a statue.

The soft sound of footsteps broke the silence. In his peripheral, a pair of legs came into view, standing near Maddie. "Yeah, she's right here," an adult voice said. "I just cover her eyes, then?"

What must this guy be seeing? Jack wondered if everyone else looked as ridiculous as he did, with his butt pointed upward and his face planted in the dirt.

A voice crackled through the static of a walkie talkie. The newcomer squatted down, and Jack could see the familiar blue of a *STAFF* shirt. The official made a motion with his arm toward Maddie, and Jack felt mobility flood back into him like water filling a sack. Limbs loosening, he sank to the floor, then shook his paws at the uncomfortable tingling. His knees knocked together as he stood and turned around.

"What is with you?" the shrew demanded. He looked between Maddie and Jack, seeming unsure of who to blame, then roared in frustration and stomped away.

Maddie was angrily readjusting her patrol cap. Jack looked in the direction she had been facing. A bright line of sunlight was gleaming off the rim of a high wall. He must have spun her right toward it.

"Well, that's that," Sprint said, looking down at the flag in his paws. "It hasn't been fifteen minutes. The other team must have made it. We're out."

Outside of the arena, the victorious teams were euphoric. They slapped high fives, pounced happily on each other's backs, and exchanged stories of their adventures into the maze. But when they were led away by officials, they left behind a rather gloomy mood. The losing teams had almost all broken apart. Some sat along the raised arena ramp, crying, commiserating, or stewing in disillusioned silence. Others seemed to decide that, now that it was all over, they might as well get started heading home.

A row of tram cars were parked just before the arena entrance, their fiberglass benches filled with silent, disappointed teens waiting to be shuttled toward the harbor.

"We came close," Sprint said, standing just before the tram. "Just a little bad luck at the end."

Jack shifted uncomfortably.

"Or we all just failed hard," Willie groused. He strode off toward one of the southward pointing trams without another word. A moment later, that tram started off, and Willie was gone without even a backward glance.

"Who knows," Sprint started again. "Now that they've reopened the sidekick program, maybe we'll be invited back next…"

He trailed off as a cheerful voice boomed nearby. Jack turned to see the giraffe's team — the team they had lost to — striding past. "I said, *If you want our flag, you'll have to get past me, Princess,*" the giraffe gloated, to the appreciative laughter of his teammates. Sprint grimaced, his shoulders stiffening as the group passed behind him.

"That noodle-neck," he growled. "I mean, we *had* their flag. If not for Maddie, we definitely would have won."

Maddie sat alone in the rearmost car, her arms folded across her chest, wearing an expression of suppressed confusion. She looked, Jack thought, as though she'd been lied to, and was trying not to show how much that hurt.

"Well, see ya," Sprint said, nodding to Jack as he climbed into the nearest car.

"Yeah. See ya," Jack sighed, nodding to Hoover. The anteater nodded in return, then slid onto the bench next to Sprint.

Jack turned toward the rear of the tram and began along the path. As he passed Maddie, she looked pointedly in the other direction, and his half-raised paw dropped to his side.

Now to find Alan. Jack had last seen the fox at the Convention Center, so he figured he'd head that way. Alan was his legal guardian now, although he hadn't seemed too thrilled about the fact. The fox was ambitious and important. Perhaps he thought that Jack would only get in his way. Where did he live? Somewhere in the city, no doubt. But Alan was a young bachelor. It seemed unlikely he would have a spare bedroom for Jack. Would he have to sleep in the attic again, like when he'd lived with The Punts? Would he be stuck there while Alan was at work? He let out a disappointed sigh. If only he hadn't knocked Maddie over.

"Jack. Hey, there you are." Jack looked up. Mr. Behr was striding up the path, his paws stretched wide as he approached. Jack was surprised to see Willie following behind, walking briskly to keep up with the much taller dog and looking very confused.

"Uh, hi," Jack said as they drew near.

Behr didn't stop, though. He passed Jack and motioned for him to follow. "Quickly now," he said. "We don't have much time." His coat trailed behind him as he took off at a jog. "Hold that tram," he shouted, waving his paws over his head.

The tram, which had started off toward the North Gate, slowed to a stop. Behr waved thanks to the driver as he reached the rearmost car, where Maddie was seated. He said something Jack couldn't hear. Looking as confused as Willie, as confused as Jack himself felt, she slid off of the bench as Behr walked to the next car, where Sprint and Hoover were watching him with interest. He said something to them, they exchanged a glance, then dropped down off of the tram car and followed Behr as he turned once more toward Jack.

"Follow me," he said as he passed again, and Jack and Willie spun on their heels. The six of them moved along the pathway as it wound between well-manicured lawns, beneath a sky bridge connecting two buildings, finally arriving at a door in the building on the left. White letters were stenciled onto the windows of the door, reading *Kelly Hall.*

"So did we make it?" Maddie asked. "Are we in?"

Beyond the door, a voice seemed to be addressing a crowd through a microphone. One paw on the door handle, Behr cleared his throat. "Er... no. I suppose I should explain," he said. "We don't have any more spaces available for apprenticeships, unfortunately. I'm sorry it didn't work out." He paused. "But we were watching you in that maze, you know. We had cameras. And your team... well, you made a good impression on some important folks, including the President." He nodded around at them, smiling. "So," he began again, clapping his paws together, "how would the five of you like to come work for me?"

"For *you*," Sprint said.

"Well, in so many words. Really you'll be working for Animal Control. It won't be an apprenticeship — we had eight teams of heroes ready to receive eight teams of sidekicks. All of those spots are now full. However, there *is* a need to get more *porters* around here."

The word was familiar to Jack. He remembered the dog from that morning, the one that had teleported into the fountain.

"*Porters*," Willie said, crossing his arms. "You mean like... errand boys?"

"Uh... *boys?*" Maddie asked.

"My son Jay is... was a porter," Behr said. "He loved it! But he's off to live with his mother next week, so..." he spread his paws wide. "Think of it as an internship," he continued with a smile. "You will spend your days helping in the mail room, or running copies around the campus. It might not be glamorous, but you get to stay here, make connections and all that." He straightened up and stuck his thumbs in his coat pockets. "So what do you say?"

Jack and Sprint exchanged glances. Sprint looked to Hoover.

"Count me in," said Maddie.

"Us too," said Sprint. Hoover nodded.

"If it's the best we can get," said the frog. "Sure, I'm in."

Behr turned to Jack. "How about it, Jack?"

The sky had turned a pleasant shade of pink, the air warm and fragrant. He couldn't think of anywhere he would rather be. "Yeah," he said, smiling around at the squirrel, the anteater, the frog, the doe. His new team. "Let's do it."

"Excellent," Behr grinned, and he yanked open the door. The amplified voice inside became clearer. Behr motioned for the group to enter. "Sounds like we'll just catch the tail end of the welcome ceremony."

## Chapter Twenty

## THE CAMPUS

"Where's D7?"

"That's the brick building near the south entrance. Looks like a train station."

"No, that's G7."

"Oh, right," Sprint said. "I'll never get used to this place. It's huge!"

It was Tuesday, which meant that today their duties revolved around delivering the mail. This was Jack's favorite assignment, as it gave him a chance to explore the campus. The place was so vast; he could hardly round a bend in one of the many pathways without seeing something new and interesting. There were greenhouses wrapped in vines like the crushing tentacles of some monstrous sea creature, buildings that plunged right down into the lakes — of which there were several — and even a glass tunnel with an impossibly huge fan at one end, which was apparently meant for training fliers. In the six weeks that had passed since the trials, he was increasingly amazed at exactly how big this place was, and the task of navigating it without getting hopelessly lost seemed an impossible one.

"Alright, so where's D7, then?" Willie repeated.

"It's by the Grove," Jack said. "I can show you. I'm going that direction too."

"No, I'm good," Willie said, and he pushed his mail cart, which he was hardly taller than, out the swinging double doors.

Jack turned to Maddie. "What about you? Where are you headed?"

She slid a bin full of envelopes onto the lower rack of her cart without looking up, tugged down the brim of her patrol cap, and followed after Willie.

"Life of the party, that one," Sprint said.

"When she's not sneaking off to make phone calls, you mean?" Jack replied.

"Yeah, what's that about?" Sprint asked. "It's at least five times a day. Who could possibly want to talk to her that often?"

"Parents?" Jack mused. The thought gave him a sort of hollow feeling inside. With Dr. Walraven gone, and Alan completely indifferent to Jack's whereabouts or activities, he felt more than ever like an orphan, which, he realized with a pang, he now was for the second time in his life. It hadn't ever occurred to him in that way. This had been more like being away at summer camp, an impression aided by the rows and rows of bunk beds they shared in the Barracks. But one day, this would all be over, and then what?

"Well, whoever she's calling," Sprint continued, taking the box Hoover was passing him and loading it onto his cart, "she sure seems to want to keep it secret. I walked in on her yesterday, and she just slammed the phone down. Hung up on whoever it was."

Still lost in thought, Jack simply shrugged and dropped a bin of envelopes onto his own cart.

"I just..." Sprint started, and he seemed uncharacteristically uneasy. "I just think since we're... you know... graded as a team... maybe we shouldn't be keeping any secrets."

Jack took his time in unshelving a large box. The conversation had been about Maddie, but he thought he knew what Sprint was really getting at. The day they'd arrived at the campus, Sprint had overheard him telling the woman at the gate that his house had been attacked, that someone had been killed. Since then, neither of them had mentioned it — how does one start a conversation like that, anyway? — but it had to be gnawing away at him inside, to know there was some deep, dark reason why Jack was even here.

And then there was the key. As part of the whole complex history of the past seven weeks, the key had remained Jack's secret. There was also the small matter of it having been stolen from the very facilities where it was now hidden. And what a terrible hiding place he'd chosen; the air conditioning vent behind his bed on the lower bunk. If anyone even suspected him, that was sure to be the first place they'd look. Well, the second, he supposed. The messenger bag he carried with him would be the first, which was exactly why he hid it.

"Jack?"

Blinking, Jack looked up. "Huh?"

"You agree with me, right? About us being a team? About not having secrets?"

Jack glanced at Hoover, who made an effort to look busy with a bin of envelopes.

"Yeah, of course," he said finally. "Anyway, I better get going. See ya in a bit." And with that, he tipped the box onto his cart and shoved it toward the swinging doors.

It was mid-December, and bitingly chilly despite the intense sunshine. Still thinking of the key, he hardly noticed, although the cold pavement was pleasant against his bare feet.

But as he rounded the side of the building, he nearly tripped. Coming up the path, right for him, was Grey Company, one of Animal Control's top teams. Heroes were easy to spot — they were the only ones allowed to wear the falcon emblem. Grey Company wore ash colored uniforms with the falcon stitched in white across the chest. They were an imposing group — the smallest of them was Kenja Hawari, the cheetah woman from the trials, and with a rhinoceros following her lead, even she seemed larger than life.

She met his eyes. Heart skipping, Jack thought again of the key, of that feeble hiding place behind his bunk bed. Could they have found it? Of course they could have! Were they coming to arrest him?

Distracted, he steered the cart right over the edge of the cement path, nearly toppling it. He managed to keep the cart upright, but a few of the boxes tumbled into the bushes.

Hawari and the rest of Grey Company walked right past, hardly seeming to notice him. Following just behind were their sidekicks, including the letterman giraffe. "Nice driving, Porter," he said with a sneer. The others laughed. Jack watched them pass, feeling about as significant as the bush next to him, which was now ornamented in boxes at odd angles.

Kelly Hall was bustling with the dinner crowd. It was everything Jack had hoped it would be, having seen pictures of it in some of Dr. Walraven's books; an open, well maintained cafeteria where the heroes and staff of Animal Control gathered for meals. But he still wasn't used to *being* here, to seeing it in person. The place was amazing. It had a high roof with rafters like polished tree trunks — in which many of the climbers and fliers were perched. The seating area was wrapped in two-story windows that looked out onto the same lake he'd seen on his first day, over which a soft purple sunset was fading.

"I'm telling you, you need a catch phrase," Sprint was saying. He set his dinner tray on the table, scooped up his tail, and dropped into a chair. "All the best heroes have a catch phrase."

"That's not a thing," Jack said, prodding his salad with a fork.

"It is! Like, mine can be, *try to keep up!*"

"That's terrible," Jack said.

"Okay then, what's yours gonna be? You've just done something amazing. Heroic. You turn to the onlooking crowd and you say…"

Jack wagged his paws. "Ta-da."

Sprint rolled his eyes.

"Mine can be *I hate walking*," said Maddie. "My mail route went all the way around that lake up in the north corner of the campus."

"Well, at least you were on the ground," Willie said, jabbing at his salad. "I was in that forest area. They have labs up in the canopy. I must have climbed a hundred trees." He lifted his fork, showing a roasted beetle. "I felt like an insect."

"Ugh," Maddie groaned, pulling the brim of her hat down. "Speaking of insects…"

"Well, if it isn't the Bench Warmers," came a pompous, boyish voice. Jack turned to see Cal approaching, his fellow apprentices in tow.

"Rain, rain, go away," Sprint sang.

"Muzzle it, *Splint*," Cal shot back. "I see your limp's gotten better. Must make it easier getting everyone's coffee."

"I see your humor's gotten better," Sprint retorted. "Must make it easier getting everyone to hate you."

"Listen, you puff tail…" Cal started up.

"Careful, pet," Maddie interrupted, jerking her head past the groundhog. "Here come your masters."

Jack followed her gaze. Grayson Conway and his team had entered the hall. Unlike Grey Company, or any of the other teams for that matter, Vanguard didn't wear matching suits, but casual attire with the falcon logo simply printed onto the fabric at either the chest or sleeve. Yet despite their dressed down appearance, every eye in the hall turned to them as they entered.

"Carl," said Dixon, the wine-snob greyhound Jack had met at the Honey Sap. "You're late for training. Let's go."

Cal jumped. "Yes, sir. On our way, sir."

"Shoo, fly," Maddie said with a smile.

Cal shot her a dirty look, and the apprentices followed their mentors.

"How is that undertail apprenticing for Firebird?" Willie seethed.

"William! That's no way to talk about your superiors," Sprint barked. "Show *Carl* some respect!" Jack and Hoover laughed. Even Willie betrayed the shadow of a grin.

"Who has the pager?" Maddie asked.

"It's in my bag," Jack said, indicating the messenger bag dangling from the back of his chair. Every team was given a pager so that they would know when their mentors were ready for them. The pager would buzz, a light at the top would blink green, and a little screen would tell them at which building to meet. Of course, for the porter team, the green light never blinked. Only a red one. Still, every time that thing buzzed, Jack's heart would skip, and he'd fish it out of his bag hopefully.

Sprint spoke again. "So I was in line behind a couple staffers. They were talking in a sort of hushed tone, like they didn't want to be overheard. They weren't doing a very good job of it, though."

"What were they saying?" Jack asked through a mouthful of dandelions.

Sprint leaned over the table, as if to set this piece of information in the middle for them all to inspect. "They said Animal Control has been *robbed!*"

A sudden hollow feeling flooded Jack's chest, and he looked away with a shrug. He scooped up another mouthful, chewing mechanically. The florets suddenly tasted very dry.

"Who could possibly rob Animal Control?" Willie asked. Jack privately considered that a slow old rat had managed.

"Petrillo could do it," Sprint said.

Jack stopped chewing and turned to look at the squirrel. He remembered Gale and the other boys threatening to summon the griffin demon in Mrs. Punts' attic. At the time, it had been terrifying. Now, it only made him laugh. "Petrillo? Petrillo's a myth."

"No, he's real," Sprint insisted. "Hoover met a guy yesterday that's seen him." Hoover nodded vigorously.

"Petrillo is just a story," Jack started, "that parents tell their kids to get them to behave. *Stop hitting your sister, or Petrillo will come take you when you're sleeping.*"

"I always heard he punished crooked heroes," Willie said. "Heroes on the take, or whatever."

Jack shook his head in disbelief. "You really believe," he said, "that a griffin, a *mythological* creature, lives in the rooftops of Triarch, beating up dirty superheroes without ever being caught or photographed?"

"Well, I mean you make it sound ridiculous," Sprint said. "But yeah, I do. There's weirder stuff going on than a griffin vigilante, to be honest. And anyway, I don't really care *who* stole it. I care *what* got stolen," he finished dramatically.

"Okay, so what was it?" Willie asked, setting his fork down and folding his arms across his chest.

Sprint looked around conspiratorially, then lowered his voice and leaned in. "Some kind of *magical heart-shaped key* or something," he said. "Not sure what it opens, but it sounds like if you touch it, you can read minds or something."

"Hearts," Hoover said, his eyes widening in an expression of pure reverence. "That's why King of Hearts was called *King of Hearts*." When he didn't elaborate, the four others stared at him, and he looked down at the table. "He could touch someone, and see what was on their heart," he said with a shrug.

"What, you mean like *who they loved* or something?" Willie asked.

"No," Hoover said, still not looking up from his food. "More like what *motivated* them. If they had evil intentions, he could see what those were. If they were being forced to do something, or if they had pure motives, he could see that, too."

Jack sat in silence, considering. *Hearts.* So *that's* what it was. When he had touched the President while holding the key, he'd seen a power-hungry monster. When he'd touched Maddie, he'd seen a frail kid, afraid of failure and rejection. It's what was on their hearts.

"Okay, so a key got stolen," Maddie said. "Someone's… what… after King's stashed fortune or something?"

"Dunno," Sprint said. "But it sounds like a pretty big deal. They were saying whoever took it, they're gonna get *banished*."

The others cringed. Getting banished meant being sent to live in Kerccia, the carnivore-inhabited badlands to the north. It was the harshest sentence, the capital punishment of Nikacia. Jack's mind went to the Barracks. More specifically, to the air conditioning vent behind his bed.

The first time an anaxopter — the dragonfly-like vehicles that flew heroes to their missions — passed overhead, he couldn't stop staring in amazement. Now, as they walked along the edge of the lake and toward the sleeping quarters, he gave only a casual glance as an anax chopped through the air just above them, its red and green lights blinking alternately against the night sky, its titanium wings beating loudly up and down.

As usual, they were the first to return to the Barracks. It was a single-story building, with a hall running between dormitory rooms filled with bunk beds. Heroes were housed in a separate village near the President's mansion. The Barracks were for new recruits and guards. But the first room on the right was designated for the apprentice teams: forty sidekicks, and the five new porters. Most teams were out late, either in training, or tagging along on actual missions. Jack felt a swell of envy at the thought. For his team, the day ended after their chores, well before dinner.

Jack entered the room first, patting the wall in search of the light switch.

There was a flash of black. Something swung down from above the door. Before he could react, it collided heavily with his jawbone. He fell backward into the hall. The black mass swung smoothly over the top of him, like an ape through branches, then landed lightly on the carpet near his head. He rolled over quickly, rubbing his jaw.

A dark figure was crouching catlike on the floor, its head cocked sideways, considering him. And in its claw, it clutched the heart-shaped key.

## Chapter Twenty-One

## PETRILLO

In the short space of time as the creature considered him, Jack took in its bizarre appearance. It was almost entirely black, with feathers sticking out at odd angles from its shoulders and head. The only part of the creature not covered in black feathers or fur was a slender mask. It was the shape one might expect to see at a masquerade, with bone white material that curved outward into a long, sharp vulture's beak. Despite these birdlike features, its body more closely resembled a monkey, with slender arms ending in paws much larger but not unlike his own. They curved out into sharp talons, which dug into the carpet as a monkey tail swished back and forth above its head, playfully.

If this was who he thought it was, it looked a lot less like a *griffin* than he would have expected. "Petrillo?" he asked, disbelieving.

The creature spun on the spot and dashed toward the door. It moved at first on all fours, like a scurrying ape, and bounded toward the other four, who had all stopped in the hallway in surprise. "Hey!" Sprint cried out as the creature bowled him to the ground.

It bounded from the right wall to the left and back, landing in the open window above the door. It perched up there, its long tail dangling, and turned again toward Jack.

Without thinking, without responding as he passed his confused friends, Jack tore off down the hall.

When he neared the door below the creature, it spun around and leapt from the window. Jack crashed through the door and into the night.

He glanced frantically up and down the path, but the creature had vanished. A few staffers were stopped along the pathway, looking in surprise toward the building across from the Barracks. Following their gaze, he spotted the shadowy figure pressed out of the wall like a gargoyle. It climbed the rain spout, gracefully crested the top, then stood erect, peering down at Jack. They watched each other for a moment.

Jack made the first move, darting toward the building. Reciprocating, the creature disappeared behind the wall. Jack rounded the corner, far enough from the building to keep an eye on the creature as it bounded along the rooftop, hurdled over the edge, and crashed feet first into the foliage of a tree. Jack jogged to a stop, expecting the creature to fall injured to the ground. Instead, it swung from the lowest branch without missing a beat, landed on all fours, then stood and took off in a dash across the lawn.

"Wait!" Jack called as the creature disappeared over a tall hedge. Moving along the dense network of leaves, he found a small gap and forced his way through. On the other side, he recognized the lawn that stretched out toward suburban housing on the far end, and the President's mansion to his left.

There was a *woosh* of wind, and Sprint appeared. "What in the world is going on?" he asked, limping along the damp grass to where Jack stood. "Who was that? Was that..." He fell silent as he spotted the dark figure.

Petrillo was standing only yards away, unmoving, its head bent to the side, seeming to size Sprint up.

"Push me one more time, I dare you," the squirrel said, his voice lowering an octave as he stepped toward the creature, doing a bad job of disguising his limp.

Without warning, the creature charged at him, ramming square into his chest. Sprint landed on his back, his wind knocked out in a cough. It stood over him, pressed a foot into the squirrel's wounded ankle, and applied pressure. Sprint cried out in pain.

Moving to Sprint's aid, Jack faltered as the creature turned on him, squatting like a jungle cat ready to pounce. Instead of attacking, however, it turned toward the President's mansion and tore off across the field.

As Jack dropped to Sprint's side, a panting figure jogged up to them. "What's going on?" Hoover wheezed.

"I'm fine, Jack," Sprint said, sitting up with a wince. "Go."

Hoping he wasn't already too late, Jack turned and ran after the creature. At first, he couldn't see it, and simply ran into the darkness blindly. The light beyond the President's gate was bright, and as Jack squinted into it, he saw the dark silhouette of the figure rushing toward the fence. The creature scaled the gate without trouble, perched itself on top, and turned again toward Jack.

"Give it back," Jack said as he approached, clutching a stitch at his side.

The creature dropped down on the other side of the gate, then moved across the driveway on its knuckles, glancing over its shoulder as if seeing whether he was following.

*What am I doing?* he thought as he neared the gate. He would lose his position on the team if he was caught. Then again, if Petrillo exposed that Jack had the key, his fate would be worse. *Much* worse. Swearing under his breath, he hooked one foot into the gate, then clumsily climbed over.

His eyes fell on a lit window beyond the oak tree at the center of the drive. Somebody was home. He walked in a crouch across the cobblestone, looking at an expensive silver car parked in a carport to the left. Petrillo stood on the carport roof, and as Jack drew closer, the creature stepped to the wall of the mansion, grabbed hold of a drainpipe, and began climbing.

Wondering how Petrillo had managed to get up there so quickly, he spotted a stack of crates along the outside pillar and pushed himself up onto them. Adjusting the strap of his messenger bag, he leapt to the nearest beam of the open carport roof, knocking the crates over with his flailing legs. When he'd pulled himself up, he stepped cautiously along the beam, arms stretched out, until he reached the drainpipe. There was hardly room to fit his fingers behind it; he'd have to find another way up. A window to his left was lit, shining upon construction scaffolding that moved up along the far edge of the house.

He crept along the roof of the carport, his eyes trained upward to the spot where Petrillo had disappeared. If he lost Petrillo, he lost the key; the key Dr. Walraven had stolen from Animal Control, had died to protect. From who? Petrillo? Had Jack, in his quest for adventure, delivered the key right to the one from whom Dr. Walraven had been protecting it? And what if Petrillo *was* on the roof when he got up there? He could no sooner catch him than get back down from this carport without that scaffolding. Whether he continued to follow, or slunk away in defeat, he'd have to make it past that window. He crouched low and moved below the light.

"...Searched every square inch of the place," a voice was saying.

"And what did you find?" This voice was President Brisk.

"Nothing whatsoever," said a third voice; a horribly familiar voice. "Little runt must have taken it with him. Why don't we just arrest him? Have him searched."

There was a brief pause. "No. No, if he doesn't have it on him, he'll know we suspect him, and then we'll *never* find it."

"And if he makes a move for the tree?" asked the familiar voice.

Brisk let out an angry roar. At the same time, there was a loud crashing sound, as though something had been toppled over. Another pause. Brisk inhaled a calming breath, and spoke again. "We have him here now. The Safehaven affair is already set in motion. I couldn't stop it, even if I wanted to, but if I don't get that key before the gate opens, it will all have been for nothing. *Nothing!*" He shouted the last word, and again there was the sound of something toppling over. There was silence again, and then he spoke, his voice calm once more. "Good thing I didn't rely on Plan A."

"So you hired him just to keep him here?"

"Yes," Brisk said. "It was Alan's idea. *Bring the kid on. He'll slip up eventually.* I hired that whole useless team just to keep him here. Looks like I made the right choice."

Feeling lightheaded, Jack lowered himself to sit on the scaffolding. Brisk had sent the wolves to kill Dr. Walraven, to get the key? Worse, Alan was in on it. And now Jack had brought it right to them. Was Petrillo about to drop in and present Brisk with the key? With this thought in mind, Jack stood slowly, gripping the windowsill, and peered anxiously into the room.

The three of them were at the center of a garage, a full story below him. Brisk was facing away, leaning against a stack of boxes, hanging his head. More boxes were scattered across the floor. A goat in a black suit and tie watched him without expression. And on the other side, the familiar wolf fidgeted with a sling around the shoulder he had dislocated at the mill.

His piercing silver eyes flicked up to the window.

Jack threw himself backward. He lost his balance. Slipped between the beams of the open carport. Landed hard on the roof of the car.

The alarm blared, a pulsating honk that seemed deafening in the still night. Jack tumbled off the roof of the car, landing on his tail bone. The rhythmic flash of orange parking lights splashed against the wall as he sat upright and scooted his back to the car.

There were footsteps. Voices. They were coming from the front side of the house. His heart pounding, Jack peeked around the side of the car. They weren't visible yet, but they sounded close.

He hid once more, holding his breath and listening.

Something dropped next to him. Turning quickly, he began to cry out, but a paw clapped over his mouth and nose. There was a sharp odor, like the chemical smell of rubbing alcohol. It burned in his nostrils. His eyes began to water and he gave a muffled yell, grabbing uselessly at the slender black arms.

His attempts to fight grew weaker, and he was lowered to his back. That same white vulture mask peered down at him through empty black sockets. As everything else faded to blackness, only the mask remained, cocked to the side, considering.

And then all was silent.

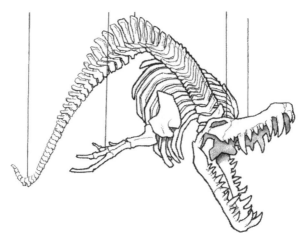

## Chapter Twenty-Two

# THE ARCHIVE

The warmth of the entryway vanished as Pontifucus Gordon pushed the oak doors open and stepped out into the snowy night. The hawk paid no attention to the chill, nor to the swirling clouds his breath made. He'd lived in the mountains since childhood, had spent his entire adult life here at Fort Safehaven. He could handle the cold. Yet he allowed himself a shiver. Now that he was outside, not observed by anyone save perhaps the guards along the rooftop four stories up, he felt no need to suppress his emotion. It wasn't fear. He wasn't *afraid* of what was happening.

He was angry.

Angry that it had come to this. Angry that President Brisk refused to help, that Lady Claythorne refused to listen. Of course, it was neither his job nor his right to make demands of her. He was an adviser, not an official. A glorified errand-boy entering the last quarter of his life. And he'd watched these changes happen slowly, bit by bit, one little compromise after another, until Fort

Savehaven was almost unrecognizable from the sentinel city it had once been.

The ranks of Safehaven were compromised. He'd seen it happening. And now, who could say who their friends were? Or who was to be trusted?

He strode across the stone esplanade and toward the descending snow bank. In the distance below, the lights of Pine Creek twinkled like yellow stars against the night. So peaceful, a perfect postcard of a town; the kind of place where everyone knew everyone. It didn't look like the setting for a murder, let alone five.

The fifth had been only two days ago. This victim was the youngest yet, hardly a man. And they were all the same species. Why?

His thoughts were interrupted by a mechanical, grinding sound. It came from the trees just down the slope from where he stood. He knew that sound.

The guard along the rooftop was pacing in the opposite direction. Gordon hesitated, thinking to gain the guard's attention. But reckless anger got the better of him, and he turned again toward the noise.

Drawing the cloak around himself, he started off down the hill. The snow was deeper than he'd expected, and he nearly lost his balance as he sank knee-deep. Righting himself, he trudged toward the growth of evergreens, beyond which that mechanical grind could still be heard.

It was dark in the midst of the trees, cut off from the moon and the lights of the fort. Somehow, the mechanical sound seemed much louder in here. It was getting closer.

Indeed, he could see the yellow lights, like the glowing eyes of some giant beast, moving between the trees ahead. They bobbed up and down as the machine stomped slowly through the glade, right toward him.

Heart pounding, he squinted against the headlights, trying to make out the shaded figure of the machine's pilot.

And then his stomach plummeted. It was a sinking feeling, a realization. He was being watched. Not from the front, but from the side. He spun to the left, taking a step backward.

A bleach white skull reflected the light of the moon. He — or it — stood in a clearing, a cloak of fur billowing out to one side like a tattered flag. Long, bull like horns extended from either side of the skull, its round sockets like big black coins.

And in its skeletal fingers, the monstrous creature clutched a burlap sack.

"We've been waiting for you, Mr. Gordon," said a wheezing voice. There was something broken, wrong in the sound of it. Gordon, a war veteran, thought it sounded like words spoken through a punctured lung. And it seemed to be coming from the burlap sack.

He turned to see the machine pass between the trees to his right. It was only yards away now, a great four-legged tank with a cage at the front. And behind the bars of the cage, he could just make out the face of the pilot. "You," he said, his voice cold, his blood boiling.

The pilot cranked his arms forward, and the machine lunged. The horned creature made no move, empty sockets staring blankly as Gordon screamed.


"Move over, I want to see."

"Hey, stop shoving."

"Wow. He doesn't even look *hurt!*"

Jack opened his eyes. A dozen faces were peering down at him. Disoriented, his head pounding, he was nonetheless relieved to see that the faces were all kids; apprentices.

"Ah, you're awake!" Sprint said, looking down at him with a combination of relief and reverence. "Had us worried there. We thought you'd been poisoned or something."

"Poisoned?" Jack said, pushing himself to a sitting position and rubbing the space between his ears. He looked around. He was on his bed in the Barracks. Morning light shown in through the window between bunk beds.

"Is it true?" asked a goat named Burson. "Did you *really* fight Petrillo?"

"Does he *look* like he fought Petrillo?" another boy responded.

"Well, he chased Petrillo, for sure," said a girl. "Tonya and I saw him."

"*And* he tried to break into the President's car," Sprint added impressively.

"Sprint!" Jack yelled, his heart leaping.

"Don't worry," Sprint muttered. "They love it. You're like a *hero* now."

Jack looked around uncertainly at the faces beaming down at him.

"Why would you try to break into the President's car?" the same girl asked. She was a pretty mouse, maybe a little older than Jack, with large round ears and fur of a soft brown.

His cheeks burned. "I didn't. I fell onto it from his house."

Some gasped. Others exchanged glances. One boy whistled, impressed.

Cal was hovering near the edge of the crowd. Jack caught his eye, and the groundhog turned away, shaking his head in disgust. His team followed as he left the room.

"So what was he like?" Burson asked. "Was he strong? Did he have any powers?"

"Who says it's a *he?*" a fox girl said, looking Burson up and down.

"Petrillo's a guy name," Burson said. "If it was a girl, it'd be *Petrilla*."

"Wait, he's up?" called an angry voice from beyond the crowd. Kids were pushed sideways as Maddie forced her way to the edge of Jack's bed. "What in the all-fours world were you thinking, Jack?" she bellowed. "Do you have any idea how much damage you could have done?" The crowd began to shuffle awkwardly away. "We're being evaluated as a *team*," she continued. "Everything you do, every stupid little bone-headed idea reflects on all five of us. If one of us messes up, we're *all* out of here. Thank God you weren't caught. Thank God we didn't get thrown out of here *today*. It was *that* close."

"He's fine, Maddie," Sprint said. "We're all fine. He didn't get caught, and we're no longer the laughing stock of the apprentices. Wins all around."

Maddie glared at him. "And if he had been caught?"

Sprint shrugged. "We'd be sent home. And if a rock fell from the sky and flattened us, we'd be dead. It didn't happen, so who cares?"

"This time. It didn't happen this time."

"You mean getting caught?" Sprint asked.

"No, you guys getting flattened by a rock," she said as she stalked away. "But there's still hope."

There was a faint buzzing sound. "Someone's pager is going off," a boy called. "The light is red. What does that mean?"

"It means *none of your business*," Willie answered, grabbing the pager from him and looking down at the screen. "Detail," he said.

Sprint groaned. "Man, I hate detail."

"What are you complaining about," Willie said. "You could finish the job for *all* of us in five minutes."

Jack laughed, which made Sprint shoot him an angry glance. "Well, he has a point," Jack said. "I mean, a job where all we have to do is dust and polish? That's a walk in the park for you."

Trapped between annoyance and flattery, Sprint simply shrugged. "It's boring though."

"Not today, it won't be," Maddie replied, taking the pager from Willie and reading it. Her tone had changed from anger to excitement. "We're detailing the Archive."

"The Archive?" Hoover said, stopping with one arm in his sweater. "I mean, *the* Archive? Oh man! I've always wanted to check it out."

"Okay, nerd," Sprint said. "What's the Archive?"

"It's where they keep all the historic, significant stuff from Animal Control's past," Hoover explained, his eyes wide as he finished with the sweater. "It's like a big museum, filled with costumes, vehicles, weapons. Everything."

"A museum?" Sprint said. "You're excited about dusting *historic* stuff in a museum?"

"I dunno," Hoover mumbled. "It could be fun."

Jack threw his arms up to shield himself as Maddie tossed the pager at him rather aggressively. Picking it up, he unclasped the messenger bag at his feet and dropped the pager inside.

His eyes caught something else in there. After making sure the others were occupied, he lifted the bag to his lap and peeked inside. There, sitting among the papers, pens, and pamphlets he'd accumulated over the past several weeks, was the heart-shaped key.

The Archive was a large steel building, the arched shape of an airplane hangar. It glinted in the morning sunlight, its great hangar doors pushed wide. Standing at the entrance was a plump mole in a maroon cardigan.

"Hello there," the mole said, her face squashing into a good-natured grin. "My name is Rose. Welcome to The Archive!"

"That's Pitfall," Hoover whispered, a familiar star-struck tone in his voice. "She's a legend! Retired ten years ago."

"Now," the mole said, clapping her paws together and squinting slightly over their heads, "The Archive is where we preserve some of Animal Control's history. Today, my little historians, we're going to learn a bit about that history, all while helping to preserve it."

"Lucky little ducks!" Sprint muttered, mimicking her sing-song tone.

"As you all know," Pitfall continued, "Animal Control was founded over forty years ago. We had just won the war against the Red Teeth, thanks almost entirely to one man." She turned and motioned for them to follow her as she passed through the tall hangar doors. They entered a green carpeted lobby decorated in flags and glass displays. Near the inner doors stood a bronze statue of a lion with a dread-locked mane. "King of Hearts," Pitfall continued, "was only a teen during the New Famine War. He was a soldier, one of the last survivors of the Battle of Pretty Fishes." She stood before the statue, her paws clasped in front of her. "The story goes, his squad was hiding in a foxhole. They were exhausted, injured, and out of ammunition. A Red Teeth soldier spotted them, and before they could react, a tank was poking its cannon straight in at them. Then King — *Aaron Harding*, I should say — did something amazing. He grabbed the cannon with both paws, and *shoved* it out of the hole. Just pushed it right out, then followed after it. Something had changed in him. Some power discovered." She paused, looking between them. "Can anyone tell me what caused this change?"

Sprint nudged Hoover with an elbow. "This guy knows."

The mole gave Hoover an encouraging smile. "Do you?"

Looking anxiously between the two of them, Hoover hesitated, then nodded. "*In Extremis Manifestation*," he half-whispered. "He was near death. That's why his powers manifested."

"Precisely," Pitfall said, her face once again squashing into a smile. "For some, heightena will not show up until the body *needs* it. It was at that moment, when he was about to die, that he discovered his power. And not just any power. *The* power; the Alpha Heightena, which hadn't been seen in a century. The story goes that his eyes began to glow red, his feet left the ground, and he hovered around that battlefield, crumpling tanks with his bare paws, causing the earth to swallow Red Teeth soldiers, calling the very roots of trees to bind his enemies. He took that field. Then the next. Within days, the tide had shifted. Within weeks, the war was over."

Jack was transfixed, staring at the statue, imagining the glowing red eyes, the hovering body. He must have been terrifying.

And then he realized something else. Dr. Walraven must have been there, must have seen that change in his friend. Without meaning to, he began stroking the falcon emblem stitched into his messenger bag.

"When the war was over," Pitfall continued, gesturing for the group to follow as she pulled open one half of the double doors and walked through, "King realized that his protection wouldn't be enough. He would need to find others like himself and unite them. I myself was the third officer King recruited."

They entered an enormous room, five stories tall and punched with skylights along its curved roof. Display cases formed a pathway that moved to the left. As Pitfall spoke, she gestured toward the cases, their shelves filled with all sorts of Animal Control memorabilia: medals, framed photographs, even weaponry. The walls of memories weaved through what Jack quickly realized was a sort of museum and trophy room, all in one. The mole pointed upward. "Here are the remains of the leviathan, defeated by Sud Flood twelve years ago." An enormous, bleach-white skeleton was suspended overhead. It reminded Jack of a whale skeleton he had seen in one of Dr. Walraven's books, only this one was longer, skinnier, and had a head more similar to a jagged-toothed crocodile.

Further ahead, they passed a wall of mannequins dressed in colorful, rather old-fashioned costumes, some of which Jack recognized. A female mannequin, sculpted to resemble a slender cat, wore a purple and black outfit with a yellow "R" patch on the chest. That was Retract. She had been on the front page of one of the newspapers in Jack's childhood collection. A much larger mannequin, a big bellied hippopotamus, wore the kind of mask a wrestler might wear. Jack couldn't think of his name; *The Murphy* or something.

"And here," the mole said, coming to a stop, "is your assignment for today." Jack looked ahead, and his stomach plummeted. They had come to an open, circular space, at the center of which sat the crumple-nosed engine of an s-train. *The* s-train.

"You might recognize S-530 here," Pitfall said, standing before it with her paws folded in front of her. "This is the train engine that ended King's life. We keep it here as a reminder: none of us is perfect. We must always, *always* be ready for the worst." She began to walk around the chained perimeter of the display. "But, as you can see, Ol' Five-Thirty could use a little spit and polish. For the next two hours, you'll be scrubbing her down. This way; I'll show you the supply room."

When they had gathered their dust rags and spray bottles, Pitfall left them to it.

"Alright, Hooves," Sprint said, tossing his rag over his shoulder and turning to the anteater.

"Alright what?" Hoover asked.

"Alright, do your stuff."

Nonplussed, Hoover raised an eyebrow.

"Just, you know," Sprint explained, wagging a paw toward the engine. "Bust the dust." When Hoover looked even more confused, Sprint rolled his eyes. "You can save us all a ton of work here."

Catching on, Hoover looked nervously toward the engine. "This is a priceless piece of Animal Control history. I'll blow it up!"

"You gotta learn to use your low settings sometime. Why not now?"

"I'm not a blow dryer," Hoover said. "I don't have high and low settings."

Personally, Jack wished Hoover *could* blow it clean. The sight of the mangled engine was unsettling to him; the idea of touching it made him queasy. As the others got to work, he walked around it, looking for an area that didn't hold a secret history between him and the train engine. Sprint had insisted that they keep no secrets. Well here was the biggest one, the granddaddy secret of all time: he, Jack, was the reason King of Hearts was dead.

As he passed around the back, examining the gaping hole where it had once joined with the passenger cars, he could practically hear his own small voice.

*King, please help me!*

And the ghost of King's voice echoed back.

*Take my paw! Quickly!*

Jack continued around the train, but stopped short of the front wheels, which were bent inward beneath a crumpled section of the body. He looked away, afraid he'd find some fleck of brownish red, some clump of golden fur caught in the iron folds.

He diverted his eyes to a door along the body of the train. The bottom of it was higher than the tips of his ears. He remembered that door being flung open. He remembered the pig grabbing him by his ears and tossing him out into the rain.

His eyes moved down to the silver plank-like object protruding like an injured wing just above the wheels. It looked like a panel from a set of hanging blinds, only it was made of metal, so shiny Jack could see his own distorted reflection looking back at him. He reached forward, sliding his paw along the thin edge. It was surprisingly sharp. This was the section that had caught his shirt collar. It had saved his life.

But as he bent lower to examine it, there was something else. Some vague memory, like a word balancing on the tip of the tongue. The underside of the train; he didn't know why, but as he looked at the dark metal pipes and bolts, some feeling of recollection blossomed. Why was the underside of the train so familiar?

He was so lost in thought, he hadn't heard Sprint approaching, and jumped at the sight of him. He winced as his paw scraped the edge of the mirror-like fin branch.

"Er… boo," Sprint said.

Jack frowned down at his paw. A small patch of red was growing on the largest of his pads.

"Youch!" Sprint grimaced. "I saw a first aid kit in the supply room." He jerked his head in that direction. Jack gave a final look at the base of the train, then followed.

"You know, I still don't understand how you did it," Sprint said. He leaned against the wall and watched Jack dab at his wounded paw.

"Did what?" Jack responded, tossing the bloodied cloth into a garbage bin, then peeling open a bandage.

"Got through the maze so quickly," Sprint said. "I mean, you didn't even seem to *try*. It's like you knew where you were going."

Jack didn't immediately respond. In the six weeks since the trial, he had thought about this very thing quite a bit. The apprentice teams had spent many nights, especially in the first few weeks, talking about the trials. It always surprised Jack to hear how difficult the maze had been for most of them. "*It just seemed unfair,*" Burson, the goat boy, had complained. "*I mean, I spent the entire fifteen minutes just wandering aimlessly.*" This was true for most everyone, it seemed. The ones who solved the maze were either fliers or climbers, those that could reach the top of the maze and solve it from there, or runners like Sprint, who solved it by simply trying every possibility. Jack seemed to be the only one who hadn't found the maze difficult. Why was that?

Before he could voice an answer, however, his messenger bag began to buzz. He flipped it open. "It can't be time to leave," he said. "It's not even noon."

Sprint shook his head, watching with stiff anticipation.

Fishing among the papers, Jack peeked into the bag. The interior was now flooded with green light. Breath caught in his chest, he withdrew the pager and read the screen.

**ANAX LAUNCH 99**

"It's green," Sprint said, stunned. "Anax launch. But what do you think *99* means?"

Jack stared at the pager in his paw, disbelieving. "Code 99. It means *bring a suitcase.*"

## Chapter Twenty-Three
## FLIGHT

"I suppose you're wondering why you're here," Mr. Behr said, a tone of excitement in his voice. He was watching them approach from the doorway of the Launch Center — a wide, single story building they knew from their mail runs. A fleet of anaxopters were lined up along the flat roof, their dragonfly-like wings turned skyward. "As you may know, during the apprenticing season, no hero may deploy on assignment without a sidekick. It's one of our bylaws; part of the Future Generations Act." He motioned for them to follow him inside. "One of the apprentice teams has been disqualified. Unfortunate for them, of course, but certainly advantageous for you!"

"Who was it?" Maddie asked as they passed through the tinted glass doors and entered a well-lit lobby. A large black map made up the back wall, small lights blinking across its surface.

Her question was answered when they spotted the five heroes standing before the map. They looked as impressive as ever, even with the disappointed scowls they wore. At the center, and slightly in front of the others, Grayson Conway watched their approach, wings folded behind his back.

"You are of course familiar with Team Vanguard," Behr said, that same excited tone in his voice. "But allow me to make the introductions. Miles," he said, indicating Sprint and motioning for him to walk forward, "this is Edward Dixon, also known as *Bullet Hound*. He'll be your new mentor. Mr. Dixon, this is Miles Greenacre. He prefers the name *Sprint*."

Sprint extended a paw. The greyhound examined him over the top of his oval-rimmed glasses, the corners of his mouth twitching in a stifled grin. When he looked away, Sprint dropped his paw awkwardly.

"Right," Behr said. "Hoover, please." The anteater stepped forward. "Hoover Fennelman, meet Llood Ristal, also called *Weed*." The grayish green sloth stepped forward, sizing Hoover up. He nodded. Jack saw an expression of relief on the anteater's face when the sloth did not offer a paw to shake.

"Maddie, this is Billy Netti," Behr continued.

A long legged and sharp faced jackrabbit strutted forward and took her hoof in his paw. "You can call me *Pan*," he said, stooping to kiss it. She looked between him and Behr uneasily.

"Willie, I'd like you to meet Hugo Ford," Behr said, indicating the muscular bull Jack had met at the Honey Sap. "Learn everything you can from him. Hugo doesn't say much, but he's got a lot of experience to share with you.

"And finally," Behr said, taking Jack's shoulder and ushering him forward. "Grayson Conway, I'd like you to meet…"

"Jack Robberts," the falcon said, stepping forward. "We've met. Tell me, Jack: how does one go from busing tables at a nowhere dive to apprenticing at Animal Control within a matter of weeks?"

Jack shrugged. "Just lucky, I guess."

Conway smiled and nodded. "Welcome aboard."

The tinted door opened once more, and Alan Kale stepped in. Jack's pulse quickened; it was the first time he'd seen the fox since he'd overheard Brisk's conversation. Something was bubbling up inside Jack; something that felt a lot like hatred.

In his paw, Alan held a manila folder. "Mr. Behr," he said. He sounded almost congested. "Here are the assignment files."

He passed the folder to Behr, who flipped it open. The eagerness drained from Behr's expression, and his eyes shot up to meet Alan's. "No," he said. "Gordon?"

The name was familiar to Jack, although he couldn't immediately place it.

Alan nodded stiffly. Jack thought his brother's eyes looked a little redder than normal. *No*, he thought, *not brother. Not anymore.*

Behr licked his chops, then shook his head. He passed the folder to Conway. "Very well. Thank you, Mr. Kale."

Jack felt his jaw tighten as the fox gave him the briefest of glances, then turned and exited the building.

"Well, let's get the safety stuff taken care of," Behr said.

"Ouch!" Sprint yelped.

The same nurse from the day of the trials, the one he had referred to as *Mother Goose*, patted him on the shoulder. "That's you done, dear," she said, removing a cartridge from the needle-ended gun she was holding and replacing it with a fresh one.

"It may sting a bit," Behr apologized, "but believe me: you'll be glad you have a tracker the moment you need it."

"Tracker?" Maddie asked. "Like, tags?" She watched the nurse moving toward her with apprehension.

"It's merely a precaution," Behr said. "In case you get lost out there, we'll be able to find you. Although," he added hesitantly, "it takes a while for the tag to become active. A few days, I should think, so let's do our best not to wander off, alright?"

The roof of the building was an enormous cement landing pad, with anaxopters in two rows along the edges. A single anaxopter was positioned at the center of a yellow painted circle in the space between, its wings fully extended. Up close, the anax looked much bigger.

A boar in a brown flight suit stood before the vehicle, watching them approach. She introduced herself as Carrie Anne. Serious and broad shouldered, she had a wide bosom and a deadpan stare that commanded attention as she spoke. "Vanguard, you already know what I'm about to tell you," she said in her deep voice, "but for the safety of our new guys, I'll reiterate it all anyway. From the moment you enter this door," she knocked on the opened sliding door behind her, "Until the moment you exit, your powers do not exist. You do not use them. You do not talk about them. You do not think about them. You do not think about talking about using them. The Captain is in charge, then his co-pilot, then me, then the fuel, then the tires, then the dirt on the tires, and *then* you."

Maddie raised a hoof, but didn't wait to be addressed before speaking. "What happens if a crisis ari…"

"If an emergency presents itself and you feel you can use your heightena to save the anax or the crew, here's what you do," the boar said, fixing her yellow eyes on Maddie. "You say, 'Excuse me, Miss Carrie Anne, but I got it in my stupid head that I know better than the Captain. May I please use my power?' to which I will respond, 'No you may not. Now sit down and shut up. Land sakes, child.'

"Now you'll find we've already installed seats to your proper size and supplied species-specific headsets. Please drop your bags where you stand and board the anax."

The interior of the anax smelled of rubber and gasoline. Seats were positioned facing each other, so that five faced forward, and five faced back. Jack crossed the cabin and settled into a seat at the far end, facing forward.

"That's my seat," barked Pan, the long-legged jackrabbit.

"Oh!" Jack said, hopping back out of the seat and moving out of Pan's way. Willie and Maddie were already buckling themselves into their seats on the opposite side. Willie's seat looked comically small next to Maddie's.

"Your seat is tagged with your ACID number, Jack," Conway said. "Look on your badge."

The end of Jack's lanyard dangled from his pants pocket. He withdrew it, and read the identification number. *1178902.* He scanned the empty rear-facing seats. Each had a silver plate mounted into the wall above it, with numbers scribbled in dry-erase marker. His seat was next to the window, directly across from Conway. Thankfully, it wasn't as small as Willie's, although it still looked tiny compared to any of the adult chairs across from them.

As he fastened his restraints, Carrie Anne slid the door shut from the outside, then climbed into the front of the anax, where Behr was also sitting.

The wings outside began beating, slowly at first. Jack watched them pump up and down, up and down, picking up speed. The cabin began to rattle, a shiver that echoed in his spine and knees. *What am I doing here?* he thought. *Minds of mice!* That was Dr. Walraven's favorite phrase. Dr. Walraven, who'd always looked out for him. Now he was gone, and Jack was alone. He swallowed, trying to keep his face straight as his cheeks rattled with the shaking anax. He looked across at Grayson Conway. The falcon looked so perfect, so confident, strapped into that bigger chair.

There was a strange rocking motion as the body of the anax swayed. They were lifting off. The tightness in Jack's chest continued to swell like a bubble. The air in here was so thin, so hot. He couldn't hear anything but the loud beating of the wings. He fixed his eyes on the roof. If he was about to be sick, he didn't want to see Conway's disapproving frown, or Edward Dixon's smug leer.

There was a tug on his sleeve. Sprint, cushioned in the fluff of his own tail, was tapping headphones on his ears, then pointing above Jack's head. After he repeated the gesture, Jack understood; a headset was locked into the wall just below the number plate. Everyone else was already wearing theirs. Jack reached up and unclasped his, then slid the frame between his long ears. He was used to the unusual design of rabbit headphones, which pressed his ears flat against the sides of his head. But these were heavier than he'd ever worn, and he had to maneuver a bendable microphone toward his mouth. He spoke into it, but heard nothing. Sprint reached across and clicked a switch on the left phone. "Can you hear me?" he asked.

"Yeah," Jack nodded.

"You alright?" Sprint asked, his tone excited.

"I'm... I think so, yeah. Though I might be sick."

"Well suck it up, Buttercup," came another voice. Dixon was staring across at him. "We've got a long flight, and nobody wants to smell regurgitated carrot the whole way there."

This was followed by the static sound of laughter from Ford, Pan, and to Jack's annoyance, Willie and Maddie.

"I'm fine," Jack said. "Just got a little motion sick, that's all."

"Motion sick?" Dixon scoffed. "We've hardly left the ground." He laughed shrilly.

"That's enough," Conway said through mild static. "Vanguard: our apprentice team screwed up. Like it or not, this is our team now. Let's not start off on the wrong foot." Dixon gave a curt nod, wearing that familiar pompous smirk.

For a while, there was radio silence. Out the window, Jack watched the campus shrink below them, until it was little more than a green patch the shape of a guitar pick. The city surrounding it wasn't nearly as colorful from above as it had been from inside. Gray white buildings stretched away from the harbor, becoming so small, Jack felt as though he could run his paw across the grooves of the city. The anax began to bank, and the window filled with the vibrant blue of the sea.

The vehicle righted itself. Jack felt his nerves settling like particles of dust. This wasn't so bad. Outside, he could still see the wings pumping up and down, moving so quickly, they looked like rectangular screens tinting the horizon beyond them. He could still feel their vibration, especially in his feet. It was almost pleasant.

Dixon and Pan talked through most of the flight, reminiscing about past adventures Jack had seen on the news. Ford, whose chair was so big he was nearly sitting on the floor, emanated a sort of boundless strength, as if one good stretch might tear this cabin in two. Llood, the sloth, sat in quiet contemplation, not breaking focus even as Pan lobbed peanuts at the side of his head.

"He calls it meditation," Pan said, "but have we ever really proven he's not just sleeping?" The others laughed. Even Conway cracked a smile, although he didn't look up from the contents of the folder Behr had handed him.

Jack was so enamored by the Vanguard team, he hadn't realized they had crossed the sea. When he looked out the window, he saw nothing but forests of evergreens and rolling foothills. Somewhere below was Hadensburrow, and the charred remains of the old watermill. Looking across the others to the opposite window, he saw a range of snowy mountains breaching the horizon. As if in response, the anax banked slightly, and they turned toward the mountain range.

"Nearly there," Carrie Anne's disembodied voice said. "We'll arrive in Pine Creek in just over twenty minutes."

Jack looked up in surprise. The team across from him made no response to the words, nor did Sprint, who was casually munching a bag of peanuts. But then, he considered, they *wouldn't* be surprised by the destination. They hadn't been there the day the wolves had attacked.

"The truth of the matter is that this is quite urgent," Dr. Walraven had said. "I *must* get to Pine Creek, and I need you with me."

Jack sighed, gazing blankly out the window beside him. *I'm here now, Dr. Walraven,* he thought. *So what did you have in mind?*

## Chapter Twenty-Four
## THE LADY OF THE MAZE

Snow was flying upward, swimming chaotically through floodlights as the anax touched down. The platform out the window was well lit, casting sharp contrast between the churning flakes and the night beyond. Jack felt as though he was inside a snow globe.

The engine died off suddenly, leaving an eerie silence in its wake. Jack jumped as the door slid open abruptly. Cold air poured in like floodwater, and he instinctively buried his muzzle in the crook of his elbow.

"Vanguard first," Carrie Anne said in her stern tone. The boar stood outside of the door, gesturing toward Conway and his team. They unclasped their restraints and slid out into the night in a perfect line.

"Apprentice team next," Carrie Anne ordered. Compared to Conway's team, Jack was sure he and the others looked like untrained monkey children, all following their own idea of what an orderly exit looked like.

The fur on his haunches rose at the chill air, and he wrapped his arms around his chest. He lined up next to Pan, feeling tiny and insignificant alongside the much taller rabbit. They stood at quiet attention as a group approached them from what looked like a stairwell hut. It was the only protrusion Jack could see on the otherwise flat concrete roof. The newcomers were silhouetted by the floodlights, striking an imposing image against the jagged line of fir trees beyond the platform. At the front of the group, and leaning heavily onto a cane with every other step, was a female wolf. Her cane clicked against the concrete as she approached, sounding like the impatient toe tapping of an irritated school teacher.

She moved in front of the light, casting a long, impressive shadow onto the ground at their feet. She wasn't alone, but somehow Jack couldn't take his eyes away from her blackened silhouette, rimmed in white light.

As she and those with her came under the nearest light, her white fur and pointed ears seemed to pop from the darkness. She was aged yet beautiful, with paper white fur and eyes like copper coins. Her gray cloak was crowned with a crimson-red scarf that trickled down her front like spilled blood.

To her left stood the biggest bear Jack had ever seen; so big, Jack wondered how he hadn't spotted him first. He was a grizzly, with a mange of thick fur around his gullet and the knitted cap of a mountaineer pulled over his ears. His limbs, beneath a blue jacket with too many pockets, were thicker than Jack's body, and his yellow eyes reflected out from below heavy brows.

To the wolf's right, a second wolf, hunched and diminished, stared at his own booted feet. Jack recognized him instantly as the wolf assistant he'd met outside of Brisk's office, the one who had accompanied Pontificus Gordon to Animal Control. He looked, as he had then, as though he expected to get a whipping as soon as he was out of sight.

There was one final, pronounced *click* as the wolf woman stopped in front of them. She eyed them all, stone faced and calculating, her head moving very little as her eyes flicked between them. "Welcome to Safehaven," she said. Her voice was low yet musical. "Which of you is Robert Behr?"

"Ah, that'll be me, Ma'am," Behr said, stepping forward and extending a paw. "And may I say how delighted I am to meet you in person, My Lady."

"Yes," she said stolidly, taking his paw briefly and continuing to appraise the rest of the group. "You bring a large crowd with you; that is good." She didn't sound pleased, however. "I don't see any familiar faces here."

"Right, introductions," Behr said, turning to the teams. "May I introduce you all to Lady Margarette Claythorne, the Seated Lady of Safehaven. Madam Claythorne, I've brought with me *two* teams." He sectioned off the groups with a paw. "Here we have Vanguard. Now I'm sure you've heard that name."

"Indeed," Lady Claythorne said in that same, unsatisfied tone. "New recruits, aren't they?"

"Oh, well, they've been around a few years. Wouldn't exactly call them *new*," Behr said. "Best recruits we've had in two decades. Broken just about every record we've got a record for."

Lady Claythorne cut across him. "I would have hoped for some more experience, given our situation."

Conway stepped forward, his beak pointed high and his chest puffed outward. "We're more than capable of protecting you, My Lady."

"Do I look like I've got flat teeth, boy?" she retorted. "We don't need protectors, we need investigators, and investigators only come with *experience*."

Conway didn't flinch. "We are up to the task, My Lady."

She looked him up and down, then took in the rest of his team once more. "Let us hope so, Mr. Conway. I would not like to think that Alexander Brisk has short-changed me."

Conway stepped back into line.

"And who are these?" she asked, turning her attention to Jack's team.

"Ah, well," Behr said uncomfortably. "This is our, well, our apprentice team."

"Apprentice team," Lady Claythorne sighed, then said something under her breath that sounded very much like "Typical." She stopped in front of Jack, her golden eyes fixed on him. She took him in for a moment, then stepped away. "Very well," she said, turning to the giant grizzly to her left. "Greenridge, please get them all checked in. No doubt they are hungry." She paused, looking around the group once more. She gave a curt nod, and as she turned to leave, she said, "We'll continue this discussion in the Great Hall."

"Yes, My Lady," the grizzly said. His voice was deep and gravelly. He turned to the hunched wolf. "Peter, see to their bags. The rest of you, follow me."

Warm air burst from the stairwell as the door was opened. Greenridge marched through, leading them down three flights of wooden stairs that smelled of the forest. At the landing, an arched opening let out into a long hallway. The walls looked, at first, as though they were made of pure gold. As the group followed Greenridge and entered the hall, however, Jack saw that they were actually made up of thick golden logs stacked on top of each other. They were beautiful in their imperfections, with dark knots here, patches of unshaven bark there. Every so often, a flat surface was ground into them, making way for wall hangings such as landscape paintings and tapestries. In one deeper recess, a bronze bust of a proud looking ape with a monocle glared out at them.

Conway was at the front of the group, talking in a formal tone with Greenridge. "I read the briefing during the flight," he was saying. "Six murders, including Gordon. And as I understand it, he was the only victim that was a different species?"

"That's correct," the bear said.

"The report didn't include a suspect. Do you have any leads?"

Greenridge was silent for a moment. He turned down a hallway to the right, and the group followed. "We *know* who's doing it," he said. "We haven't made a move yet out of sheer diplomacy. We need proof, which is why you're here. If we were to make a move on our own, we'd end up with a small war on our hands."

"With the Kerccians?" Dixon asked from Conway's other side.

"The Kerccians?" Greenridge shook his head. "No. The gate is enough to keep us safe from our Northern neighbors. It's the locals we have to worry about, which is exactly why the fort was built this way."

"This way?" Dixon inquired.

"Look around you, Mr. Dixon."

They passed another alcove in the log wall. Jack did a double take. A bust of an ape wearing a monocle peered out at them; it was identical to the one they'd seen before.

"We're not going in circles," Greenridge assured them, pressing his massive paw against the wall opposite the sculpture. The wall swiveled, revealing another hall beyond. "It takes years of living in Safehaven to find your way around. Invaders would become hopelessly lost. Safehaven is a maze."

Dinner was served in the Great Hall. It was a large cafeteria room similar to Kelly Hall, although far more luxurious, with red tablecloths beneath golden plates and crystal glasses that sparkled like diamonds. The food was much fancier than Jack was used to, and it seemed Sprint felt the same way. He flagged down a falcon server to complain about a pine cone in his salad. The server looked at him with suppressed irritation. "I'm sorry, sir?"

"It's undercooked," Sprint repeated, holding the little pine cone up for the falcon's inspection. "I don't even think it's been cooked at all, in fact."

"Sir," the falcon said, "that pine cone is a garnish. Merely for decoration."

Sprint plucked a dry bit from his mouth. "Uh… right."

The server nodded and walked away. Maddie was giggling. She caught Sprint's eye, then looked away quickly, excusing her laughter with a cough. Jack felt relief; he'd been equally confused about the brush of pine needles in his blossom salad.

At the other end of the table, the discussion had turned to the murders.

"Now don't take her Ladyship wrong," Greenridge was saying. "We *are* pleased to have you here. It's just that…"

"I can articulate for myself, thank you General," Claythorne interrupted. "I don't care for softening the blow, nor for padding a firm word. The fact is, had your President listened to our pleas to start with, I might still have my adviser." The wiry falcon to her right shifted uncomfortably and prodded at his plate of fish.

"We might also have prevented the numerous murders before," Claythorne continued. "Let us hope that your lack of experience will not cast a further shade upon our difficulties."

Behr laughed. "I think these guys will surprise you."

"I pray that you are right," Claythorne nodded. "I will make no more mention of the fact. You are here, and that is that. Let us get down to business. General?"

Greenridge nodded, then explained in detail about the murders. According to his report, all of the victims were residents of the neighboring village of Pine Creek; all except Pontificus Gordon.

"And how far is it to Pine Creek," Conway asked.

"As the falcon flies, about five miles," Greenridge responded through a mouthful of trout, "but it's at the foot of the mountain. You can see the village from the south wall."

"And is that where you discovered the bodies?" Conway asked.

"We still haven't found any of the bodies, but…" Greenridge started, but was cut off by Dixon.

"Hold on; if you haven't found any bodies, how can you classify these as murders rather than, at the most, abductions?"

"You misunderstand me," Greenridge responded, shaking his great head. "We've found the victims. We just haven't found their *bodies*."

Many around the table cringed. Pan rubbed his throat.

"That's the key piece of evidence," Greenridge went on, chewing loudly as he spoke. "The ritualistically displayed heads. It's a characteristic trait of the coyotes."

"General," Lady Claythorne warned.

"The coyotes?" Pan repeated, looking across the table to Greenridge. "The locals you mentioned, I presume?"

"Ferals," said the wild-eyed falcon to Claythorne's right. He wore a leering smile; Jack thought he looked a little crazy. "They don't follow the same laws we have. Next to impossible to track them down, though. Reckon that's one area you can help us with."

Conway looked to Lady Claythorne. "Have these ferals been a problem in the past?"

Claythorne seemed troubled. "No, they have not. In fact," she glanced sideways, reproachfully toward Greenridge, "we've been at peace with the ferals for ten years now. I see no reason to suspect them."

"But the evidence…" the wild-eyed falcon retorted.

"…Is purely circumstantial," Lady Claythorne said. "Faked, I believe."

"With permission, My Lady," Greenridge added, "I must reiterate that the evidence does incriminate the ferals. Now, it's possible it was planted. It is; I agree. But it's *also* possible, and to be frank, more likely, that our peace treaty with the ferals is simply decaying."

"I think not," Lady Claythorne said. "Magdalia Nofski is a fair woman. Now I don't approve of the ferals' way of life — and we've arrested more than a few of them for thievery, but so long as Magdalia Nofski is in charge, they will remain our allies."

"Well, perhaps there's a rogue among them," Conway reasoned. "Perhaps these killings are the work of a single coyote, or a group, acting outside of Nofski's authority — and knowledge.".

"If that were so, the culprits would be very foolish to incriminate themselves with the ritualism," Claythorne said. "Their traditions are not religious — they are a mark of honor, intended as a display of respect toward their victims. If such rogues were acting out of their own volition, there would be no honor in the killings; there would be no displayed remains."

"It's possible that they…"

"Enough," Claythorne said, though her voice didn't rise. "We must make plans for tomorrow." She paused, looking around the table. Her eyes held on Jack for a long moment. He preoccupied himself by chasing a dandelion around his plate. "Vanguard will accompany General Greenridge and his men to the areas in which the remains were found."

"Excellent, excellent," Behr piped up. "And what about my boys — er, excuse me, Maddie — my team?"

"Mr. Behr," Claythorne started, turning her full self toward him, "this is no field trip, nor is it a classroom. My charges have been targeted for murder, for reasons unknown. We need answers, we need resolution, and we need them *fast*. I am sorry that you've troubled yourself with the apprentice team, but we cannot afford any liabilities. They'll have to stay behind."

"We're not a liability," Willie said, masking a heated tone with little success. "We're an asset." The other interns nodded in agreement.

Lady Claythorne fixed eyes on Willie, and he faltered.

"You don't understand the situation just yet," Greenridge said.

"Yes we do," Maddie piped up. "It's horrible, but it's what we're here for; we're not afraid."

"It's not a question of being afraid," Greenridge said. "You would present an unnecessary target. We can't be worried about you while…"

"Worried about us?" Sprint said. "We're sidekicks. We're no more likely to…"

"Enough," Lady Claythorne repeated, standing up. Her voice remained even, but her expression was cold. "There will be no more argument, no more discussion on the subject. The..." she looked at Sprint, "*sidekicks* will stay behind in Safehaven, where they can be kept under watch." She fixed her eyes once more on Jack. "Mr. Behr, I must add that I question your judgment in bringing the snowshoe along."

Jack felt his ears droop.

"Oh, Mr. Robberts is harmless enough," Behr responded, sounding surprised. "In fact, he's about the luckiest rabbit I've ever met. Never knew if I believed that old fairytale until I met him."

Jack noticed Greenridge's eyes flick interestedly toward him.

"I'm not worried that he's dangerous," Claythorne replied. "I'm worried that he'll be in danger, and that he'll pose an unnecessary risk for the rest of you."

"Why?" Jack blurted out before he could stop himself. He was looking at Lady Claythorne with what he realized too late was an angry glare.

"What have you heard, Mr. Robberts?" Lady Claythorne said in a businesslike tone.

Jack flushed beneath his fur, looking at his own paws. "That there have been a bunch of murders up here, that only their... their bodies weren't found. Mr. Gordon and some others." Wanting to sound as informed as possible, he added, "And the remains are similar to the traditional displays of feral killings, but the ferals are at peace with Safehaven, so... so it doesn't make sense."

"What you *haven't* heard," Claythorne added, "the reason you pose such a danger in being here, both to yourself and to others, is that with the exception of Pontificus Gordon, all of the victims have been snowshoe bunnies."

She dropped again into her high-backed seat. Jack felt a shudder through his spine that had nothing to do with the chilly mountain air.

## Chapter Twenty-Five
# NOT MUCH OF AN ADVENTURE

The gangly white wolf turned out to be Peter Claythorne, only son of Lady Claythorne. He had once been an Animal Control apprentice himself, back before the program had closed, although they were told this by Greenridge, and Peter seemed too embarrassed to talk about it. He was stooped and silent all through breakfast, as though he expected to be reprimanded for picking up his fork. When Lady Claythorne tasked him with giving the apprentice team a tour — her exact words were "keep the children occupied" — he jumped and looked around as if an explosion had gone off.

Still, once he warmed up to the group, he was quite friendly, and very knowledgeable about the fort. He was older than Jack would have thought, qualifying his stories with "you're probably too young to remember" or "way back when *I* was an apprentice," yet there was a boyish immaturity to him. He'd delighted in showing them the dungeon. "The prison cells are still useable," he'd said, "but the torture stuff is really just there for historical purposes, like a museum." The *torture stuff* was pretty horrific, Jack thought; a large iron casket called an "inverse porcupine," a series of pulleys and chains that Peter called "the giraffe maker." There was even something that looked horribly like a guillotine lying on its side. "Pretty gruesome, huh?" Peter said with a smile.

The room Jack found most interesting was simply called "Munitions." It was also underground but, unlike the dungeon, this space was broad, not the least bit claustrophobic. One side of the room was lined with a security cage, behind which every imaginable type of weapon was mounted on a wall.

When Peter flipped the light switch on, row after row of fluorescent lights shuddered to life throughout the room, revealing an arsenal of four-legged machines with caged seats on their fronts. They looked to Jack like monstrous bears on all fours, so enormous that even Greenridge would be dwarfed standing next to them. There were about twenty, in one neat row stretching back into the expansive room. They were all pointing toward an upward sloping ramp through which daylight poured, glistening against the remaining bits of icy sludge left from a recent shoveling.

"These are the Ice Cats," Peter said as he gestured toward the machines with a sweeping arm. "Mostly, they're used for plowing the roads." He pointed to one of the machines, which had an enormous shovel mounted to the front like a big steel bib. "But they were created as war machines, used for our protection. Imagine coming up against one of these guys." He paused. "They're piloted by the strongest, the best. Not frail little wolves," he added, unable to disguise the bitterness in his voice. He turned toward them and shrugged. "So my mother says, anyway." He was quiet for a moment, nodding and pursing his lips awkwardly. "Well, that's Munitions," he said. "Who's hungry?"

They ate in the Great Hall again. Jack noticed that Peter chose a seat as far from the head table as could be found, even though it was empty. As the group ate, Peter shared a little more of the history of Safehaven.

The Helmet mountain range, he explained, was a natural barrier between Nikacia and Kerccia. The carnivore-infested country to the north was an ever present, yet currently dormant threat, he said, like an inactive volcano. Animals such as wolves and bears got along mostly fine, but non-predatory animals, "which includes all of you," Peter pointed out, were preyed upon, even "farmed," as he called it.

Maddie seemed to lose interest in this part of the conversation. She asked Peter if there was an accessible phone nearby and excused herself.

"What do you mean by 'farmed'?" Sprint asked, wearing an expression that suggested he wasn't sure whether he wanted an answer.

"'Farmed' might be the wrong word; I'm not sure. Enslaved; bred. Two centuries ago in Nikacia, quads such as horses were slaves, bred and raised, the strongest with the strongest, to make powerful work animals that had no rights, and were considered the property of others. In Kerccia, that practice is still taking place, although it's not just for work animals. The fattest are bred with the fattest. You ever met a Kerccian pig? They're enormous. And they're bred for... well, food."

"But that's illegal," Jack said, horror-struck.

"Not in Kerccia, it's not," Peter said. "That's why we have Safehaven. Because the Axe Wound is an open ravine that leads directly through the mountains, easy access for the next invasion. Safehaven is the plug. Centuries ago, a barrier was built; an enormous gate that closes off our end of the ravine. We call it

*Hard Stop.* We safeguard the gate. If Safehaven falls, it's open season in Nikacia."

"Animal Control will—" Willie began.

"Will what?" Peter fired up. His shy demeanor was all but gone. "Will stop an invasion?" He scoffed. "How long did it take you to get here? I've made that flight many times. By the time Animal Control arrived, the damage would be done. There's plenty of space out here for enemies to hide. They're Kerccians, not aliens from outer space. They look just like the rest of us. A whole lot more like me, to be fair," he added under his breath. Then he gave a gesture as if throwing off his own bad mood. "Ah, it doesn't matter," he continued, his voice much more cheerful. "We've got Greenridge. We've got the Ice Cats, and a whole lot more where they came from. We'll be ready for an attack. It's what this place was built for, after all."

There was a commotion in the entryway. Jack turned toward the noise. Greenridge, the massive grizzly bear, was dragging someone roughly into the Hall. The newcomer was a coyote, raggedly dressed and trapped in a headlock under the bear's left arm. "Let go of me, you big idiot," the coyote said, tugging at his captor's arm. "You've already got shackles on me, haven't ya? Where you think I'm gonna go?"

"Shut your mouth," Greenridge growled, dragging the coyote further into the room and looking around. "I've seen more than one of you gnaw themselves free of a shackle. I'm not taking any chances."

"Why… would I… run?" the coyote demanded, jerking his head so hard, his words sounded broken. "Ain't done nothin' wrong."

"Where's Lady Claythorne," came a voice from behind them. Grayson Conway stepped into the Great Hall, covered from head to toe in snow gear.

A rhythmic click came from the entrance to the left. "What is the meaning of this?" Lady Claythorne demanded, limping into the room on her cane.

Greenridge turned, dragging the coyote — with a yelp — around with him. "Mr. Conway and his team are to be commended, My Lady," the bear said in his deep voice. "Together, we've apprehended our murderer."

Claythorne looked the coyote up and down as though inspecting an item for sale. "And what has convinced you so thoroughly of this?" she asked without taking her eyes off of the suspect.

"We found these in the coyote's tent," Conway said, gesturing behind him. Llood, the meditative sloth, was holding a stack of what looked like oddly-shaped white blankets.

Hoover groaned.

"That's disgusting," Sprint said, his voice faint.

"I see," Lady Claythorne said, leaving the coyote and approaching Llood. She grabbed the outermost in the stack, turning it over to expose dried leather skin on its underside. Jack turned away, unable to stomach the grotesque pile of furs. How could Llood stand to hold them? "And these are the rabbits, I presume?"

"Robberts," Conway called. "Come here, please."

Jack's heart skipped a beat. "Me?" he asked.

"Yes," Conway replied. His voice was gentle, but firm. "We need you."

Jack stood from the table and approached, his knees feeling weak. Dixon grabbed his arm, pushed up the sleeve, and placed it alongside the pelt Lady Claythorne had been examining. Jack felt his fur rub against the dead animal's. His head spun.

"Different color," the greyhound said, releasing Jack's arm. "But it's the same fur."

"Without a doubt, these are the victims," Conway concluded. "And this is our killer," he added, thrusting a flight feather toward the coyote.

"No! That's a lie," the coyote said, his voice panicked now. "These pelts are not mine!"

"Holding them for a friend?" Dixon jeered.

The coyote's terrified words became inaudible as he dissolved into tears.

"Get this mongrel out of my sight," Claythorne said. Greenridge obediently dragged the sobbing coyote out of the room, followed by Llood and several Safehaven falcons. When they had gone, Claythorne turned again to Conway and his team. "Well done, Mr. Conway," she said. But her tone was troubled and uncertain. "Was he acting alone?"

Conway shook his head. "We found the feral colony," he said. "Near the river. I can see why you've had so much trouble locating those mutts. The whole camp is buried in the snow, tents and all."

"You raided their camp?" She turned with an exasperated growl, taking a few cane-aided steps away, then turning again. "I thought I had made it clear, Mr. Conway, that I wanted you to *investigate*." She limped toward him. "You have no idea what you've done."

"My Lady, we *did* uncover the murderer," Pan protested.

"And you've destroyed ten years of peace. Before Magdalia Nofski returned, we were at *war* with the ferals. You think 'snow-covered tents' are hard to find? The coyotes set hothead traps. They know the trees. They're a pack of ghosts for all the good tracking does." She paused, regaining her composure with a sigh.

"I'll send an envoy to the ferals. If Gordon were here… well," she looked to her wiry falcon assistant. "I suppose I'll have to make do with what I've got. Lowder, gather the Table. I want a team ready to meet the ferals in the next hour."

"We'd be happy to do any outreaching…" Conway started.

"You have done quite enough," Lady Claythorne interrupted. "I want you and your team — and the children," she gestured to the apprentices, "out of here tomorrow morning."

"May I reiterate," Conway said, "that my team apprehended the murderer. We did so with minimal force, and in only a few hours."

Lady Claythorne clicked her way toward Conway again. He was a head taller than she, but her aged face was fierce, tough as iron, and he faltered in his glare. "If Magdalia Nofski had something to hide," she said, her voice firm and level, "it would have been hidden."

"How can you be certain?"

"Because Magdalia Nofski," Claythorne explained, "is a clairvoyant. She sees events before they unfold. She will have known you were coming before *you* did, and yet she did not order the evidence to be destroyed. Do you see the paradox?"

"My Lady," Conway started, but Claythorne held up a paw to silence him.

"The coyote will remain here for questioning." She began limping away, speaking over her shoulder as she left. "You will leave in the morning."

The hall seemed to echo with the *click* of Lady Claythorne's cane as she strode away.

Jack turned toward Conway and smiled. "Guess you could have used a sidekick after all."

He didn't know why he'd said it; a feeble attempt at levity, perhaps, but he knew instantly that he'd said the wrong thing. The look Conway gave him was of deepest disgust, a look he'd never seen on the hero's face before. "Exactly what is it that you think *you* could have done, *Jack*?"

Jack felt his ears droop. "I… nothing. Nothing."

"Nothing," Conway agreed. The jackrabbit, Pan, stared at Jack with a furrowed brow, while Dixon smiled broadly, as if in amused disbelief at what he had just heard. The team followed Conway out of the Hall, leaving a ringing silence in their wake.

Hours later, Jack lay awake in his bed. It was dark, with only moonlight through two narrow windows, and dying embers in the fireplace between them. For the second night, they'd found a fire crackling there, and for the second night, Willie insisted they extinguish it. "Do you have any idea what that will do to my skin?" he had groused.

Jack stared blankly at the glowing embers, pulling the quilt tight around him and trying to forget the look Conway had given him. He didn't care much about what Pan or Dixon thought, but the more he knew Firebird, the more he came to respect him, even feel a sort of fandom toward him. Being made his sidekick, no matter how temporarily, still felt like some kind of daydream. "Exactly what is it that you think *you* could have done, Jack?" he had asked. And then, "Nothing." The words came back to him loudly in the dim quiet, and every time he thought of them, he felt another punch to the gut.

He pushed his ears back and looked around the room. Sprint and Hoover were asleep in beds against the opposite wall, Willie in the bed to his right. A row of thick, wool-lined coats hung from hooks next to a heavy oak door. They'd been provided the previous night, presumably by the same housekeepers that had lit the fire. And much like the fire, they wouldn't get to serve their purpose.

Of course, neither would the apprentices. Their first — and perhaps *only* — "mission" wasn't much of a mission at all. It wasn't much of an adventure, either. Fly to Safehaven, be babysat, fly home. Was it because of Jack? Because he shared a species with the victims? Or was there just something about him; something in need of coddling, protection? Dr. Walraven had kept him away from Triarch; hadn't wanted to take him to Animal Control; had, for some reason, wanted to bring him here instead. For what?

His thoughts were interrupted by a metallic grinding sound. It reminded him of the trash compactor back at the Honey Sap. The sound was joined by a soft crunching — that sound he recognized. It was the crunch of something pressing into snow. There was another grinding. Another crunching. Footsteps. Heavy, mechanical footsteps.

Kicking the quilt off, he moved to the window to the left of the fireplace. Several floors below was the cement ramp that sloped down into Munitions. The snow that mounted up on either side of the ramp was deep, burying the first two floors of the fort.

He traced the snow-plowed cement with his eyes. The ramp ended at a T junction, carving a trench-like road that ran parallel to the fort. To the left, a section of the trench wall had collapsed, like a birthday cake that had been scooped at by a toddler. Along this newly formed trail, two of the mechanical Ice Cats were crunching their way through the snow, away from the fort and into the darkness.

There was a louder grinding directly below him. He flattened his nose against the cold glass and peered straight down. A third

Ice Cat was stomping its way up the ramp, its caged cockpit rattling with each mechanical step.

But there was something odd about this. It was early, maybe three in the morning. Admittedly, Jack didn't know anything about how things were done here at Fort Safehaven. Maybe they plowed the roads this early. But none of these Ice Cats were adorned with the giant shovels he had seen before. The early hour and the lack of shovels weren't what bothered Jack. What bothered him was that, despite the darkness of the early morning, neither of the machines in the distance, nor the one below him, had any lights on. Jack was certain he'd seen headlights and little orange lights along the legs when they'd been up close to the Ice Cats. But the further machines were now completely hidden in darkness, and as the nearer machine reached the top of the ramp and turned left, its pilot turned his head toward the fort. In the light cast from the rooftop, Jack could make out the face of Greenridge, the grizzly general. There was something suspicious in that look, as if he was ensuring he hadn't been seen or followed.

*Exactly what is it that you think you could have done, Jack?*

As he watched Greenridge follow the other Ice Cats into the snowy darkness, Jack thought of the response he had given. *Nothing.*

Well, perhaps it was time to do *something.*

## Chapter Twenty-Six

## INTO THE WOODS

Sprint and Jack were practically bouncing on their paws at the end of Maddie's bed, trying to wake her. Willie leaned against the door frame, arms folded across his chest. Hoover hadn't dared come into the room at all.

It had taken a lot of smooth talking on Jack's part to convince them that Greenridge was up to something, that they should follow him and, as Lady Claythorne had so adamantly demanded, "investigate." But Jack knew the real trick was going to be convincing Maddie to go along with the plan. She'd be furious at first, he was sure of that much, but the reasoning he'd used with the others had worked, and now he had them on his side.

Despite the bouncing mattress, Maddie woke slowly at first, looking confused. When she saw Jack and Sprint at the end of her bed, she shuffled back against the headboard, pulling the quilt to her shoulders. "What are you guys doing in here?" she asked, looking both confused and alarmed. "Why are you wearing those coats?"

"We're going out," Sprint said.

"Going... what? Where?" She turned to her bedside clock, which read "5:28 AM", then groaned and flopped back down onto her pillow, her face buried in an elbow.

"Greenridge is up to something," Jack said. "We... *I* saw him take an Ice Cat into the woods. I don't know what for, but he's definitely up to something."

"So let him be up to it," Maddie said, her voice muffled by her arm.

"We're going to follow him," Sprint said.

Maddie dropped her arm and stared, bewildered, at Sprint. "Are you out of your bushy-tailed mind? 'Follow him'? Follow him where?"

"Wherever he's going," Jack supplied. "To see what he's doing."

"He's not doing anything," Maddie groaned in irritation. "He's probably just plowing the road."

"No," Jack said. "He was headed *up* the mountain. All the roads go *down*."

"You'll get kicked out," Maddie said, looking past them, to the door where Willie stood. "You *do* realize that, right? If you get caught, you'll get kicked out. All four of you." She turned on her side, away from them. "Good luck with that."

"You mean all *five* of us," Jack corrected her. "Team evaluation and all that."

Maddie rolled over again in her bed. The look she gave him was of purest venom.

The stairwell leading to Munitions was just around the corner from their rooms — Peter had pointed that out during their tour. They found it, descended, and gasped at the sudden chill as they entered the enormous room. The lights had been turned back off, but a yellow light from the access ramp illuminated what they were looking for: a row of snowmobiles lined up before the farther Ice Cats.

"I don't know," Hoover said as they drew near. "I mean, we could get in *real* trouble for this."

"Relax, Hooves," Sprint said. "Peter said these were for *everybody's* use."

"Yeah, but..."

"Let's go," Willie interjected, throwing a leg over the nearest of the machines and turning the key. The motor wasn't loud, but it echoed in the quiet of this dark room.

"Is it just me," Maddie said, looking toward the lit ramp, "or does this seem too easy. I mean they can't leave this stuff unguarded all the time."

Jack thought she had a point. This room was where they kept their weapons and vehicles. There was an iron gate along the ramp opening, the kind that rolls downward like a garage door. But Greenridge had left it wide open, as though he didn't care who came out — or in.

But despite the nervousness they all felt, within moments they were gliding across the powdery snow, skirting the edge of the lumpy trail the Ice Cats had carved. They left the headlights off, not wanting to be spotted, but it was a full moon, or nearly, and it wasn't hard to follow the jagged trench. They cut between snow covered pines, avoiding the bowls beneath them where the snow had not fallen.

They were ascending the mountain at a gradual climb, but soon it tapered off, and they found themselves gliding along a flat expanse between trees. The peak of the neighboring mountain was just visible ahead, connecting halfway down with a stark horizontal line. Jack recognized the striking image — this was Hard Stop, the gate Peter had described. It had been depicted in a tapestry outside of the Great Hall. Only the gate that stretched between the peaks was more enormous and imposing than any image could convey, even from several miles off. Whether it was of steel or wood or stone, Jack couldn't tell — in the faint moonlight it looked solid black.

Willie brought his snowmobile to a sudden stop. Maddie, seated behind him, turned to the others and waved emphatically for them to do the same. They let their motors burp to a stall. Jack, seated behind Sprint, perked his ears up, hearing nothing but the faint sound of crashing water — there was a river nearby.

He followed as Sprint dismounted, sinking knee deep in the snow and trudging toward Willie and Maddie.

"What is it?" Sprint asked.

Willie put a long finger to his mouth, then pointed ahead. The snow sloped modestly downward. Fifty yards along, the Ice Cat trail peeled left, vanishing behind a cluster of tall boulders. There, jutting out from behind the rocks, the rear legs of an Ice Cat were just visible.

"Good eye," Sprint whispered.

Together, they pushed the three snowmobiles to their left behind a group of trees with low foliage. On the other side of the trees, the snow sloped steeply downward, and the trail they had been following doubled back around, making a U shape, with the abandoned Ice Cat at the apex.

"Look!" Maddie whispered, pointing toward the lower trail. The second and third Ice Cats were standing several yards into the snow, apparently vacant.

The group stumbled gracelessly down the hill, crossed the path, and moved toward the Ice Cats. The cages around the cockpits were swung upward, and small craters indicated where the drivers had dropped down into the snow.

They moved cautiously between the machines, Willie in the lead. Jack felt as though he was passing between two sentinels, the kind that might strike him down if he was found to be unworthy. This was the closest he had been to the Ice Cats. They stood on mechanical legs as thick as tree trunks; their underbellies higher than the tips of Jack's ears.

An uneven line of footprints cut between the trees ahead. They followed. At first, they attempted to keep inside of the existing prints, but Hoover had all the balance of an egg on its nose, and soon they gave up, although they maintained a single file line all the same.

Willie stopped abruptly. Maddie bumped right into him, and was midway through blurting out "Watch it," when he quickly turned and clamped his over-long fingers over her muzzle. She jerked away, her eyes like daggers. He pointed to the side of his head, which Jack understood to mean "Listen." Jack held his breath, ears perked high, and heard it immediately. The deep, booming voice of Greenridge was coming from just over the brow of the small hill ahead. The words were indistinguishable, but he sounded angry. The group exchanged looks of apprehension and nervous excitement — all except for Maddie, who maintained a vigil of resentful compliance.

They reached a downward slope in the snow too steep to walk. The footprints they had been following ended here, transitioning to a thick trail that plowed thirty feet downward, then turned once more into footprints that disappeared into a cluster of trees at the base of the slope.

The snow gave way beneath Willie. Quickly, his elastic pink tongue shot from his mouth, connecting with a fir tree to their right. He hung over the ledge at an angle, flailing his arms for balance "That wath clothe," he said around his extended tongue, accepting Sprint's paw as the squirrel pulled him back up.

"Yeth it wath," Sprint agreed, releasing his grip on Willie and looking once more over the edge. "Looks like they slid," he said, observing the trails running down the hill.

Retracting his tongue with a snap, Willie looked once more down the slope. "We'll have to do the same," he said, picking a pine needle from his mouth.

"Huh uh," Maddie protested. "No way."

"It's a long way down," Hoover said. "How are we going to get back up?"

"Fine," Willie said. "You two stay here. Jack? Sprint?" he added, looking at them with an expression that said "are you going to wimp out, too?"

"I'm in," Sprint said. "Snuffles, you stay here and keep an eye out. Probably better that way."

Jack was the last to slide down the hill. He picked up speed quicker than he'd expected, his stomach lurching, but the ground leveled off again, and he plowed into a small bank of snow.

"First place," Sprint whispered, raising his paws over his head in mock celebration. "You passed Willie's mark by a full ten feet!"

"Shhhhh," Willie hissed.

The voices were clearer now, just on the other side of the trees. The trio moved forward, catching the end of something Greenridge was saying. "I know that Gordon was no fool. Even so, he couldn't have stopped us. But his murder has summoned those who can."

"Have faith," said a second voice. It was a horrible sound, dry and raspy, as if the speaker was inhaling at the same time. "Vanguard is here because I wanted them here."

Willie, Sprint, and Jack dropped down into a snow bowl beneath a tree. They peeked cautiously over the opposite side like soldiers in a trench. Jack could see Greenridge now, just ahead with his back to them. His coat looked as large as a tent, the haunch of his neck pronounced by a wool-lined hood. He was flanked by two Safehaven falcons. "It's my head on the chopping block here," he said. "If Claythorne realizes the pelts had been planted…"

"Everything has now fallen into place," the voice interrupted. "Vanguard are leaving in the morning. The one you need has been delivered to you. I see no reason why Claythorne should live to see another sunset."

"The one I need?" Greenridge asked. "The boy; the rabbit? How can I be sure he's the one?"

"Oh, he is the one," the voice said. "When you have him, and when Claythorne is dead, you will fire a green flare into the sky. My army awaits this signal."

Jack's eyes darted around, searching for the source of the voice. At first, he saw only the two falcons on either side of Greenridge.

"All fours," Willie swore under his breath, sounding as if he was going to be sick.

"What?" Jack whispered. Then he saw it. At the lip of a small snowbank, three shadows stood framed against the moonlight, looming down upon Greenridge and his men. At the center was a tall, square shouldered figure, a cloak of fur wrapped around him like a sleeping bat's wings. From the front of the cloak, a horned, chalk-white skull protruded on a vulture's neck, below which a skeletal arm extended, clutching something that looked like a potato sack.

But even more strange and unsettling than this monstrous figure were the creatures that stood to its right and left. They were much smaller, naked, pink and bald. They stood limply, off balance, as if they were suspended on strings reaching down from the gray clouds above. Most horribly of all, a flat space extended from one shoulder to the other; they were headless.

Jack felt his knees weaken, and he folded his head into his arms against the brim of the bowl. Sprint ducked down too, but Willie stayed upright, a look of pained disgust on his face.

The raspy voice was speaking again, responding to something Greenridge had said. "You don't understand the Red Teeth. Their commitment is unyielding. For an entire year, you've kept them waiting. Some of the weaker ones have been sacrificed to the meager rations. The faction grows stronger by ebbing off the weak, but it grows smaller, too. I can't deny that they might not feel so warmly toward you once they're on this side of the gate."

"Then why should we let them in at all?" another voice asked. It was familiar; the oily voice of Lady Claythorne's falcon assistant. Greenridge growled a hush, but the eerie voice of the skull creature laughed. The sound was chilling, and despite his fear, Jack pushed himself up slowly and peaked over the edge of the bowl.

The headless figures were walking — stumbling — toward the falcon, who took a single step backward. They glistened in the moonlight, shiny and smooth, like two headless pink frogs. They bobbed weirdly up to the falcon and caught him under the wings with surprising speed. He struggled to pull away as they dragged him forward.

"Because there is no rock, no nest, no god forsaken cave that can hide you from me," the voice said. To Jack's surprise, the voice seemed to come not from the horned skull, but from the bag it carried. A second skeletal arm protruded from the cloak, holding a jagged knife. "I am the eyes of the dead," the rasping voice said. It sounded like an incantation. "The manipulator of the dead."

The falcon cried out in pain as the pink creatures jerked his head roughly backward, exposing his feathered throat.

The skull creature raised the dagger high into the air. "I am the maker of the dead."

"No!" Jack yelled.

It just came out; he hadn't even felt the cry forming. The horned skull snapped in his direction, the dagger still high in the air.

The three of them dropped down behind the edge of the bowl. Willie turned to him, eyes wide and furious.

There was a moment of silence, only the sound of pine needles brushing each other on the wind. And then the raspy voice spoke.

"Kill them."

# Chapter Twenty-Seven
## JAGGED TOOTH

Willie was the first to move. He sprang from the hole and into the clearing. Sprint blasted off, plowing through the snow. Jack stood and trudged after them. He felt heavy and sluggish in the powdery snow, as if running in a dream.

Ahead, he saw Sprint arrive at the slope. He crouched, then ran full tilt, moving effortlessly up the incline.

Willie arrived next, squatted, and sprang up the slope in one great bound, disappearing over the crest.

Jack reached the base, charging forward. He got a good start, upright at first, then using his paws as the hill steepened. He lost momentum, clawing desperately at the snow, slipping downward, taking a panicked peek over his shoulder. Greenridge came to a stop at the base, his arms stretched like the jaws of some hungry beast. Jack kicked uselessly, sliding closer and closer.

Something pink and sticky collided with his shoulder. He was jerked roughly upward, pulled through space like a fish on a hook. The slope passed beneath him in a blur. He flew up over the edge of the hill, then crashed down into the snow.

The pink object released his jacket, snapping away quickly and reentering Willie's open mouth. The frog let out a disgusted groan, and swatted at his own tongue. "Don't *ever* make me do that again," he said, repulsed.

"What happened?" Maddie demanded.

"Ask Jack," Willie said.

Jack felt his cheeks burn. "He was about to kill—"

"Guys, can we do this later?" Sprint said. He'd taken Hoover by the crook of his elbow and was leading him toward the pathway. "We still have another hill to climb, remember."

They passed between the Ice Cats, crossed the trail and began up the incline. This hill wasn't as steep, with rocks and trees to aid their progress, and soon enough they were at their snowmobiles.

"Let's get out of here before one of those things eats us," Sprint said.

"How they gonna eat us," Willie said, mounting the snowmobile behind Maddie. "They ain't got no heads."

"Did you just hear yourself?" Sprint asked as Jack mounted the seat behind him. "*They ain't got no heads?* How does that make it better?"

There was a loud *crack* from the hill below, like a blast of compressed air, then the coppery sound of cable unspooling. Turning, Jack looked just in time to see a silver object flying up between the trees.

"Look out!" Sprint cried. He and Jack dove off the snowmobile in opposite directions just as the object crashed into the vehicle's seat. It didn't crush it, but closed around it like a claw in an arcade game. The cable snapped tight, dragging the snowmobile toward the edge of the hill. Jack, who lay between the snowmobile and hill, scrambled to get out from behind it, but the snow beneath him gave way, and he tumbled over the edge.

He was somersaulting backward, head over heels. He struggled to stop himself, to roll onto his stomach. The snowmobile was tumbling after him, crashing into the ground every few feet.

He slammed into the lower pathway on his side, his head narrowly missing a protruding boulder. The full weight of the snowmobile crashed onto the boulder, mere inches above Jack's face.

The metal claw slithered through the snow, re-spooling on its cable until it reconnected with the outstretched front leg of the Ice Cat. The grizzly was strapped into the pilot seat at the head of the machine. "After the others," he barked, grinning down at Jack from between the cage bars. "The rabbit's mine."

There was another sound. He'd heard it when they'd arrived — maybe he'd been hearing it this whole time. It was pronounced now, as if someone had slid the volume up. As if it was beckoning for his attention.

It was the cackling sound of water; more specifically, of a river. Unsure of exactly why he was doing it, Jack stood on wobbly legs, gained his balance, and bolted toward the sound. It was just beyond the trees ahead, at the U bend in the path where the first Ice Cat had stood. The Ice Cat was gone, after the others perhaps.

He crossed the path, passing between a row of trees. They grew closer together here — he could outstretch his paws and brush the tree on either side of him. They formed a single line, a perimeter on the other side of which Jack came to a sudden, off-balance halt. He stood at the edge of a ravine, looking down at blue-gray walls of boulders as big as cars. To the right, thousands of gallons spilled over a dam of river-smoothed logs. They seemed to have been piling up here for years, maybe centuries. The water poured over and between them, plummeting into a vaporous cloud that rose up from the ravine to Jack's nostrils. After the fall, the river roared and spat and slammed its fists against jagged rocks and pieces of tree like upturned spears.

He was cornered.

And then, for the briefest moment, something caught his eye. It had made a movement at the crest of the opposite wall. When he looked again, it was gone, but he could swear he'd seen gleaming green eyes.

*Crash!* The heavy metal claw of the Ice Cat slammed down behind him, so close that he felt the swoosh of the wind. The arm raised, then slammed down a second time. The Ice Cat was wedged between the trees; a great metal beast swatting hungrily at its prey, just out of reach.

Heart thumping, mind racing, Jack stepped carefully to the edge and looked down. It wasn't scalable, not by someone without experience, or Willie's sticky fingers.

Greenridge had withdrawn from the gap. He drove the machine up against the rightmost tree, placing the enormous metal claws against its trunk. The hydraulic whine it made grew louder, until it was joined by the creaking and snapping of wood. Bits of bark began to fall from the tree, then the whole thing began to bow toward the river.

There was a final crack, then a crescendo of splintering snaps as the tree slowly toppled, nosing into the ravine. Jack threw his arms over his head, although the tree's lower end crashed down several feet to his left.

The Ice Cat mounted the stump, Greenridge's mad eyes fixed on him.

He turned toward the ravine. Jumping might not be a more pleasant way to die, but it was a less sure death than waiting on Greenridge. Weak kneed, he stepped to the edge and peered once more down into the dark chasm.

The rocks below were jagged, a thousand blue-gray teeth waiting for Jack to jump into their maw. Even the mist rising out of the pit looked like icy breath, curling around the downward sloping body of the fallen tree, which spanned the gap as if pinning the ravine's jaws open.

The tree!

It sloped downward, its top end folded against the boulders on the opposite wall. He would have to fight the limbs to get across, have to climb the wall once he got there. But it was his best hope, his *only* hope.

He leapt at the trunk, sliding back off on his first attempt. He tried again, this time digging his claws into the bark. He felt the sharp sting of his own weight tugging at his fingertips, but he maintained his grip, struggled upward, and threw an arm over the top. There was a heavy jolt, and he almost slipped back off. The Ice Cat had mounted the tree, climbing up the splintered end, its metal claws crushing into the bark with vice-like strength.

Pushing himself to stand, he adjusted the messenger bag and started down the angled surface of the tree. Balance wasn't difficult — the trunk was broad enough — but the angle was steep, and every step the Ice Cat took made the tree buckle.

He was halfway across now, no longer willing himself to look down. Naked trunk was replaced by branches thicker than his arms, their foliage a dense network of green needles. He thrust himself headfirst into their midst, pushing aside smaller limbs with his outstretched paws. The branches stood so high, so full, that once he was deep within them, he could barely see through the darkness and the cloud of mist.

Behind him, branches collapsed as the Ice Cat stomped through them like a plow in tall grass.

He quickened pace. Early daylight pressed through the foliage ahead, the stone wall peeking between limbs.

The tree rattled heavier than ever. The loud crunching of branches was joined by a low, slow splintering sound. The tree was beginning to give way beneath the Ice Cat's weight.

He swung around the left side of a thick branch. The right side of another. He reached the wall. Black crevices cut between the large boulders, enabling him a hold, first with his paws, then, tentatively, his feet.

The sound of compressed air once more, then a metal *clank* as the Ice Cat's grappling claw connected with the wall somewhere above him. The cable snapped tight, and a boulder jerked just overhead. It pivoted sideways like a loose tooth. With a final jolt, the boulder was pulled free. It plummeted over his shoulder, nearly clipping him.

He lost his grip.

The mist enveloped him as he fell, his arms swinging wildly. With an abrupt jerk, he came to a painful halt.

It was the Ice Cat's grappling claw. The strap of his bag had snagged on it, catching Jack by the armpit. He threw his other arm around and hugged the bag, then looked upward. The thick black line of the fallen tree was broken by the Ice Cat, silhouetted against the faint morning light. It leaned over the side of the tree, its grappling arm outstretched toward Jack.

"You're still alive down there?" Greenridge roared, his voice intermingled with the hissing of mist and rapids. "You're luckier than I'd hoped! Have y'up in a minute." The winch whined as Jack began to rise upward, pulled toward the machine like a meal on a dumbwaiter.

But the winch stopped suddenly, and Jack began to swing like a pendulum. Hugging his bag tighter, he turned upward to see that some kind of struggle was happening overhead. A second figure had mounted the body of the Ice Cat, and Greenridge had flung the cage enclosure upward, struggling with one paw to unclasp his restraints while fending off the figure with his other.

The wedged tree groaned ominously, sagging visibly under the weight of the machine.

Jack looked desperately toward the ravine wall. It was too far to reach, even to jump, and the boulders down here were much larger. He would have a hard time finding a hold.

There was a roar — it didn't sound like Greenridge — and the second figure tumbled over the side of the Ice Cat, catching wildly onto the trunk of the tree with what must have been long, powerful claws. The figure began to scramble toward the machine again, but stopped suddenly and looked downward. From the darkness of a hood, two reflective green eyes peered down at Jack. Changing direction, the figure descended the curved body of the tree, dangling from its underside, then leaping skillfully to the grappling cable.

Jack moaned in fear, looking desperately around for anywhere to go. The morning light now illuminated the jagged rocks of the river below, teeth of a frothy monster just waiting for Jack to gain his nerve and jump.

But before he could make a move, the hooded figure was on him. He threw a desperate kick, catching the figure in the groin.

The figure barked out in pain. "Cut it out, kid. I'm trying to save you."

Jack froze, mid struggle. The face was of a lion. A strikingly, impossibly familiar lion.

The log sagged further, dropping them another few feet.

## CHAPTER TWENTY-SEVEN

"It's not going to hold," the lion said. "Move to my back."

Jack threw an arm around the lion's shoulder, awkwardly climbing over him. His fingers felt weak, his elbows wobbling with delayed shock. He wrapped his arms around the neck, clasping his paws together.

The lion kicked his legs forward, then back, then forward again. After a few attempts, they began to swing. He pushed forward, back, forward, back. They were swinging wide now, the mist wisping around Jack's face. They arched backward. The lion's muscles tighten at the top of the swing.

"Hold on tight!" he yelled. He kicked his legs forward again.

They swung quickly through the mist. The lion pulled upward. Pounced. Released the cable.

They flew through the air. With a sudden, final jolt, they slammed against the far wall of the ravine, the lion's thick, black claws digging into the surface, struggling for purchase.

There was a loud crack overhead. Greenridge roared. The sound was angry and afraid, and for a wild moment Jack imagined the bear flying through the air toward them. But as the two halves of the tree fell, they clapped together like the jaws of an enormous crocodile, crushing the Ice Cat between them. There was a final splashing, crashing, metal rending explosion of sound. Jack turned in time to watch the limp limbs of the Ice Cat tumble away down the river.

There was silence for a moment. Relative silence, the kind where the growling river and fizzing mist were like the white noise of a television that had lost its signal.

And then there was a crack, like a gunshot. Something heavy and black shot past, just over their heads.

The lion looked upward, then turned his head sharply to the right. Jack, following his gaze, saw the towering face of the waterfall, its countless logs piled high above their heads. But at one spot, just above them, water gushed outward from a gap between logs, like a child's missing tooth.

The dam began to moan, a thousand voices groaning in protest. Then plunking sounds as several logs shifted suddenly, ominously forward.

The lion turned upward once more. Jack followed his gaze again. Halfway up the ravine wall, a gap was left where Greenridge had dislodged the boulder.

With surprising strength and agility, the lion began paw-over-paw up the wall.

The logs groaned louder. Water spat through wounds opening in the dam face.

They were nearly there. Up and up. Only a few stones left.

Another gunshot crack. A log flew just below their feet, connecting with the wall, taking a chunk of stone with it.

The lion roared; a deep, wildcat roar. He lunged, threw his arms into the open gap, struggled upward.

Two more loud cracks. Then three. Four. Then, as Jack was pulled up and into the muddy smelling crevice, there began a chorus of plunking, crashing, thudding, and banging. The dam gave way completely. Endless logs tumbled past them, shutting them into momentary darkness.

## Chapter Twenty-Eight

## PINE CREEK

The water subsided, and they climbed the rest of the way up the ravine wall. When they reached the top, Jack dropped into the snow and looked out to his right. A frozen lake twinkled in the early morning light, small drifts of ice floating gradually to the lip of the waterfall, picking up speed and slipping over the edge. For some reason, the shattered ice made him think of his friends, and his happiness at surviving was replaced by a plummeting sensation in his stomach.

The lion stepped to a nearby tree, stooped, and snatched up a rucksack that had been laying there. As he threw it over his shoulder, his hood fell backward. There were no ropes of dread locked mane. There was no mane at all. As he turned, Jack saw that he was slender, with high cheekbones and gaunt features. His tall frame was exaggerated by narrow shoulders and limbs more slender than any lion Jack had ever seen. He looked half starved.

Jack hadn't believed he was King — not really — but the illusion of King's likeness ended when the lion spoke. His voice was not the smoky baritone of Aaron Harding, but a high, soft tenor.

"Who are you? You're not a local." This second part wasn't a question. He looked Jack over, then shrugged off his rucksack, unclasped it, and rummaged around inside. "Take off your coat," he said. He withdrew a tightly woven blanket and tossed it to Jack.

Jack did as he was told, then wrapped himself in the blanket. "Thank you," he said. "I'm Jack. I'm… I came here with Animal Control. We were investigating the murders."

The lion shouldered the sack once more, then turned and started walking, indicating with his head that Jack should follow. "Mystery solved," he said. "Any idea what Greenridge wanted with you?"

Jack trudged after him, drawing the blanket tightly around himself. It made him think, briefly, of the fur cloak the horned creature had been wearing. He considered the strange appearance must be some kind of costume. But the word that came to his mind wasn't *costume*. It was *puppet*, and although it made no sense to him, there was a strange certainty in the word.

He shook his head. "I… we followed him into the woods. My friends and I." He paused, afraid to ask the question, afraid of what the answer might be. "Did you… see anyone else?"

"No," the lion said. "Why was Greenridge after you?"

"He wasn't after me, specifically. He was after all of us."

"Trust me, kid," the lion said without glancing over his shoulder, "I know an obsession. Greenridge was after *you*. Whatever he wanted you for, it's the reason all the other rabbits have died. Did he lure you out here or something?"

"No," Jack said. "He was meeting someone… well, something." The word *puppet* came back to him. "It was a sort of creature. Like a bull or something, but… dead. Instead of a head, it…"

"It had a skull?" the lion asked, turning sharply toward Jack, his eyes suddenly intense. "Big, circular eye sockets, like a baboon with horns?"

Surprised, Jack nodded.

"And what did he want? Was he looking for me? Did he say my name?" He took an aggressive step toward Jack. "Think! Did he say my name?"

"I don't think so," Jack stammered. "I don't… I'm sorry, I don't know your name."

The lion's mouth worked silently for a moment. Then he gave a curt nod and turned once more away. "Let's get you back."

Jack had to jog to keep up, hugging the blanket around himself. "How did you know? That I wasn't a local, I mean."

"Your fur," the lion said without looking back. "You haven't been here long enough for your fur to turn white. Never seen a butterscotch snowshoe up here."

"Oh," Jack said. Now that he mentioned it, it seemed obvious. He remembered Dixon jerking his arm up against those horrible pelts. Exactly the same texture and length, but the pelts had been solid white.

They headed down the mountain, skirting the edge of the river. The crunch of their footsteps was the only conversation for a long while. Then Jack built up the courage to ask another question. "The skull creature; you know him?"

The lion didn't respond.

"He said something about an army," Jack continued. Then the words came back to him. "The Red Teeth! He said the Red Teeth were waiting at a gate."

"The Red Teeth are extinct," the lion said.

Jack considered this. What had that mole said? The one at the Archive. Pitfall was her name. "That's right," he said, remembering. "King destroyed them. The ones that survived, he chased back to Kerccia, but even their own country denounced them. But they're here. The skull creature definitely said *the Red Teeth*."

"That's impossible," the lion said.

For the first time, Jack remembered something President Brisk had said. Not Brisk himself, but the horribly transfigured creature he had appeared as under the influence of the key. *"Red Teeth. Red Teeth. Red Teeth."* Jack had learned later that the key shows what is on someone's heart. Was Brisk a member of the Red Teeth, then? Or perhaps sympathetic to their goals? Unconsciously, Jack withdrew the key from his pocket, turning it over in his paw beneath the cover of the blanket.

"Anyway," he started again, his mind too busy to stay silent, "I haven't thanked you for saving me."

"Forget it," the lion said.

"No, seriously," Jack started again. "You risked your life for me. If you hadn't…"

"I said forget it," the lion barked. He whirled on Jack, and for a wild moment, Jack thought he might tackle him and took a step back. He felt something plunk to the ground, hitting one of his feet. But before he could react, the lion lunged at the object, scooped it up, and thrust it into Jack's face. "Where did you get this?" he snarled. It was the brass key, which Jack had been absently clutching. "I said where did you get this?" the lion roared, grabbing Jack by the throat and slamming him against the trunk of a tree so hard, snow cascaded from the lowest branches.

But immediately, a change came over him. Not the kind of change Jack had seen in Maddie or the President, morphing into unworldly creatures. This change was more real, more internal. It was as if the anger and aggression had been replaced by something else, some kind of grim comprehension, like he was seeing Jack clearly for the first time. He looked Jack up and down, his mouth forming words he did not voice. His grip loosened, and he stood upright. "Don't drop this again," he said, thrusting the key at Jack. Then he turned, adjusted his rucksack, and continued down the hill. "Come on," he ordered over his shoulder.

Nonplussed and shaken, Jack pocketed the key and followed.

They walked in silence. Jack had much more trouble than the lion in vaulting the fallen trees and descending the rock faces they came upon. They walked across a bed of river-smoothed stones, a trickling stream weaving through its center. The lion had to help Jack up the opposite bank.

Eventually, the trees opened to a broad valley, ornamented in the pleasant sort of village that belonged on a post card. A tall steeple pointed at the sky from a quaint white chapel. The windows of a shop declared *Deli & Bakery* in big blue letters, the paint beginning to chip away.

They saw only moderate signs of life at first. The lights of the deli were on, and Jack espied shadowy figures walking around inside. A plump chinchilla in an apron was sweeping the covered patio of a shop called *The Dust Bath*. When he spotted them, he stared for a moment, then stepped into his shop, a bell tinkling as he entered.

"Kind of a quiet town," Jack said, breaking the silence as they moved across an icy parking lot.

"They're afraid," the lion said. "There's a killer on the loose." He looked down at Jack, who now walked alongside him. For the first time, he cracked a small smile. "And we don't exactly look subtle."

This was true, Jack thought. The lion, while he no longer wore a hood, was dressed more similarly to the feral Conway had arrested than to the townsfolk that lived here. He, Jack, was still draped in the blanket, looking he supposed like the victim of a house fire.

The street connected with a broader road that wound east, up the base of the mountain. Jack traced it with his eyes. It cut between tall trees, curved right, and disappeared behind them. High above, pressing out of the woods like a mask on the mountain's face, Fort Safehaven looked down upon Pine Creek. It looked as big as a castle to Jack, who had only seen it at night and from too close up to appreciate its magnitude.

It also looked very far away. "We still have to walk all of that?" he asked.

"Walk?" the lion repeated. "No. This way." He approached a plain gray building, its small parking lot cracked and potholed, with painted lines that had almost entirely faded.

Inside, the lobby was narrow, with a single potted plant to one side, and a single restroom door to the other. The shop smelled of rubber and tobacco, and nearly every surface looked as though the dust had become permanently affixed. Country music was playing somewhere in the back, along with the whine of a power tool. Black letters stenciled on the wall behind the counter read PUCHERELLI'S PINE CREEK TOW.

The lion clapped his paw down on a service bell. It chimed loudly. "Yep!" called a voice from the back room. "Be right up."

Jack stared at the stenciled sign. "Pine Creek," he read out loud. "How can we be in Pine Creek? We never crossed the river."

The lion glanced at him briefly, then leaned into his elbows against the counter and looked straight ahead.

Jack racked his brain. He couldn't remember ever crossing any bridges. They'd crossed over several fallen trees, but none of them had been bridging a river. The only water he could remember crossing was that damp riverbed with the small stream. How were they now back on the other side of the river?

Behind the counter, a door with a porthole window swung open, and out stepped a weasel in blue coveralls. "What can I do…" he started, but he fell silent at the sight of the lion. "What in the name of King Sindle's magical manure brings *you* into the land of the living?" the weasel asked, wringing his paws in an oil stained towel. His eyes fell on Jack. "Looks like a newcomer. Bad time for a snowshoe to come to Pine Creek," he said. Then his eyes grew wide, and he looked back at the lion. "Hey. He's… he's not part of that whole thing, is he?"

"It's a long story, Pooch," the lion said. "Right now, we need a ride up to the fort."

"Safehaven?" the weasel said in surprise. "You so sure that's a good idea? You so sure they won't just nail you to the wall up there? Haven't you got yourself in enough trouble with them?"

"Well, I'm either out of it, or I'm in a whole lot more. I killed Harland Greenridge this morning."

The weasel leaned back, his bulgy eyes widening. "You killed Greenridge?" He drummed his claws on the counter top, chewing on his lower lip. "I can't help you. Guilt by association. I got a kid to feed, man."

"They won't even know yet." The lion jerked his head toward Jack. "He was trying to kill the rabbit. I stopped him. If I got a little revenge on the side, well, that's just a bonus."

"Kill the rabbit?" Pooch said, amazed. "So was Greenridge the one killing all the rabbits then?"

"I don't know," the lion answered. "I don't really care. I need to get the kid back up to the fort and get out of there before nightfall. You got a truck I can take?"

The weasel continued to drum his fingers nervously. "I don't know," he said. "I owe you one, I know that… but this… this is a lot to ask." He seemed to be struggling with himself. "I could lose my shop. Times are tough, you know."

"Tough?" the lion repeated. "I've been surviving off hot heads in a snow cave for nearly six years. And yes, you *do* owe me one; forget about your shop, you're *alive* because of me."

"I know," Pooch said, unable to meet the lion's eyes. "You're right. But if you did what you say you did, you must be out of your mind to go up to the fort." He was quiet for a moment. "I'll take the kid. I'll take him up there without you; how's that?"

The lion shook his head. "From this point on, the kid doesn't leave my sight."

The weasel let out a long, slow sigh. "Alright, Harding," he said. "I'll take you both. I've got a truck out back. Let me get some chains on it and we'll get going." He left without waiting for thanks, which the lion didn't seem likely to offer.


"This is far enough," the lion said. The brakes whined, and the truck rocked softly to a stop. He cracked open his door and stepped out into the snow.

Jack shimmied along the bench and made to follow, but the weasel made a whistling sound, as if to get his attention.

"Be careful, kid," he said in a low voice. "Harding's a good guy, but his paws are dirty, you understand me? Folks around him tend to get… well, just be careful."

Not knowing what to make of this strange advice, Jack simply nodded and lowered himself out into the snow.

They watched the truck make a three-point turn and start off down the icy road again, then turned themselves and began in the opposite direction.

Jack had intended to ask about the lion's name. Clearly, he *was* related to Aaron Harding. But the weasel's final words made him apprehensive, and he held his silence.

They didn't have to walk far before they stood at a gate made of naked tree trunks wrapped in black iron. Torch brackets were mounted on either side, but the torches were not yet lit. In the dimming light, it looked ominous.

"Hello there," a voice called from somewhere above the gate. Looking upward, Jack saw an ape in plated armor — the same armor worn by the sentries inside the fort. He was leaning over a railing just above and to the right of the gate. "What are your names and business?"

"This is Jack Robberts," Harding called up to him. "He's a guest here, up until your General Greenridge tried to kill him."

Jack thought this seemed a rather aggressive way to start things out.

"We need to speak to the Seated Lady immediately," the lion added.

The ape gaped at them for a moment, then clasped a radio on his armored shoulder, spoke a few words into it, and turned back down to them. "Wait right there," he said in a suddenly commanding voice, then disappeared behind the wall.

Snow had begun to fall. Jack hugged himself tightly, wishing he hadn't given the blanket back to the lion. "What do you think we're waiting for?" he asked through clenched teeth.

"No idea," Harding said, but he sounded uneasy, and he turned to look back down the road.

After several minutes of silence, there was a loud clattering, as though something was being removed from the gate, and then a deep groan as the doors slowly opened.

The lion moved first, and Jack followed him through the gate. As they passed beneath it, a group of guards approached, then formed a circle around them, guns poised to fire.

There was silence for a moment. Then the sound of heavy footsteps. Several guards parted, and a tall figure entered the circle.

He came to a stop before them, his large paws balled into fists as he smiled dangerously down at Jack.

"You are one lucky bunny," Greenridge said, looking Jack up and down as if he was a meal.

The flare gun looked comically small in his paw. He raised it, and fired off a single green flare.

Behind them, the gate clapped loudly shut.

## Chapter Twenty-Nine

## HARDING

The smell of moss and mildew made Jack feel like he was a mile below the earth. This sensation was aided by the stones that made up the dungeon walls, and the torture devices and swinging chains that belonged in a morbid painting of the afterlife. Peter Claythorne had said these devices were here only for historical purposes, not to be used. But then, what rules applied anymore, now that Greenridge was in charge; now that Lady Claythorne was dead.

And Claythorne was definitely dead; that much he did know. Greenridge had fired that green flare into the sky, as the horned creature had ordered.

Somehow, in all of the chaos and madness of the day, this one fact scared him the most. Claythorne had not been friendly, nor altogether likable, but from the moment she'd limped onto the landing pad, authoritative and sure, she had been a foundation. She was what held this place together. With her gone, with Greenridge now in control, the fort would be as anarchical as its tangled maze of halls. A madhouse.

Harding, who lay heaped in the corner into which he'd been thrown, let out a groan of pain.

"Shut up in there," an ape guard barked, slamming the butt of his rifle against the prison bars.

Jack turned to look at Harding. He didn't look good. When the guards had brought them down here, they had left Jack mostly alone. They'd jostled him and dragged him through the maze halls, but they'd left him unharmed. Not Harding; they'd used him as a living punching bag.

"He's hurt," Jack said to the back of the guard's head. "He needs help."

The guard adjusted his grip on his rifle, the only sign that he'd heard Jack at all.

"Jack?" came a voice to his left. Jack turned to see Mr. Behr peering at him from between the bars dividing this cell from the next. "Jack, thank goodness. I thought…"

"Mr. Behr!" Jack said in surprise, running to the bars. He hissed sympathetically when he got a closer look at the old dog. There was a gash along his muzzle, still damp with blood, and one of his eyes was swollen almost completely shut. "Mr. Behr, what happened? Where are the others?"

"The others?" Behr asked, confused. "Vanguard left, and…"

"Vanguard left?" Jack asked.

Behr nodded. "The coup was well-executed. Greenridge returned, battered up pretty bad, and fed us this story about the ferals wanting blood. He got Conway all worked up, wanting to go to war. It's brilliant, really. Get Conway and his team ready for a fight, when Claythorne wants peace. They argued for a bit, but of course Claythorne is… was in charge. She sent them packing, just like she said she would. The anax wasn't even out of sight yet. Greenridge came up behind Claythorne and…" He made a gun gesture with his finger and thumb. "*Pop*, right in the back. Coward." He shook his head in disgust. "There were a few loyalists, but they were outnumbered. The ones he kept alive," he gestured around the room. Looking around, Jack saw that several cells across from them were occupied. "Must need them or something," Behr reasoned, then paused. "It just doesn't make sense. Animal Control will find out what's happened. This isn't something they can hide. At most, there are fifty of them. They can't hold the fort forever, not against Animal Control."

"Maybe they don't have to," Jack said.

"What do you mean?"

"Maybe they don't *plan* to hold the fort." He met Behr's visible eye. "What is Safehaven?"

"It's a defense," Behr said. "Against Kerccian invasion."

"Exactly. A *plug*," he said, remembering Peter Claythorne's words, "positioned at the end of the Axe Wound."

"Which is the only way for a Kerccian army to enter Nikacia," Behr said, nodding.

"Right," Jack said. "So what if he didn't want to hold the fort. What if he wanted to uncork the bottle?"

"Kerccia," Behr responded, comprehending.

"Yeah," Jack said. It made perfect sense. Animal Control *would* come, but that would take hours, maybe days. By that time, an army could leak in. Start small.

And recruit.

"When we came back," Jack started again, "Greenridge fired a green flair into the air, to announce that Lady Claythorne was dead. But I think it was more than that. I think it was a signal, to tell the Red Teeth the time has come."

"*Whoa*, hold on Jack," Behr said, standing upright. "The Red Teeth? The Red Teeth have been extinct for forty years. King himself saw to it."

"I know," Jack said. "But the skull headed creature definitely said '*The Red Teeth*.'"

"Skull headed creature?" Behr said. He was watching Jack with concern. "Maybe you should rest."

"I don't need to rest," Jack said, flinging out his arms in frustration, forgetting to keep his voice down.

"I said quiet in there," the guard barked once more.

Jack approached Behr again. "Look, we followed Greenridge this morning. He went into the woods, he met with this skull headed creature…"

The word *puppet* came to him again.

"…and the creature told him that the Red Teeth were ready at the gate. Ask Willie. Ask Sprint. They were there; they'll tell you." He looked around the dungeon, trying to spy out the other apprentices.

"Willie and Sprint?" Behr said, confused. "Jack, I thought you… Oh Jack, I thought you already knew."

There was dead silence between them. Jack could feel his pulse rising, and a small ringing started in his left ear. "Know what?" he heard himself asking, clenching his teeth in the infinite silence that seemed to follow.

"I'm sorry Jack," Behr said as he looked slowly up at him. "Your team; they're all… they didn't make it."

The ringing was now in both ears, as though an explosion had gone off right by his head. Without knowing he was doing it,

Jack sank to the stone floor, clutching the bars that separated him from Behr.

"It's my fault," Behr said in a flat tone. "I shouldn't have got you involved. Apprentices are supposed to start on easy assignments."

Behr continued to speak, but Jack could barely hear him. A flood of images were washing through his mind. Sprint ordering up the menu after beating Jack at cards. Hoover's eyes lighting up as they stood between the skyscrapers of Triarch. Willie swatting disgustedly at his own tongue after rescuing Jack. But mostly, he thought of the angry glare Maddie had given him when he'd explained to her that she would be kicked out with the rest of them, whether or not she came along to follow Greenridge.

"No," he said. "It's my fault. This *was* an easy assignment. *Too* easy. I talked the others into going out this morning, because..." He tried to steel himself, to say the words. Conway had snapped at him, making him feel small and unimportant. But no matter how that had made him feel, no matter how suspicious Greenridge had acted, Jack hadn't followed the grizzly to prove anything. The truth was much simpler. "...Because I was bored."

Behr watched him, not seeming to know what to say.

There was silence for a long while. Jack felt, more than ever, that he was buried under the earth. The weasel tow-truck driver — what had Harding called him? Pooch. He had warned Jack about Harding; or at least he'd started to. "Folks around him tend to get..." To get what? Hurt? Killed? From where Jack was sitting, he himself seemed like the real danger. First Dr. Walraven, and now his only friends.

But Dr. Walraven hadn't been first at all. There was also King of Hearts. King, the indestructible, seemingly *immortal* hero, who had rid the world of the Red Teeth, was dead because of

Jack. Now the Red Teeth were back. And who was left to stop them?

"I've been thinking about it," Behr said, breaking the silence. "There's something strange about this whole thing. The mutiny, I mean. It's like everything worked in Greenridge's favor. Claythorne sending Vanguard home. You and your ragged friend returning too late to tell anyone what had happened. By all accounts, his plan *should* have failed, but it seems to be going *perfectly*." He paused in thought. "Maybe he's part rabbit," he added with a weak grin.

Then Behr's eyes shot past Jack, fixing on something behind him. Jack turned. Harding, who had looked like little more than a pile of dirty rags heaped in the corner, was standing. He rubbed his head, as if recovering from a massive headache, and turned around. He made no acknowledgment of Jack, Behr, or their surroundings. He simply walked to the bars where the guard stood. In response, the guard took a hesitant step away. "Stay back, you," he ordered.

"Water," the lion said. His voice sounded more gravelly than usual.

"I said get back," the guard barked, clutching at his rifle, his eyes flicking between Harding and the stairwell.

"I need water," Harding repeated. He raised a trembling paw as if begging for a scrap.

The guard relaxed a bit, lowering his rifle. "You want some water, huh?" he said. He reached for his hip flask, uncapped it, and took a swig. "Here ya go," he gargled, then spat the mouthful at Harding.

But the water never hit him. It hung in midair, a thousand crystal beads dangling from invisible strings. And then the beads came together. For a half a second, the crystal blob of water simply levitated, reflecting the dim torchlight of the dungeon.

And then it shot back at the guard. It burst against his face like a water balloon. But the water stayed there, wrapped around his muzzle, a crystal-clear mask that covered his mouth and nostrils.

Immediately, the guard dropped his rifle, swatting at his own face with both paws. He stumbled back against the bars of the opposite cell, letting out a scream that bubbled its way through the water.

"Drop the keys," Harding said, but the guard didn't seem to hear him. His eyes worked maniacally, back and forth, then snapped suddenly to the stairs. He made to run for them.

But his steps became shallow, and eventually he collapsed, first to his knees, then his face.

Jack stared through the bars. "You can control water," he said. "You… killed him with water."

"He's not dead," Harding said. He seemed fatigued, leaning against the bars to look out at the collapsed guard.

"Well, we're not in a worse situation than we were," Behr said. "But we'll never get the keys now."

But Harding was focusing on the limp body. He gripped the bars of the cell, staring at the fallen guard as if trying to see through him.

By now, the other prisoners were standing at the bars of their own cells, watching with interest.

The guard's leg shifted suddenly sideways.

"What exactly are you trying to…" said a gray cat in the cell opposite them, but Behr waved him down. They watched in silence. For a moment, the guard didn't make any other movements. But then the leg shifted again. This time, the boot raised up off of the ground. It pointed toward Harding, and began moving through the air as though being pulled by an invisible paw. The guard slid along the stone floor, face down, dragging behind the elevated foot.

He passed close to Behr's cell. The dog stooped, reached through the bars, and snatched the key ring from the guard's belt. "Got it!" he said.

Harding let out a sigh, relaxing his shoulders. In response, the guard's foot dropped to the floor with a thud.

"Someone's coming," said the gray cat.

Behr flicked through the keys. He jammed one into the lock. It didn't work.

Jack could hear the footsteps now, coming from the stairs.

Behr tried another key. Wrong. He swore as he fumbled the ring. The keys clattered to the stone. Jack, who was nearest, reached through the bars and picked them up, his fingers pinched around a small black key. He passed it to Behr, who immediately stuffed it into the hole.

It worked!

Behr pushed the door open, slipped out, then clicked it gently shut once more.

He stooped, grabbed up the rifle the guard had dropped, then bolted for the stairwell.

"What in the sharp toothed world? Hey, you can't leave us here!" the gray cat yelled after him. The other prisoners cursed and swiped at him as he passed, but he paid them no attention.

Instead of leaving, however, he came to a stop just to the side of the opening, pressing his back to the wall and inclining his ear toward the stairs. The other prisoners continued to bark threats at him.

A voice yelled out from the stairwell; an approaching guard. "Fadden, you useless undertail. Keep them quiet down there." The guard came stumping into the room.

Behr flung out a leg, sending the guard sprawling, then fixed the rifle on him. "Keep your head shut if you don't want it open," he growled.

They made it to the rooftop, eight of them in total. It was snowing in full force now, and the sky was a dense black. Harding had an arm draped over Behr's shoulder, limping heavily on his left leg.

"The anax pad," the gray cat said, pointing ahead of them.

"Can you fly?" Behr asked.

"'Course I can," the cat said. "That's why they kept me alive."

By the same miracle that had kept the halls more or less free of guards, the rooftop seemed to be clear. But as they reached the anax, a voice called out. "Hey! Hold it!" Jack spun around. A guard was yelling something into his shoulder mounted radio. He pointed his rifle at them and let out a spray of bullets, which sparked against the cement roof and the body of the vehicle.

Behr heaved Harding's weight into the anax, then spun around. He raised his rifle and returned fire. "Get in, Jack! Aaaaargh!" he cried out in pain as he took a hit to the shoulder.

"Mr. Behr!" Jack yelled, but was pushed bodily into the anax. The cat climbed in after him, slamming the bay door shut just as more gunfire pinged against the window.

"Wait!" Jack cried, reaching for the door. "We can't leave Mr. Behr!"

Harding gripped his shoulder with surprising strength and shoved him into the smallest of the seats. "He's gone, Jack," he said.

The gray cat crawled from the bay to the cockpit — in the Safehaven anaxopters, the two were not divided — and within seconds, the anax wings began to pump up and down. Snow started to curl upward, then swirl wildly around the body of the machine.

There was more gunfire, now pinging against both sides.

As the anax rose and tilted sideways, Jack saw Mr. Behr surrounded by soldiers. Several raised their weapons and fired at the anax.

"Don't worry," the cat yelled from the cockpit. "This thing's meant to take a lot more than bullets. It's the SAMs we gotta worry about."

"Sams?" Jack asked, fumbling his safety restraints with trembling paws.

"Surface to Air Missiles," the cat yelled. "Safehaven's the first defense up here, so you can imagine we're very well armed."

The anax lifted up into the air. Jack shut his eyes and gripped the sides of his seat.

"Then let's get out of here," Harding said. "Triarch, as quick as you can."

"That's the plan," the cat agreed. The body of the anax leaned forward, and they cut through the snowy air. "At this point, it's just a matter of... uh oh."

Jack opened his eyes. The cat was looking at a circular screen on the console. "We've got company."

Out the left window, a bright light was moving toward them; moving much too quickly.

"Is it a missile?" Jack yelled, hearing the panic in his own voice.

"It's an anax," the cat said, his paws working across the console, flipping switches, turning dials. "...Aaaaand there's another one."

## CHAPTER TWENTY-NINE

Sure enough, a second light was approaching from the other side.

"They've got us pinned," the cat yelled. "Sorry boys. Triarch'll have to wait. First step is survival." The anax banked hard to the right. They flew past the second light, narrowly missing it.

Out the window, Jack now saw the peak of the tallest mountain. They were moving north, toward the Axe Wound.

There was a loud shrieking sound. It whistled past the window to the left, a flickering light that left an unmistakable trail of smoke behind it. A missile! "Don't worry," the cat called back. "I've still got a few moves."

But just as he said this, there was an explosion of noise, a heavy jolt, and brightest orange lit up the interior of the craft. Jack felt heat licking his face. When he opened his eyes, he looked out into open sky. The cockpit was a gaping hole on the face of the machine. The pilot was gone.

As the anaxopter began spinning out of control, someone pounced on top of him.

Harding unclasped Jack's harness. There was an immediate sensation of weightlessness; they were in a free fall. Pulling him into a one armed hug, the lion used his free arm to move himself along the floor of the falling craft, then planted both feet against the remains of the cockpit and leapt into the roaring wind.

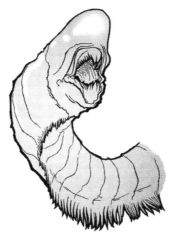

## Chapter Thirty

# THE RED LIGHTS

They fell through space, smoke and deafening noise. Jack felt a scraping all across his body and face. His back collided with something firm. He pinwheeled downward, then collided chest-first with another one. A branch. He didn't mean to catch it. His arms and stomach curled around it, and he dangled like a sheet on a clothesline. He coughed, trying to catch his breath, which was both labored and quick.

From somewhere below him, Harding let out a roar of pain. Adjusting his hold, Jack peered downward, and was instantly amazed he had heard Harding at all.

A plume of smoke rose from the forest floor, orange lit against the fiery wreckage. The anax, which had landed in a clearing between the trees, writhed like a wounded creature; a black, skeletal frame with a belly full of fire, pushed in uneven circles by the broken but relentless dragonfly wings. Its missing cockpit was an anguished mouth, toothless, screaming. The *chop*

*chop chop* of the wings was joined by a whistle, loud and shrill. Louder. Shriller. Until...

*Shuckaah!*

The explosion was concussive. Jack shielded his face as bits of shrapnel tore through the foliage. He jerked his paw away as a triangular bit lodged into the wood like an ax head.

Crackling silence followed.

He stared at the now motionless remains of the anax, grabbed at the branch, and vomited.

"Watch it," said a weak voice below him. He adjusted himself again, wiped his lips with the back of a paw, and looked downward.

Harding was working his way up the tree, claws digging into the trunk, feet seeking out each branch along the way. He rose to Jack's level.

"Are you okay?" Harding asked.

Unable to answer, afraid that he might sob if he opened his mouth, or maybe vomit again, Jack jerked his head side to side. No. He wasn't okay.

Harding let out a sigh of understanding, and looked back down. "Let's get you out of this tree."

But as Jack moved to reach for him, Harding snapped a finger to his own lips, his body suddenly motionless, his ears perked up.

"You stupid bag of fodder," said an angry voice. "Greenridge wanted them alive."

"At least they didn't escape," said a second voice.

"Escape?" said the first voice. "You disintegrated them!"

There was silence. Two dark figures moved into the light of the crackling fire. "They're dead as dead. Nobody could survive that, not without a serious heightena."

"That's a possibility," the first voice said. The beam of a flashlight bloomed. It swept across the snow surrounding the wreck. A second flashlight clicked to life. The lights criss-crossed the area, scanning. One of them turned upward, straight into the tree in which they hid.

The light froze, held on them.

Jack's breath caught in his throat.

And then the beam moved on.

"They're toast," one of the voices said, and the lights clicked off. "Quite literally," the voice added with a laugh. They left the firelight, and a moment later, the *chop chop chopping* of anax wings carried them away.

The tree was tall, and it took a long time for them to work their way down. Jack released Harding's shoulders as they reached the forest floor, dropping into the snow. He wasn't able to look at the wreckage. The warmth of the fire turned his stomach. "So now what?" he asked.

Harding started to answer, winced, clutched at his waist, and then doubled over.

"What is it?" Jack asked in alarm.

The lion opened his paws. Something slender and metallic stuck out between them. Shrapnel. It looked like some sort of wire or very thin bar, like the spoke of a bike wheel. Jack hissed. "Is it deep?" he asked.

Harding tugged at it, then winced and let it go. Instead of answering, he limped past Jack, away from the wreckage, into the snowy forest.

Jack followed, watching him apprehensively. "Harding?" he called. It had started to snow again. "We have to get out of this. We have to get somewhere warm." He thought of the fire they were leaving behind. The thought sickened him, and he shook it away. Harding must have somewhere warm to go. Hadn't he said something about a cave?

But the lion was unresponsive. He limped through the snow, as wobbly and off balance as a sleepwalker.

Jack began to feel sleepy, too. His limbs were numb, his jaw sore from chattering. And his eyes seemed to be playing tricks on him. In the darkness ahead, he seemed to see a faint red glow just below the snow's surface. He blinked at it, thinking he'd stared at the firelight too long. But as he shifted his eyes around, the light did not follow. It moved through the snow at its own slow pace, weaving below the surface. It was almost beautiful.

Then there was another, moving alongside the first.

Suddenly, Jack saw three, four, then a dozen, the way a thousand stars become visible once the first one is seen.

The lights weren't bright, but they were unmistakable now. They drew near, at least two dozen strong, and began a bizarre, slow-turning whirlpool beneath Harding and himself. They no longer appeared as simple red lights. Each glow was emitting from the front of a long, tapering shadow. They reminded Jack, in his daze, of a bendable flashlight Dr. Walraven had once owned, which he could wrap around a pipe or…

*SHOOF!* Harding disappeared into the snow as though falling through a trapdoor. Jack hardly had time to react. The ground beneath him suddenly felt as weak as an eggshell. It crumpled under his weight, and he was swallowed into the red light.

He became aware of a low chorus of hissing, like sand across paper. The lights swirled all around him. Something brushed his fingertips. It was warm.

A tube-like shape slithered just past his face. He registered the rubbery white texture of translucent skin. Arms flailing, he half crawled, half swam backward, jerking away as his arm contacted another one.

Then he felt a quick tug, a nip at his sleeve. Another at his leg.

There was a shrill squeal. Then another. Then several more.

The nips turned to bites. A pinch at his neck. Another at his hip. It only hurt a little. He felt sleepy. He just wanted to sleep. The weird squealing sound and the bright red light enveloped him. The tube-like shapes were slithering across him now, wrapping between his knees, under his arms. It was a nauseating feeling. He heaved, but he'd already emptied the contents of his stomach in the tree.

Just then, there was a sharper pain at his back. Had one of them made it through his shirt, through his skin? *Just let it be over quickly,* he thought. He closed his eyes, waiting for the tearing, the burning.

But instead, he felt a sudden, powerful tug. He was yanked upward, out of the red light. The tube creatures fell away from him, and he landed on his back in the powdery snow. The darkness and the cold surprised him after the red pit, and he wretched dryly once more.

"Get the other one," he heard a voice yell out. "Howl at the moon, this one smells like barf." Someone was leaning over him, looking at him, *smelling* him. In the now faint red light, he registered a sneering coyote face.

## Chapter Thirty-One

# THE FERAL CAMP

Jack was draped over a burly shoulder. He hung there, too weak to struggle, watching snowflakes shrink into the open flame of a torch.

Just beyond the flame, Jack could see Harding's bloodied face. His eyes were closed — he might have been dead. His arms swung limply across the back of the coyote carrying him.

The trees seemed to be thickening, the darkness around them more dense. Ahead, a faint glow bloomed over the crest of a hill. It flickered softly and irregularly, and as they drew nearer, the light seemed to expand. There were voices, crowds of them, talking, laughing, even singing. There was also a steady drumming, up tempo, with some sort of stringed instrument rattling along with it.

As they passed over the peak of the hill, Jack saw that the light was contained under a wide canopy that stretched between the trees. The top of this makeshift cave was covered in snow, blending with the surrounding hills. This made it impossible to guess at its size, but even before they passed beneath it, Jack counted at least six separate campfires inside. They lit upon a lively group of musicians and dancers, an old woman telling stories to a group of wide-eyed children, a circle of men laughing and swigging from mugs.

They were greeted at the entrance by a coyote so big, he might have been a bear. As he drew nearer, Jack could see the white of his muzzle, and the aged sag in his lower lids. "Sasha," he said in a deep voice. "What have you brought us, my son?" He looked Harding up and down. "What have you done to this one? My goodness, Sasha — with so many of you against one?"

"That wasn't us," said the coyote carrying Jack. "We pulled him out of a hothead pit, along with this one." He stood Jack up on the dirt floor in the mouth of the tent-cave.

The elder coyote eyed him. "Hmmm… you were in the worm pit, too?" Jack gave a weak nod. The coyote laughed, plucking at the torn sleeve of Jack's coat. "Well, they seemed to have liked your jacket more than you." He swept an arm invitingly, and they followed him inside.

More and more campfires became visible as they moved deeper into the tent-cave. The canopy was of white plastic, and used the thick trunks of living trees as architectural support beams. Jack supposed that from above, these trees would add to the camp's disguise. Below the surface, though, they looked more like works of art. They were carved and decorated, their bark chipped away into ornate patterns of fish, snowflakes, and rushing rivers.

"What is this?" asked a voice from ahead of them. "More of them?"

"Survivors," Sasha said, "of an anaxopter crash. The rabbit, I'm not sure about, but this one," he indicated Harding, who still appeared to be unconscious, "is familiar. He lives in the mountain, like us."

"Certainly not like us," the newcomer said, drawing near. He had a long, bent snout and sunken eyes that gave him a menacing look, despite being much smaller than most of the others. "He looks next to death. You say an anaxopter crash? What happened?"

"That army we've been watching; one of their Hogs shot it out of the sky. I suspect they're getting ready to make their move."

"That's no concern of ours," the hook-nosed coyote said. "Let them have their war."

"It *is* your concern."

Jack turned in surprise. Harding, who was still draped over the largest coyote's shoulder, had rolled his head to face them.

"What did you say?" the hook-nosed coyote asked.

Harding tried to speak, took a few steadying breaths, then tried again. "I said it *is* your concern. The fort has fallen. Claythorne is dead."

There was a murmur from the surrounding coyotes. Even Sasha looked at Harding with sudden alarm.

The hook nosed coyote collected himself quickly and took a step closer to Harding. "Are you *sure?*"

"We weren't shot down by a Hog," Harding said. "We weren't even near the gate. We were shot down by two Safehaven anaxopters."

Sasha's father, the bear-like coyote who had greeted them at the entrance, looked frantically between Harding and the hook nosed coyote. "Ramses," he said. "Ramses is still in there. We have to go get him."

"Calm yourself, Armel. We will decide what is best," the hook nosed coyote said.

"*I* will decide."

The surrounding ferals began to part, and an elderly coyote woman stepped into their midst. She wasn't much taller than Jack, and wore garments of so many colors, she looked bizarrely mismatched: a deep green top wrapped in a blood red shawl; a purple skirt stitched with golden lace. Her eyes were tired, sad even, and fixed on Jack. "You have finally arrived, Jack Robberts. I am Magdalia Nofski." The hint of a smile touched her eyes at the surprised look on his face. "I know much, and see much," she said, "but the universe did not tell me your name. We have a mutual friend."

Jack watched her silently. She said nothing for a moment, but walked in a slow circle around him, looking him up and down. She reached forward, snatched up the messenger bag resting against his hip. He didn't make a move. She seemed to weigh the bag in her paws, like a child guessing the contents of a gift, then released it. She moved to Harding. He watched her through slits.

"There is much to be done," she said. "This is only the beginning of the journey, for both of you. And I'm afraid the darkest times are yet to come." As she said this, she turned her eyes to the floor at Jack's feet. Her expression was somber, holding none of the jubilance or music of her tribe. When her eyes met Jack's once more, he saw a hollowness there, as though she wasn't looking at him at all, but straight through him. She drew closer, speaking into his ear. "Jack Robberts," she whispered, "you don't know who you are."

Jack was shown to a small, curtained room. "I guessed these were your size," Sasha said, placing a bundle of clothes in his arms, then allowing the curtain to drop, leaving Jack in privacy.

The clothes were a little big, and mismatched in that same quilt-like way: a hooded maroon sweater with ash gray sleeves, and blue jeans covered in purple and yellow patches. Still, it felt wonderful to slip into clean, dry clothes.

They moved deeper into the camp, Magdalia at the front of the procession. Every eye turned to watch as they passed.

Colorful quilts formed a curtain between two carved trunks. Magdalia grabbed the opening between them, but before she could pull it back, Sasha spoke up.

"We can't leave him here. We need to question him."

"We will question the lion," Magdalia responded.

"The lion," Sasha protested. "He's half-dead. My brother is in the fort. We need answers now."

"And we will get them," Magdalia said, her tone gentle. "The lion's wounds aren't as deep as the rabbit's, nor are they as easily remedied." She turned to Jack. "That is why I've brought you here, Jack. Your wounds are invisible; to mend them requires something I cannot give you."

She pulled back the curtain, revealing a small, oddly shaped room with quilt walls. A campfire emitted a dim red light, its smoke rising to the canopy and escaping through the gaps along the tree trunks. And staring back at him were five surprised faces.

"You will stay here tonight," Magdalia said. "When the lion is recovered, I will want to speak to you both."

Jack nodded, although he'd barely heard her words. She walked away, the others following, and Jack was left speechless, staring into the room.

"You look a lot less dead than we thought you were!" Sprint said, a broad smile stretched across his face.

## Chapter Thirty-Two

## SURVIVORS' TALES

It felt wonderful to laugh, huddled around the campfire, the darkness of recent events seeming to fade behind the relief at finding each other alive and unharmed. Sprint, Hoover, Maddie, and Willie all seemed as fresh to Jack as the new clothes he wore. And with them, to his surprise, was Peter Claythorne.

"When you got dragged over that hill," Sprint explained, his eyes wide, "we thought you were gone. I tried to go after you, but the Ice Cats were practically on top of us, so I..." He faltered.

"Well, I made it," Jack said, holding his paws up as if displaying himself for inspection. "So how'd you escape the Ice Cats?"

"We split up," Sprint said. "Maddie and Willie went one way. Hooves and I went up the hill. We climbed up some rocks, and found a frozen lake up there. We figured the Ice Cat would be too heavy for the ice, so we took off across it." He looked at Hoover and smiled. "In the end, it *was*, sort of. The pilot was yelling at us, language I shan't repeat in the company of a lady."

"All fours, you undertail," Maddie swore, to which the others laughed, including Sprint.

"Right, well," he continued. "He drives the Ice Cat out onto the lake, kinda slip-sliding like someone learning to ice skate. He gets it stable, then lunges at us. I don't think he wanted to catch us; just flatten us. But then Hooves... ha!" He laughed, and clapped Hoover on the back. "So the Ice Cat is coming down on us, about to smash us, and Hooves points his trunk straight down and *BOOM!* Blasts a hole right into the ice. We drop into the water. The Ice Cat crashes through right behind us. We're able to bob back up to the surface, but the Ice Cat's too heavy, obviously, so it sinks like a stone, bringing the pilot with it."

"Wow!" Jack said, giving Hoover an impressed look. "Good thinking!"

The anteater shrugged modestly.

"It's like I'm always telling you, Hooves," Sprint said, nudging him with an elbow. "You're too powerful *not* to be a hero. If you and I ever got in a fight, you'd..."

"I know, I know," Hoover said, looking suddenly uncomfortable. "I hate when you say that."

Sprint laughed, and then continued. "Only when we get to the surface, the water is moving, like a river. I think Hooves' ice trick burst a dam or something. So now we're being carried toward a waterfall. Hoover can't swim. I'm usually a motorboat, but with his weight, plus the fact that I can't feel my limbs, it's all I can do to keep our heads above the water. We're just about to go over the edge when..." He let the anticipation hang for a moment, his paws suspended in the air. Then he deflated like an untied balloon and pointed to Peter.

"Then I showed up with my stick," Peter said, trying to pick up the same energy with which Sprint had told the story.

Sprint laughed. "Peter is standing on the edge of the lake, and fishes us out with a tree branch. But of course, we're soaked, and it's freezing, so it's just dying later rather than sooner. I doubt we'd have made it, if the coyotes hadn't come along."

"How did they find you?" Jack asked, privately wondering the same thing about himself.

"This camp is just west of the lake. I think they must have heard all the commotion or something. A few of their scouts came along and surrounded us, and here we are."

For the first time, Jack noticed that Sprint and Hoover were wearing mismatched clothes similar to his own. Maddie and Willie, however, were still in their snow coats. "So what about you guys?" he asked.

Willie was looking at his own fingers, touching the index and thumb together, watching them stretch and then separate. "We tried heading for the fort," he explained, "but we couldn't outrun the Ice Cat, especially not with two of us on the snowmobile. Just before it caught us, Maddie turned left into a kind of roofless cave, like a crack in the mountain. It sloped downward," he made an angle with his forearm, "and ended at a drop off. But across the gap were more mountains, and the first sign of daylight, which gave me an idea."

"A *suicidal* idea," Maddie added, although the corners of her mouth twitched.

"Right," Willie said. "'Just keep the throttle down,' I told her. By this point, the Ice Cat had made it into the cave, and was coming at us full steam. We could feel the ground shaking. When we got closer to the drop off, the peak of the opposite mountain became visible, and just like I'd hoped, the snow cap was reflecting the sunlight; it was blinding. I shot my tongue at the wall to the right, grabbed Maddie as tight as I could, and took off her hat."

## CHAPTER THIRTY-TWO

Jack looked between them, enthralled. "So then what?"

"What do you think?" Willie said. "She saw the sunlight, and we froze. I could tell it worked on the pilot, too, because we couldn't hear the pounding footsteps anymore, just a kind of scraping noise. We slid over the edge. The snowmobile dropped out from beneath us, and we swung sideways on my tongue. Just in time, too — the Ice Cat fell after us, straight into the gorge."

"As I recall," Maddie said, her brows lowering, "You then said something about 'female drivers.'" She said this last part while holding her tongue, so that it sounded more like *thee-nale dly-thuths*. She rolled her eyes at him. "Always the classy one, *Lilly*," she added, pinching her tongue again.

He shrugged unapologetically.

Jack looked at Peter. "What about you? How'd you get mixed up in this?"

Peter looked as though he'd been accused of something. For a wolf nearly twice their age — and size — it was remarkable how helpless and delicate he could seem. "Oh, well," he said. "I saw you guys sneaking out, and so I... I followed you. Didn't catch up until you were being chased, so I..." he paused, not meeting Jack's eyes. "So I hid. When the Ice Cats were gone, I followed Sprint and Hoover, and found them in the lake."

"But what about you, Jack?" Sprint asked. "We thought you were gone when you got dragged down that hill. How'd you get away?"

They listened with rapt attention as Jack explained how he'd crossed the ravine on the fallen tree. They were amazed at Harding's harrowing rescue, and the race to the top before the dam burst. Jack began to tremble excitedly as he spoke, partly because he was so thankful to be alive, partly because they were such a good audience.

"But I don't get it," Maddie said. "Why you? What did Greenridge want with *you*?"

"I think I know," Jack said, drawing his messenger bag onto his lap. He'd made up his mind the moment he saw his friends alive. They were a team; their lives depended on each other. They shouldn't be keeping secrets. Still trembling, he unbuckled the flap. "I think he was looking for *this*," he said, stretching his arm over the fire and holding out the key palm upward.

There was silence for a moment, then Maddie broke it. "The stolen key?" she said, eyes fixed on the brass object. "*You* took it?"

"Not exactly," Jack said. "I… *ended up* with it, for safekeeping."

"Safekeeping for who?" Willie demanded.

"For… well, I'm not really sure actually."

"Not sure?" Maddie said. "Jack, if anyone finds out you have it, we're all…"

"I know," Jack said. "Look, I'm sorry. I should have told you all a long time ago. I ended up with it, and I haven't known what to do with it ever since."

"Give it to President Brisk, obviously," Maddie said. The others nodded in agreement.

Jack shook his head. "The one who took it, I think Brisk was the one he was keeping it *from*."

"He's the President of Animal Control," Willie reasoned.

"Yes, but…" Jack began, then faltered. "Look, you all know what this thing does. It shows what's really on someone's heart. And when I saw what was on Brisk's heart…" He explained about the horns, the decayed flesh, the demand for power. "Just, please trust me. We'll figure it out."

275

Hoover and Sprint exchanged uncertain glances. Maddie seemed to be chewing her lip.

Willie, however, seemed to lose interest. "Okay, so as you were saying, you escaped the ravine..."

"Right," Jack said, thankful for the change of subject. "We made it to Pine Creek, where the lion — Harding — had a friend, who gave us a ride up the mountain. We got to the fort, ready to tell Claythorne what happened, but she..."

He stopped, feeling his heart leap to his throat, and his eyes shot to Peter.

"What?" Peter asked. "Did my mom have you arrested or something? That sounds like her."

Jack could feel his cheeks and the insides of his ears burning. He shook his head. Now it was his turn not to be able to meet Peter's eyes.

The wolf drew in a breath, comprehension dawning. "No." He stood, shaking his head. He strode to one of the quilt walls, grabbed at it, fumbled to find an opening, became frustrated, and punched it. He dropped to his rear, burying his face in his paws.

The crackling fire was the only sound for a moment. Even the camp outside of their room seemed to have fallen silent.

"So the fort," Maddie said, but she didn't finish the question. She didn't need to.

Jack nodded. "Greenridge beat us back. He was there, waiting for us — alive. I don't know how."

"The necklace," Peter said to the curtain he was facing, his voice a flat monotone. "It's the necklace. I don't know what it's made from, but it's like a heightena. It keeps him... safe. Like a... like a good luck charm."

Peter let out an anguished groan, fell onto his side, and said no more. One by one, the others scooted back to their own corners of the room. Jack was glad to end the conversation here, not only because exhaustion had finally caught up with him. There was also the matter of their mentors abandoning them.

And of course, they still didn't know about Mr. Behr.

# Chapter Thirty-Three
# MAGDALIA NOFSKI

Someone was barking orders, and Jack woke up. He pushed himself to sit, rubbed his eyes, and looked around. The curtain walls had been pushed open, leaving him in the much larger space of the main tent cave.

Four coyote men were unfurling a large tarp just yards away. The oldest looking one, a burly and shirtless coyote with a whitening muzzle, was loudly shouting orders. "Coran, pull your side good and tight if you please. It's going to roll in every direction." He stomped to the middle of the tarp, reached up, and grabbed at a knotted rope dangling from the plastic canopy. When he had returned to his corner of the tarp, he gave the rope a good, hard jerk. Immediately, sunlight spilled in through an opening created in the canopy, along with a sloshing flood of snow. When the snow stopped pouring in, they lifted their tarp corners and brought them together. "This load goes to the baths," the leader said, and the group marched off, dragging the snow-filled tarp with them.

Another group was marching in Jack's direction, led by the hook-nosed coyote from the night before. Jack looked over his shoulder, intending to wake the others, and realized for the first time that they were gone.

"Mr. Robberts," the hook nosed coyote said as his group came to a halt. "I hope you got a good night's sleep." His tone and sneer suggested that he couldn't care less, and he motioned for Jack to stand.

Jack did so, looking at the empty blankets. It was as if last night had only been a dream. "Do you know where my…" he started.

"Come with us," the coyote interrupted.

Jack looked at the rest of the stony-faced group, wondering whether they might take him by *force* should he refuse. He gave one more glance over his shoulder, then followed.

Magdalia Nofski's living space was not much larger than the one in which he'd slept. Like her clothing, the room was colorful and mismatched. The walls were made of wool-lined blankets, and an orange shag rug covered the floor. At the center of the room, warmth emanated from a space heater that looked as if someone had bronzed a tiny juke box.

"I want to apologize for my discourtesy," the feral woman said. She settled herself into a chair made of tangled branches, and motioned for Jack to take a seat. He dropped into a chair across the space heater from her, next to the room's only other occupant. Harding looked much better than he had last night; fully alert, with no visible wounds, although his left brow still looked puffy. "It is not my intention to intimidate either of you, nor to make you feel unwelcome."

Another coyote entered the room, this one wearing dark red robes. "Bring the compass," Magdalia instructed. The red robed woman nodded and left.

Magdalia extracted a small knife from within her layered garments. "Are you familiar with deracin root, Jack?" she asked.

Jack saw himself on a wooded trail, squatting alongside Alan and Dr. Walraven to inspect what looked like a translucent white carrot. "It's a plant," he said. "A poisonous root."

Magdalia gave a small nod. "It won't kill you — not in small doses — but it *will* nullify your heightena. In other words, you will be left powerless." She laid the knife in her lap, fixed Jack with a stern stare, and continued. "You are wondering where your friends have gone," she said. "I have taken them. They will not be harmed, but neither will they be released; not until I have what I need from you."

"From me?" Jack asked, surprised at the sudden turn. "What do you want from *me?*"

"Two things. First, your compliance. There is something that must be done, something only *you* can do. I don't expect you to fully appreciate its necessity. I do, however, expect you to cooperate."

"And if I don't," Jack said, "you'll kill my friends?"

"We are not killers, Jack, and we don't need to be."

She withdrew a vial from her garments. It was nearly filled with a milky blue liquid. "I will not harm your friends, but unless I have your compliance, I will take away their powers."

Jack swallowed, watching the vial. It was the wrong color to be deracin, he knew, but her point was made. "You haven't told me what you want," he said. "Why threaten me before you know my answer?"

"Because I know your answer," she said, setting the vial alongside the knife. "Just as I knew about the fort. Just as I know what you do not know about yourself. You were going to reject both of my demands. Now you will accept them."

"And they are?"

"You will go to the fort," she said. "And release our ally."

Surprised, his mouth began framing a question, but it was Harding who responded, speaking for the first time. "Why Jack?" he asked. "Unless I'm mistaken, you have Claythorne's kid. Why not send him?"

Magdalia's eyes never left Jack's. "Peter Claythorne could navigate the fort without aid. Miles Greenacre could navigate without capture. Jack is the only one who can do both."

"How?" Jack asked. In his opinion, Magdalia was putting far too much faith in him.

"You must answer that for yourself," she said. "How did you navigate the maze in the Animal Control trials?" Her face softened into a faint smile. "That one I *did* get from the universe."

"Then I'm going with him," Harding said. "I'm not letting him out of my sight. And don't think you can threaten me with deracin root. There's nothing I'm afraid to lose."

The curtain parted once more, and the red robed coyote returned. Instead of a compass, however, she held a large, dead salmon. She placed it into Magdalia's outstretched paws, then bowed herself once more from the room.

"Your crimes are known to me, Toby Harding," Magdalia said. The lion made no response, but his posture became a bit more stiff. "And it is time that you pay for them." As she said this, she laid the fish across her lap, gripped the small knife, and slid the blade beneath its eye. She worked smoothly, in one quick circle, until the disk-like eye came free.

She dropped it into the bowl on her lap, then uncapped the vial and poured out its contents, massaging the white fluid into the eye. When she finished, she wiped her paws on her garments and inspected her work. It hardly looked like an eye anymore, its green-gold coloring had been replaced by that milky blue, nearly transparent at the edges. Its pupil had narrowed to a small black point, and when she tapped it on the edge of her chair, it made a solid clicking sound, as if it had turned to stone. Satisfied, she picked up the knife once more and pressed it firmly into one end.

"My second requirement," she said, turning her eyes upon Jack, "is the key."

It took a moment for the words to register. Realization dawned too late, and Jack did a bad job of playing dumb. "Key? A key? What key?"

Magdalia set the knife down again. She plucked a strand from her garments, and threaded it through the new hole she had whittled into the eye. "You are right to protect it, Jack. The key must not fall into the wrong paws." She let the eye dangle like an ornament for a moment, examining it, and set it down once more. "What you don't know," she continued, "is that Dr. Walraven — yes, we are acquainted — had intended to bring the key here."

"To give it to you?" Jack asked.

"No," she responded. "To give it to *him*." She nodded toward Harding.

The lion looked between them. "To *me*?" he asked.

"The heart belonged to your cousin," Magdalia responded. "And now it falls to you. You will make amends for your deeds. You will take the key to the Harbinger."

Harding's posture became more rigid still, and he gripped the armrests tightly.

Magdalia looked again to Jack. "So do we have a deal?" she asked.

Jack thought of his friends; reduced to being powerless, their dreams crushed, their lives forever changed, all because of his choice here and now.

Snatching up his bag, he unfastened the buckle, withdrew the bronze key, and passed it to Harding, who seemed as reluctant to take it as he was to surrender it.

"And the fort?" Magdalia asked.

"When do I leave?" Jack asked. The words formed as if someone else had spoken them.

Magdalia did not smile. On the contrary, her eyes seemed to fill with regret. "Immediately."

# Chapter Thirty-Four

## THE FALLEN FORT

A strange vehicle was cutting its way through the snow. Mostly, it looked like a motorcycle, although the front wheel had been replaced by a single ski, which carved a zigzagging path across the white terrain. In place of a rear wheel, a triangular tread kicked a rooster tail of snow into the air behind. The snow bike wove between the peeking heads of snow-capped rocks and the sugar bowls at the bases of trees.

With every bounce of the bike, Jack felt as if he might lose his grip on Sasha and fall off the back. The chainsaw whine was quieter than he would have expected, but they still couldn't get too near the fort without being heard, so Sasha let the motor die just as the high walls came into view above the trees.

Jack dismounted, readjusted his messenger bag, and tried his best not to look scared out of his mind.

The coyote withdrew an old tape player from his coat pocket. "A bit retro," he apologized, "and I hope you like R&R, 'cause it's the only tape I own." He passed the tape player to Jack, along with a tangled pair of ear buds. He worked his jaw back and forth, looking as though he'd like nothing more than to come along. Jack privately hoped Sasha might forget his promise to Magdalia Nofski and join him in entering the fort, but instead the coyote added, "I'll be here when you get out."

Not knowing what to say, Jack simply nodded and turned toward the fort.

When he drew closer, the guards along the roof became easy to spot against the gray sky, and he was able to time his movements between the trees so as not to be seen. Remembering the lack of security around the munitions bay, he worked his way in that direction and found the gate was still open. He had a slight scare when a twig snapped beneath his foot, but the rooftop guard didn't seem to have heard, and when his back was once more turned, Jack sprinted across the snow and into the darkened ramp.

The space was black and eerie, and echoed hollowly. The shadows of the inactive Ice Cats were like giants looming at him from the darkness, and he found himself running the last few steps to the stairwell door.

Entering, he stood for a moment at the base, untangling the ear buds and watching the stairs above him.

His heart was hammering. If he had thought Magdalia had placed too much faith in him, it was nothing compared to the faith he was about to place in her. Her plan seemed insane, if he was honest with himself.

He placed a bud in one ear, then the other, and hit play.

An electric guitar screamed into his ears. He knew this song. *Rhodekill & the Rabies* was his favorite group.

"Let the music *blind* you," Magdalia had said. At the time it hadn't made much sense to him. Music couldn't blind anyone — it was sound, not sight. But as the guitar solo transformed into the voice of R&R's female singer, Jack understood. How had he made it through the maze in the trials? By *not thinking* about it. He'd felt useless, hopeless, and let his mind wander to other things, allowing his feet to carry him "blindly" through the maze.

The answer was that simple: he didn't need to focus on finding the prisoner. He needed to do exactly the opposite.

He was lucky, and now was the time to embrace it.

Eyes squeezed shut, he started forward.

*"Scream it in my face if you're so brave. Am I to be your lover, or am I to be your slave?"* the musician sang.

He was at the top of the stairs now. He'd made it without tripping — that had to be a good sign. *No. Don't think about it.*

*"Our good deeds can't blot our sins, 'Cause goodness knows that badness wins."*

He was moving quickly along the corridor, his eyes shut, his arms splayed at angles. To anyone who saw him, he would look ridiculous. But then if anyone saw him, he would also be dead.

The thought alarmed him, and he cracked an eye open. The hall looked familiar, although his immediate impression was that the prison had been the *other* direction. Maybe this wasn't working.

*No.* He squeezed his eyes shut and focused on the song.

*"I'm wore out fighting for you, I won't be fighting with you. I cannot let you fall again, I'm far too weak to lift you."*

He turned sharply. Pushed through what must have been a hidden door disguised as solid wall. Took another left.

*"Our love and hate reciprocate, yet I still feel invaded. I cram my face in your embrace, but get asphyxiated."*

His outstretched paws connected with a barrier. Maybe a door? He patted around for a handle or knob. Instead, his paw fell on a sliding bolt. He raised the latch and gave it a hard jerk, but it clanked unyieldingly. He tried again. Nothing. Eyes still jammed shut, he groped along the bolt until he found something that made him open his eyes. A padlock. He gave it a tug, but knew it was useless. If only he'd brought some kind of bolt cutters.

*Wham!* Something hit him upside the head. He yelled out, although he couldn't hear himself over the music. Panicking, he spun around.

He was standing at the end of a long, narrow corridor with a polished wood floor reflecting dim recess lights. The room would have looked fancy, even posh, if it wasn't for the row of jail cells lining one wall.

In the nearest cell, a pair of arms were wind-milling around frantically, a shoe held in one paw. Ramses! The coyote's mouth was moving.

"Oh," Jack said, taking out the ear buds. "Sorry."

The coyote's eyes went wide and he made a shooshing sound. He pointed past Jack. Turning, Jack nearly tripped over himself. Only feet away from him, an armored guard was clutching a rifle with both paws. He was seated, the rifle across his lap, and to Jack's relief, his head was resting uncomfortably on one shoulder. Asleep.

The coyote pressed against the bars of his cell and peered along the corridor, then looked at Jack again. "Who are you?" he whispered. "And why are you wearing my old clothes?"

Jack looked down at the mismatched attire. "Never mind," he whispered. "We need to get you out of here."

"Great, yeah," the coyote agreed. "Key's on him." He pointed to the sleeping guard. "And would you mind getting me my other shoe?"

Finding their way back out was much more difficult. Not only were there two of them now, but they kept having to duck through doorways or behind coats of armor as guards passed by. They came across guards with such frequency in fact that Jack was amazed he'd managed to blindly navigate these same halls undetected.

They found a stairwell and descended. If it didn't take them to the munitions bay, Jack thought, they might at least find a window at snow level.

They entered the second floor corridor. A double door stood open opposite the stairwell, leading into a large conference hall. Chairs were stacked against one wall, and a blue and green patterned carpet stretched across the space. At the far end, muted daylight spilled from in between elegant golden curtains.

They entered the room cautiously, but found it empty. The nearest window was just above snow level, but to Jack's disappointment, it was one solid sheet of glass. "It doesn't look like it opens," he said.

Turning just in time, he moved out of the way as Ramses swung a chair overhead and released it. The window shattered loudly, large splinters of glass crashing to the carpet and snow. "Shall we?" he asked, gesturing toward the outside.

He took off his shirt and used it to pick away the remaining glass, then vaulted the window and into the snow. He stretched his arms wide and looked up at the sky. But when he turned, his face dropped. "Hey! Behind you!"

Jack whirled around. Greenridge was taking the room in massive strides, charging straight for him. Jack scrambled for the window. He got one foot into the sill. Then he was yanked back by his ears.

He caught only a glimpse of the coyote's tail disappearing into the snow, and he was spun around, face to face with the dangerous smile of General Greenridge.

"You're back," the bear said. "I'm not taking chances this time. I'm putting you to use right now."

There wasn't much room behind the Ice Cat's caged seat, especially with Greenridge's fat body pressing it backward. Wrists taped together, Jack squirmed on his shoulder and, with great difficulty, pushed himself into a sitting position. A brown bag of tools lay in the opposite corner of the small space, along with a tangle of red and black jumper cables. Perhaps he could hit Greenridge over the head with a wrench, or maybe strangle him with the cables. He wondered if he'd be brave enough to try either, even if his arms weren't taped up behind him. He looked to the cage bars. They weren't quite wide enough for him to squeeze through, not without a struggle. And besides, even if he did manage to get through them, he'd fall straight into the path of the Ice Cat's elephantine legs.

Instead, he watched through the bars as the machine passed beneath the trees, and listened to the crunching of snow through the sounds of the engine and legs.

After what seemed like hours, a sudden darkness fell like a thick cloud blocking the sun. When he looked up, Jack thought at first that it *was* a cloud, spanning the gap between the sheer mountain faces on either side. It was dark gray and imposing, but its edge was too perfect, too flat. As his eyes adjusted to the shade, he spotted a thin black line running down the object's surface, as though the entire thing might divide in two, right down the center. And looking closer, he saw that the entire surface was made up of metal plates, riveted together like a mountain-sized quilt.

They had arrived at the Gate.

## Chapter Thirty-Five
## HARD STOP

The elevator whined mechanically as it rattled upward. The overheads gave off an uneven bluish light that didn't quite fill the space. Jack made no effort to hide his trembling. He stood quietly next to Greenridge, watching the door like a greyhound watches a starting gate. As soon as it opened, he would run as fast as he could. What he wouldn't give to swap powers with Sprint right about now. He'd seen a ladder on their way to the elevator. It stretched the full fifty yards up the wall, looking like it had seen a thousand years of corrosive winters, but he wasn't heavy. His arms were still taped behind his back, but the ladder was angled; maybe he could lean against it. Risky, sure, but what choice was there? If he could take Greenridge by surprise, make it over the edge before the grizzly had time to react… well, that was as far as his plan got. Once on the ground, he'd still have to run a good mile of treeless snow at the mouth of the canyon.

But even this faint hope was crushed the moment the doors opened. A fleet of eight armed soldiers stood waiting for them.

Greenridge shoved Jack roughly forward, and they stepped out onto the top of the wall.

There wasn't much up here, only rusted railings along either side of a cement path stretching to the opposite mountain face. The path was wide enough to land an anaxopter, and marked with potholes and oil stains throughout. Halfway across, a thick black stripe marked the point where the wall divided into two separate gates.

"Another one? Do we get to eat him this time?" one of the guards sneered. He was a gray wolf, with yellow eyes that matched his yellow teeth.

"He's not much to share," said another, this one a chubby black bear.

"We're not eating him," Greenridge said. "This little guy's gonna open the gate for us. Isn't that right, Jack?"

Jack made no answer, not only because he didn't know what Greenridge meant; he was too afraid to speak, even if he'd wanted to do so.

That's when the numbers came to him.

One One

Seven Eight Nine

Zero Two

He didn't know what they meant, or why they came so easily — and there was something oddly familiar about them. They rolled around in his mind like a song he couldn't get out of his head.

One One

Seven Eight Nine

Zero Two

One One

Seven Eight Nine

Zero Two

Greenridge shoved him once more — he nearly toppled over — and the group moved to the northern edge of the wall and looked down.

The army fifty yards below them was bigger than Jack could have imagined, seeming to fill the canyon as far as he could see. They moved around like a hundred thousand ants, climbing over one another, onto the backs of tanks and other war machines.

*Some of the weaker ones have been sacrificed to the meager rations,* the horned creature had said. The thought made Jack feel faint.

"My brothers!" Greenridge roared. "Today we take back what is ours! Today, we reclaim the home from which our fathers were banished! Today, the Red Teeth will rise!"

The crowd hadn't quieted during this speech, and they didn't seem to grow louder as it ended, but guns were raised over heads, and many let out triumphant roars.

"Thing of beauty, isn't it?" Greenridge said, turning to Jack. "The strongest of the strong down there. They don't need your super hero heightena. Hard work and belief; that's all they need. We live in a world where the weak are given the same rights as the strong, thanks to bleeding hearts like Aaron Harding and Margarette Claythorne. But is that how it's meant to be? Look at you, Jack. Shaking like a whipped pup. Without the protection of stronger animals, you don't stand a chance. Can you honestly tell me that isn't how it's meant to be? Can you honestly say that we weren't *designed* this way? For the strong to rule the weak?" He grabbed Jack by the jaw, squeezing his cheeks together. "Look at those teeth," he said, showing Jack's face around to the others. They laughed. "You were meant to eat grass, kid," he continued, throwing Jack's face back. "But what about me? What are these for?" He curled his lip and tapped a yellowish fang longer than

Jack's finger. Then he laughed. "Look at me, justifying myself to you. I've been in this country too long."

Without another word, he stood to full height and shoved Jack once more. The group moved along the top of the wall until they arrived at a small metal keypad mounted into the railing, with silver buttons for 0 through 9, along with the pound and asterisk keys. It looked like an old phone, but in place of a receiver, there was a big red light.

"I've tried this several times," Greenridge said. "Every rabbit I've brought before now has failed. So I thought I'd… combine their efforts." He reached into the neck of his coat and withdrew a necklace of thick rope, with several large pendants dangling from it. They were the shape of large slugs, wrapped in glossy black tape. In several places, white fur protruded from between the tape. Rabbit feet. "It's not going to start any fashion trends," Greenridge continued, "but it's more than paid off. I survived that river barely scathed. You rabbits… well, it's a wonder you don't rule the world. Proves my point, doesn't it?"

As Greenridge spoke, Jack looked up at the canyon walls. Sun bounced off of blinding white sheets of snow. If only Maddie was here, he thought.

"But after watching you survive again and again and again," Greenridge was saying, "I'm certain you are the one I've been waiting for. See I can't just sit here punching in numbers. There are *two* codes. I'm just as likely to enter the code for *self-destruct* as the one for *open*. Only Claythorne knew them both. If I'd tried to force her to open the gates, she could enter the self-destruct code instead. Self-righteous fleabag." He gripped Jack roughly around the back of the neck, shut his eyes, and tapped out several keys on the pad.

The response was immediate. The red light blinked to life. The ground beneath Jack's feet rumbled steadily as it began to shift sideways, accompanied by a long, low moan.

Jack looked toward the opposite half of the gate. The two sections were turning a slight angle from each other, the concrete road forming a V that angled further and further outward, away from the army below, until finally splitting into two enormous doors.

"Yes!" Greenridge roared, nearly knocking Jack to the ground as he released him. He walked to the edge once more, joined by his guards, and leaned over the railing, balled fists raised to the sky. One of the guards withdrew a pistol from his belt and fired it into the air, but Greenridge caught him around the wrist. "Are you crazy?" he roared, pointing to the canyon walls. "You wanna bring the whole thing down on us?"

*Do it now*, a voice seemed to say. It was so clear, it took Jack by surprise and he looked around. There was no one else — Greenridge and his guards all stood at the railing with their backs to him. He didn't hear the voice again, but his stomach tightened, and he understood. Claythorne had a secret code, one that would cause the canyon to self-destruct. If Greenridge could use Jack to enter the correct code, surely Jack himself could enter the alternate.

By the time Greenridge had realized his mistake in letting him go, Jack was already at the keypad, his bound wrists shifted around his right hip.

"Hey, wait!" the bear yelled, charging toward him.

*One One*

*Seven Eight Nine*

*Zero Two*

As abruptly as they had started opening, the gates came to a grinding halt, stopping at a shallow angle from each other. The ground, the mountain, *everything* began to shake so violently, Jack had to grip the keypad to keep from falling, and watched in numb terror as several guards toppled over the railing and into the canyon.

The canyon walls began to growl. Boulders from the lower section tumbled down the face. Then clumps of snow. Then the large sheets along the mountain's upper crest tore away and began to slide.

"What have you *done?*" the bear roared. He grabbed Jack around the throat and hoisted him into the air. "I'll *kill* you for this!"

Panic flooded Jack's senses as the bear's grip on his throat tightened. He couldn't breathe. His head began to feel light.

And then, over Greenridge's shoulder, someone was smiling at him. At first, the face was shaded, and Jack recognized it as the farmer with the blue tractor. Only his hat was missing, and instead a mane of tangled dread-locks dangled around his shoulders. King of Hearts' expression was soft and warm. He opened his mouth, and a voice rose from inside him as though he were a radio. A voice Jack knew immediately as that of Dr. Walraven. "I know you won't understand this now, but sometimes... sometimes you have to lose in order to win." And just like that, King was gone.

Blinking, gasping for air, Jack kicked and fought and struggled. He caught Greenridge in the chest, although the bear hardly seemed to notice. He kicked again. His windpipe felt as though it had collapsed. He kicked again. This time, his foot caught in something, and he jerked his leg upward.

The rabbit feet! The necklace came up over Greenridge's head, flew over the railing, and fell into the gorge.

The effect this had on Greenridge was terrifying. He roared furiously, swung Jack around, and dangled him over the empty air. He was leaning far out, his waist bent around the railing. "Any last words, kid?" he yelled over the roar of the avalanche below them.

*Sometimes you have to lose in order to win.*

And then Jack understood.

It was the choice King had made for everyone on that train; the choice Dr. Walraven had made for Jack.

Now it was Jack's turn.

He gripped Greenridge's massive paw with both of his own, swung his feet upward to connect with the railing, and pushed.

Fear flashed into Greenridge's eyes as he toppled over the bar, and the two of them fell toward the cascading avalanche below.

They split apart in the air, Jack pinwheeling until he faced the sky. He felt as if he would fall forever, watching the half opened gates stretch upward before him.

A sort of peace flooded him like warm fluid. *Sometimes you have to lose in order to win.* He had chosen to lose, so that others could win. So that *good* could win.

He clenched his teeth and braced for impact.

There was a flash of light. The gray clouds were broken by a white hot missile, arcing over the gate and plummeting down, straight toward him. He could just make out the brilliant white figure, crackling like a holiday sparkler.

And then he was swallowed by the avalanche.

## Chapter Thirty-Six
## THE NEW DEAD

The world around him was engulfed in white. It fell past on every side, a roaring waterfall broken up by tumbling boulders of snow. They didn't hurt much when they hit him, only broke into smaller chunks and continued to plummet past his feet.

He looked upward. Wings spread wide and beak pointed toward the sky, Firebird glowed so brightly, the snow around him looked dim blue by comparison. The only part of him not flickering with white hot light was his bare black legs, and the talons that gripped Jack's shoulders. They caught mostly jacket, but their razor sharp points pressed firmly against his collar bones.

Soon, they broke into daylight. They passed through the narrow gap between the gate doors, over the mound of snow spilling through, and landed softly next to the inactive Ice Cat.

Heart still hammering, Jack fell to a seated position in the snow. "Thank… thank you," he panted.

The falcon's flames dimmed, licking with finality from between feathers, and Firebird was replaced by Grayson Conway. He nodded, watching the gap in the gate expectantly.

Jack sat for a moment, catching his breath. "How are you here?" he asked.

Seeming satisfied that nobody was coming through, the falcon turned to Jack and indicated a small device attached at his waist. It had a dark green display on which several blinking dots were visible. "Your tracker finally kicked in," he explained. "Once we saw that you were alive, we rushed back. The others came by anax; they may be a while behind." He jerked his head toward the gate. "So you want to tell me what happened here?"

Jack explained everything; the fall of the fort, the death of Claythorne, the horned monster, Greenridge's betrayal. He explained about the ferals, Harding, and the army behind the wall.

When he was finished, Conway seemed to consider this information. He then looked Jack up and down.

The sound of engines roared from the direction of the forest, and feral snow bikes pulled into the clearing, one by one sputtering to silence.

"Jack!" Sprint called. He dismounted from behind one of the coyotes and zipped across the snow, spraying the pair of them as he came to a sliding halt. "Oh, sorry," he said, seeing the annoyed look on Conway's face. Then he turned to Jack. "You're alright!" He laughed. "Shoot, how many times are we going to be saying *that* in our careers?" He looked past Jack, seeing the partly opened gate and the spill of fresh snow. "Wow! Did you do that?" he asked, amazed.

Jack raised his paws and wagged them. "Ta-da!"

Hoover, Willie, and Maddie trudged through the snow to where they stood. "So it's over then?" Maddie asked, looking toward the gap in the gate.

"Not quite," Conway said, his stern eyes still fixed on Jack. Then he seemed to soften. "There's still the fort. Dixon and the others are headed there now. I…" But he stopped abruptly.

A palpable silence had fallen. Every approaching feral stopped in their tracks. Hoover's eyes grew wide. Maddie looked as though she might be sick.

"Ah, what in the world?" Sprint groaned.

Conway spun around. Jack did the same, and his legs instantly felt weak.

Greenridge stood in the gap between the gate walls, looming down on the crowd from the mound of snow that had spilled through. Only he didn't look like Greenridge. He looked broken and misshapen. One arm hung further down than the other, his head rested loosely against his shoulder, and his knees turned inward as if he was being supported from behind. Just like the pink headless creatures, Jack thought he looked as though he was suspended on great strings coming down from the clouds overhead. His teeth were bared, and his eyes were wide, fixed madly on empty air.

Wind whistled through the gap, a mournful, ghostly sound, and for a moment Greenridge's undead body simply stood there like a nightmarish statue. Then something — someone — bobbed up to his left. Then his right. Then more. The gap began to fill with limping, broken bodies of the avalanche victims.

*Puppets*, Jack thought once again.

There was a cackle of laughter from overhead. Jack looked, and so did everyone else. Cutting against the cloudy sky, the cloaked, skull headed creature grinned down at them from the top of the wall, those perfect circle eye sockets seeming to take them all in.

The creature lifted the sack it carried into the air, and from it emitted a shrill war cry. As the cry continued, the creature lobbed the sack from the brink of the wall. It fell through the air, the yell growing louder, and landed with a *thoop* twenty yards from the line. The sharp black tip of a beak protruded from the darkened opening.

"Gordon," Conway said, a bitter note in his voice.

The undead soldiers burst from the gate, pouring out like fluid, charging down the mound. A cacophony of shrieks filled the canyon, echoing off the walls.

Terrified, Jack turned to Conway. "What do we do?" he yelled over the noise.

"What do you think?" Conway yelled. "Run!" But instead of turning with them, he looked upward and burst into the air, straight for the horned creature.

"Let's go!" Sprint said, grabbing Hoover by the arm. "Jack, what are you waiting for? Let's go!"

Jack took his eyes away from the top of the gate, turned, and followed the others as they did their best to run through the snow. Like the rest of them, Jack's movements were slow and labored. He felt like he was wading through shallow water.

Ahead, it seemed the entire feral camp had come out, ready for war. They stood their ground in several uneven rows. Their weapons were as mismatched as their clothing; everything from wood carved spears to old fashioned rifles. Armel, the bear-like coyote, stood before the rest, his sons Sasha and Ramses at his sides.

Jack glanced over his shoulder as he ran. The undead climbed over each other, stepping on the backs of the fallen, crushing them into the snow. They were gaining.

Jack and the others reached the line of the ferals and turned.

A blinding white light arched up from the gate, passing over the approaching army. Conway landed near Armel and his sons.

His flames died out, and he shook his head, tossing something big and white at their feet; the horned skull. "There was nothing under that costume. Just a bunch of bones."

"We didn't come here to fight an unstoppable army," Sasha said.

"He's right," Armel shouted, gripping his rifle anxiously. "We can't beat an enemy that's already dead."

"Well, you can't outrun them either," Conway said.

Armel considered this, then gave a defeated nod. "Hold your ground!" he shouted.

"Jack, what are you doing?" Conway yelled. "I told you to run! Now!"

"No. We want to fight," Jack argued. Since he'd entered that code, he felt a certain hardening within him. He'd really done something now, really *saved the day*. He wasn't about to turn and flee. "I'm not a coward," he said.

Conway fixed him with a stern look. "We can't beat this army, Jack," he said in little more than a whisper. "Everyone here is about to die. And I won't have five children dying with us." Then he burst into white flame, and spoke in that godlike voice he'd used at the Honey Sap. "Now *go!*"

There wasn't time to argue. Jack turned helplessly toward the approaching army. They charged in a tight cluster, a great black wall of claws and teeth, growling, roaring, chomping, snarling.

"You heard him," Sprint said, shoving Hoover from behind. They moved through the crowd of coyotes until they came out the other side. Ahead, pure snow stretched out before a forest of white-powdered trees sparkling in the sunlight. Safety.

Behind them, the sound of gunfire, clashing weapons, and screams broke the peaceful illusion.

## CHAPTER THIRTY-SIX

*Everyone here is about to die.*

Jack came to a stop, staring ahead.

"Jack," Sprint said, releasing Hoover and turning back. "Jack, what are you doing?"

"This isn't who we are," Jack said. The others stopped and turned also. "We can't run and hide the moment things get dangerous."

"Jack," Maddie reasoned, "did you see Greenridge? Did you see his men? They're not even *alive*. They're like machines. Even if I could see direct sunlight, it might not stop them. It might only stop the ferals and Conway. What good would that do?"

"*Being a hero is not about heightena, it's about heart,*" Jack quoted. "King of Hearts." And despite his fears, he smiled. "Maybe you've heard of him."

Maddie opened her mouth to speak, then shut it again.

Willie sighed resignedly, then moved to Jack's side. "You're right. He's right. We can't hide. We're heroes."

Hoover gulped and nodded, then joined them. He shrugged apologetically to Sprint, who rolled his eyes and followed.

Maddie stared at them, then turned toward the open snow.

"If you want to leave, that's okay," Jack said. "The four of us are going back."

Maddie folded her arms across her chest and glared at him, but her mouth twitched. "You mean the five of us," she said. "Team evaluation and all that."

Jack smiled, but before he could turn, Hoover pointed toward a line of trees to their left. "Isn't that Peter Claythorne?"

Jack followed his outstretched claw. The white wolf was sitting in the bowl below a tree, his back pressed to the trunk.

"Hiding *again*?," Sprint said, disbelieving. "Shoot. That guy's a real hero."

"But if he's afraid," Jack voiced, "why isn't he running?" And there was something else. His eyes were open, staring transfixed, as if he was in some kind of hypnosis, and held out in front of him were both paws, their fingers splayed out as if manipulating a…

*A puppet.*

"It's him!" Jack said, taking off in the direction of the trees. "It's Peter! He's doing this!"

The others raced to catch up. Sprint was by his side immediately. "What do you mean?"

"I mean, *he* is the horned creature. Didn't you hear Conway? There wasn't anything under that cloak. It was a puppet. So the first night we saw it, somebody had to be controlling it. And who came to your rescue at the lake?"

Understanding, Sprint zipped off toward Peter. Just as he entered the shade of the trees, something swung out from behind a trunk and clothes-lined him, sending him pin-wheeling into the snow. He skidded to a halt on his face, unmoving.

"Miles!" Hoover cried, picking up pace. But he stopped short — they all did — as a figure emerged from behind the tree. His brown fur was matted, and he had that same lopsided posture, the same lifeless expression on his face.

"I thought I might need protection," Mr. Behr said. Only it didn't sound like Mr. Behr. The voice was wheezing, as if the air was being squeezed out rather than spoken, just like the voice from the sack.

Trembling, Jack looked past the reanimated body of their handler. Peter still had his back to the tree, still wore a transfixed expression, still held his paws in front of him as though manipulating a marionette. "Why are you doing this?" Jack yelled. "Your army is already dead; you've lost!"

A high, cold laugh erupted from Behr's mouth. "Yes," the voice said. "I really should thank you for that. I confess I was in over my head with the invasion plan. Perhaps too much faith was placed in me."

"By Brisk?" Jack asked, trying to see Peter from around Behr.

"President Brisk is a fool. Foolish enough to believe this invasion was his idea; a Red Teeth rebirth that would scare the nation, have them *begging* him to access the Alpha Heightena. And while he thought he was manipulating me, it was truly my master who was manipulating *him*."

Edging slowly to the left, Jack tried to keep Peter talking. "But you were an apprentice. A hero."

The voice issuing from Behr's mouth became cold. "You all think being an apprentice is a dream come true," he snarled. "For me, it was a nightmare, just a way for my mother to pawn me off, make me someone else's problem. Please don't move," he barked, and Behr's head snapped toward Maddie. She stopped midway through a step backward. "I loved my father," the voice continued. "The sickness that took him, it worked quickly. I never even got to say goodbye. Imagine my surprise, to wake up from a dream about better times only to find him standing beside my bed." Behr's face did not change, but the voice became wistful. "I had my father back. Of course, I didn't realize at first that it was *me* doing it; my sadness, my pining reanimating his dead body. But my mother..." His pensive tone was replaced with hollow disgust. "She locked me away, both horrified and ashamed of what I had done. Punished me, for the simple crime of loving my father too much to let him go. Then her adviser, Gordon, suggested the apprenticeship program. She couldn't be happier with the solution. But where my mother and Gordon saw me as filth to be swept under the rug, my master saw my true potential. He incorporated me into his plan. A train hijacking that would end King's life."

Jack froze. "Train…?"

"Yes," the voice said. "Your lion friend, King's cousin, was so overflowing with envy, so bitter at being rejected from King's team, he sold him out. Sold us his weakness: *a broken heart*. This information positioned me perfectly; my mentor was White Stripe, the badger from King's team. I saw firsthand King's interactions with his own sidekick, and knew that they'd become quite close, very much like a father and son."

"So you killed his sidekick to break his heart."

"Oh, it's better than just that," the voice said with oily satisfaction. "I was on the train that day. I had the apprentice brought on board. I made them *fight*."

Jack remembered the anguished roar King had issued from the roof of the train. "All of this because you wanted King's power?"

"It's not King's power. It's *the* power. The Alpha Heightena. King was merely a vessel; a jar to contain the power. My master had to break him in order to take it."

"Well, he failed," Jack said, surprised to hear the laughter in his own voice. "*You* failed. King beat you both. Before he died, he hid his power where you'll *never* reach it. You want the key, right? Well I don't have it anymore. It's gone. Sorry."

In the distance beyond the forest, the sounds of battle grew louder and closer. Screams. Gunshots. The clanging of metal.

"The sapling?" the voice inferred. Then it laughed that horrible, shrill laugh again. "And now we come to it," the voice said, tremulous with excitement. "The big secret. Surely you don't think you're here by coincidence, Jack. Surely you don't believe your pathetic little team of *porters* actually qualify as Vanguard's sidekicks. I wanted you here. The moment I met you, I understood."

"Understood what?" Jack spat. "That I could open the gate for you?"

"No. Although the gate *did* confirm my suspicions. Perhaps you noticed today that when you triggered the avalanche with your code, there weren't any explosions. The snow just... did what you wanted it to do."

"What are you saying?"

"Dr. Walraven has been hiding you away all these years, his own private secret. The sapling is a fake. *You* have the Alpha power, Jack."

His head suddenly light, Jack saw the train wreck play out in his memory as though watching it through a long tunnel. He had been soaring through the air, clutched tightly in King's arms. The engine was toppling end-over-end just behind them as they crashed through the stone wall of an old chapel. He had blacked out. Woke up in Dr. Walraven's arms. But there was something between, some narrow sliver of memory, like a single photograph spliced between frames of a film reel; so minuscule, it had never before surfaced in his attempts to block out that horrible day. He'd been shut in blackness beneath the train. Arms pressed the engine up and off of him in a dead lift.

But the arms weren't King's.

They were Jack's.

His memory was interrupted as Willie made a move. He leapt for the nearest tree, landed high up the trunk, and shot his tongue toward Peter. But a paw snatched the tongue as easily as if it were an underhanded pitch.

"NO!" Hoover howled.

Sprint, his face fixed in a hollow stare, jerked the tongue. Willie was yanked bodily through the air. He connected with an opposing tree with a loud *thud*, then collapsed to the ground.

Behr moved to Sprint's side, the two of them blocking Peter from view. And then they spoke together in an eerie drone. "The Red Teeth *will* rise again. Safehaven is only a spark. But the flame is coming. And when it does, Nikacia will burn to ashes." The two of them sniffed the air dramatically. "Mmmmm... delicious ashes."

"Maddie," Jack said, "get to the sun. Stopping him will stop them all."

Maddie turned to leave the shade of the trees, but Behr lunged for her. He grabbed her around the arms, lifting her kicking into the air. "I don't think so," the voice said.

Hoover made a move toward Peter, but Sprint zipped in front of him. "Not so fast, Fatso."

Not knowing what he planned to do, Jack darted toward Peter. He was caught around the ankle, and tumbled to the ground. Willie's tongue released, and the frog tackled him. "Would you please stop distracting me," he seethed. Willie wasn't particularly heavy, but he was strong. He pinned Jack's arms behind his back as if placing him under arrest, shoving his head into the snow. Jack struggled against the restraint, rolled his face to the side.

Hoover, still blocked by Sprint, wore an expression of deepest anguish. "You're my best friend," he said. "You've always been there for me."

"Fatty," Sprint sneered. "*Blubber-butt!*"

"I know it's not you talking," Hoover continued, raising his voice over the string of insults. "But I hope you're in there somewhere, listening."

"*Thunder-thighs.*"

"I didn't want to be a hero," Hoover continued. His voice rattled, as though the words, and what it cost to speak them, was taking everything he had. "I wanted to be a writer, like—like my dad. But you said something to me. Something you meant as a joke, but which I think – I hope – that deep down, you—you really meant."

"Did I tell you what a walrus you are?" Sprint mocked. "Because I wasn't joking."

"No," Hoover said, and he took a step toward his friend. "You said that in a fight, I'd kick your ass."

He raised his snout like the barrel of a rifle.

*Crack!* The noise of the blast made Jack's ears ring. Sprint flew through the forest, crashing into the snow somewhere out of sight.

The anguished look replaced with deepest rage, Hoover turned toward Peter.

For a fraction of a second, the wolf came back to himself, his eyes focusing fearfully on Hoover.

*Crack!* Peter was blasted backward, straight through the trunk of the tree against which he had been positioned. Splinters filled the air as the tree fell forward. Peter smacked against a second tree, bringing the snow down upon himself, and was buried. Instantly, Behr and Willie collapsed like marionettes whose strings had been clipped.

Jack pushed out from beneath Willie's unconscious figure. Fighting his own wobbling legs, he stood and moved to Hoover's side. "Are you okay?"

Hoover gave a single, slow nod.

"And Sprint?" Jack asked, looking in the direction the squirrel had flown.

"He's alive," Hoover said. He turned toward the jagged remains of the fallen tree. The air was thick with splintery confetti as bits of wood drifted toward the ground. "High and low settings," he said, smiling tearfully.

## Chapter Thirty-Seven

## STRONGER

"Just drop him anywhere," Sasha growled.

Hoover shrugged off the unconscious body of Peter Claythorne. The wolf flopped into the snow alongside one of the fallen Red Teeth soldiers.

Looking around at the field of bodies, Jack had to remind himself how many had *already* been dead. The ferals had fought bravely, and while a few sustained serious injuries, not a single life was lost. "At least no lives not already lost," Sasha pointed out, nodding toward the heaped form of General Greenridge. "Claythorne seemed to have bitten off more than he could chew, trying to control that many. None of them seemed able to focus or defend themselves, they just sort of ran around swinging their weapons wildly."

Maddie approached Jack, arms folded across her chest. "Do you have a second?"

He had been afraid of this. Clenching his teeth, Jack followed as she stepped away. They didn't walk far before she seemed satisfied that they wouldn't be overheard, and she turned toward him. For a moment, she seemed to struggle with what exactly she wanted to say, opening and closing her mouth several times, and moving her weight from one foot to the other. "You probably wonder why I've been making all those phone calls," she said.

Bemused, Jack shrugged. "I guess, yeah." What did that have to do with Peter's big revelation?

She folded her arms once more across her chest and spoke to her own feet. "I have a little brother." She said this in a whisper, as though confessing her deepest sin.

"Oh," Jack said. This was not at all what he had expected, and he was unsure of why this information was important, or seemingly embarrassing.

"I should say," Maddie continued, "I *only* have a brother. Rather, he only has *me*." Her eyes met Jack's, trying to assess if he'd understood her meaning. "He's staying with a friend while I... while we do this whole *sidekick* thing. That's who I was calling all those times."

"Gotcha," Jack said, his face fixed in what he hoped was an understanding smile.

"I can't fail, Jack," she said, looking again at her feet. "My brother, Luke, he... he depends on me."

"Understood," Jack replied.

"Just..." She took a step closer and lowered her voice. "Just please keep it between us."

"Sure," Jack said, rubbing the space between his ears. "But... why tell *me?*" he added, trying his best to sound supportive rather than uneasy.

She met his eyes, and there was something in that look; something like apology. But at that moment, Conway appeared from among the crowd, and Maddie gave a start and hurried away.

"What was that about?" Hoover asked when Jack returned.

"No idea," Jack responded. He didn't like the appraising look Conway was now giving him.

Sasha spat, then wiped his lips with a shaking paw. "So much for the return of the Red Teeth."

"We'll see," said Conway. "First things first, we'll need to get that gate sealed. I've received word from my team that the fort has been recovered. Looks like we've got a lot of arrests to make." He shot a brief glance at Jack, then walked away.

The fort grew smaller out the anax window. When it had disappeared beneath a cloud, Jack rolled his aching neck the other way to look at his team.

Still very weak, Sprint was tearing off bits of a pinkish fruit Hoover had peeled for him. "What is this I'm eating?" he groaned.

"A grapefruit," Hoover answered, peeling a second.

Sprint picked a piece from his mouth. "Bleeegh! You eat these? It's like someone weaponized an orange!"

"You need to finish it. And stay awake!" Hoover demanded. Sprint raised his eyebrows and gave a small, surprised laugh.

Willie laughed too, something Jack wasn't sure he'd ever seen, and laid his head against the cushion of his anaxopter seat.

Only Maddie seemed unchanged by the events of the past few days. In fact, Jack thought she looked more stern and uneasy than ever. She kept giving Conway sidelong, guilty glances, repositioning herself as though she was sitting on something uncomfortable, and then looking pointedly out the window. Once, she caught Jack looking at her, but instead of cocking her neck sideways and giving him the usual "can I *help* you?" glare, she simply dropped her eyes and turned away.

The remainder of the flight was mostly silent. The Vanguard team only spoke on occasion, and only to recount facts about the mission, or to bemoan the stacks of paperwork they would be required to fill out upon returning. Conway, however, never commented on any of this, and never seemed to look away from the window.

Jack watched the other anaxopters fly alongside them, remembering the harrowing chase through the mountains. Remembering Behr. His kindness and bravery, his faith in Jack and the others. *"He's not dead,"* a medic had announced. *"But he's close."* He hadn't sustained more than the single gunshot wound in his left shoulder, but had been rendered unconscious by what the medic described as "the kind of hit he'll be feeling for a long while."

Jack and the others had protested when the medic insisted on restraining Behr with shackles. "Only until he's awake," the medic had reassured them. "After all, Peter Claythorne is here too."

Indeed he was; bound and blindfolded in another of those anaxopters, about to spend the rest of his life in prison.

At this thought, Peter's words came to Jack once more. *Dr. Walraven has been hiding you away all these years, his own private secret. The sapling is a fake.* You *have the Alpha power.*

But it couldn't be true. No matter what he thought he might have remembered, if he'd had King's powers, why had others always needed to come to his rescue? Dr. Walraven at the mill. President Brisk at the harbor. Harding at the ravine. Conway at the gate. Surely Jack wouldn't have needed their help, if he'd had King's powers all along. And if Dr. Walraven knew, then why hadn't he told Jack? The day the wolves attacked, why hadn't he told him then that Jack could save them both?

It just *couldn't* be true.

Darkness had fallen by the time they reached the southern edge of the sea. In contrast to the bland gray tone the city had when they'd left, it now looked as vibrant and alive as the insides of a pinball machine. Neon lights stretched across the faces of sparkling glass buildings. Veins of headlights weaved throughout the grid-like network of roads.

The campus formed a dark patch along one edge of the city, flecked throughout with yellow path lights. The anax was low enough now that Jack could see figures walking along those paths, could see the detail of the trees. They passed over Kelly Hall, across the black water of the lake. Smoothly, they set down on the roof of the Launch Center, the wings ground to a stop, and Jack became aware of his own heartbeat. Something felt wrong.

Carry Anne, the boar in the brown flight suit, pulled the door open from the outside and stood to one side.

But instead of unhitching their seat belts, the Vanguard team looked toward Conway.

He sighed, cleared his throat, and spoke. "Vanguard, please take responsibility for your apprentices. Exit the craft and return them to the Barracks." He met Jack's eyes. "Jack, please remain seated."

Heart hammering, Jack began to speak, but Sprint beat him to it. "This was you, wasn't it?" he said, looking at Maddie. Then he turned to Conway. "Whatever she told you, it's not true." He nudged Hoover, who looked uneasily at his own paws.

And then Jack understood. Sprint knew about the key, of course, but he'd been unconscious when Peter had spoken. The others had heard everything. The crash. King's death. King's *power*.

And Maddie had told Conway.

Dixon, Pan, Llood, and Ford unclasped their restraints and hopped out onto the concrete. Maddie followed them, looking as though eye contact with anyone might turn her to stone. But Sprint, Hoover, and Willie remained in their seats.

"What's going on?" Willie asked, looking between Jack and Conway.

"Never you mind," Conway said. "Exit the craft and join your mentors."

The sound of footsteps brought their attention to the door. Armed soldiers came to a stop outside the anax, raising their rifles and pointing them into the anax bay.

"Whoa, what is going on?" Sprint echoed, his tone both alarmed and demanding.

"They're kids. Lower your weapons," Conway called without looking at the guards. "Greenacre, Driyoute, Fennelman. I want you out of this anax immediately."

Reluctantly, and with mutinous glares, they did as they were told. When they had joined their mentors and the flight crew and had left the rooftop, Conway spoke.

"Don't think too harshly of her, Jack," he said, jerking his head to where Maddie had disappeared. "She has an adult's burdens. She has to do what's best for her."

Jack gripped his pant legs to keep his paws from shaking, and said nothing.

Conway met his eyes again, then sighed. "Where is the key?"

Jack blinked. This was not the question he had expected. The key? The key was the least of the secrets he was now harboring. Mistaking the confusion on Jack's face, Conway continued. "Several months ago, a key was stolen from Animal Control. I was told that you know something about it."

So he only knew about the key, then, and nothing about Peter Claythorne's wild theory about Jack having the Alpha power. This was poker. Maddie might have sold him out, but she hadn't given Conway all of Jack's cards; she'd left room to bluff. Now it was time to hitch on that poker face.

He looked out the open door. Those soldiers, with their faces obscured behind glass face plates and their black rifles, looked truly menacing. "I don't have it anymore."

"You *lost* it?" Conway said, his eyes widening.

"No," Jack said. "But someone else has it now."

Conway looked uncertain. "Okay. Who?"

"I can't tell you," Jack said.

Conway's eyes grew wider still and he seethed. "What do you mean you can't tell me?"

"It's safe," Jack said. "That's all I can tell you."

Something unusual caught his eye. The soldiers were standing almost completely still. But one of them made a subtle movement, one nobody else seemed to have noticed. It looked to Jack as if they were pickpocketing the soldier in front of them.

"Jack, do you have any idea what that key *is*? If the wrong side get a hold of it..."

"They won't," Jack said confidently, thinking of President Brisk.

There it was again. This time it was a shorter soldier to the left. They took one paw off of their rifle, withdrew something from their belt, expertly reached to the soldier in front of them, and returned their empty paw to the rifle.

"But that's not your decision to make," Conway said. "If I don't get the key, you'll leave me no choice."

Jack tried to meet Conway's eyes, found it impossible, and simply shrugged and shook his head.

"In that case," Conway sighed, and unclasped his restraints. He dropped to the roof, paused, then looked back at Jack. "Arrest him."

The soldiers moved in, their rifles half-raised.

But a shrill noise behind them brought them all to a stop. One of the anaxopters along the opposite end of the rooftop was whining to life. Its dragonfly wings pumped downward. At first the wings simply slapped the bodies of the other anaxopters to the right and left, but as the wings picked up speed, the other anaxes were pushed sideways, scraping along the cement until they pressed up against the next ones in line.

A pair of paws gripped Jack's chest, taking him by surprise. He found himself face to face with the familiar bleach-white vulture mask. The black creature had climbed into the anax bay while all eyes were pointed the other way. Its empty eyes seemed to glare right through Jack while in one smooth motion it unclasped the restraints and pulled him from the seat. Claws digging into Jack's upper arm, the creature dragged him from the anax, but their movements were interrupted by Conway's voice.

"Let him go!" he shouted over the chopping of the wings. "There's nowhere to run!"

Looking at Conway, Petrillo released Jack, then slowly raised its paws, elbowing Jack, who did the same.

For a moment, Conway and Petrillo simply stared at each other, the wind from the active anax blowing across them. Then Petrillo held up a finger as if to say "if I may," and cautiously reached to its waist. The creature unclasped a small black device. It looked to Jack like a remote control for a toy car, with a small green light at the top.

The soldiers raised their rifles in unison. The red dots of a dozen laser sights popped up on Petrillo's chest and forehead.

"Drop it!" Conway ordered. "Don't do anything stupid."

Petrillo raised his paw in surrender again, but still clutched the small remote.

"I said *drop it!*" Conway repeated.

Petrillo complied, tossing the object aside, but not before mashing a thumb down on one of the buttons. As the remote clattered to the floor, the chopping sound grew louder, and the anax behind Conway lifted off into the air.

Jack watched as the machine floated away like a released balloon, no pilot at the controls. Just as he began to wonder if Petrillo's only plan was to make Conway mad, something thin and black caught his eye. It looked like some kind of rope. It dangled from the body of the anax, writhing wildly on the wind coming from the wings. Then, with a sudden pop, it snapped tight.

"Hey! HEY!" yelled a soldier. He was pulled violently to the pavement, and was dragged across the rooftop. The soldier next to him fell also, then the next. Seeing what was happening, the others dropped their rifles, grabbed wildly for the rope strung between them, and squatted down as if preparing for a tug of war. The moment the rope grew taut, however, they were pulled roughly to the ground as well, dragged along the rooftop, and one by one were hoisted into the air as the anax gained altitude and carried them screaming into the black sky.

The night grew silent once more, and Petrillo lowered its paws. Conway and the creature considered each other for a moment. If looks could kill, Jack thought, Petrillo would have dropped dead on the spot.

He shielded his eyes as Conway exploded into flames. "Jack comes with me," the falcon said in his godlike voice.

In response, Petrillo turned to Jack and jerked its head toward Conway. Squinting in the brilliant light, Jack walked forward, past Conway, and was grabbed around the collar by one of the two remaining soldiers.

"Get him out of here," Conway commanded, his white-hot eyes still fixed on Petrillo. The shorter soldier tugged Jack roughly, and they passed between the rows of remaining anaxopters that lined the rooftop.

The other, taller soldier threw the stairwell door open. Jack was shoved inside, and the door slammed with an echo. They stopped on the upper landing.

"We gotta go," said the taller soldier. His voice was deep and husky.

"Just a moment, Darlin'," said the shorter one in a high, sing-song voice. She shrugged off a duffel bag, dropped it to the floor and unzipped it, then extracted a black helmet with a plastic faceplate identical to the ones they both wore. "Put this on," she said. "Tuck them ears in. And these. Quickly." She dumped out the contents of the bag, revealing gloves, boots, and armor. "For real! We have maybe seconds."

Bemused, Jack threw the items on as quickly as he could. The helmet wobbled on his head, and he was absolutely swimming in the body armor. The boots fit, though.

"Close enough," the female soldier said, then pushed him forward once more. They jogged down the stairwell, crossed through the Launch Center lobby, and out into the night on ground level. There was a loud crashing sound, a burst of flames over their heads, and the scraping noise of metal.

"Look out!" the larger soldier said, pulling Jack backward just as the tail section of an anaxopter crashed before them in a ball of fire.

There was a blur of motion. Dixon appeared so quickly before them, Jack might have thought he had teleported, if not for the way the smoke was curling where he had passed through. "What happened?"

"Petrillo," the larger guard said, pointing toward the roof.

Without waiting for further explanation, the greyhound zipped off into the building.

"Is it me," asked the larger soldier, "or are they getting dumber? Wait, what are you doing?"

The female soldier, who wasn't much taller than Jack, was rummaging through the duffel bag once more.

"No, come on!" the male one demanded. "We don't have time for your urban habits."

"Urban habits?" the female said in a mock hurt voice. She withdrew a silver can from the bag, shook it briskly back and forth, and turned to face an Animal Control logo that stood out from the exterior wall. "This, my brawler friend, is *art.*" She began spraying white paint across and around the falcon shape, moving the can skillfully in small arcs. She took a step back, examining her work, although through her faceplate Jack couldn't tell if she was happy with it or not. In any case, she snapped the lid back onto the paint, dropped it into the duffel, and nodded forward. They jogged around the burning remains of the anaxopter and into the night.

White paint dripped down the falcon and the wall behind it, although it no longer looked like a falcon. A face had been painted across the body, turning the wings into great, flopping ears. The tail was extended into a long trunk, on either side of which two large curved tusks swooped downward. And above the newly created elephant's head, thin white lines trickled from letters spelling a single word:

STRONGER

## Chapter Thirty-Eight
## THE NIGHT CLUB

"I think I'm out of white paint," said the shorter of his rescuers, who turned out to be a teenage black cat. She unsnapped her shin guards, stuffing them into the duffel bag between her feet in the passenger seat of the gray sedan. "Swing by the store on the way, would you?"

The other rescuer, a muscular brown Pitbull with a row of scars along his jowl that looked very much like a tiger had taken a swipe at his face, gave a small laugh. "Yeah right. I'm just glad we made it out. Can't believe that worked." He eased the steering wheel to the left and passed a slow-moving trailer.

"And Petrillo?" the cat asked. "For all we know, he's a ball of ash right now."

"He can take care of himself," the Pitbull said, checking his mirror.

Watching them from the back seat, Jack sat in quiet dread. What had just happened? In a matter of moments, he'd gone from hero to convict to fugitive. Now here he was, abducted by two strangers about whom the only thing he knew was that they were connected to Triarch's most wanted thief.

They moved along a darkened highway. An hour out of the city, the Pitbull exited onto a single lane road that cut between the shadowy shapes of grain silos and orchards. Finally, they pulled into a half circle driveway before a mansion of a farmhouse. A porch wrapped around the house, covered in so many potted plants and small trees, it looked like a boxed-in jungle. At the center of the porch, a single light was on beside large double doors with inset doors similar to the President's Mansion. The cat wrapped her knuckles against them, then stood back. Almost immediately, the porch began to rumble. Jack looked uncertainly toward the others, wondering whether a dinosaur was about to burst through. The cat winked and smiled.

The medium sized door swung open, a palm like a large gray trashcan lid pressing it outward, and a single eye peeked through. "Welcome home!" the eye boomed. "I see your mission was a success."

"So far," the cat said, half skipping, half walking inside. The eye pulled out of the opening and let her pass. "We'll feel more relaxed when Petrillo gets back. I hate leaving him behind."

"Oh, I'm sure he'll be just fine," the eye said, and as Jack moved through the door and into the large entryway, he saw that it belonged to a plump, kind-faced elephant. Plump, in fact, might have been too subtle a word, Jack considered. The elephant filled the space, as though someone had fitted a tuxedo onto a small gray mountain. "And you must be Jack," he said, his cheeks pressing into his tusks in an even broader smile. "Glad we got you here."

"Er... thanks," Jack said. He looked around the space in awe. Everything was made of polished wood, from a floor so shiny that he could check his reflection in it, to a curving staircase that led to what seemed like a library, to rafters overhead that looked like each had been an entire tree at one point in its life.

"Oooh, do I smell peanut butter?" the cat asked, sniffing the air hungrily.

"I made cookies," the elephant said. "And keep your grubby paws off them."

"Of course we will," the cat responded. She and the Pitbull marched down the hallway to the left, and Jack found himself alone with the elephant.

"Now, there's someone who would like very much to speak with you," the elephant said, motioning for Jack to follow him. As they moved through the hallway, Jack was amazed that the elephant, who was nearly as wide as he was tall, didn't knock the frames from the walls on either side. They stopped in front of a door too small for the elephant to pass through. He opened it, looking like an oversized child playing with a dollhouse, and gestured for Jack to enter.

"Would you like some tea?" he asked, squatting down and peering after Jack as if looking through a keyhole.

"Uh… no, thank you," Jack said.

"I'll get some anyway."

Turning into the room, Jack was greeted by a warm fire burning in a stone fireplace taller than himself. Two high-backed armchairs sat unoccupied before the fire, a small round table between them.

Jack's eyes were drawn to a painting mounted above the mantle, and he stared disbelieving. It was a portrait of two lions — a man and a woman. The man's mane draped around his shoulders in long ropes. His mouth was stretched into an almost goofy smile. The woman, whose paw was pressed to her husband's breast, wore a more serious expression. Her brows were high, her lips closed in a one-sided and nearly imperceptible grin. Jack thought she looked like someone not to be challenged.

He looked back at the man. That face, that mane, and the brass, heart-shaped pendant that dangled over a thick-knotted tie, were unmistakable.

A voice spoke from the doorway behind him. A voice so impossibly, wonderfully familiar that his heart seemed to both leap to his throat and sink to his stomach.

"Beautiful portrait, isn't it?"

Jack spun around so quickly, he nearly fell over, and when he saw the figure standing in the doorway, he thought he might fall over anyway.

The newcomer stepped into the room, the firelight bouncing off of his circular spectacles. He opened his mouth to speak, then shut it again.

Jack stared blankly, not breathing. He took a single step toward Dr. Walraven, as though the latter might disappear if he drew too close. The doctor spread his arms wide, inviting an embrace, but Jack moved no further. "Where were you?" he asked, hearing the accusation in his own voice.

Dr. Walraven lowered his arms slightly. "I'm sorry Jack. I know you've been through a lot."

"A lot?" Jack repeated. "I was nearly murdered. Several times."

A silence fell between them, broken only by the crackling of the fire.

"You want to tell me about it?" Dr. Walraven invited.

Tears came sudden and heavy. Jack strode across the room, crashing against the doctor. His arms wrapped so tightly, Dr. Walraven let out a surprised cough and a laugh, but he reciprocated the hug.

They sat in front of the fire, and Jack tore into recounting every detail of his adventure, from the moment he fell into the river, to his return, arrest, and rescue at Animal Control. Some memories were wonderful to relive: meeting Sprint and Hoover in that overcrowded diner; the excitement of the trials; even the simple act of delivering mail around the Animal Control campus. Some moments, which seemed terrifying at the time, he retold with enthusiasm. He sat on the edge of his armchair as he recounted the climb up the canyon wall as the dam had begun to burst. Dr. Walraven seemed interested in Harding, but didn't press for details.

And then some memories were almost too horrible to speak out loud; the terror he'd felt at the sight of those headless creatures, the crash of the anaxopter, the violence at Safehaven. When he got to the part about falling from the top of the Gate, he saw that Dr. Walraven was gripping his armrests, although his expression was unreadable.

The door creaked open. "More tea?" the elephant asked, peeking an eye into the room.

"Yes, thank you," said Dr. Walraven, and he began to stand.

"No, no," the elephant said. "You sit." An arm reached into the room, daintily pinching a teapot between two stubby fingers. The wall groaned as the arm reached full extension, still several feet from Dr. Walraven.

"I can get up," Dr. Walraven said.

"No, no," the elephant repeated. He withdrew his arm from the room, there was a tinkling of china, and the tea pot reentered, now supported by the elephant's long trunk. "*How's... this?*" he growled, his forehead pressed against the door frame, his tusks narrowly clearing its edges.

Dr. Walraven positioned his cup directly below the suspended teapot. "Yep," he said, smiling at Jack. "You're right there. Go ahead and pour."

"Okay, say when," the elephant sang. When he'd splashed tea into Dr. Walraven's cup — and much of the floor — he withdrew the pot and peered in again. "And you, Jack?"

"I'm okay," Jack said, stifling a laugh. The elephant winked, then pinched the doorknob and pulled it closed once more.

"I wish I could have been there for you," Dr. Walraven said. "For all of it. I did try to find you, but was unsuccessful until you reached Triarch. There were other things I had to take care of, and I..."

"You knew King's power would protect me."

The doctor met Jack's eyes.

"Yeah, I figured it out," Jack said, his gut tightening. In the beginning, he hadn't believed Peter's words, but the look on Dr. Walraven's face, as though Jack had just said the doctor's darkest secret out loud, served as confirmation.

The silence seemed to grow heavy, even the crackling fireplace grew dim, as Jack began, at long last, to understand.

The earthquakes in Hadensburrow. He did that.

The avalanche at Hard Stop. There hadn't been any explosions. The mountains themselves had shaken. *Jack* had shaken them.

He remembered the train crash again. Remembered pushing out from under the engine. No, pushing the engine off from *him*. He stared into the fireplace without seeing the flames. "So then it's true," he whispered. "The sapling was a fake. King passed his powers on to me."

Dr. Walraven set his tea aside, eyes fixed on Jack.

"Why?" Jack asked. "Why would he do that? I'm just a kid."

In response, Dr. Walraven turned to the portrait. "Because he knew, in that moment, that one of you was going to die. It was him or you. As Aaron always did, he chose the hero's path."

A hollow feeling grew inside Jack. "Then I *am* the reason. I'm the reason he's dead."

"No," Dr. Walraven said. "He died to save…"

"I know, I know," Jack interrupted, rolling his eyes. "He died to save all of us." That argument might have worked when he was younger. It didn't work now.

"Yes he did," Dr. Walraven replied, his tone understanding. "And in his place," he met Jack's eyes, and there was a glistening pride there, "he gave us *you*."

Not knowing what to say to this, Jack remained silent. His eyes moved back to the painting above the mantle. "So what is this place? Is this… is this King's house?"

Dr. Walraven looked up at the painting too. "Yes. This is the home Aaron built for his wife Evangeline. She lives here still, and has kindly offered to allow us to use it as headquarters for the Night Club."

"The Night Club?"

Dr. Walraven dabbed his lips with a cloth napkin, pushed himself to stand, and turned to Jack. "I think it's best if I show you," he said, and motioned toward the door.

The hall seemed much bigger without an elephant filling it up. As they walked, Jack admired the artwork, photographs, and newspapers that covered every square inch of the walls.

"When Aaron and I first conceived of the idea of Animal Control," Dr. Walraven said, indicating the same newspaper clipping Jack had seen at the campus, depicting a young Aaron Harding with his arm draped across a young Dr. Walraven's shoulder, "we understood that no hero should go unchecked. Too much power could go to their heads. What we needed was an antihero. At first, it was only Petrillo, a persona we'd invented that would be faceless and feared. But as Animal Control expanded, it became impossible for one vigilante to do the job. So together, we founded a secret society, a group of antiheroes, to keep watch on the heroes of Animal Control."

Jack looked at Dr. Walraven incredulously. "King of Hearts hired vigi – whatever that word is – to beat up his superheroes?"

Dr. Walraven began walking again. "Vigilantes. And only when they crossed the line. You saw what happened at the mill. You saw with your own eyes what Brisk was plotting. The corruption of Animal Control has reached peak levels. That's why we had to get the key away from them."

"But if the tree is a fake," Jack started, confused, "if King gave *me* his... I mean, why would it matter if Brisk got to the tree?"

"It's precisely *because* the tree is a fake that we must keep Brisk away from it," Dr. Walraven explained. "The longer he doesn't know about you, the better off we'll all be."

They walked quietly for a moment, Jack deep in thought. Finally, he spoke his fear aloud. "But it's only a matter of time, isn't it?" he said. "I mean, Brisk doesn't know about me, but Peter does, and so does *his master*. And it sounded like..."

Dr. Walraven looked sideways at him as they continued along the hall. "It sounded like this *master* worked for Animal Control?"

"Yeah," Jack said, surprised. "You think that's possible?"

"I made a grave mistake in hiding too much from you for too long," Dr. Walraven apologized. "I don't want to make that mistake again, but I'm afraid there's not yet much I can tell you. I've known for a long time that the hijackers were just a distraction. Your story about Peter Claythorne fills in a lot of those blanks. And as he was an apprentice, it stands to reason he may have met this master at Animal Control."

They passed the front door and entered the opposite hall, which opened into a dining room adjacent to a polished kitchen. Along windows that stretched to the rafters, a long table was positioned, with a red cloth running down the middle and two dozen empty chairs surrounding it. The teenage cat and the scar-faced Pitbull were seated at an island with a silver counter top, a plate of cookies between them. The cat shot Jack a serious look. "You tell Henderstaut about the cookies, I will *cut* you." She opened her paw, and long silver claws popped outward. She smiled and winked, then retracted the claws and scooped up another cookie.

Jack forced a smile, then turned to Dr. Walraven. "Peter's master knows about me. It's only a matter of time before Brisk figures it out, and Animal Control comes looking for me, too. So what are we going to do?"

Dr. Walraven met Jack's eyes, his expression grave. "We do what we've always done. We fight."

As if on cue, a window overhead swung open, and a dark figure climbed in onto the rafters.

"Hey, there you are!" the cat said through a mouthful of cookie.

Petrillo cocked his head sideways, staring down at the room.

"As you said," Dr. Walraven continued, "it's not over. In fact, this is only the beginning. I hope you'll stick with us."

Jack looked up at Petrillo, who seemed to be staring right through him. Looking around, he saw that the others were staring at him, too.

"It's going to be dangerous," Dr. Walraven continued. "But I need you to trust me, Jack."

"Of course I trust you," Jack said. "You're my father."

A smile touched the edges of Dr Walraven's mouth, and he seemed momentarily unable to speak. Then he nodded, and looked around the room. "Well, first things first," he sighed. "We're going to need to build up our team."

Now it was Jack's turn to smile. He had a few names in mind.

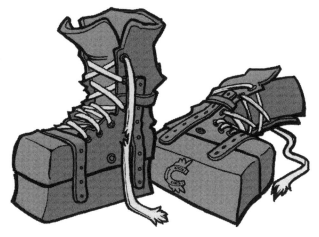

Epilogue

# PENANCE

Gravel crunched beneath Toby Harding's boots. Somewhere, a twig snapped, and he spun around. The road was empty, bathed in moonlight. He laughed, small and humorless, and wondered why he was feeling so skittish. He hadn't been this jumpy since the day Aaron died. Maybe that was the reason. Tonight he was on the other side of that equation. Tonight he would pay for his sins.

The forest disappeared, replaced by an uneven terrain of mud and stone, a cliff overlooking an endless black plane that stretched to the horizon. It wasn't the Heartbreak Sea that divided the northern and southern land masses of Nikacia. It was the Chillic, the black, ice cold sea known variously as the 'Spawn of Monsters,' the 'Lawless Chillic,' or the 'Neversail'. He inhaled the salty sea air, unshouldered a tattered backpack, and dropped to one knee. The boots he withdrew were heavy, with four-inch soles made of solid lead. He got to work putting them on, lacing tight enough to hurt. The pain wasn't necessary, but he loathed himself today more than ever. Not that anyone was around to witness his self-chastisement.

Yet for the past six years, he'd lived in self-imposed banishment, alone in a hut buried in the snow. He knew what it was to be alone. He also knew when he wasn't.

"Hello there!"

Toby jumped and spun around again. Beaming headlights glared at him, as high as his head and as bright as searchlights. He shielded his eyes and squinted against the glow. It was a tractor, a big four-wheeled one that made a rust bucket rattle as it sat idle in the middle of the road. How had he not heard it approaching, or seen the lights, for that matter?

A figure dropped from the cab and stepped toward him, a black shadow against the light, but even in silhouette, Toby knew him. How could he not? Maybe he'd even expected him.

"How are you here?" he asked, surprised to find that he wasn't scared.

"I'm here to help you on your way," the other said, and he pointed a thick finger toward the sea.

Recognizing that this wasn't an answer to the question, and wondering whether he deserved one, Toby turned and stared out at the blackness. He was near to the cliff's edge now, standing alongside a lonely, naked tree that leaned out over the drop off as if considering a jump.

He reached a paw into each pocket and withdrew the items there, raising the first to eye level and looking at it blankly: Aaron's key. It was small in his paw, an imperfect brass with purple swaths of oil here and there. The heart shaped head was pocked with little dents, and the two teeth on the opposite end seemed to be slightly bent. Closing his fingers around it, he held the other item up. He let the fish eye dangle on its string. It didn't rotate, as an ornament would. Instead, it snapped to a northwestern bearing, and held perfectly still. Toby looked out at the ocean in that direction, then stuffed both items once more into his pockets.

"You going to be alright?"

The figure was leaning against the large rear wheel of the tractor. Toby hesitated in his response. In truth, he had no idea. "I guess we'll see."

"Yes we will," the other agreed.

Toby tried to speak, but his throat had tightened. He coughed and tried again. "I'm sorry. I know that doesn't mean much now, but if I could take it all back…"

The figure stood and approached him. "I know, Toby. But we can't go back. All we can do is move forward." He pointed once more at the ocean. Toby looked too. And when he turned back, Aaron Harding was gone. So was the tractor. He was alone, probably for miles in every direction.

Placing one paw on the tree, he leaned over the lip of the cliff and looked down. Death didn't scare him, but he'd rather avoid those rocks if possible. It would take a pretty good leap; he'd need to get a running start.

It was almost pleasant to feel his heart hammering in his chest, to feel the trembling in his paws, and the way his knees didn't seem to want to support his weight. At least he was feeling *something*. He stomped out into the long grass, wrenching the heavy boots upward with each step, and turned once more to face the ocean.

The wind blew around him, rippling through his cheek fur; how he would miss that.

He charged forward.

One bound. Two. Three. He crouched low. He kicked the earth with all his might and soared over the edge. Arms wind-milling, he fell and fell. The boots dragged him downward. He hit, and for a fraction of a second, he thought he *had* landed on the stones. His legs crumpled beneath him, and he became submerged in the icy water.

Darkness pulled him down. A trail of bubbles chirped in zig-zags toward the surface. Pressure began to squeeze at his ears and behind his eyes. The pain would continue until he made the transition, but the transition itself had always been pure agony. He steeled himself, claws digging into his palms, and inhaled.

It was as if ice water was flooding his skull, a thousand needles pushing through the roof of his mouth. It filled his lungs, seeming to turn them into two bags of wet cement. He struggled to push the fluid outward again. A few bubbles escaped. He continued to sink, drawing in another labored lungful, then pushed it out again. No bubbles this time.

His leaden boots hit the ocean floor, churning up a cloud of murk that would be brownish green, if there were any light down here. He opened his eyes. They were meant for darkness, but he was so deep, the terrain looked like nothing more than an endless landscape of shadowy tombstones disappearing into salty fog.

He withdrew the eye once more and let it float before him. It snapped around, locked dead ahead. Satisfied, he closed his fingers around it, replaced it in his pocket, and bowed his head. He didn't know if he was saying a prayer, or mentally preparing, or searching for strength from the ether around him. His brain kept repeating, "Please. Please. Please." Drawing the water in once more, now owning the pain, he opened his eyes.

And took the first step.

www.AnimalControlBook.com
1178902

Made in the USA
Las Vegas, NV
14 July 2021

26441916R00190